M000009268

Praise for Linda Crist's *The Bluest Eyes In Texas*

Ravigo Zomana, <u>The Virginia Gayzette</u>

"Crist has done an excellent job of keeping the adventure hopping, as villains come from all different angles, and our lead characters struggle to find balance and safety in their lives. The action is seemingly real and doesn't feel contrived."

Blayne Cooper, Author of *Cobb's Island, Echoes from the Mist, The Last Train Home,* and *Unbreakable*:
"Linda Crist's debut novel is a winner! The novel's easy-to-read style, realistic dialogue, and good pacing make it a pleasure to read. The plot is two-fold and well-crafted. Office intrigue allows for plenty of action and conflict while the women's budding romantic relationship is allowed to progress at a solid, believable pace. The author takes her time, treating the reader to hours of great reading and drawing you into the storyline inch by inch. I'm anxious to see other works from this new author."

Stephanie Solomon, Editor of *Telltale Kisses*:
"What a *fantastic* book! I can't recommend it highly enough! It's a must-have for any home library."

Borderline

Linda Crist

Yellow Rose Books

Nederland, Texas

Copyright © 2006 by Linda Crist

All rights reserved. No part of this publication may be reproduced, trans-
mitted in any form or by any means, electronic or mechanical, including
photocopy, recording, or any information storage and retrieval system,
without permission in writing from the publisher. The characters, inci-
dents and dialogue herein are fictional and any resemblance to actual
events or persons, living or dead, is purely coincidental.

ISBN 978-1-932300-62-8

First Printing 2006

9 8 7 6 5 4 3 2 1

Cover design by Donna Pawlowski

Published by:

Regal Crest Enterprises, LLC
4700 Hwy 365, Ste A
PMB 210
Port Arthur, Texas 77642

Find us on the World Wide Web at
http://www.regalcrest.biz

Printed in the United States of America

Acknowledgements

Thank you to:

Cindy Cresap—once again, your insight was spot on, and made this a much better book.

Donna, for a rocking book cover.

Joob, Wendy, T-Spoon, and Lauren, for creating the Chapter 12C artwork and charity shop.

Lucy, Renee, and Rob, for bringing us all together in the first place.

Dedications

To the readers, without whom there would be no book.

To the Posse, the sisters I never had.

To Suzanne, Jay, and Henry, with much love, and especially in this case, for introducing me to the beauty of Big Bend National Park.

To Sandra and Renee—for one wonderful day, you put the "magic" in the Magic Kingdom, and gave a room full of readers and writers memories to last a lifetime.

Chapter
One

A RED 4RUNNER topped the rise, and the driver immediately slowed down, tapping her foot on the brakes in a steady motion, trying not to appear too obvious in her attempt to decrease her speed. The truck passed the county sheriff's car at the side of the road, and the 4Runner's driver pumped her fist in the air, smiling at her companion in the back seat. "Close call that time."

"What was a close call?" a sleepy voice replied. "Ouch."

"Ouch?" Kennedy glanced in the rearview mirror, and spotting nothing amiss, gazed forward again at the long flat stretch of road ahead of them, noting a tumbleweed as it rolled across the highway, buffeted about by the stiff wind, until it lodged itself in a barbed wire fence. "You okay?"

"Yeah. Fine." Carson's face scrunched up as she worked the clasp on one of two seatbelts that had been holding her securely in place during her nap. She'd forgotten about the entrapments and had tried to sit up without unfastening them first. The seatbelts appeased her lover and so she complied, one of many concessions she was learning to make in their relatively new relationship. It was a small sacrifice if it gave Kennedy peace of mind.

"Glad you're up." Kennedy gestured toward a sign as they passed it, 'Welcome to Fort Stockton' emblazoned across it in bold, western-style letters. "Last chance for a decent bathroom break and whatever else you might need to do before we get there."

"Already?" Panic rose in Carson's voice and she sat up, shifting until she was sitting to the right in the back seat, where she could see Kennedy's face in profile. She dutifully pulled the shoulder harness part of the seatbelt over her head and snapped it into place. "How much longer? I need to touch up my makeup, and comb my hair, and..." She covered her face with her hands, shaking her head slightly. "Oh, dear lord. I am so not ready for this."

"Relax." Kennedy pushed a map back toward her from on top of the center console, and then leaned forward just enough to turn down Shania Twain on the stereo, so she could hear Carson better. "We still have over fifty miles to go. Just that there isn't much between here and home, unless you happen to be terribly fond of roadside rest stops."

"Ewww." Carson wrinkled her nose in disgust. "No, thank you. I need hot water and some semblance of something sanitary, thank you very much. How about a McDonald's? They always have good bathrooms. And good mirrors. I must look a sight by now."

"That you do," Kennedy mused, studying the disheveled hair in the rearview mirror with an appreciative eye. Blonde, unruly locks stuck out appealingly in all directions, and Carson's purple fleece pullover was askew and partially unzipped, open just enough to offer a brief hint of curved flesh. Kennedy realized Carson's shoulder harness was keeping her from having a better view, and briefly pondered her staunch stance on seatbelts.

"What's that supposed to mean?" Carson dug frantically through her purse, searching for a mirror. "Do I look that bad?"

"You're beautiful," Kennedy replied, receiving an uncertain smile in response. "My folks are going to love you, sweetheart. Quit fretting."

"It's just..." Carson's face reddened and she looked down, brushing the never-ending assortment of pet hair from her faded jeans with agitated flicks of her wrist. "Your mother..."

Ah. Kennedy suppressed a grin, recalling a phone call from her mother the morning after she and Carson made love for the first time. They were still cuddled up in bed when she took the call. Her mother had intuitively deciphered the situation and given her daughter a gently teasing hard time about it. Carson, in turn, had figured out what was being said on the other end of the line, and had been mortified. "Carson, it will be fine. Trust me. Mama has been dying to meet you. She called last night to check on when we thought we'd get there, and she was extremely excited about you coming home with me."

"Really?" Carson ran her fingers back through her hair in an attempt to order it. "I'm just afraid I'll die of embarrassment when I see her. It's so different from the way I grew up. If my folks were still alive, they'd be assuming I'm still a virgin because I'm not married."

Kennedy chuckled under her breath. "See, and mine thought I wasn't one, when I still was. Go figure. Pa had 'the talk' with me about the heartbreak of teenage pregnancy and birth control and all that. He sure was surprised when I told him that not only did I already know about all that, it wasn't applicable in my case. Took some convincing too. Besides drinking, drugs, and drag racing, sex was one of the main weekend pastimes at my high school. Not much else to do in these parts. There were too many girls who did get pregnant, and he wasn't taking any chances of it happening with me. I finally told him I wasn't interested in boys, and that led to a whole other discussion."

"Wow. Your father had that talk with you? I can't imagine having it with my mother, much less my father. It was just assumed I wasn't having sex. Which I wasn't. At least not in high school. I— Kennedy?" Carson's attention was diverted out the window. "What in the heck is that?" A tiny creature was running along the grassy space between the road and the fence, a small brown blur just a little bit ahead of the truck.

"Roadrunner." Kennedy slowed a bit, so they wouldn't pass the bird too quickly, giving Carson a chance to see it better. "Fairly common around here. Never seen one before?"

"No, other than the cartoon version." Carson pressed her nose against the window and fogged the glass, drawing back when she realized it was cold outside. "Hey, are those mountains way off over there?"

"Yep." Kennedy gazed off to the distant left at the hazy-looking brown hills. "We'll be driving through the Glass Mountains once we turn off I-10 onto 67. Be a nice change, huh?"

"Yeah." Carson continued to look at the mountains as they grew close. She noted a large state flag on a tall pole in front of a ranch house as they passed it, with no American flag above it. "Another Republic of Texas sympathizer."

"Lots of them in these parts, that's for sure." Kennedy spotted a pair of golden arches as they entered the town and exited, pulling up to the side of the building. Carson hopped out and made a beeline for the restroom, while Kennedy chose to step out of the truck and stretch her long legs, which had been screaming in cramped protest for the last hundred miles.

The unrelenting wind whipped around her as she walked around in a circle, and she reached up and pulled her leather jacket collar up higher against her neck. It was mostly clear, but cold, with only a few puffy clouds floating way up above in the thin blue fall sky. The air was much drier than what they were used to in Austin, and she briefly hoped her mother had remembered to put a humidifier in their room.

In a bit, Carson returned bearing a white paper bag and two cups. Kennedy eyed the bag and the cups, peering over the top of her sunglasses at Carson as she waited for her to put them in the car. "Back in a minute." She gave a quick pat to a denim-clad backside and took off, darting inside the fast food restaurant.

Carson merely shook her head and smiled, leaning against the passenger door until she returned. "You joining me up front now?" Kennedy noted a hint of freshly-applied perfume as Carson drew closer and placed a hand at the small of her back while she opened the door for her. As Carson got situated, Kennedy leaned in, resting her hand on her knee. "You smell good." She leaned closer still, kissing Carson on the cheek. "And you look great. I think you'll pass muster with the folks, no problem."

"You're sure?" Carson's eyes narrowed as three men passed in front of the truck, watching the two women with great interest. "Redneck jerks," she whispered, nodding toward the men.

Kennedy glanced over her shoulder, feeling her feistier side rise up. "Screw 'em," she muttered under her breath. She pecked Carson's lips and slowly drew back, smiling at the green and gold flecks dancing in her gray eyes. It was sweet, the life she was living, and she'd be damned if a few hometown bigots were going to spoil it. It was nice having someone in her life that made even simple things like a pit stop at a fast-food chain special. She peered curiously at the paper bag in Carson's lap and opened it slightly, catching a whiff of French fries. "Hey, what did you bring me?"

"Orange juice," Carson replied, picking up a chocolate shake she'd purchased for herself. "And you can share the extra-large fries with me if you're in the mood to live dangerously." She winked at her vegetarian lover.

"All right." Kennedy smiled. "French fries sound kind of good right now."

"Yeah. I always seem to crave junk food right before a holiday. Guess it's to store up before eating all that home-cooked stuff." She poked a straw in her shake cup lid and paused, looking up as Kennedy prepared to close the door. A thought occurred to her. "Kennedy, you don't eat turkey, do you?"

"Nope." The tall woman gave a tug to Carson's seatbelt.

"Then what do you eat for Thanksgiving dinner?" She tossed the straw wrapper back into the paper bag.

"Tofurkey." Kennedy closed the door with a solid thunking noise.

"Oh." Carson sat back, watching as Kennedy rounded the front of the car. She had the sexiest swagger Carson had ever seen. "Tofurkey?" She spoke aloud, enjoying the view. "What in the heck is that?"

CARSON PRESSED HER nose against the window again, as the 4Runner cruised down Holland Avenue, the main street, in Alpine. Every now and then she pulled back long enough to clear the fog from the window with the cuff of her pullover, making a spot so she could watch the town roll by. It had proved to be more charming than other West Texas towns she could recall. Just as Kennedy had said, there were several art galleries, and the streets and buildings seemed cleaner and more cared for than she had anticipated. She noted a coffee shop and swiveled around toward the driver's seat, batting her eyelashes fetchingly. Kennedy rolled her eyes and without a word, turned in and parked the truck, then followed her into the warm, aromatic shop.

While Carson ordered up a large mocha latte, Kennedy shoved her hands in her pockets and meandered about, carefully looking around the shop. A few people were scattered at small round tables, either reading or conversing in low tones among themselves. She didn't recognize any of them and immediately felt a knot relax in her stomach that she hadn't realized was there. *Hmm.* She stored that away to ponder later, smiling as Carson approached her with two cups. "And what did you bring me this time?"

"Soy decaf." Carson handed over the hot paper cup and took a cautious sip of her own beverage, careful not to burn her tongue or the roof of her mouth. She had a home-cooked Thanksgiving dinner to look forward to the next day and had no intention of doing anything that might dampen the experience.

"Thanks, sweetheart." The endearment slipped out quite naturally and earned her a frown from a woman seated behind her. The expression was lost on Kennedy, but not on Carson, who briefly glanced at the woman before she deliberately tucked her hand in the crook of Kennedy's elbow.

"You're welcome. It's cold out there." She glared at the woman, who was pretending to read a book but in reality was scrutinizing them over the top of the pages. Carson recognized the author's name on the book jacket as one from her Southern Baptist days. "Thought you might need something to warm you up. Besides me that is." She bumped hips with Kennedy as they started toward the door.

Kennedy's brows rose in puzzlement, but she appeared pleased, nonetheless. "Why, Miz Garret, are you flirting with me?" She tilted her head as Carson held the door open and gave her an insistent push through it.

"No, I'm propositioning you," she raised her voice a little louder than necessary and looked back over her shoulder once more to see the woman openly scowling at them. With a little wave of her hand in the woman's direction, and a perky smirk, she closed the shop door.

Heh. Carson buffed her nails on her jacket collar. Kennedy had missed the entire exchange.

"All rightttt." Kennedy fished the keys out of her jacket pocket and opened Carson's door, feeling the tug of the wind as she held the handle. "This might be the best trip home ever." She closed the door and went around, climbing into her side and pausing halfway in for a moment to take in Carson's expression. "What?" She slid into her seat and felt a light touch to her arm.

"I love you, that's all." It hurt to think someone found something so beautiful to her to be abhorrent. "Couldn't remember if I'd said that to you today or not."

A charmed smile lit up Kennedy's face. "Well, you said it now." She reached across, cupping Carson's cheek and brushing her thumb against her skin before she leaned over and kissed her, taking a moment to savor the sweet contact. "I love you too, sweetheart. You ready to go meet my family?"

"Ready as I'll ever be." Carson dropped her hand down, resting it on Kennedy's thigh, enjoying the play of muscle as her leg moved from the brake to the gas pedal. She suddenly felt braver and rejuvenated. She'd just stood up to an obviously bigoted stranger. How bad could a couple of parents be?

They drove to the end of the street, or at least what was the end of a continuous row of buildings, then passed a long expanse of open area between the edge of town and a large Victorian-style house. It had three stories and was painted pale blue with white trim. One corner was a rounded tower that went all the way from the ground level to the third floor, and an inviting wide covered porch appeared to go all the way around the house. A few of the upper rooms had balconies, and several tall pecan trees graced the yard.

Kennedy turned into a long, winding driveway and pulled up to the side of the house, parking under a long, low carport that was big enough to shelter a half dozen vehicles. Besides the 4Runner, Carson noted a navy blue Ford F150 extended cab pickup, a black Chevrolet Avalanche, another 4Runner, this one in forest green, and Pete's Ford Ranger. Kennedy's younger brother had left Austin on Monday, two days earlier, having finished up all the class work he needed to prior to the holiday.

"This is where you grew up?" Carson studied the place in wonder. "It's like a giant gingerbread house. How cool."

"Yep, this be home." Kennedy made no further comment, a dozen emotions flicking across her face as she observed the stately house. Slowly, she opened the truck door.

As her feet hit the ground, three dogs came bounding around from behind the house, an Akita/wolf mix who was a littermate to her own Talia, a German Shepherd, and what appeared to be a Rottie-Mastiff mix. "Whoa, whoa, hey!" She found herself pressed against the side of the car as three sets of paws pushed her back and three lolling doggie tongues vied for the honor of licking her face. "Ugh!!" She tried to push them off as Carson came around the side of the truck laughing so hard she was almost doubled over.

A screen door opened off the side of the house, and two more little dogs came running, a dachshund and a small terrier mutt that was so ugly he was cute. "Awww." Carson plunked down, as the two tiny canines both leaped into her lap, quite oblivious to her status of stranger. "Kennedy, you didn't tell me your folks ran a kennel and a bed and breakfast.

"Ahh." She finally managed to shove the larger dogs away. "Nah, all of these are their dogs, but we do have some stables." She nodded toward the edge of a barn, which peeked out from behind the house. "One of the perks of staying here are guided horseback riding tours in season."

"Are we in season?" Carson stood, carefully setting the two dogs down, before she brushed yet more dog hair off her jeans.

"If the guests are willing to pay extra, we're always in season." Kennedy grinned at her, then turned as the screen door opened again. "Uh..."

"Shea!" A bubbly redheaded woman approached them, her face shining like the sun. Carson liked her immediately. "My baby girl. Get over here and give your mama a hug." The woman's arms opened wide and Kennedy automatically moved into them, hunching over and kissing her mother on the cheek.

"Hi, Mama." Kennedy stepped back, suffering her mother's attentions as she fluffed her dark bangs, patted her cheek, and finally clasped her by the shoulders.

"Introduce me to your Carson." She turned, and Carson suddenly felt self-conscious, hoping beyond hope that she would meet with the woman's approval. "Oh, aren't you just lovely!"

"Th-thank you," Carson stammered, as she found herself engulfed in a hug similar to the one Kennedy had just received. It lasted a lifetime, as her senses and emotions were overwhelmed. Mrs. Nocona's hair was softly coifed in curls and waves, and her eyes were the same vivid blue as Kennedy's. She was warm and solid, and her voice was melodic with just a hint of a drawl-twinged brogue. She smelled...like a mom...of flour, and sugar, and Estee Lauder perfume, and she wore a feminine lavender blouse and a pair of pleated dark navy mom-style jeans, complete with white Keds sneakers and white lace socks. How long had it been since she'd received a mom-hug?

Finally, they parted. "Welcome."

"Mama, this is Carson," Kennedy cut in, her brows scrunched together in question at the mix of emotion on Carson's face. "Carson, this is my mother, Aileen Nocona."

"Thank you." Carson smiled shyly. "Pleased to meet you, Mrs. Nocona."

"Call me Aileen, Carson." She draped an arm over first Carson's and then Kennedy's shoulders and steered them toward the house with the dogs in tow. "Come on in the house. I just took a batch of peanut butter cookies out of the oven and brewed a fresh pot of tea. I don't think our weekend boarders will be back from their hike in time for afternoon cookies, so y'all can join Pete in the parlor."

"All right" Kennedy glanced over at Carson, whose head was bowed in silence as she listened. "How many boarders for the holiday?"

"Just a young couple. Not much to deal with, thank goodness. Your father isn't here right now. He rode down toward the park on Shadow. Took his sketching pencils and a fresh canvas with him. We didn't expect you two for a few more hours, so I imagine he'll be back in time for supper." She gave a squeeze to her daughter's shoulder. It was no secret Kennedy was a daddy's girl, something Aileen Nocona had accepted from her daughter's infancy. She herself was hopelessly in love with the man, so it stood to reason their daughter would adore him as well.

"Oh. Okay. Hold on, I forgot the bags." Kennedy trotted back toward the truck and quickly returned with their luggage in hand, and all three women ducked inside the house. The scent of fresh baked-goods wafted into the entryway, and Carson looked around, taking in the mix of Southwestern furniture and décor. It was strangely comforting, and she wandered over toward a painting similar to the one that hung over their fireplace back in Austin. She recognized Kennedy's father's fine hand in the bold brushstrokes and earth-toned pigments, and she smiled as she felt Kennedy's hands clasp her shoulders from behind.

Aileen smiled at the sight and prudently disappeared into the kitchen. "I'll put the cookies on the plate and bring them out shortly, and then I'll go roust out your brother. I think he's upstairs."

"Thanks, Mama." Kennedy rested her chin on Carson's head. "You all right?"

"Yeah." Carson patted one of the hands at her shoulder. "Just a little overwhelmed. Been a while since I've had mom-type contact, is all. Kinda threw me off balance."

"Oh." Kennedy drew in a deep breath, pondering Carson's words. "This gonna be a tough weekend for you?"

"No. Well, maybe just a little." Carson turned, placing her hands on Kennedy's hips, giving them a little pat. She looked up, blinking hard for a minute. "Your mom's real nice." It had been an overwhelming meeting already, and she silently hoped Aileen's niceties were genuine acceptance of her in Kennedy's life and not just company manners.

"You sure you're okay?" Kennedy hugged her tightly. "Mama is a force of nature, no doubt. Seems like all the women in my life are."

"I'll be fine. Just might need some time to sort things out, okay?" Kennedy nodded, and Carson stood on tiptoes, pressing their foreheads together. "As for the other...it's good for you. Keeps you on your toes."

Kennedy frowned and nodded again, accepting the change of subject for the time being. "Seems to me like I'm keeping you on your toes right now." She picked Carson up until she was about a foot off the ground and gave her a healthy squeeze before setting her back on her feet.

Carson felt her entire spinal column pop into alignment and groaned in relieved bliss. "Lord, I needed that after that long drive. I've got a severe case of fanny fatigue."

"Need a massage?" Kennedy asked hopefully, as she raised both hands and wiggled her fingers in anticipation.

"I just might take you up on that later, honey." Carson looked around, spying a wide wooden staircase. "Speaking of, where are we sleeping tonight?"

"I've got the both of you in Shea's room," Aileen answered as she backed through the kitchen door with a large platter of cookies.

"Mama, in the twin bed?" Kennedy groaned in consternation.

"Not any more. Took it out and put in a long antique queen a few weeks ago." She set the platter down on a shadowbox coffee table. "Figured it was time you had a grown-up bed to sleep in here."

"Oh." Kennedy sat down on a dark brown leather couch, motioning Carson to do the same. She picked up a cookie and broke off the edge, popping it in her mouth. "Cool. A bed I can finally fit in without hanging over the end."

"Hopefully the both of you will fit," Aileen answered

absently. "I'll go get the tea and be right back."

Carson covered her face with her hands, trying to scrub the blush away. "I'm never going to get used to a parental unit approving of their child sleeping with someone," she whispered. "It's just not right."

"Better than having to do the sneak down the hall routine." Kennedy nudged her shoulder. "I'd hate to have to crawl out of a warm bed early in the morning to sneak back, when I'd much rather be snuggled up with you."

"Hmm." Carson attacked a cookie with a healthy bite. "You do have a point. Oh. Wow." Peanut butter and sugar melted on her tongue. "These are fantastic. Peanut butter is my favorite, you know."

"Yeah, I do." Kennedy's eyes twinkled at her. "So does Mama. She asked."

"Oh." Carson retrieved another cookie and looked around the room again as she savored this one more slowly, tasting a hopeful hint of acceptance. So far, Thanksgiving was turning out much better than she'd anticipated.

CARSON OBSERVED THE interior of the barn with a somewhat educated eye as she wandered slowly through it, feeling the springy hay underfoot. She'd lived with Kennedy in Austin for almost a month, and they'd squeezed in a week in Mexico, sailing and scuba diving, earlier in November. The other two and a half weeks, she'd spent her fair share of time both feeding and caring for Missy and Storm, Kennedy's champion quarter horses. It was normally Pete's job to take care of them, but she'd taken pity on him as he worked extra hard to finish up some research papers and studied for tests prior to the Thanksgiving break. Since she had not started job hunting, caring for the horses helped occupy her time.

She still wasn't certain exactly what Pete was studying at The University. He had kept to himself much of the time since she'd moved to Austin, and she suspected he was perhaps a bit upset at her presence in the house. At Kennedy's insistence, her Honda had taken Pete's space in the garage, relegating his truck to the elements, and neither of them had quite recovered from the first time he forgot she lived there, and had come flying though the back door one morning in just his boxer shorts. He lived in an efficiency apartment over Kennedy's garage, but ate many meals in the main house, taking advantage of his sister's grocery bill and using their washer and dryer for his laundry. She'd also done a few loads of laundry for him, if she happened to be doing some for herself and Kennedy.

Between her and Pete, the two of them were beginning to change the contents of the refrigerator and pantry to a balanced mix of Kennedy's ultra-healthy fare and their own more common tastes. She'd expected Pete to come bounding down the stairs earlier, as he also loved peanut butter cookies. Aileen had gone to roust him out and had come back downstairs, announcing she'd found him sound asleep and she hesitated to wake him, as he seemed to still be catching up after the hard week of tests prior to his drive home.

So they'd shared half a plate of cookies and a pot of herbal raspberry tea, after which Kennedy's restless side surfaced with a vengeance, fueled by the large dose of sugar her system was unaccustomed to. She'd decided a trip to the barn was in order to visit her father's ten horses, two cows and chicken coops. The horses were all quarter horses, with the exception of two plucky mustangs. Carson had willingly gone along for the tour, smiling as Kennedy practically dragged her across the backyard area in her exuberance to simply get up and move.

Carson took her time, stopping to look at each horse in turn, scratching a nose here, offering up an apple bit there, and occasionally stepping inside the stalls to get a better look, if a horse seemed amiable enough. After fifteen minutes or so, she realized Kennedy had disappeared. Emerging from a stall, she carefully dropped the latch in place before she went in search of her missing lover. The scent of hay, leather, and horseflesh was thick and pleasant around her, and farther down, she heard the distinct moo of a cow and beyond that the continual clucking and scratching of the free-range chickens.

In addition to the indoor pens, the chicken coops had small doors that led to very large outdoor wire-enclosed pens, where the chickens had extensive room to run and flap about. However, on the brisk, windy day, most of the hens were sensibly inside the barn, roosting and keeping warm. Carson nodded in approval at the nice arrangement for the chickens. She'd seen a documentary on the conditions of the average chicken farm and it had almost been enough for her to join Kennedy in the land of vegetarians.

She smiled, humming under her breath, as she thought about the drastic turn her life had taken. New lover, new city, and for all practical purposes, a new life. She still had no new job and was not quite ready to call Kennedy's house her home just yet. The jury was still out on her decision to find a place of her own or stay with Kennedy permanently. Her independent side wanted a space of her own, but the part of her that was head over heels in love was slowly winning the debate to stay.

Kennedy had done everything she could to encourage the move to be permanent. She'd completely cleared one of the guest bedrooms so Carson could set up her computer desk and her bed there. She had yet to sleep anywhere but Kennedy's bed, which was just fine with Kennedy, but she did understand her only-child lover's need to have a part of the house that was hers alone. Many of Carson's boxes from the move were still packed and she'd had to go digging for her winter clothing just prior to the drive to Alpine.

Carson was drawn out of her musings of Austin as she rounded a corner, making a ninety degree turn into another whole room of the large structure. She stopped and let out an appreciative whistle. Kennedy was seated on her red and black Harley Heritage Softail Classic and had donned a pair of black leather riding chaps that perfectly matched the black jacket and boots she was already wearing. As Carson entered the storage area, Kennedy turned and winked at her and motioned her over with a crook of her finger.

"Nice." Carson sidled up to her, running her hand up and down the buttery-soft leather that covered Kennedy's thigh.

"Thanks, I like her." Kennedy trailed her fingertips along the chrome handlebars.

"Oh." Carson patted her thigh. "The bike's nice too." She watched, pleased to see a slight blush to Kennedy's cheeks at the compliment. "So this is your baby, huh?"

"No." Kennedy turned, snaring her closer. "You're my baby. This is my Harley." She tilted her head and spent a moment indulging in a lengthy kiss. "Mmm." She pulled back just a little, but still close enough to feel Carson's warm breath against her face. "Raspberries and sugar." She licked her lips and raked her eyes suggestively over her lover's toned body. "Almost as tasty as the rest of you." She stole another quick kiss. "Wanna go for a little ride? I've got a couple of helmets over there."

Kennedy gestured toward a shelf that held five helmets, along with a variety of gloves, boots, and other items she assumed went with the bike. A rack next to the shelf bore a few pairs of chaps in various sizes, along with a couple of jackets. "That sounds like fun." Carson looked down at her own black leather jacket, which almost matched Kennedy's. "Got some extra gear for me over there? Maybe some gloves and chaps? It'll be cold in the open air."

"You bet." Kennedy swung her leg over the bike and sauntered toward the rack, picking out a pair of chaps and holding them up. "These should fit you. Mama has worn them a few times, and they were mine back in junior high school, before I hit my full height. I actually wore them for rodeo, but they'll do for the bike too."

"Cool!" Carson stood still, allowing Kennedy to buckle the foreign garment in place. A hand trailed suggestively up her inner thigh and around and over her backside as Kennedy fastened the buckles to the smooth, slightly-heavy garment. Carson chuckled and ruffled her hair, receiving a kiss to her stomach as Kennedy stood, and stepped back.

"Damn. Just when I think you can't possibly look any hotter." Kennedy wolf-whistled. "Look at you. You're gonna be a road hazard. People will be having wrecks trying to catch a closer look."

"Thanks." Carson blushed and looked down uncertainly. She'd never worn chaps before and spent a moment walking around a little, getting used to the weight of them, and the slight creaking noise they made when she walked. Her own black Doc Martens complimented the ensemble, as Kennedy added a pair of soft leather gloves and, lastly, a sparkling bright blue helmet.

"You ready?" Kennedy checked the helmet's fit.

"You bet." Carson watched while Kennedy snapped a red helmet in place and held out her hand, leading Carson back to the bike, making sure they both had their sunglasses safely in place as well. "We'll just go for a short ride down the road to start out, until you get used to it. Once I get on, just climb up on that little higher seat behind me and hang on. I'll do all the work. You should be able to feel me leaning into turns. Just follow my lead and you'll be fine."

"I think I can do that. You're a good lead." Carson smiled, thinking of the few times they'd danced together. She waited, following a safe distance behind as Kennedy wheeled the bike out of the barn, climbed aboard, turned the key, and with a loud rumble, brought the engine to life. "Sweet." She carefully climbed in behind Kennedy, pressing her body against her and wrapping her arms around her middle. "Very sweet." The extra height to the back part of the seat put her on a level with Kennedy, and she was able to see over her shoulder as they took off. It was like flying, but without the protection of the body of the plane.

The wind was cold, but the leather and face shields on the helmets protected them from much of the icy breeze as it whipped past them. Kennedy felt an involuntary grin spread across her face. She'd missed this greatly and wondered if perhaps she should reconsider getting a bike to keep in Austin as well. The smile grew wider as she got used to Carson's presence behind her.

That was something new, but her body quickly adjusted to the extra weight and altered balance as she expertly steered the bike around the curves in the road. Having Carson at her back was keeping her warmer than she usually was, and she laughed as she felt her snuggle closer, her cheek pressed against Kennedy's shoulder. They couldn't talk very well, so she settled back, enjoying the physical sensations as they shared the ride and the view together.

The Big Bend area was different from the hill country they lived in. These were real mountains, maybe not by Colorado standards, but compared to the hills west of Austin, they were huge. The leaves on the deciduous trees were turning, lending a bright spectrum of red, orange, and yellow, in contrast to the evergreens that also dotted the mountains in the distance. The sky overhead was crisply blue, and the air smelled fresh and clean. Carson looked up and spotted a hawk circling way over head before it suddenly dove quickly down behind a grove of trees, emerging again with some small creature in its claws. It flapped its wings faster and faster, flying high above them before disappearing behind the nearest mountain. "Wow," she murmured as much to herself as to Kennedy. "Awesome."

Carson felt a brief pat to one of her own glove-covered hands, indicating she had been heard. She gave Kennedy a little squeeze in response, then released it and dropped her own hand, running it up and down Kennedy's leg. Kennedy was all motion and warmth and Carson could feel the energy rolling off her as they ate up the road ahead of them. Even between two layers of leather she could feel the subtle movement of her leg muscles as she compensated for the miniscule dips and turns they took.

It was an interesting combination of sensations, being so close to Kennedy that she could smell the leather and the clean, unique scent of her skin, and even the herbal shampoo that lingered in her hair. Despite the cold, she was very warm, and suspected Kennedy was too. Her own legs were pressed tightly against Kennedy's hips and she suddenly realized just how pleasant the vibration of the bike itself was.

It was almost a sexual sensation. She recalled Kennedy speaking of it in those terms. *Hell,* she acknowledged, it *was* a sexual sensation and she was beginning to understand the underlying lure of the expensive powerful bikes. They couldn't be much closer together without removing their clothing and she laughed out loud as she realized just how appealing that thought was.

Her hands were back around Kennedy's middle, and she

received a questioning pat to her leg. *Ah.* Kennedy had heard her laughing and wanted to know what was so funny. *All right,* she laughed again. *Let me see if I can show her.* She pressed as close as she possibly could, giving Kennedy's behind a little bump with her own pelvis before she settled back down, again running one hand up and down Kennedy's leg before it came to rest on her hip. She allowed her other hand to snake inside the halfway-unzipped opening of Kennedy's jacket, giving her belly a rub before it sneaked higher, just below a tempting breast. She grinned wickedly and cupped the breast in question, laughing again as she felt Kennedy jump just a little in surprise.

Kennedy glanced briefly over her shoulder, smiling before she turned back to face the road. It was sweet torture as she became aware of the humming engine between her legs and Carson's pleasantly wandering hands. The need to pull off the road was growing exponentially, and she slowed a bit, carefully leaving pavement for a wide open patch of land that led to a large outcropping of rock. The rock jutted out from the side of a hill, which had been cut clear through to make room for the road. Behind the outcropping, she recalled a sheltered spot where she had spent many a night in high school, partying with her friends and six-packs of pilfered beer.

She pulled into the hidden space, and with an economy of motion, shut off the engine, popped the kickstand in place, and jumped off the bike, turning only long enough to climb back on, facing backward. "Grrrowllll," she purred, pulling Carson close until Carson's legs were draped over her own. She wasted no time in removing both their helmets, tossing them to the ground before she located the zipper on Carson's jacket, anxiously tugging it down, watching as Carson did the same with her jacket. With the barrier of leather removed, she pulled her lover still closer, pressing their fleece-clad bodies together. She removed a glove, quickly running one hand under Carson's top, finding her sports bra and tracing the tempting curves there. "Damn, you feel good."

Carefully keeping one foot planted firmly on the ground for balance, she laced the fingers of her other hand through the hair at the nape of Carson's neck as their lips met in a hungry exchange and they attempted to devour each other. Soon both hands were under Carson's top, running up and down a smooth back, then down, lifting Carson slightly and engulfing her butt, guiding her in a slow grind against Kennedy's lap. "Sweet Jesus," she gasped. "If it weren't so damned cold, you wouldn't be wearing anything by now, Miz Garret."

Carson slowed, her chest heaving, and buried her face into

Kennedy's neck, nipping at sweet salty skin, tracing an ear with her tongue, then finding full, moist lips once more. She pulled back, teasing her with tiny nips before she deepened the kiss again. Her own hands were busy with a pair of perfectly shaped breasts, and she could feel and hear Kennedy's groans of pleasure as she shoved her bra up, finding warm sensitive skin. "Wish we could..."

"Me too." Kennedy pressed her forehead against Carson's, smiling as she looked down at the movement under her pullover. "Chaps and stuff would make it kinda tough, not to mention the cold." She kissed Carson with abandonment, aching to give in to the sensations coursing through her body. "Lord, much more of that and the cold is gonna be irrelevant."

"Yeah." Carson reluctantly slowed some more, sliding her hands down and rubbing Kennedy's stomach before engulfing her in a warm hug, laughing giddily as they both caught their breath. "Cold?" Carson raised her head up, her eyes sparkling in the late afternoon sunlight. "What cold?"

"That was deliciously hot, sweetheart." Kennedy traced a flushed cheek with her fingertips. She watched Carson's eyes flutter closed in response and heard a catch in her breath. "You okay?"

"Yeah." Carson drew in a deep breath. "Yeah, fine. I just...I...I almost..." She could feel the heat of her own blush beneath her skin. She hugged Kennedy again, pressing her lips against her ear, whispering into it as if someone might hear them.

Kennedy found it endearing in the extreme. "Oh?" She smiled and simply held her, listening intently. One hand wandered down, toying with the buckles on Carson's chaps. "You want me to help you out with that?" She looked up, grinning as Carson's cheeks flushed pinker.

"Oh." Carson moaned in frustration. "That is so very tempting, but no. Thank you. Later..." She grasped Kennedy's teasing hand and lifted it, brushing her lips across it. "...later, I'm definitely going to need your helping hand, stud."

"Ooo. 'Need.' I like it." Kennedy cradled Carson's face with both hands and gently kissed her lips and then each closed eyelid. She released a pleased chuckle. "Riding back might be a little painful, huh?"

"Oh, yeah." Carson re-zipped her jacket while Kennedy jumped down to fish their helmets off the ground. "Definitely painful."

"Come on." Kennedy gave her calf a squeeze before she climbed back on the bike, facing forward. "Bet Pa will be home by the time we get there. Can't wait for you to meet him."

"Oh, dear lord." Carson buried her face in her hands. "I am in no state for that. He'll know. I swear he will."

"Sweetheart." Kennedy turned around as much as she could. "No matter what you're feeling inside, I promise, you don't have 'I'm horny' stamped on your forehead."

"Promise?" Carson was grateful for the face shield, hiding her return blush.

"Promise. Because if that were possible, I'd not be able to go out in public very often." Kennedy winked at her before dropping her own face shield.

"Oh?" Carson pondered that as Kennedy kicked the engine on. "*Oh.*" She smiled and snuggled closer, careful to keep her hands politely against Kennedy's stomach as they began the fast ride back to the house.

"PA HOME?" KENNEDY opened the back door, which led into a large kitchen that bore commercial-sized appliances.

Aileen turned from the counter where she was beating cornbread ingredients in a green ceramic mixing bowl. "No. Why don't you go get your bags put away and see if you can get Pete to wake up? He'll be up all night if he sleeps much more."

"Wouldn't be much different than his usual hours in Austin," Kennedy muttered. She ushered Carson through the spacious room and into the short hallway between there and the parlor. Their suitcases were still sitting at the foot of the stairs and she hoisted hers up.

"I'll get mine." Carson grabbed her own smaller red duffle bag and followed her up the wide oak staircase. Along the walls were more small art prints with "Joseph Nocona" signed in a bold hand. The Southwestern décor extended to the second floor, and she climbed a bit slower than normal, just taking it all in. A rich rust and forest green mixed rug ran down the second floor hallway and led them to a third staircase, which Kennedy took at a brisk pace.

"Second floor is the guest rooms; third is where we actually live." She looked over her shoulder, slowing a bit when she realized Carson was almost at a standstill. "Oh." She grimaced. Carson was studying a hodgepodge of family photos that covered the wall going up to the third floor. "I'll tell you about all of those later if you want."

"Oh, how cute!" Carson stopped completely, smiling at a naked brownish-red baby, stomach-down, on a fuzzy sheepskin rug. The baby had a big blue bow wrapped around its thick head of black hair, her only clue it was a girl. The baby's eyes matched the bow. "This is you, isn't it?"

"Uh, yeah." Kennedy cursed internally at whatever led parents to think it was fun to capture their children naked when they were too young to know to protest. She ran the rest of the way up the stairs and dropped her bag, then hustled back down. Carson had moved on to another photo a little farther up.

"You again?" The girl in the photo was probably around fifteen or so, not smiling, arms crossed, chin jutted out in a defiant manner. Her hair was wild and long, and she wore jeans that were ripped out at both knees. Her feet were bare, and she wore a black tank top that showed off muscles that were already developed very nicely. Next to her on the floor in the photo was a two-foot tall trophy. "What was that for?"

"State archery championships." Kennedy touched the wooden frame for a moment, remembering the contest. "I was grounded and they only let me out of the house that day for the competition. It was held up in Odessa. We'd just gotten home and I'd changed clothes. They snapped the picture and sent me back to my room." She remembered a quiet ride home, with her pressed against one window in the back seat, Parker against the other, and a very small Pete strapped into a car seat between them. "I was so mad at them," she recalled. "I thought winning should have gotten me off the hook. No such luck."

"What did you do?" Carson looked over, noting the slight twitch in Kennedy's jaw and a swallow as her sight turned inward in memory.

"What hadn't I done?" Kennedy smiled sadly for a moment. "I'd beaten up a boy at school. Roger Bradley. Beat him up good, too. Caught him behind the school cafeteria and broke his nose, and a rib, I think. Then I ran away from school and skipped the rest of the day because I knew I was in trouble. He'd been mean to me for so long, always calling me names when none of the teachers could hear him — half-breed, squaw — you've heard those stories. He tried to trip me in the hallway too. Stuff like that. He'd asked me out and I turned him down, so I think that had something to do with it. He wasn't mean to me until after I turned him down. He spread some stories about me too, and that was the last straw." Her cheeks turned red in shame. "Remember I said I didn't mind if I went out with boys and they told stories in the locker room saying I'd slept with them when I hadn't?"

"Yeah." Carson remembered her lover's sad story. "'Cause it kept people from finding out you were gay?"

"Yep. One boy at a time was one thing." Kennedy looked away, back at the picture. "The stories Roger told were different.

He started telling guys that I'd gang-banged some of the football team at a party up in the hills. Of course I hadn't, but it didn't stop some of them from believing him, especially since I really had been at a kegger the night he said it happened. I don't think that particular story ever completely blew over. I never told my parents why I'd beaten him up. I was too ashamed of the story, so I just told them about the name-calling."

"I'm sorry." Carson reached out, rubbing Kennedy's arm through her fleecy soft top.

"Thing is, I'd hurt him bad enough that his folks called the sheriff to press assault charges against me. Sheriff found me at a bar, a litle dive, out on the edge of town. I was too young to be in there, but the owner was soft on me. He'd let me come in and drink a Coke in the afternoons if no one else was there." She pressed her lips inward, her forehead scrunched up as she remembered her younger self. "When he walked in, he caught me smoking. Then he sniffed my Coke. I'd snuck some whiskey in there when the bartender was in the back room. My folks grounded me for three months and made me work off Roger's medical bills. I ended up in county juvy court and the bartender got fined for serving alcohol to a minor, even though he hadn't really served me. The judge kept the charges off my record because I was a straight-A student and because I was headed to the state championships."

"Oh, my lord." Carson studied the photo more closely. "Is that the worst thing you ever did?"

"Mmm. Maybe worst thing I did that year." Kennedy glanced at her, still feeling the shame of her much younger self. "Carson, I was a mean, angry, cocky kid in high school. I don't have many nice stories from then, other than my grades and sports achievements. Outside school, I was a terror. I was almost always in trouble for something. Just so angry..." she trailed off.

"I know. But, honey, it sounds like you had reason to be." Carson had heard about Kennedy's troubled childhood, especially the prejudice she suffered for her Comanche background. "Still wish we had known each other then."

"Me too." Kennedy finally smiled, wondering if Carson could ever truly understand just how differently they'd grown up. "You ready to see my room?"

"I'd love to." She took Kennedy's hand, and they rounded the top of the staircase and went to the end of the hallway, to the last door. Kennedy opened it and dropped her bag inside the doorway, taking Carson's and depositing it next to it.

"Kinda crowded in here with the queen bed," she remarked. "The twin one took up a lot less room."

"What a cool room." Carson looked around, taking it all in. The bed did indeed fill much of the space, but tucked against a sloping outer wall was a desk that bore a very old computer and a stack of reference books. On the other side of the bed, next to the interior wall, were a dresser and a tall bookcase. The bookcase was half filled with books, the other half filled with trophies of various sizes. A door led to what she assumed was a closet, but the far corner was what drew her eye. "Oh, wow, this is so awesome." She moved to the corner, which was part of one of the rounded towers she'd seen from outside. It was an alcove, a large round bench of sorts, covered with a thick navy blue cushion. Matching navy blue curtains were drawn back, revealing a view of the mountains in the distance. The sun was starting to set behind them, painting the sky in bright rich reds and oranges.

"Yeah." Kennedy joined her as they scooted up on the cushion until they were next to the window. "Spent a lot of time sitting in this window, figuring out how to get out of this town." She picked up a very tattered old stuffed black and white horse, unconsciously hugging it to herself in a way that led Carson to believe the horse had received and given a lot of love in its day. "Funny." She turned. "Now that I don't live here, I always like coming home, at least to the house itself, and down in the park. The town..." She sighed. "I don't know. Folks still see me as that young punk, I think. Kinda tough sometimes, if we actually go into town for anything."

"Maybe it would be different now because I'll have you by my side, and I can't think of anything that would make me prouder." She rubbed noses with Carson, and found her lips, dropping the horse as she held her close. "Damn them all." She came up for air, her smile almost outshining the sun behind her. It was amazing to her. Despite all the hell she'd raised growing up, she'd been lucky enough to find Carson. Many days she simply pinched herself, trying to believe the acceptance was truly real.

Carson hugged her tightly, her chin pressed over her shoulder as they rocked back and forth in the window. "I'd be proud to be seen with you anywhere." She felt Kennedy's embrace tighten and the puff of air next to her ear as she released a long, shaky breath. Kennedy was trembling, and for a moment Carson thought she was crying, but when she pulled back, she saw a tentative smile, only the faintest hint of unshed tears shining in bright eyes.

"God, I love you." Kennedy sat back, her arm around Carson as they watched the sun continue its journey behind the mountains. Off in the distance, a charcoal-colored horse rounded the bend, a tall proud rider on its back. Kennedy bolted up, crawling across the cushion and flipping the latch on the window before she flung it open. "Pa's home." She looked over her shoulder, and then leaned out the window, bracing herself on the windowsill as she waved wildly.

Carson slipped in next to her, partly to hold on to her for fear she'd fall out the window. She smiled as Kennedy's father waved back. He was too far away for them to hear each other. She saw the man crouch low over the horse's neck as they began galloping toward the house, eating up the space on the road.

"Let's go downstairs!" Kennedy closed the window and leaped off the cushion, dragging Carson with her. "When I was real little, I always used to meet him at the barn door when he came back from a ride."

"All right." They made their way quickly back down to the first floor and sped past Aileen, who was bent over the oven.

"Your father must be home." She looked up, her hands covered with two peach-colored oven mitts.

"Yeah." Kennedy hurried out the back door and took off at a run for the barn. Carson stopped short on the back porch, somehow sensing that maybe Kennedy needed this moment to herself. Aileen joined her, wiping her hands on her apron.

"Took a long time for her to feel that way about him again," she remarked as she clapped Carson on the shoulder. "Oh, she adored him as a child, but they clashed as she got older. She was almost ready to leave for college up in Santa Fe when they finally made their peace with each other."

"Glad to see they've patched things up." Carson watched as the horse rounded the side of the house and continued galloping toward the barn. It pulled up in a cloud of dust and Joseph Nocona jumped down, pulling Kennedy to him and lifting her slightly, spinning her around in a circle once before he let her down. They spoke low enough that the women on the porch couldn't hear them. Finally, after an animated conversation, they walked arm in arm back toward the house, identical expressions of adoration etched on their faces as they spotted Aileen and Carson.

It was too cute for words, and Carson smiled as Joseph mounted the back steps and pecked Aileen on the cheek before he turned to study her. She felt vaguely like a prize steer at the state fair, his gaze piercing right through her as if he could see into her soul. Finally, he smiled. "Welcome to our home, Carson." He took her hand, leading her into the house. "Come in by the fire and tell me all about yourself. Aileen, have you any coffee made up? I believe I recall hearing Carson is as fond of it as I am."

"I'll brew up a pot." Aileen turned toward the counter where a triple coffee maker sat in a corner next to the stove.

Carson felt Kennedy fall in beside her, her long arm automatically draping across her shoulders in a comforting gesture. It was comforting and unnerving at the same time, the familiar warm presence helping calm jittery nerves, even as the public display in front of parents set her equilibrium off center.

"Shea," Joseph addressed his daughter. "Why don't you go roust your lazy brother down here, while your Carson and I have a nice long chat over our coffee?"

Oh boy. Carson looked up at Kennedy in panic. Kennedy smiled at her and bent over, whispering in her ear, "It'll be okay. I promise. I'll hurry back down."

KENNEDY KNOCKED SOFTLY on the door at first, then stood back and waited a reasonable amount of time before she rapped her knuckles against the stained wood a bit more forcefully. She leaned against the doorframe and crossed her arms, tapping one toe impatiently as she listened for any sound indicating Pete had heard her. She frowned and looked at the door speculatively, then shrugged. "Hell, if he's naked, it's not like I haven't seen him that way before. Just been about sixteen years is all." Cautiously, she grasped the cool brass knob and turned it, poking just her head around the edge of the door first.

Pete was still crashed diagonally across the bed, clad in his jeans and a T-shirt. The covers were rumpled and shoved toward the footboard. He was facing away from the door, stomach-down, with one foot hanging off the side of the bed. The room was a wreck. "Figures," she mumbled. "He's been here all of three days and already managed to trash it, just like he does at home." She tiptoed across the room, intent on tickling her brother's exposed foot to wake him, when she stopped short, wrinkling her nose.

She frowned and looked around for the source of a subtle old familiar scent. It wafted up around her, brushing across her memory and stirring up long-forgotten emotions and a sudden sadness at what she didn't want to believe. Pete's heavy denim jacket was tossed haphazardly over the back of his desk chair across the room, and she slid silently across the thick braided rug, lifting it and pressing it to her face.

Damn. Two things struck her at once—strong, stale whiskey, and the sickly sweet odor she'd dreaded to find there. *Dammit,*

Pete. She glanced at her sleeping brother, and without further thought, felt the jacket all over, her nimble fingers locating the slight bulge in the hip pocket. Dipping inside, she retrieved a small baggie of pot, with one joint rolled and ready, stashed inside with the loose weed. A box of matches fell out with it, hitting the floor with a muted rattle.

Her blood boiled to the surface, faster than she could stop it, and she shot across the room, grasping Pete by the shoulder and roughly rolling him over with one swift jerk of her arm. She tossed the bag in his face and stood back, her hands on her hips and her feet at a wide stance. "Wake up, dammit!"

"What!?" Pete's eyes flew open and both hands fumbled around at the bag that was now on his chest, his mind trying to catch up with his shocked and shaking body. "What the hell?" He looked first at the bag and then at Kennedy, dropping the bag as if it had burned him.

"Exactly." Kennedy crossed her arms. "How long have you been smoking, Pete?" She knew her face was red. She could feel the heat all over, especially in her cheeks and neck. "You got a stash back in Austin, too? I could lose my law license if we ever get raided!" Her voice rose with each word.

"Shhh." Pete started to stand and thought better of it. It had been a long time since he and Kennedy had come to actual blows, but from the expression on her face, it was a definite possibility if he got too close. "Damn, Shea. Do you go looking through my stuff very often?"

"No." She began pacing back and forth next to the bed, while gazing through the window at the dusky mountains in the distance. "It didn't take rocket science to find it. Your room stinks of the stuff. I'm surprised Mama and Pa haven't found it before now. And don't try to turn this back around on me. I don't give a damn about your right to privacy. It's wrong and it puts more than just you in jeopardy, and you know it."

"You did it, back when you were in school." He sat up and raked his fingers through thick tousled dark hair, still trying to order his thoughts.

"Yes, I did. *Did* being the operative word. I thought you were smarter than that." She strode toward him and grabbed his face, tilting his chin up as she turned on the bedside lamp. "Your eyes look like roadmaps." She let him go and snatched up his stash, which had landed next to him on the patchwork quilt.

"Ouch." He rubbed his jaw and squinted at the harsh light. "Hey!" He watched her as she disappeared out the door, baggie in hand. "Where are you going?" He ran after her, trotting down the third-floor hallway in his bare feet, catching up just in time to have the bathroom door slammed in his face. The lock clicked from the other side. "Let me in, Shea. I mean it!"

The toilet flushed and he bumped his head against the door in frustration. "Shea! That cost me half a day's pay. Let me in!" He pounded on the door and almost fell on his face as Kennedy suddenly yanked it open, grasping him by the collar and hauling him inside.

"You want in here, fine!" She bodily picked him up and tossed him into the tub, fully clothed. "Come on in." She turned on the shower full blast and stood back. "Take a shower. You stink."

"God dammit, Shea!" He scrambled around, sliding on the smooth enameled surface. He glared up at her, his fists balling as she moved closer. "Don't you come any closer."

"Save it, Pete. I can still kick your ass and we both know it." She sat down on the toilet lid and leaned forward, her forearms on her thighs, ignoring the droplets of water that were hitting the top of her head, and the water beginning to pool on the floor. "Listen to me, because I'm only going to say this once. If I ever find any drugs in Austin in the house or your apartment, anything stronger than ibuprofen, you're out. No more free rent, no more free meals, no more help with your tuition. If you ever get arrested for possession or use, don't bother calling me. Are we clear?"

He snorted, rubbing water out of his face, and continued to glare at her. "You going to tell Mama and Pa?"

"Are we clear?" She sat back, grabbing a hand towel from a rack and patting her face dry.

"Are you?" His demeanor slowly shifted, from defiance to petulant child, as he silently pleaded with her for mercy.

"Are...we...clear?" No mercy was forthcoming.

"Yeah." He looked completely miserable and was starting to shiver. He stood up, holding the side of the tub for balance, and began stripping off his T-shirt. He was taller than her now and she was glad he hadn't challenged her on her ability to best him in a fight.

Kennedy also stood, turning her back on him, leaving him to bathe in privacy.

"Are you...?"

She stopped, her back still turned, and held up one finger above her shoulder, next to her head, where he could see it. She heard his jaw click shut as she slowly dropped her hand and continued on her way, slamming the door behind her. At the top of the stairs she stopped, feeling her knees go weak, and leaned against the wall for a moment, drawing in deep breaths until the sensation passed.

She had no answer for his question just yet. Telling her parents seemed to serve no real purpose other than to upset and worry them, and she figured she could be upset and worried enough for all of them. She certainly understood what he was dealing with better than they would, having been in his shoes herself. Her skin burned with shame, remembering all the pain she'd caused her parents at the height of her own partying days. With quiet resolution, she continued down to the second floor. There was no need for them to go through that again. Pete would simply straighten up and that was the end of it.

As she rounded the top of the banister and headed for the first floor, she heard two voices rising up to greet her ears in companionable discourse. *Carson.* She chastised herself, remembering her promise to return quickly. *Oh, well,* she mused. At least the third floor was far removed enough that most likely no one had heard her and Pete shouting at one another. As she reached the bottom of the final staircase, she stopped again as her father's words washed over her.

"...I was always proud of her." His voice sounded clear and deep and she smiled and sat down on the stairs just out of sight. She didn't intend to eavesdrop, but felt even more awkward at the thought of walking into the middle of the conversation. "...But never more proud than when she decided to move to Austin and start that firm she runs, helping people. That was when I knew Aileen and I had done something right. She turned things around by sheer force of her own will."

It was a revelation and it took her breath away. She felt the sting of unshed tears as her vision rapidly blurred. "I have some stories," she heard Carson's voice pipe up, "that I think might make you even prouder."

Uh-oh. Kennedy stood. *Time to make my appearance.* She quickly swiped at her eyes and rolled her shoulders, then stepped down and rounded the corner into the parlor. Her father and Carson were seated on the edge of the wide stone hearth, their heads close together in conspiratorial discussion as they shared coffee and enjoyed the roaring warm fire.

"Hey." Kennedy smiled, thinking of their conversation. "Sorry I took so long. Pete...will be down after he showers."

"Ah, my cha-nawoonit ecka-peta, come join us." Her father patted his leg and she blushed, but complied anyway, sidling up and taking a seat, draping an arm across his shoulders. He shifted his coffee cup from one hand to the other and wrapped an arm around her waist, bouncing her slightly.

"I'm going to squish you." She laughed in protest. "And

make you spill your coffee. And I'm not your first daughter. I'm your only daughter, but thank you for the 'beautiful' part."

"You won't squish me. I can still lift you up, can't I?" Joseph set down his coffee cup and made a muscle, a rather nice one, much to Carson's surprise, visible even through the long-sleeved Henley shirt he was wearing. "But it would be a shame to waste your mother's good coffee, so scoot." He nudged her toward a leather-covered footstool near the hearth.

She pulled the stool over and wriggled in as close as she could get, looking over and catching Carson's eye for a long moment. Her lover smiled back at her, a genuine expression that lit up her face, and she felt a matching one grace her own lips. Pure sweet love shined back at her, and she got lost in Carson's eyes for a bit before she realized her father was watching them. She felt the blush all over again and looked down, scrubbing her hand against the side of her neck.

Joseph made no comment, but picked up his cup and took a long thoughtful sip, giving her time to compose herself. He swallowed and looked from Carson back to his daughter. In less than thirty minutes he'd come to like his daughter's companion, but his final question had just been answered. It was one thing to see Carson become animated when she spoke of his daughter, but to see both their faces when they looked at each other, the love between them was obvious, an honest emotion neither one seemed to be able to hide. He smiled and looked over the rim of his cup. "I believe you were about to tell me a story."

"Oh. Yes." Carson glanced at Kennedy and saw resignation...and permission...in her eyes. "All right. Let's see. It's about a real hero, something rare these days. It started a few months ago, when I discovered I was working for some very bad men. I became suspicious of their activities and began to question my boss regarding some of the work he asked me to do. Next thing I knew, they were trying to blackmail me. I went to Kennedy for help, but once they knew she had information that could send them to prison, they kidnapped me to try to silence her. While the police were haggling with the law over how to rescue me, Kennedy just up and tracked me down, and broke into the hotel room where they were holding me, just in the nick of time. If not for her, well ..." she trailed off for a moment, her words catching in her throat. She looked over at Kennedy and her voice softened, "It was the first time in my life anything like that ever happened. A real, live superhero came to my rescue and saved my life. It was amazing..."

As Carson continued, Kennedy half-listened, the words rolling over her, as she watched her father taking in the story of her rescuing Carson when Nick Giovani had kidnapped her. She sighed in silent relief when Carson left out the part about her shooting Nick, and her brows rose in surprise in a few places. It was interesting to see herself through Carson's eyes and to hear the genuine awe in her voice as she told the story from her viewpoint. It was the first time she had heard Carson talk about it to someone else and she found herself drawn in, as if she were hearing a story about someone other than herself.

Not until Carson had finished did she realize that her mother had been listening quietly from the kitchen doorway and Pete from the stairs. Pete's eyes met hers in question and she turned away, choosing to let him sweat for a while longer. He was a smart boy. The fact that their mother wasn't screaming at him should have been clue enough that, for now, his secret was safe with her. As she turned back to the fire she felt Carson's gaze and looked up. Carson's brow was scrunched in worry, her face one big unspoken question.

'Later,' she mouthed quietly, and received the slightest nod of recognition. "Well." She stood and stretched. "Guess it's about to time to rustle up dinner, huh?"

"It'll be ready shortly," her mother answered softly. Kennedy studied her and realized she was still overwhelmed from hearing the kidnapping story.

"Guess Parker didn't share that part, did he?"

"No." Aileen drew her into a quick hug. "He didn't, and I'm a mind to turn him over my knee when they get here in the morning." She squeezed Kennedy again and released her. "I'm proud of you, Shea," she whispered and gave her a swat on the behind. "Now go give Carson a proper tour of the house while I check on the cornbread."

"Shea," Joseph's voice beckoned her, just as she was starting up the stairs.

"Hold on." She placed a hand on Carson's shoulder. "I'll meet you up top in a minute, okay?"

"Okay." Carson gave her a little pat on the side and trotted up the stairs.

"Pa?" She shoved her hands in her pockets and looked down as she approached him.

"I'm proud to call you my daughter." He looked at her, his face shining in pride.

"Thanks, Pa." Her voice caught and she kicked at the floor with the toe of her boot.

"Shea, whatever is between you and your brother..." He glanced toward the kitchen where Pete had followed Aileen. "Is it under control?"

"Never could hide anything from you, could I?" She cocked her head to one side and flashed him a half-hearted smile. "I don't know, Pa. I just don't know. Is it enough for now that I promise to ask you if I decide I need help?"

"More than enough." He pulled her forward and kissed her on the forehead. "Now go. My new daughter is waiting for you." He laughed quietly at her startled expression.

Chapter
Two

DINNER WAS A relatively quiet affair on the part of the majority of the family, with Aileen doing most of the talking, filling Kennedy and Pete in on the comings and goings of the bed and breakfast over the past few months. The second floor had six guest rooms and four bathrooms. Two of the rooms had private baths and the other four each shared a bath with one other room. The rooms were decorated in Southwestern style, with a touch of cowboy cool chic on the side. Guests had a choice of a full sit-down breakfast in the dining room, or a continental basket left at their door in the mornings.

Guest traffic had picked up considerably during the year after an article on Big Bend National Park was published in a popular outdoor magazine. As a bonus, the bed and breakfast, Big Star Lodge, had been mentioned in a sidebar article on places to stay.

Carson was properly impressed with the layout of the house. She'd seen Kennedy's room earlier in the day, but on the tour learned that the third floor was another complete living space, including a tiny kitchenette. There were five bedrooms, three baths, a small dining area, and a comfortable family room complete with fireplace, television, DVD player, and bookshelves that covered all of one wall.

For the time being, the one young couple booked for the evening and on through the weekend had come back from their hike, changed clothing and gone back out again for dinner at the Gage Hotel down the road in Marathon, leaving the larger downstairs parlor vacant to an evening of peace. Pete had volunteered to clean up after dinner and had quickly made himself scarce, driving away to parts unknown as soon as the last dish was put away. Joseph suggested an evening of movies and popcorn up on the third floor for the rest of them, and Kennedy quietly told him she and Carson would join them later in the evening.

She excused herself and squeezed Carson's leg under the table, indicating she wanted some company. They got up and Kennedy headed for a coat rack near the front door, grabbing her leather jacket and holding Carson's up while she shrugged into it.

Carson glanced over, studying Kennedy's drawn face and her troubled, brooding eyes. They'd not discussed whatever was bothering her during the tour of the house, as Kennedy had seemed to need some time to mull things over and Carson had chosen not to press her, figuring she'd talk when she was ready.

They stepped outside into a cold, cloudy night, with only a faint scattering of stars peeking through the wispy darkness overhead. Carson looked up, spinning in a circle, taking in the vast expanse of land and sky around them. "It's so big out here. Home on the lake feels big, but this is gigantic in comparison." Her breath fogged as she spoke, the vapor floating up over her head before dissipating into the dry air. "It must be beautiful when you can see all the stars."

"Yep. It is." Kennedy shoved her hands in her pockets and started down the driveway, her boots crunching in the finely-ground gravel and packed dirt. Carson had called the lake 'home,' adding to her already discombobulated emotions. She'd steadily avoided mentioning Carson's non-existent search for an apartment, hoping Carson would simply forget to look. Unconsciously, her stride lengthened until she was a few steps ahead.

Carson trotted after her and cautiously tucked a hand in the crook of her elbow, tugging at her until she slowed, and they walked along in a rare uncomfortable silence. Carson wrestled with that, trying to decide if she should wait or speak up. She was literally on unfamiliar turf, her own emotions off kilter as she sorted out her feelings concerning Kennedy's family and their apparent acceptance of her. She sighed a bit unhappily, wishing she could just let it all go and feel a part of the family, and more importantly, figure out how to draw out her reticent lover.

She stopped for a moment as a pack of coyotes yipped off in the direction of the hills, their howls and barks almost like a disorganized song. "Wow. Just like out in Chaco Canyon, New Mexico." The sweet happy canine songs settled over her, a bit of familiarity from her past, helping restore some of her good humor.

"Yeah." Kennedy smiled into the darkness. "I spent many a weekend camped out there when I was in school up in Santa Fe. I know those ruins like the back of my hand. I almost stayed there to work instead of going on to law school."

"Really? What changed your mind?" Carson loved the desert park, full of Anasazi pueblos, which hikers could actually walk through. She also enjoyed the remoteness of the area. It was only a few hours' drive from Albuquerque, but the rough roads and spare facilities kept the park from getting crowded. There was only one campground for tents and RVs, no store and no showers available, although it did have toilets and sinks in a cement washhouse.

"I applied for a park ranger position but didn't get it." They reached the end of the driveway and Kennedy steered Carson to the right toward the mountains.

"Would've been kind of a lonely life out there, huh?" She could only recall a single visitor's center and no other separate ranger stations. "Talk about rolling the sidewalks up when the sun goes down."

"They don't have sidewalks." Kennedy gave her a playful kick to the behind, trying to shake the dark cloud over her head.

"Hey!" Carson tried to kick back and ended up half falling as Kennedy smoothly anticipated and evaded her foot. Kennedy caught her and spun them both around before making sure she was standing steadily on her feet. "Thanks." Carson looked up and reached out, watching Kennedy's eyes close as she pushed her bangs back. "You wanna tell me what's wrong?"

Slowly, Kennedy reached into her jacket pocket, withdrawing a baggie. "Found this in Pete's room."

"Is...is that...?" Carson took it from her, trying to hold it where she could see it better in the darkness. "I've never...Pete had that? Really? I mean, I knew he drank quite a bit sometimes. I've been kind of worried about him."

"Yeah." Kennedy took it back and re-pocketed it. "He thinks I flushed it, but I kept it. I hid it in the linen cabinet until he finished his shower."

"Why?" Carson recalled stories of drunken high weekends on Galveston Bay and felt a brief surge of fear, shooting adrenaline through her system and making her skin prickle. "You don't want to...do you?"

"No. Oh, no." Carson's response was disappointing, but she tried to shove it down. It was a logical conclusion, wasn't it, given what Carson knew of her past? "He said something...said he paid a half day's salary for it."

"Well, honey, he is a student. He's not exactly rolling in the dough." Carson relaxed, the cool air refreshing on her face on the heels of the retreating rush of heat.

"You've really never done drugs?" Kennedy's voice was

thoughtfully quiet. "Ever?"

"No." Carson felt the slightest stiffness in the body next to her as she answered. "Just...never was curious about it and never really was exposed to it. The crowd I ran with in high school and college, mostly church kids and all, we just didn't..." she trailed off.

"Oh, yeah. I forget sometimes you were one of the really good kids." Kennedy released a long, foggy breath, feeling a sad gulf between them. "I still think a half day's salary is too much for this tiny bag of weed. I haven't checked on what he makes lately, but it seems too high, pardon the pun. Makes me wonder..." She sighed and grew silent, looking out toward the mountains.

"Wonder what?" Carson gently probed, finding Kennedy's arm and wrapping her hand around it again.

"Wonder if it's mixed with something more potent." Kennedy kicked savagely at a rock in the road, sending it flying and tumbling off into the ditch. "Stupid kid," she huffed. "Anyway, I thought about it and I'm going to give it to Parker. He knows people. I'd like to have it analyzed. See what Pete has gotten himself into, if anything. Anything other than pot," she amended.

"What would it be mixed with?"

"Cocaine, maybe. Or PCP, which is pretty dangerous stuff. I've not kept up with the more sophisticated drugs available these days. Most of my clients who get in trouble go the way of crack or garden-variety weed. They can't afford the more pricey stuff." Kennedy sighed. "I've heard heroin is on the rise again, and that sometimes they smoke it. Damn!" Her voice resonated across the open field next to them. "I can't figure out what to do about it."

"You planning on telling your folks?" Kennedy shook her head and Carson started to open her mouth in protest, but stopped herself, deciding she didn't know enough yet about Nocona family dynamics to interject her opinion into the fray. "Why not?" she asked instead.

"It would only worry them. Legally he's an adult. And he lives with me most of the time. In a way he's more my responsibility now than theirs. I just figured, unless he gets himself into trouble here at home, it serves no purpose to tell them. They don't support him financially at all. He works for his fraternity dues and fun money. He pays for his books. He's got a partial scholarship for being Comanche. I make up the difference in tuition and give him free room and board." Kennedy veered off toward a small grove of trees, carefully stepping through the tall grass. There was no worry of snakes in the cold, but she wanted to give any other small creatures plenty of chance to get out of their way.

They reached the trees and she smiled briefly, giving a spin to a large old tractor tire that hung from a thick rope. "Cool." Carson immediately climbed into the tire and looked at her expectantly, laughing as Kennedy gave her a spin, then pulled back on the rope and released it, sending her flying back and forth between the trees. "Is this still y'all's land?" she yelled from high off the ground.

"Yeah." Kennedy caught the tire as it sailed past, running with it a ways and making it stop. She gave it another spin and walked around it in a circle as she spoke. "I have to decide what I'm going to do with him. I already told him if I find drugs back in Austin, he's out. I...just...I know how those threats go. He won't listen. At least not the first time. I didn't."

"You got caught?" Carson dug her toes into the ground, grinding to a halt.

"Yeah." Kennedy's head dropped and Carson saw the slight rounding in her shoulders, the stoop in her posture, indicating she was ashamed. "I was fourteen, freshman year of high school. Some friends and I decided to get high up in the loft in the barn one rainy afternoon. Colossal stupidness." She shook her head. "My mother saw the open loft window from the kitchen and went out there to close it against the storm. We'd opened it to let the smoke escape. When she found us we were too screwed up to even try to get away. I'm surprised we didn't burn the barn down."

"Whoa. What did they do to you?" Carson got up and grasped the inner edges of the tire, hanging back from it, her feet still on the ground, peering at Kennedy's silhouette through the large round opening.

"Sent my friends packing and turned me over a sawhorse and whipped my ass but good. Used a saddle strap, if I recall." She rubbed her backside in memory. "I know that sounds abusive, but damn. It did make an impression. I think that may have been the last time she spanked me."

"Ouch." Carson's feet slid beneath her, and she hopped a little before leaning back again. "What did your father do?"

"Remember that this was when I still hated him for my heritage." She walked back over to the tire, mimicking Carson's stance from the other side, causing the tire to dangle slightly more in her direction due to her extra weight. She chuckled. "If I let go right now, you'd fall on your butt."

Carson quickly let go and watched as Kennedy lifted herself, swinging up and landing seated in the middle of the tire. "No fair!" She stepped forward and found herself standing between Kennedy's legs with two large hands resting on her hips.

"My father told me if I did drugs again, I'd have to go sleep down in the park in a tent for a week." She pulled Carson closer, trapping her in the circle of her legs.

"But you like camping." Carson leaned back some, smiling as Kennedy held her up, strong calf muscles pressed against her backside.

"It was winter. Temperatures can drop into the teens down there." Kennedy playfully loosened her grip, tightening it again as Carson started to fall backward.

"Oh." Carson leaned forward, placing her hands on Kennedy's thighs. "I guess you did some snow camping?"

"Yeah, a couple of times, before I finally quit getting high. At least at home. Didn't stop me from doing it away from the house and on through college and law school. You've heard the rest." She hung her head, hiding behind her hair, and felt a gentle touch to her cheek. She slowly looked up as Carson pushed her hair back and continued to stroke it. "Never any drugs at all, huh? Regular cigarettes?"

"No." Carson moved in as close as she could, feeling Kennedy's legs tighten around her. "You almost sound like you wish I had." She patted a cool cheek, taking the sting from the honest observation.

"No!" God, could she mess things up any worse? "Just...Never mind. I think finding that bag has me not thinking straight." She gazed uncertainly at Carson, who was still running her fingers back through her hair. "That feels nice." She closed her eyes.

"And I, for one, am really glad you don't think 'straight'." Carson chose to lighten the moment, still feeling residual tension between them, but deciding there was too much going on inside Kennedy with her family and childhood issues, to add to them at the moment.

"I love you." Kennedy hugged her tightly, squeezing her with her arms and her legs, feeling the little gasp of breath as Carson eagerly returned the hug, holding on for all she was worth. "I keep forgetting I don't have to face this stuff by myself anymore. Do I?"

The insecurity in those words broke Carson's heart. "No, you don't." Carson turned her head, finding her lips, nibbling at them tentatively before they made a more solid contact, reaffirming their budding partnership. She pulled back and resumed stroking Kennedy's hair. "I'm here for you. Don't you forget that. I know you'll figure out the best thing to do about him."

"Thanks." Kennedy sat there for a bit, simply holding Carson close, feeling some semblance of peace as they breathed the cold air, their lungs rising and falling almost in sync. She finally shook herself out of a pleasant lethargy, feeling a slight tremor run through Carson's body "Getting cold?"

"My front is nice and warm, but my back is a little chilly, yeah." Carson smiled as Kennedy's face drew closer and they spent another few minutes in slowly escalating kisses. "Not so cold now." She laughed as they drew apart slightly, very warm breath clouding the slight space between their lips. "But I think we promised your father we'd watch some movies with him."

"That we did." Kennedy slid out of the tire, releasing her hold while she straightened her leather jacket. "And I think I promised to lend you a hand later, so to speak," she teased, taking Carson's hand, swinging their arms as they walked back toward the road.

Carson bit her lower lip, listening to the swish of their footsteps in the grass. "Is that a little strange for you? I mean, in the room you grew up in, with your parents just down the hall?"

"Don't know." Kennedy dropped her hand and wrapped her arm around Carson's shoulders. "Guess I'll find out. Might have to make sure there aren't any photos of them in the room watching us or anything." She laughed quietly.

"You've never?" Carson looked up at her in shocked disbelief. She'd just assumed, based upon everything else Kennedy had done growing up, that sneaking around with someone in her parents' home would have been a natural course for her to follow.

"Nope. You get to be the first." She looked down, her heart skipping a fearful beat. "And the last, I hope," she spoke softly, looking down at her booted feet as they walked, almost hoping Carson hadn't heard her. All of a sudden two boots moved in front of hers and she looked up. "Whoa."

Carson pulled Kennedy to her so fast it made her head spin, drawing her swiftly forward into a warm embrace. They stood there in the middle of the road with coyotes howling behind them and a growing wind blowing around them, stirring the tall grasses and the leaves on the nearby trees and brushing softly through their hair. Carson tilted her head back and pulled her lover's face toward her, kissing her soundly for a long while, until they forgot where they were. They didn't break apart until bright headlights illuminated them and a horn sounded loudly, making them jump.

"Hey," a familiar voice called from the idling vehicle. "Break it up, you two. You're scandalizing the children."

"Parker?" Kennedy peered past Carson, who simply buried her face into Kennedy's chest in utter embarrassment. "Come on." She led her mortified lover toward the mini van. "Hi, Katie." She nodded at the woman in the passenger seat. "Thought you weren't getting in until tomorrow morning."

"Howdy, Carson." Parker grinned, taking in her blush, obvious even in the faint evening light.

"Hi, Parker." Carson leaned heavily into Kennedy, still flustered. She felt Kennedy give her a little squeeze before her arm dropped down and she slipped her hand into Carson's back pocket, unseen in the darkness.

"We weren't, but I got off a little earlier than expected, and the kids were whining about missing the Macy's parade on TV if we drove out in the morning, so...here we are." He looked behind him toward the inside of the van, where the sounds of video games and serious banter could be heard. "Hey, hush up for a minute. Your Aunt Shea is out here."

"Auntie Shea!" Three voices piped up all at once, and one small body wriggled forward, leaning over Parker out the window. "Hi, Auntie Shea." A small boy with a shock of red hair peered up at her. "Is that your wife?"

"Hi, Nathan." She bent over, accepting a hug and a kiss on the cheek. "Um...no, no, not exactly. She's my girlfriend. This is Carson. Carson, meet Nathan, Parker's youngest."

"For now." Parker winked at her. "Hey, let me get this thing parked and we can go in and talk with the folks and make proper introductions." He put the van in gear and turned into the driveway, leaving them to catch up.

"Did he say...?" Kennedy looked to Carson for affirmation.

"'For now?' Yeah." She grinned.

"Oh, boy." She took Carson's hand, dragging her toward the house.

JOSEPH AND AILEEN stood as the noise of multiple pairs of feet sounded on the wooden stairs just outside the third floor family room. Their quiet evening was suddenly shattered as their grandchildren entered the large room, all three of them flinging themselves at them at once, threatening to bowl Aileen over in their exuberance.

"Grandpa! Grandma!" Nathan managed to get a hand on one leg of each of his grandparents, fighting for space next to his two taller siblings, who eagerly hugged each of the older adults in turn. Aileen knelt down and hefted him up for a moment, ruffling his hair before she set him back down.

"Land sakes, but you've gotten big!" Nathan was the sole other redhead in the room, a testament that Parker actually was her son, despite the fact he so strongly favored Joseph. "Look at you. You've grown a foot since I saw you last month."

"Hi, Mama. He has. We've had to buy him all new jeans this past week." Parker kissed her on the cheek, pushing his way through the excited children, "Pa," he grasped his father in a man-hug as they patted each other on the back but didn't touch anywhere else. "Hope it's okay we came down tonight."

"More than okay," Joseph answered, beaming down at Ryan, Parker's nine-year-old middle child. "Look at that shirt." He plucked at an orange and white miniature University of Texas football jersey. "Wonder who sent you that?" he teased.

"Auntie Shea." He smiled proudly. "She promised me she'd play football with me this weekend."

"That I did." Kennedy entered the room carrying a large bowl of popcorn, followed by Carson, who bore a pitcher of cherry Kool-Aid. "Who wants to watch a movie?"

"Me! Me!" Nathan and Ryan shrieked as they clamored for the smaller bowls of popcorn Kennedy was dishing up.

"How about you, Erin?" She smiled as Parker's eleven-year-old only daughter shyly stepped out of a corner and joined her at the table.

"Can I hang out with you?" The girl looked up at Kennedy, obviously full of hero-worship for her aunt.

"Sure." Kennedy winked at her. "But we might end up watching the movie with everyone else."

"That's okay. As long as I'm with you, we'll have fun." Erin turned to Carson. "Hi," she greeted the pretty blonde stranger.

Erin accepted a cup of Kool-Aid, curiously studying Carson's face as her long, slender fingers wrapped around the cup. She smiled shyly. *My god,* Carson took in the girl, a miniature Kennedy clone. She recalled some of the photographs on the staircase wall, feeling as if some of them had suddenly come to life. Erin was at that awkward age, all legs and arms. She was on the thin side, yet appeared sturdy, and as she talked with Kennedy, their expressions and smiles mirrored one another. Her eyes were the same vibrant blue, her skin the same rich reddish-brown, and as she nodded her head in answer to a question, the same auburn highlights flashed from her dark hair, illuminated by the fire and dimmed lamps in the room.

"Um...hi." Carson wiped her hands on her jeans and extended one, smiling warmly as Erin took it. Even the firm grip was the same. "I'm..."

"Carson." Erin grinned. "Pleased to meet you." Her soft West Texas drawl added extra syllables to a few words as she shook Carson's hand.

"Pleased to meet you, too." Carson looked up as Katie approached them. She briefly wondered if there were any ugly genes in the entire family. Parker's wife was cute as a button, with short brown hair and tanned skin, and only a little taller than Carson. "Hi." She held out her hand again, clasping Katie's. She smiled charmingly at Carson, her own accent even more pronounced than her daughter's.

"Hi, Carson, I'm Katie. Welcome to the family." She nudged Kennedy good-naturedly with one hip, watching as mortified blue eyes begged her not to make Carson uncomfortable.

"Thank you." Carson blushed slightly, ducking her head and fumbling for a cup. "Kool-Aid?" She laughed lightly.

"Might be best." Katie joined in her laughter and patted her own belly as they looked across the room. "I don't think I'll be joining them tonight." Joseph, Aileen, and Parker had already popped the tops on long-necked Mexican beers and were sipping at the cold, frothy beverages as they tried to get the wrestling boys settled in front of the television. "Go on and join your brothers, Erin." She gave her daughter a little push.

"But Auntie Shea said—"

"Just for a little while, sugar, while I chat with her, please?" Katie's expression was no-nonsense and Erin closed her mouth, her shoulders slumped in defeat. She shuffled away from the table, mumbling unhappily under her breath.

"I'll come get you to play with Carson and me in a little while, okay?" Kennedy called after her, receiving a brilliant smile in response. Erin skipped the rest of the way to the television, plopping down on the floor in the middle of her brothers. "So." Kennedy shot a meaningful glance at Katie's stomach, where her hand still rested. "I suppose y'all have a little announcement to make, huh?"

"Yeah." Katie laughed giddily, her entire face lighting up, and Carson realized it was really true that pregnant women glowed, although Katie was no where near showing just yet. "This is your fault, you know."

"My fault?" Kennedy stepped back and poked a finger into her own chest. "Firstly, if I got close enough to you to...um...Parker would kill me, and secondly, last time I checked, I'm not equipped right."

"Oh, I don't know, stud." Carson bumped hips with Kennedy. "I bet if you tried hard enough..." Carson trailed off when she realized what she was saying and her hand flew to her mouth as her blush returned in full force. She looked around and realized only the two women next to her had heard her.

Katie was shaking in silent laughter, and Kennedy's face was a mixture of outrage and well-stroked ego. Carson realized Kennedy and Katie were very comfortable with each other, and she released a relieved breath. Kennedy draped an arm across her shoulders and leaned over, whispering in her ear, "Careful. I just might try to prove that theory later, babe." She nipped the ear quickly, looking back up as Katie cleared her throat meaningfully.

"I meant your fault, as in both of you." She shook her finger back and forth at them, watching as they looked at each other in shock, and then back at her. "This little bun was baked the weekend Parker came back from Dallas. Seems there was enough chemistry going between the two of you to leave him a little hot and bothered. By the time he got home, well..." She buffed her nails against her collar. "It was a very good Sunday." She smirked.

"That weekend? But back then we hadn't even done any — " Carson felt Kennedy's hand clamp over her mouth. "Mmphh." She frowned indignantly, trying to bite the warm skin against her lips.

"I am sure Mama and Pa do *not* need to hear that version of conception, do they? Ouch!" Carson finally succeeded and Kennedy jerked her hand away, shaking it and peering at her stinging palm suspiciously. "Hey, you left teeth marks!" She swatted Carson on the behind and received a return swat. "I give up." She moved well out of the way. "You want a beer?"

"Yes, please." Carson's eyes sparkled with mischief as Kennedy stalked toward a mini-refrigerator on the counter of the wet bar which was tucked into the far corner of the room.

"I can see you're going to fit in just fine. I needed a partner in crime. Someone has to help keep Shea on her toes, and you seem like just the woman for the job." Katie took a sip of Kool-Aid and grimaced at the overly sweet taste. "Ugh. Seven more months."

"Congratulations." Carson smiled warmly, deciding she liked Katie very much. Besides, it was nice to have another person around who wasn't born into the family.

"Thank you." Katie swirled her cup around. "We decided we'd save the big news for dinner tomorrow, assuming those three can keep it a secret for that long." She glanced at her three children, who were all engrossed in an animated movie. She squinted at the television and smiled. "I always did like that version of the Hercules movie better than the Disney one. That woman, she sure can sing."

Kennedy rejoined them, handing Carson a cold bottle, then holding up her own. They clinked the necks together and Katie joined them, touching her cup to their bottles. "Glad I'm not driving." Kennedy took a long swig of her beer. "I think I need this. Been a long day."

"Oh?" Katie looked around the room again. Parker and the elder Noconas were engaged in low but lively conversation, having staked out spots on the plush leather couches that bracketed the television. "Where's Pete?" She finally did the math, realizing who was missing.

"Long story." Kennedy's voice was curt, the anger evident as her sight turned inward. "And don't ask right now. I think my blood pressure just shot up a notch."

"Alllriigghhtt." Katie shot a glance at Carson, who just shook her head slightly. "Am I going to be filled in later?"

"Yeah." Something settled inside and Kennedy's features softened a bit. "I need to have a little chat with Parker about our dear baby brother, and I imagine he'll tell you all about it. Or maybe I'll just kill Pete. It would be a lot easier."

"Well, this I can't wait to hear." Katie smiled as Erin made her way back toward them, tucking herself under her mother's arm. "Hey, sugar." She kissed her daughter's head. "Thank you for giving us some girl time."

"I'm a girl." Erin rolled her eyes. She looked down and tugged absently at a small locket on a chain around her neck, the gold metal catching the light.

"That's pretty." Kennedy reached over and took a look at it, popping it open. Inside was a picture of Erin on one side and a blonde-haired girl on the other. "Who's that?" She clicked the oval case closed.

"Oh," Erin's voice perked up. "That's my best friend, Jessica. She gave me this for my birthday. Jessie...I wish she could've come this weekend, but her parents made her go to San Francisco to visit their family. I wish I could go to San Francisco someday." Her voice was full of longing, and she looked down thoughtfully at her locket. "Are you going to watch the movie, Auntie Shea?"

"No." Kennedy shrugged at Katie as she spoke, silently seeking approval to tear Erin away from the group. "I was thinking of having some more girl talk in my room. You want to join us?"

"Oh, that would be so cool!" Erin's voice bubbled over. "I wish Jessie was here so she could have girl talk with us. I told her all about y'all's house. It's just rad. She was jealous I got to come here and ride horses and play football and stuff."

"Why don't you take a couple bowls of popcorn on down to my room and Carson and I will join you in a few minutes?" Kennedy was still watching Katie, and she gave Carson's shoulder a little squeeze as Carson handed Erin the requested bowls.

"Hurry!" Erin shouted as she danced out of the room with the popcorn.

"Jessie?" Kennedy eased from one foot to the other, feeling Carson lean against her.

"I need to talk to you sometime." Katie glanced over her shoulder at the rest of the family. Even the adults were engrossed in the movie, having been drawn in, and were laughing at the antics of some cartoon animals. "Erin and Jess are inseparable. A few months back they were sleeping over at our house and I went in to say goodnight and caught them experimenting."

"Experimenting?" Kennedy frowned and then Katie's meaning struck her. "Oh. I see. And you think it's something more than just typical stuff? A lot of kids their age..."

"I know, but I just sense it, Shea." Katie sipped thoughtfully at her Kool-Aid, wishing she could have a beer. "I think Erin does, too. I know she feels like she's different. She's already come to me a few times, confused about her other little friends' budding obsession with boys. All she can talk about is Jess. I think Jessie is starting to like boys, too, and my baby's about to be left alone to figure it all out."

"She won't be alone." Kennedy took Katie's hand, holding on to it for a long moment. "Have you talked to her at all?"

"We've tried not to make a big deal out of it. She was embarrassed enough to be caught. They had their shirts off when I walked in. We only talked about it briefly. I wanted to make sure they were only experimenting to a certain extent, and not going too far with it. Far as I can tell, they haven't." She shook her head in frustration. "Parker was pretty shaken when I talked to him. You know he loves you, Shea, but..."

"I know." Kennedy's voice was soft as she spoke. "I know. But it's hard on any parent to think their kid might be gay. It was really hard on Mama when I came out to her. I'm her only daughter, just like Erin is Parker's only one. It's tough to give up dreams you have for your children, even if those dreams won't make them happy. I'll certainly talk with her if she seems like she needs to, assuming that's all right with you and Parker."

"It is." Katie smiled weakly. "Parker and I talked about it. She adores you."

"And I adore her," Kennedy replied thoughtfully. "I won't push, though. She's going to have to come to me with her questions."

"Thank you, Shea." Katie smiled warmly in gratitude. "You two are cut from the same cloth, you know."

"Yeah." Kennedy's expression was troubled. She fervently hoped Erin didn't completely follow in her footsteps as she grew older. "I know."

"Well." Katie eyed her husband. "I guess I'll go join the family, and let y'all go bond with my daughter. Ladies." She nodded her head graciously and turned, sashaying across the rug and bending over, wrapping her arms around Parker's neck from behind and shrieking with laughter as he grabbed her and hauled her over the back of the couch and into his lap. She quickly joined in conversation with her in-laws as the children continued to be engrossed in the movie.

Carson laughed. "I like her."

"So do I." Kennedy took her hand as they walked down to the other end of the hall. "She and Parker are a great match. I swear they're even more in love now than they were when they got married, and it's been, gosh, thirteen years."

"Wow. That's pretty impressive. Most couples I know that have been together that long have lost that spark long before then." She stopped, feeling Kennedy's grip loosen just a little. She glanced over at the tense set of her jaw and deliberately entwined their fingers more tightly. "What do you think Katie and Parker have that all those other couples don't?" She kept her voice casual.

"Oh, I guess partly, they talk about everything." Kennedy smiled, guessing at the nature of her lover's gentle prodding. "And they make time for just the two of them. They have a date night at least once a week. They also try to go away for at least a long weekend once a year, just the two of them. I know they don't take each other for granted. They work and play together. And judging from their behavior and Katie's current condition, I'm guessing they've kept their love life pretty spiced up." She bumped against Carson on those words. "They're pretty good examples, I think. My parents are the same way...still very much in love. You'll see more of that the more you're around them."

"Hmm. I like all those ideas." Carson nodded in approval. "So it's kind of a family tradition to have strong, long lasting relationships?"

"Yeah." Kennedy grinned. *She got me good.* "You could say that." They reached Kennedy's room and Carson found herself pressed against the closed door and kissed soundly. Kennedy pulled back, just enough to look into her eyes. Carson's heart sped up at the banked passion there, an unmistakable fire that simmered and threatened to erupt. Kennedy trailed her fingers against Carson's face and twined them in her hair as she kissed her again, her entire body pushing Carson against the smooth wooden door. "I want you," Kennedy whispered into her ear, sending chills skittering down her spine.

"Umm." Carson quickly stood as she felt the door starting to give way. "Hold that thought. We've got a confused kid to entertain for a while first."

"Grrrrrr." Kennedy's voice trilled, tempered with an agreeable, yet very sexy smile. "I hope these kids have a reasonable bedtime." She also stood up as the door opened and Erin poked her head out.

"What you doing?" She eyed Carson, who was hastily straightening out her mussed shirt. Erin snickered knowingly. "Come on in. I brought my boom box and CDs in here, and a deck of cards. And I have a bag of M&Ms. We can play poker."

"Ooo." Carson's voice rose. "M&M poker is the best. You get to eat your winnings when the game is over."

Kennedy sighed in frustrated resignation. Bedtime, it seemed, was going to be a long ways away.

THEY SLIPPED EASILY from poker, to tossing M&Ms in the air and catching them in their mouths, to Erin giving a very impressive impromptu hip-hop dance lesson, to a giggle fest and pillow fight, and ended up with the three of them sprawled out on large pillows on the floor, drinking more Kool-Aid and eating the last of the popcorn. Without much thought, Kennedy had flopped down on her back, her head on Carson's thigh, her hands folded across her stomach. Carson and Erin were deep in discussion about fashion, mountain biking, rollerblading, and a variety of topics Kennedy was more than happy to listen to as she tried to process the day.

From time to time she opened her eyes and looked up long enough to catch Carson's eye. Each time she did this, Carson fed her either a piece of popcorn or a handful of M&Ms, or both. It was an arrangement that was working rather well, she mused, and she smiled as Carson's other hand unconsciously stroked her head while she talked. She could feel Erin watching them and decided if her niece was indeed headed down the rainbow path, she might as well see a healthy example of love between two women. Briefly she hoped it might also turn out to be an example of long-lasting love between two women.

"Auntie Shea." Erin finished chewing a mouthful of popcorn, washing it down with Kool-Aid.

"Yes?" Kennedy rolled her head to the side and one eye drifted lazily open. "You have a red moustache."

"Oh." Erin swiped at her upper lip and drew in a deep breath. "Auntie Shea, did you ever like boys?"

Well, Kennedy mused to herself. *Nothing like diving right in headfirst.* She sat up and crossed her legs, her forearms resting loosely against her thighs. She felt a warm hand at the small of her back and smiled as she continued to look down, collecting her thoughts.

"I've always liked boys," she answered carefully. "Some of my best friends growing up were boys."

"You know what I mean." Erin rolled her eyes and sighed dramatically.

"Yeah, I do." She swallowed and glanced over at Carson. "Why do you ask?"

"Well..." Erin made a concentrated effort at arranging M&Ms into piles by color, as her brows furrowed and she pressed on. "All my friends, all they talk about are boys. Even Jessie. Every day we have to eat lunch in the cafeteria with Tyler."

The way she spit out Tyler's name left no misunderstanding as to Erin's feelings toward the poor boy. "And you aren't very happy about that, I take it?" Kennedy felt a light, comforting scratching at her back as Carson's fingers wandered just beneath her shirt.

"No!" Erin grabbed a pillow and hugged it to herself. "Before Tyler came along, we used to talk just to each other, and we'd go play on the playground afterward, and talk about riding horses, and movies, and all kinds of fun things." She frowned. "Now they sit there and stare at each other and trade lunches, and it's all just stupid. Why can't everything just stay the same?"

"Nothing ever stays the same," Carson interjected. "If it did, you'd never grow up, or get to go to high school, or college, or fall in love. You're going to be a beautiful woman someday, Erin. Have you ever compared your pictures to ones of your Auntie Shea when she was your age?"

Erin blushed and she smiled shyly. "Sometimes people see her pictures and think they're me."

"Well." Carson smiled. "I agree with them and your Auntie Shea grew up to be a very beautiful woman. At least I think she is."

"So do I." Erin giggled as Kennedy ducked her head in embarrassment. "But you never did answer my question."

Kennedy looked up thoughtfully. "No, sweetpea. I never did like boys like that, even when all the other girls did."

"Sometimes I feel like a freak." Erin's eyes teared up. "I try so hard to like them, but I just don't. I...I don't think I ever will."

"Don't try." Carson reached across and patted her leg. "Forcing yourself to be something you're not, it only leads to unhappiness. I should know. If it comes naturally to you, it will, if not, well..." She hesitated, wondering just how much to say.

"If not," Kennedy took up the mantle, "just remember that no matter what, you are a beautiful, smart, perfectly normal girl. And you're certainly no freak."

"But all the girls — all of them — it's all they talk about at slumber parties and in the gym and at lunch and at Indian Princess meetings. I don't fit in with them much anymore. Sometimes..." Her voice grew very soft. "Sometimes I think I'm the only one like me."

Kennedy sadly remembered her own confused teenage self. How could she explain to an eleven-year-old girl that there was probably a whole lot of loneliness in her future before there would be happiness? Small town West Texas was no place to grow up gay. She, of all people, should know that. "You're not the only one." Kennedy opened up one arm and Erin slid beneath it.

"You listen to me." She kissed her niece's head. "I will always be here for you. Anytime you need me, you call me."

"Anytime?" Erin looked up hopefully.

"Anytime." She hugged her close. "Hey, maybe you can come stay with me in the summers, once you get older. Would you like that?"

"That would really be okay?" She looked from Carson to Kennedy and back again.

"Absolutely," Carson confirmed quietly, receiving a kiss to her own head in turn.

"Awesome!" Erin smiled and sat up, drawing her legs up and wrapping her arms around them. "Auntie Shea, did the kids make fun of you for not liking boys?"

"A few did, yeah." Their eyes locked in understanding, one pair much too mature for their years

"But everything turned out okay?" Erin glanced at Carson, her meaning all too clear.

"Sweetpea, everything turned out better than I could ever have hoped for." Kennedy felt Carson's leg brushing hers, and she dropped a hand to squeeze a well-toned calf. "And they will for you, too."

"Promise?"

"Promise," Carson and Kennedy answered in unison, and then touched heads, laughing quietly.

"Hey, how about some more dancing?" Carson decided it was time to lighten the mood and got up, choosing a bubble-gum dance CD and placing it in the boom box. Before too long all serious talk was forgotten, as three kindred spirits danced their cares away on a crisp fall evening.

It was close to midnight before everyone was settled into various rooms on the third floor. All three adult Nocona children were conveniently assigned to their childhood rooms, although Pete was still not home. Joseph and Aileen of course slept in the master bedroom they always shared, leaving one guest room next to Parker's for his children. Joseph and Parker carried the two sleeping boys down the hall from the family room, and tucked them into the comfortable queen-sized bed, while a none-too-happy Erin had to settle for a pull-out trundle on the floor next to them.

"I want to have a sleepover with Auntie Shea and Carson." She scowled, crossing her arms and poking her lower lip out. "I'm a big girl. I don't want to sleep with the little kids anymore." She looked up hopefully at Carson, who merely ducked her head and rubbed the side of her neck before glancing up at her partner.

"Sugar, there isn't room for you in Aunt Shea's room, so you'll have to go on in with the boys." Katie shooed her oldest out of Kennedy's corner spot, smiling as Kennedy mouthed a giant 'thank you' at her.

Kennedy bent over and tousled Erin's hair. "Hey, sport, you beat me but good at poker." She coaxed a reluctant smile from her niece. "How about a rematch before the end of the weekend?"

"All right." Erin placed her hands on her hips, her stance matching one Carson had seen many times before. "But I'll just win again."

"We'll see." Kennedy pecked her on the cheek and closed the door behind her, then moved over to the desk where a variety of CDs were scattered across the ink blotter. Carson leaned against the door and watched as Kennedy's hips wiggled slightly. She could just make out Kennedy humming something as she sorted the CDs and replaced them in their cases, and she moved closer to try to hear her.

Carson burst out in a fit of giggles and Kennedy turned and raised one eyebrow at her. "What?"

"You're singing that Pink "Get the Party Started" song." She laughed again.

"Am not." Kennedy frowned. "Was I?"

"Yep." Carson chuckled and moved in behind her. "Cute moves too, by the way."

Kennedy was just about to turn and tackle her in retaliation when she felt Carson press up against her, wrapping her arms around her and encouraging her to keep up her little dance. She smiled and complied as they began to move together while she finished putting the CDs away. Carson's hands began to wander, and Kennedy picked out something a bit more sensual and popped it into the boom box, her hips swaying suggestively as Carson plucked her shirt from the waistband of her jeans and quickly found her breasts, pushing her bra up and teasing her sensitive skin.

"Oh, god." Kennedy began unbuttoning the brushed cotton shirt, allowing it to drop off her shoulders. Carson's lips traveled along her partially bare back, a scattering of goose bumps following the tiny butterfly kisses she placed there. She unclasped Kennedy's bra and stepped back long enough to allow it and the shirt to fall to the floor.

"I love dancing with you." Carson pressed against her again, placing her hands on Kennedy's hips and guiding her in a slow grind as she moved with her in time to the saxophone playing from the boom box. Her hands snaked around and unbuckled Kennedy's belt, then unpopped the button on her jeans and slowly unzipped them. She slid the jeans down past her hips, moving back just long enough to let them slide on down her legs before she pressed against Kennedy again, slipping her hand inside the waistband of her underwear.

"Thought I was lending you a hand tonight," Kennedy gasped and leaned forward, bracing her weight on the desktop as Carson began teasing her with light strokes of her fingers. She groaned as Carson's lips assaulted her back again, moving downward while she knelt to remove the last remaining article of clothing.

"I want you," Carson purred against her skin as she guided Kennedy back, pushing her down on top of the bed. Carson crawled up with her, creeping up her body on her hands and knees like a cat, and found her lips, kissing her fiercely, smiling against the soft skin as Kennedy fussed with her clothing, managing to get most of it off as they rolled over a few times, warring for dominance before Kennedy ended up on her back again, arms and legs wrapped around Carson as she kissed her way down Kennedy's very appealing body.

"I could absolutely devour you right now," Carson whispered against her lower belly, nuzzling her lover, nudging her legs further apart. "Will you let me do that?" She paused, turning her head to the side and closing her eyes as Kennedy cupped her cheek, stroking her face with her thumb. Those fingers moved back, threading through her hair and urging her downward. Their eyes met once more, desire mirroring desire, before she turned to her task, Kennedy's musky sweet scent making her mouth water.

The first warm breath against her almost made her cry out before Kennedy remembered where she was. She gasped quietly, then hissed in pleasure as Carson put her lips and tongue to good use, her hips moving against Carson until she felt one arm wrap across them, keeping them under some control. She felt Carson's other hand behind her knee, her blunt fingernails dragging slowly down the back of her sensitive leg, until Carson grasped one butt cheek, pressing her more firmly against Carson's mouth. "Oh, sweet Jesus." Kennedy's body tensed and then stilled completely for a split second before her climax hit with unexpected force.

One hand remained lightly at the back of Carson's head, while the other grabbed up a fistful of blanket, and her heels dug into the mattress as she forced down the scream of pleasure that threatened to escape her lips, her breath coming in soft whimpers instead. Slowly her body began to settle, and she looked down, tilting Carson's face up. "Come up here," she whispered, still feeling residual spasms as her lover did just that, crawling upward until their lips met again.

"Gonna have to get these insured by Lloyd's." Kennedy smiled, tracing Carson's lips with one finger. The smile turned to a laugh as Carson engulfed it, circling it with her tongue. "That too." She felt Carson's body rubbing against her and reached down with both hands, finding her ass and kneading it, settling her on top of her as they ground together, much as they had while dancing next to the desk.

"Need to feel you." Carson found her lips again, and their tongues danced together in the space between them before they got lost in another long exchange of kisses. Kennedy gently rolled her over, pressing one knee between her legs and pushing them apart, before her hand tickled its way down her belly to tease her inner thighs.

"Mmm." Kennedy found a nipple, closing her mouth around it as Carson arched up into her. "Need to feel you too." She moved to the other breast as she slipped inside her lover, stroking her gently at first, then feeling the rhythm Carson established and matching it. Carson cried out quietly and Kennedy stroked her head, brushing her bangs out of her eyes.

"Look at me." Carson forced herself to look up, and Kennedy smiled at her, kissing her forehead. "Your eyes are so beautiful." Carson was panting now, her release very close, and Kennedy nipped at her throat, nibbling back toward the very sensitive skin of her ear. "Feels so very nice. Let go, baby." She buried her face into Carson's shoulder, her lips teasing the soft skin. Carson wrapped her arms around her and cried out again as the waves crashed over her.

Kennedy watched her face as Carson slowly came back down to earth. She rolled over and pulled the compact body against her, rubbing Carson's back and smiling as she pressed against her hipbone. "Need more?" She chuckled, patting a firm backside and feeling a long, shuddering, warm breath against her chest.

"No." She shook her head slightly, tickling Kennedy's skin. "Just. Sometimes, right afterward, it feels good to..." She trailed off, ducking her head, and slid down, hiding her face against Kennedy's stomach, pulling the covers over both of them in the process.

"Hey." Kennedy dug under the covers, pulling Carson back up. "Feels good to what?" She stroked damp locks, arranging them back behind Carson's ear. "I need to take notes for future reference."

"Um..." Carson blushed. "Feels good when I grind against you like that. Gives me another little jolt without you having to do any more work." She grinned sheepishly. "Feels really good."

"Grind away, sweetheart." She waggled her brows and flashed a sexy little smile, watching it matched on Carson's face. "But if you need me to help out, I'll be glad to oblige." She held Carson as they lay there quietly for a few minutes, while she rubbed Carson's back and Carson traced circles around her navel. "We've managed to do a lot in the past month or so, but we haven't really talked about this stuff a whole lot, have we?"

"Nope." Carson's hand moved up, cupping a firm breast. She kept her hand still, more a comforting gesture than anything else. "Do we need to talk about it? Everything okay?"

Kennedy pulled her up some more until they were eye to eye. She smiled, guiding Carson toward her and kissing her, a long, languid exchange, as she felt her lover relax more fully against her. She could taste the lingering evidence of their lovemaking on Carson's tongue and she moaned a little, deepening the contact. "I don't think they could get any more okay." She broke off and studied Carson's face, the deep love and passion evident in her shining eyes. "You really enjoy going down on me, don't you? Not that I'm complaining in the least.

It's a huge turn on just watching you, actually."

Carson fought the urge to hide her face, realizing it was an honestly curious question, not meant to tease. "Yeah." She dipped her hand down, running it along the curve of Kennedy's hip. "When we started dating, and when I knew we were eventually going to...you know..." She smiled. "It was just about all I could think of." She wandered across Kennedy's stomach, rubbing it with the flat of her hand as she spoke. "I've loved your body from the moment I laid eyes on you. I knew I had to love you in that way. So that first time, after you made love to me, I just had to, in case something happened and we didn't make love again. Not that I was really afraid we wouldn't. Just, I had dreamed about it for so long."

"Really?" Kennedy combed her fingers back through Carson's hair.

"Yeah." Carson closed her eyes, enjoying the loving touches. "It seemed like the most natural thing in the world. I never really thought about if I could do it right or anything. I wanted you so much there wasn't much thought involved."

"You surprised the hell out of me." Kennedy laughed quietly. "At first because I didn't expect you to go there, and then because it was the most mind-blowing experience of my life. I really thought the top of my head was about to explode."

Carson's body shook in silent laughter. "Glad it was good for you, honey, because it was spectacular for me." Her hand drifted down, cupping her lover, feeling her heat. "Just felt good, like this does right now." She kept her hand where it was, feeling the love between them, equally as strong as the physical sensations had been moments before. "I think I like it because you make yourself so completely vulnerable to me, and your face is so beautiful when you do that. I can't describe it. And it's knowing that no one else gets that close to you, that you trust me enough to allow me to love you like that."

"Mmm. That feels good. I love it when you do that." Kennedy squeezed Carson's hand between her thighs a little before releasing it, reaching down and holding her there. "I think that's why I like being inside you. Sort of the same idea. I like feeling you when you come. It's so completely erotic and beautiful to me...something we only share with each other. It's why I sometimes ask you to look at me. I love your eyes all the time, but at the height of passion, they're absolutely breathtaking, like I can see into your soul."

"You are the keeper of my soul." Carson kissed her lightly on the lips. "Take it, it's yours."

Kennedy took her hand and pulled it up from its warm nest,

kissing her palm. "You are my soul." She hugged her tightly. "I love you so much." She pulled the covers up over them, tangling her legs with Carson's.

"Love you too." Carson hugged her back, settling against her as they sank down into the warm covers, their bodies tired and pleasantly sated. "You know, it's too bad we can't explain to Erin just yet what an awesome life she can have when she's older."

Kennedy laughed silently. "True. Guess I need to have another talk with Katie before they go home." She yawned sleepily. "But it can wait until after dinner tomorrow." She briefly hoped no one would expect them up early, then closed her eyes, surrendering to a deep dreamless sleep.

A CLAP OF thunder rolled across the mountains, echoing through the valley and shaking the house. Carson stirred beneath her warm layer of blankets, reaching next to her and feeling for Kennedy. She frowned, not quite awake, and rolled over, finding the space next to her empty. Her eyes fluttered open and she looked around, slowly remembering where she was. The curtains were still drawn in the rounded alcove, and there was only the faintest suggestion of daylight indicating it was morning.

She thought about getting up, but she was naked and warm, and the air outside the covers bore a hint of chill. Stretching and yawning, she searched around for a clock and spotted the green glow of a digital clock radio on the desk next to the computer. It was 7:00 a.m. and she groaned. "Where'd she go?" she croaked to the empty room. She had little time to wonder, as the doorknob clicked and Kennedy slipped into the room.

"Morning." She flashed a cheery grin in Carson's direction and set a bundle down at the foot of the bed before walking past it and pulling the curtains partway open to reveal a panorama of ominous billowing dark clouds, pouring rain, and streaks of lightning over the mountain tops in the distance. Kennedy was wearing a thick white terry robe and was toweling her hair dry as she walked. "Big thunderstorm out. Kinda rare around here, especially this time of year. Gullies will be flooded in a few more hours." She noted the question in the sleepy eyes and smiled. "We're high up enough not to worry."

"Oh." Carson yawned again as Kennedy stretched out on the bed next to her.

"You're not awake yet, are you?" She leaned over and planted a light kiss on Carson's lips. "I need to go downstairs and see how I can help out. Mama will be prepping our dinner and Pa will most likely be out in the barn, so it's a tossup where they'll want me, but rest assured, they'll find something for me to do."

"Mmm. You smell great." Carson nuzzled the wet head, drawing in a fresh clean green sort of scent that reminded her of something she couldn't quite place.

"Agave cactus shampoo and conditioner. One of the perks of living in a bed and breakfast. We always have top of the line toiletries and fresh clean robes to wear. And the thickest, softest towels."

"Just like the towels you keep at home." Carson smiled.

"Yeah, I got spoiled growing up and order mine from the same place Mama does." Kennedy ruffled Carson's scraggly hair and rolled on top of her, engulfing her and the blankets in a hug, burying her face into her shoulder, nibbling a little bit at her salty skin. "You smell pretty darned good too." She lifted her head and raised a flirtatious eyebrow.

"But I haven't had a shower yet." Carson enjoyed the attention, reaching up and tracing the raised brow, watching as Kennedy's eyelids lowered halfway and her nostrils flared.

"I know." Her voice was low and sexy and sent a little shiver down to Carson's toes, which she wiggled in reflex. The animal magnetism was palpable, this close, covered by Kennedy's warm, strong, clean-smelling body, and before she could stop herself, her hands were wandering, slipping inside the soft robe and finding warm softer skin. She felt the ripple of movement at her touch and heard the faintest frustrated groan as Kennedy tugged the covers partway down, and got so close her face blurred. Their lips met in a heart-pounding exchange that left them both breathless.

Kennedy slowly rose up again. "Better stop before I can't." She smiled watching Carson's chest rise and fall. The smile turned to a frown as she traced a red strawberry mark near Carson's left shoulder just above her breast. "Oops." She bit her lip and glanced up at Carson's face. "I think I got a little carried away last night. Left a mark. Sorry about that."

"Huh?" Carson looked down and made a little ticking noise with her tongue. "At least it's in a place that usually stays covered this time of year." She touched the tip of Kennedy's nose. "Go check yourself out in a full-length mirror, stud. I think I may have returned the favor."

"Where?" The indignant tone was charming and Carson giggled as Kennedy parted her robe further, looking down at her own body. "Didn't see anything in the shower." She tilted her head to one side in question, studying Carson's face.

Carson swatted her on the butt, then ran her hand down to the really sensitive skin just below it, rubbing it through the thick terry. "Would've been tough to see in the shower."

"Why you little wench." Kennedy rubbed her behind, tugging the robe up. "Did you really?" She presented her backside to Carson for inspection and felt the gentlest of kisses at the back of her thigh.

"Afraid so. Guess you'll have to lay off the Daisy Duke shorts for a few days," she teased, pulling the robe back down. "I don't recall you complaining at the time. Actually, I don't recall you speaking English at the time. Hey!"

Kennedy pounced, pinning her down and tickling her ruthlessly until Carson was begging for mercy. "Oh! Oh, please. Kennedy...oh lord. Hey. Stop it. Please? Heheh. Arrggghhhh!" She wriggled around and mumbled a few more unintelligible pleas, trying to toss Kennedy's weight, but there was no escape. She laughed until the tears rolled down her cheeks, then sighed as the tickles turned to light caresses, and Kennedy relented, sliding back down and kissing her for several languid minutes until Carson's sighs morphed into whimpers.

"Now who's not speaking English?" Kennedy pulled back, looking rather pleased with herself.

She stroked Carson's face, tracing a flushed cheek. "Hey." She glanced down at the foot of the bed. "I brought you a set of clean towels and a robe to wear down the hall. I think they may have fallen on the floor. Here." She crawled down to the end of the mattress and leaned over, plucking the items off the rug, then crept back to Carson's side, depositing them next to her. "Should be plenty of hot water left. Pa had an industrial-sized water heater installed in the basement back when we were little. We almost never run out, unless we're completely full up with guests and they all decide to shower around the same time."

"Thank you." Carson pulled her over and kissed her again. "For the towels and for making waking up so much fun." She sat up, holding the covers around her against the chill. "You want me to come find you after I shower? You had breakfast yet?"

"Yes, and no." Kennedy sat up too, swinging her legs over the side of the bed. "Go on and shower while I get dressed. I'll go on downstairs, but I'll wait on you for breakfast. If Pa wants me in the barn, grab one of the rain ponchos next to the back door and come get me when you're ready."

"Sounds like a plan, Stan." Carson reluctantly crawled out of bed and stood next to it, then felt warm terry at her back as long arms wrapped around her.

"No fair." Kennedy nipped at her ear.

"What's no fair?" Carson managed to pick up the robe on the bed, finding the front of it.

"You're just so damned sexy standing there naked. Makes me want to crawl right back in bed with you." She helped Carson shrug into the robe. "Tomorrow morning I'm going to wait and shower with you."

"Not a good idea." Carson hugged her, then slipped from her grasp and headed for the bedroom door.

"Why not?" Kennedy stood with her hands on her hips, a slightly hurt expression on her face.

"'Cause we would run out of hot water." Carson winked at her and slipped out the door.

Kennedy just laughed, all traces of hurt vanished. She looked up at the ceiling, then out at the mountains. It was so different with Carson. After five long years of solitude her mornings were suddenly lively and fun and made her look forward to each new day. The passion between them was undeniable. That had existed from the start, a chemistry that simply was, with no explanation.

But as they slowly recovered from Carson's kidnapping and the crisis that had overshadowed the beginning of their relationship, something else had emerged. They had become friends and were able to laugh and play together and tease each other in a way that Kennedy never had with anyone else before. It was new and comfortable, all at the same time. "I am the luckiest woman on God's green earth." She shook her head slightly, then rummaged around in her duffle bag for clean clothes.

Whether that luck held out remained to be seen. She waxed melancholy, wondering again what Carson saw in her, beyond a hero who had rescued her from kidnappers. More importantly, what would Carson see in her when the heroism wore off?

MORNING WAS A flurry of activity as Joseph, Kennedy, and Parker mucked out stalls in the barn and got all the livestock fed. Carson got egg-hunting duty in the chicken coop, searching about for nests in the different levels of deep shelves that served as roosting areas for the hens, placing the eggs in a softly padded basket. Inside the house Aileen and Katie were preparing an aromatic meal that made everyone's stomachs growl, despite being full from breakfast. Erin got babysitting duty upstairs in the family room, keeping her younger brothers out from under foot, since they couldn't go outside to play in the storm. Pete had not yet emerged from his room, and Parker mentioned to Kennedy that he heard him come in after 4:00 a.m.

Kennedy made little comment, wanting privacy away from their father to discuss the baggie she had locked up in a drawer in the desk in her room. She resisted the urge to go check out his car, which she noted was parked askew beneath the carport. Texas penalties for driving while intoxicated were severe and she found herself wondering if an arrest might scare some sense into her brother. Not that she would instigate it, but given his behavior, she figured it was only a matter of time.

She kicked herself silently, thinking of all the partying she knew he had done over the past few years. She had pretty much looked the other way, excusing it as typical college frat boy behavior, but the drugs drove home just how serious things had become. Now she wondered if perhaps she had nipped things in the bud, it wouldn't have gotten as bad as it apparently was. She suddenly realized that she and Pete kept such different hours that she rarely knew when he was coming or going anymore, and really only kept up with him by noting that the horses back home were cared for just as well as they always had been. "At least he's still got some sense of responsibility," she muttered to herself.

"Shea, you say something?" Parker stepped out of the stall next to her, toting a pitchfork full of soiled hay. He dumped it in a bin kept for mulching the garden and returned to the stall, repeating the process several times. He finished and poked his head around the corner and over the half door of the stall Kennedy occupied. She was absently brushing down one of the mustangs, talking to it so quietly he couldn't hear her. "Oh, you were talking to the horse." He chuckled. "Never mind."

"Huh?" Kennedy jumped slightly as he spoke, drawing her back to the present. "Oh. Yeah. Just thinking."

"About what?" He rested his forearms on the door, leaning over and studying her troubled face. "You okay? Everything okay with Carson and all?"

"Oh." Kennedy smiled. "Yeah, Carson and I are great. I was just thinking about Pete. I need to talk to you sometime before you go home."

"All right." He frowned, opening the door and stepping inside. "Is he okay?"

"No." She sighed. *Might as well talk now.* She knew her father was out of hearing, down near the cows. "I found a bag of pot in his room yesterday."

"Great." Parker didn't sound completely surprised. "I knew he was drinking like a fish, but drugs, I had kind of hoped he would avoid that road."

"Does anyone from this godforsaken town avoid that road?" Kennedy stood up taller, finishing her task and scratching the chocolate brown gelding beneath his halter strap, receiving a tickling nuzzle to her hand for her efforts. "I know some do, but my gosh, seems like our family sure didn't. And it's not like Mama and Pa are to blame. Boredom and peer pressure drew me into it, and the high kept me there for so long. High school, college, and on into law school. It's a miracle I had enough brain cells left to pass the bar exam. Down in Houston I was drunk or stoned almost every weekend." She looked down, giving a little kick to the bed of straw. "If not for what happened to Angela, lord only knows where I might have ended up."

Parker just managed to avoid a visible reaction to the mention of Angela. His sister rarely spoke of her and past discussions had usually ended with her either in tears, or storming away to be alone until she could get her emotions in check. Now, much of the sorrow from the past seemed to have disappeared. He swallowed and decided to make no comment regarding the greatest tragedy of his sister's life. "Took Katie to straighten me out." He leaned casually against the stall wall, plucking a sweet strand of oat from the trough next to him and chewing on it thoughtfully. He rolled it over to one side of his mouth and crossed his arms. "She put the clean into my living, that's for sure. Pete, dunno what to do with him. Have you talked with him at all?"

"Yeah, but he's pretty obstinate and defensive about it. Can't imagine that, him being from our family and all," she remarked drolly. "I took the bag and locked it up. I want you to send it to your buddy in the lab and have it analyzed."

"Why? Oh." He spit out the oat straw. "What's it laced with?"

"Don't know if it's laced at all, but he said he paid half a day's pay for it, so I figure either it's laced, it was grown in gold dust, or he's stupid. Since I know he's not completely stupid, despite doing drugs, and since plants don't grow in gold dust, I'm guessing he's into something more serious than pot." She signed heavily, giving the gelding one last scratch before she trudged to the stall door.

"You told Mama and Pa?" Parker followed her out, latching the door behind them.

"No, and I don't plan to unless absolutely necessary. No sense in worrying them over something they can't do anything about. Not with him in Austin and them here." She glanced toward the other end of the barn as Carson emerged from the chicken coop. "He's my responsibility, Parker. Promise not to tell them?"

"For now," he agreed. "But Pete is his own responsibility, Shea. He's an adult, not a child. Short of you locking him up at night, he's going to have to figure things out for himself."

"Now there's a thought." She held out one arm as Carson slipped under it, keeping quiet as Kennedy and Parker talked.

"What's a thought?" Parker replied, eyeing the basket hooked over Carson's arm. It bore a dozen eggs and he nodded his silent approval.

"Locking him up. Maybe a nice thick padlock on the efficiency door." Kennedy gestured with her free hand. "Or a chain across it maybe. Hey, a boot for his truck tire to force him to stay home at night." She rubbed her hands gleefully at the possibilities.

"You're not serious," Parker's voice wasn't at all certain. Unfortunately, taking things to extremes ran in the family.

"No." Kennedy's shoulders slumped in defeat. "Not really. Just, I told him if I find drugs back in Austin, he's out. No support, physically or financially. Knowing him, he'll test me on that."

"And if he does?" Parker led them toward the main barn door. The horses were all cared for, and he had seen Joseph enter the one remaining cattle stall at the far end. He retrieved a rain poncho from a hook along the wall as Kennedy and Carson did the same.

"I'll make good on my threat." She pulled the poncho over her head and held the door as Carson stepped out into the rain. They all wore tall Wellington boots, and walked back to the house, heedless of the mud and puddles liberally scattered across the backyard.

"We'll talk some more tonight after dinner, okay?" Parker pushed the poncho hood off his head as they reached the shelter of the back porch.

"Okay." Kennedy followed suit, shaking her head of the confining sensation any head covering always gave her. She led Carson into the large downstairs living area, where they both sat down near the fire, the crackling warmth a welcome respite after the damp chill outside.

Katie followed them shortly, bearing a tray with a fragrant steaming teapot and three cups. "You two look like you could use this." She poured two cups and handed them over to the apparently grateful women

"Thanks." Kennedy sipped at the sweet herbal beverage, enjoying the sensation as it washed over her taste buds and began to warm her.

"How was your girl time last night?" Katie asked. "Erin was in a good mood when I tucked her in. Not that she isn't usually in a good mood after spending time with you. It's just...she seemed a lot more contented than she was when we left Odessa. Calmer, I guess. No offense, Shea, but you don't usually have a calming effect on my children."

"I know." Kennedy sighed. "You were right." Her eyes met Katie's in meaningful acknowledgement. "Seems our girl talk took a serious turn last night."

"Oh." Katie sat down, her hands shaking a little bit. "Wow. That talk came a lot faster than I expected."

"Yeah, for me too. Although I doubt it was an isolated conversation." Kennedy reached up, pushing damp bangs out of her eyes. "I think we did an okay job of it." She glanced at Carson.

"You did, mostly." Carson wondered if it was strange for Katie, to have two lesbians confirming to her that her daughter was probably gay. "Poor kid. I wasn't that tuned in at her age. I was mostly clueless until my early twenties."

"I was just like her," Kennedy commented quietly, seeing the flicker of pain in Katie's eyes. Her sister-in-law realized her emotions were showing and quickly tried to mask them. "Hey." Kennedy looked up. "It's okay to be upset. You're not going to offend me. Hell, I was upset when I figured out I was gay."

"Sorry." Katie studied both women carefully, not wanting to say the wrong thing, despite Kennedy's reassurances. "Shea, you know me. I'm not a bigot. I just hate that my little girl is going to have some extra tough times ahead."

"Completely understandable," Kennedy responded, and Carson nodded in agreement. "If you can get her through high school in one piece, it should get easier for her after that. But I won't lie to you. High school in Odessa is going to suck."

"Mmm." Katie agreed. "I've thought about that a lot, even before this. Never was fond of the idea of my daughter going to school where being a bubble-headed, boy-crazy cheerleader is considered life's highest aspiration. God, Shea." Katie shifted, flopping back in the overstuffed chair across from them and draping her legs across one of the high arms. "I came from Van Horn to the great city of Alpine, Texas, to go to college. I'm the only one of my friends who did. Half my friends were pregnant by high school graduation. When Parker graduated Sul Ross and we escaped Alpine, Odessa looked like the promised land. Hell, it even has a mall." She smiled.

"But the truth is, high schools are all the same, aren't they?"

Carson joined in. "Even in Dallas, being a bubble-headed, boy-crazy cheerleader was considered life's highest aspiration."

"What do I do?" Katie honestly asked them. "You've been there, Shea. Do I send her to some all-gay school? That would just delay her learning how cruel the world can be, don't you think?" She started to cry. "I'm sorry." She sniffled, swiping her shirt cuff across her eyes. "Things turned out fine for you two. But I remember, Shea. Parker told me what all you went through. I just don't want my little girl—"

"To end up like me?" It popped out before she could stop it, and Kennedy wished she could take it back as soon as she heard herself. Katie's face reddened in shame and she dropped her eyes, fiddling with her tea bag. "Katie, I'm sorry. I didn't mean—"

"Neither did I," Katie answered sadly. "Guess I'm not so different from your mother after all, am I?" She shook her head. "Seems my baby is going to need her Auntie Shea an awful lot these next few years. I don't think her mother is going to do such a great job of it."

"The fact we're having this conversation tells me her mother is going to do just fine." Kennedy managed a smile. "Listen to me. There are no easy answers. But I think the most important thing you can do is treat her like your perfectly normal daughter, who just happens to be gay. If she ends up at a special school, let it be because she wanted to go there, and let it be for art, or science, or whatever she ends up being interested in."

"And if she ends up at Odessa Permian?" Katie raised her eyes, hoping for a lifeline.

"We'll all help her get through it," Kennedy answered firmly.

"Yeah, I guess we will." Katie released a long, shaking breath and stood, setting her mug on the coffee table. "Thanks." She leaned over, hugging each woman in turn. "Now I need to go find Parker and have a little chat with him. Excuse me, ladies."

She left the room and Kennedy remained silent, studying her cooling mug. "You know what I think?" She glanced over at Carson.

"What?" Carson eased the mug from Kennedy's hands, setting it aside and snuggling up to her.

"I think it was a lot easier being the family fuck up than the family counselor, that's what I think." She sighed. "I'm so tired. And I don't even want to think about Pete right now."

Carson couldn't resist any longer and hugged her tightly, rubbing her back. "You've got knots on your knots back here." She gently probed the muscles along Kennedy's spinal column, which were stretched as tight as piano wire.

"Mmm. Feels good." It was all the encouragement Carson needed and she got up and slid in behind Kennedy and dug into a few spots. "Family fixer-upper is a relatively new role for me. I'm not used to it just yet."

"Anything I can do to help?" Carson moved up to the hearth behind them and urged Kennedy to slide back, before she dug in in earnest.

"That helps." Kennedy dropped her head and gave a little grunt of pained pleasure. "Just love me. That's all I need." She felt the hands still for a second, a slight tremor running through them, before Carson continued her massage.

"I think I can manage that." She worked her way down Kennedy's back and back up, ending with a soothing scalp massage.

At last, Kennedy reluctantly stood, rolling her shoulders in appreciation. "Much better." She leaned over and kissed Carson quickly. "Thank you. What say we go upstairs and hang with the kids for a while? I think we still have *Spiderman* on DVD somewhere up there."

"Ooo. Sounds great." Carson reached out as Kennedy helped her up. "Promise me you'll take a nap during the movie if you feel the need?"

"That's already part of the plan." As they rounded the corner, Pete appeared at the top of the stairs, his hair sticking out and his T-shirt halfway tucked into wrinkled flannel pajama bottoms. "Afternoon." She nodded curtly as they passed each other. "Lord, Pete, can you at least shower and get dressed? It's almost noon."

"Leave me alone, Shea." He resisted the urge to lash out physically. "Sleeping in on a holiday was still legal last time I checked."

"Fine." She went by, listening intently.

"Peta Braden Nocona!" Aileen's voice carried up the stairs. "You march right back up there and make yourself presentable. I might allow breakfast in your pajamas, but it's near on to lunch, so go get some proper clothes on and comb your hair before I take a razor to it."

"Might be legal outside these walls." Kennedy laughed to herself. "But the laws of Mama's kitchen will prevail."

Chapter
Three

IN A MIRACLE of orchestration, the entire Nocona clan gathered around the large oak dining table, with Joseph at one end and Parker the other. The other five adults and three children were scattered evenly along both sides, and platters and bowls heaped high with food covered the tabletop. The smells sifting through the air made noses twitch in anticipation, and more than one stomach rumbled as the family settled in their seats, with the best linen napkins in their laps and a large glass of iced tea at each spot.

After a few moments of fidgeting, each face eventually turned toward Joseph, who waited patiently for his brood to quiet down. It was dusk out and the rain was still falling, a steady, light soaking of the desert, bringing promise of an explosion of late fall color over the next few days as thirsty foliage drank in the welcome moisture. The thunder had dissipated, and the weather forecast predicted sun and much warmer temperatures by Friday afternoon.

Joseph cleared his throat and smiled at his family. "Here we are again." He paused and took a sip of tea. "This year we welcome a new member to our gathering. Carson, we're honored to have you at our table. It's been many years since any of my children brought someone home for the holidays. You must be very special to my daughter, and therefore, you're special to me." He turned to his daughter's companion, who blushed to her roots and smiled shyly.

"Thank you," she almost whispered. "I'm honored to be here." She reached out and squeezed his hand briefly, having drawn the chair immediately to his right. She felt a light caress to her thigh under the table before Kennedy rested her hand on it, leaving it there.

"We have a tradition in our home for the Thanksgiving holiday. We don't say a prayer, for to us, prayer is a private matter between a person and whatever being they worship.

Instead, we go around the table and each of us names at least one thing they're thankful for. So..." He looked toward his wife. "Aileen, my love, I'll start us out, and then you go, and we'll give our guest the courtesy of going last."

Carson breathed an inaudible sigh of relief and glanced over at Kennedy, who smiled and winked at her.

"I'm thankful to have all my children and grandchildren back this year, safe and healthy, and thankful for another year of prosperity here at Big Star Lodge, and most thankful for another year walking this earth with my lovely wife." He picked up Aileen's hand and brushed a kiss across the back of it.

"You flatterer." Aileen's eyes sparkled, and Carson finally saw the one characteristic Kennedy had inherited from her mother. The blue was the exact same shade, and the sparkle, she realized, was the exact same expression she had often seen gazing back at her. It spoke volumes of love and she understood a bit more of the depth of Kennedy's love, seeing it in the expression of someone who had been in love for so many years. "I'm thankful we have a full house through the holidays." She chuckled. "It means the Christmas tree will have lots of surprises under it this year."

She turned expectantly to Katie, who smiled and looked down the table at Nathan, who was seated next to his grandmother. "What are you thankful for, sweetie?"

Nathan rolled his eyes upward in thought, kicking his chair legs as his face grew sober. "I'm thankful to have my two front teeth back." He grinned, showing off said teeth, and everyone broke into laughter.

"My turn!" Ryan bellowed out proudly next to his brother. "I'm thankful for the Dallas Cowboys and the Texas Longhorns." This resulted in more mirth, as the adults enjoyed a child's simple view of the good things in life.

"Good, sweetie." Katie kissed him on the head. She took a breath and clasped Parker's hand. "Shall we, honey?"

"I think so. Katie and I are thankful for the same thing, so we're going together." He caught his father's eye and broke into a wide grin. "Mama, Pa, by this time next year, you'll have another grandchild at the table."

"Oh my stars, you scamp!" Aileen flew out of her seat, giving both her daughter-in-law and her son hugs before she returned to her chair. She looked around at the table, then at her husband. "Seems to me everyone else was keeping this secret from us, judging by your lack of surprise."

"True." Parker fended off her accusing glare. "But not for very long. We just found out this past week and only told Shea and Carson yesterday."

"Congratulations, son." Joseph nodded, his face beaming. "And to you, Katie. My quiver overflows with the blessing of grandchildren."

"We're pretty excited about it." She smiled back at him. "This will be the last one, so we're looking forward to having our family complete."

"Ah, but look around us." Joseph waxed wise. "Our family is growing and two of my children have yet to start families. Who knows what we'll bring to this table in the years to come? I may have to add a leaf to it. Pete?" He studied his rather quiet younger son, who was busy arranging and re-arranging his silverware.

"I'm thankful to have my midterms out of the way," Pete mumbled, not looking up from his plate. Joseph frowned but let it pass, moving on to Erin.

"I'm thankful for my best friend Jessica," she warbled. "And for Auntie Shea spending time with me this weekend." She glanced adoringly at her aunt, who ruffled her head in response. Parker and Katie both made eye contact with Kennedy, confirming they had had the talk.

"We're glad Auntie Shea spends time with you too, pumpkin." Parker smiled at his daughter and then at his sister.

Kennedy nodded at him and took a deep breath. Finally, it was her turn, and she took Carson's hand, chafing it as she looked deeply into her eyes. "I'm thankful, this day and every day, for the miracle of Carson in my life." She bent forward, lightly pecking her stunned lover on the lips. "I love you," she whispered as she pulled back.

"I...I..." Carson's eyes welled up and spilled over, and everything became a blur. "I can't." Suddenly it was all too much, this family business, and she buried herself into Kennedy, sniffling as she tried to regain her composure. "I'm just thankful to have you," she gasped out, grateful as someone found a tissue and pressed it into her hand.

"Well." Aileen attempted to draw some attention away from the couple. Kennedy was gently stroking Carson's face, wiping the tears away, and as she watched, Kennedy leaned over and whispered in Carson's ear. The words seemed to have their intended effect, as Carson finally sat up and sheepishly glanced across the table. "Who's ready for turkey with all the trimmings?" Aileen hefted up a large platter. "Shea, love, at one end of this plate is your tofurkey."

"Bleck." Ryan wrinkled up his nose in disgust. "Auntie Shea, you may have good taste in girls, but your taste in food sucks." At that, the entire table burst out in laughter, as plates were passed back and forth, and they all received more than they could possibly finish as they loaded them down.

FRIDAY DAWNED SUNNY and clear, and an afternoon game of tackle football was in full swing in the large open area next to the barn. On one team was Kennedy, Erin, and Ryan, and on the other, Parker, Carson, and Nathan. It was a modified game, in deference to the children, especially since Nathan could not yet actually catch or throw the football, although if someone handed it off to him, he made a valiant effort at running with it. Basically, whichever team scored three touchdowns first won, one point per touchdown, no extra points or field goals involved. There were very few rules, many of them made up as they went along.

It was tied up at two to two, and all six players were covered in a liberal layer of mud, leftover from the previous day's storms. It made running a slow prospect, and tackling an ugly experience on several levels. Kennedy and Ryan had scored a touchdown each and Parker had scored the two for his team.

Kennedy crouched behind Erin, who hiked the ball back to her. She pivoted, backing up and looking for Ryan, who was supposed to run by and take the ball from her, after which she would follow after him to block any would-be tacklers. As she backed up, her shoe caught in the mud and came off, and she cursed, hopping on one foot, still trying to find Ryan. As Ryan approached her, he slid down and took her out, tangling with her one stable foot, and she flipped over, landing flat on her back and releasing the football, which bounced once before Carson swooped by and scooped it up.

"Hey!" Kennedy rolled and jumped up, running with one socked foot and one shoed foot as fast as she could, closing in on Carson, who was doing her best to sprint, given the two-inch thick globs of mud that coated the bottoms of both shoes. Carson looked back and realized Kennedy was going to tackle her. She held her breath and grinned as Nathan came running across the field in his bare feet.

"Here! Nathan, over here!" Kennedy's arms closed around her waist, and as she fell, she handed the ball to Nathan, who whooped with all his might and took off. He had two advantages: he was light enough that he didn't sink into the goo as badly as the others, and both Ryan and Erin were too far downfield to catch up with him, although they both screamed in outrage and put forth their best effort.

It wasn't enough, and his short legs were a blur as he neared the bales of hay that marked his goal.

Carson hit the mud, bracing her fall with her hands, but not enough to avoid getting a face full of mud as Kennedy landed on top of her. Both women looked up as Nathan crossed the goal line and spiked the ball, doing a dance that would have earned him a celebration penalty in the NFL. "Yeah. I'm the man!" He did a little rooster-like strut and both women burst out laughing. Parker ran to the end of the field and picked up his youngest son, swinging him around with pride.

Carson rolled over with Kennedy still sprawled on top of her. "Is that you under there?" Kennedy ran one finger down Carson's nose, collecting a scoop of mud and wiggling it in her face. "Man, you've got to be the dirtiest one out here."

"Oh yeah?" Carson grabbed up a handful of reddish-black goop and smeared it onto the top of Kennedy's head, then grabbed her face with both hands and applied the rest to her cheeks. "Not any more." She smiled in satisfaction, which lasted all of two seconds before the wickedest grin she'd ever seen graced Kennedy's lips. "Oh, no." She tried to scramble away but found herself pinned under two strong thighs, as Kennedy sat on her and spread handfuls of the thick mud everywhere she could reach.

"Heheheh." Kennedy reached for more mud and Carson took a chance, twisting her body and flipping her off. She tried to gain her footing, but slipped and found Carson wrapped around her legs, as she effectively dragged her backward through the almost liquid mud puddle. She grimaced as her shirt came untucked and she felt cold wet mud make its way inside her shirt, coating her stomach and sports bra. "Oh, you are going to pay for that."

"You'll have to catch me first...ooopmh." Carson's face was one inch from the thick mess, with one of Kennedy's arms wrapped firmly around her body, while the other one pushed her closer and closer, and she took a deep breath, right before she got her second mud mask of the afternoon. "You!" She stood, wiping her eyes, and spied her nemesis only a foot away. "Aaagghhhhhhh!"

She body slammed Kennedy, and they both rolled over and over, getting more and more covered with mud, grass, and leaves, until they both resembled bog beasties more than humans. An all out mud wrestling match ensued, both women dropping great handfuls of mud down each other's shirts and into the waistbands of their sweatpants. They were both laughing hysterically and ended up in a tangled mess in the middle of the puddle, Kennedy sprawled on top of Carson, pinning her with both hands and knees.

"You surrender?" Kennedy released one hand long enough to gather another scoop of mud.

Kennedy's face was completely covered, only the whites of her eyes and her very blue irises giving a clue as to her identity. "Oh, like that's a threat at this point." Carson retorted, then slapped the mud out of her hand, and it landed with a thwacking sound next to them. "But yeah, I surrender, so we can go shower."

"What do I win?" Kennedy felt two fingers, swiping the mud from her lips, and realizing Carson's intent, returned the favor, right before a muddy hand threaded through her equally-muddy hair, and their lips met for a timeless moment. The kiss lasted until suddenly both women were hit with a strong spray of very cold water.

"Yikes!" Carson released her, looking over toward the edge of the field where Aileen stood holding a hose that was aimed at them with deadly accuracy.

"Get up, the both of you." She watched as two sheepish smiles appeared, the white teeth in sharp contrast to their blackened faces. "I know this is cold, but neither of you are going anywhere near the house until I've hosed you down, so stand still and it will be over with faster."

"Yes, ma'am." Two voices spoke in unison as they held hands and braced themselves against the icy blast of water. It moved slowly and thoroughly from their heads to their feet, stopping in any spots that were especially muddy. They both turned on command while she got their backsides, and they were visibly shivering by the time she finished.

"Done." The water stopped and they turned as she tossed two towels at them. They were old towels, reserved for just such activities, and they both gratefully wrapped up in them against the chill. "Take your shoes and socks off when you reach the porch, and don't touch anything on your way upstairs. Leave your clothes in the trash bag I've put in the bathroom up there. Bring them down to wash when you've done showering."

"Yes, ma'am." They watched her stalk off methodically toward the house before Carson looked warily over at Kennedy.

"She mad?" She snuggled against Kennedy's side, trying to borrow some warmth.

"Nah." Kennedy draped an arm around her shivering lover and guided her toward the back porch. "We had many a weekend that ended with a good hosing when I was growing up. She's used to it. She just wanted to make sure we don't track any mud inside."

"Oh. Never played much football growing up. Kind of hard with only three of us." Carson stepped carefully through the still-muddy backyard, and stopped as they reached the bottom step and removed their basically-ruined tennis shoes.

Parker sat on the top step, sipping at a fresh cold beer and chuckling as they both started up the steps. Katie had already taken all three children inside and down to a large shower that occupied one corner of the basement, rather than trying to get small muddy hands all the way up to the third floor. "Man, oh man, what I wouldn't give to be a single college guy again." He looked up at his sister and her companion, his eyes twinkling with merriment.

"Why?" Kennedy stooped down, rolling up her sweats pants legs, so as to be extra careful not to get mud on the carpet inside.

"Because it would have been so much fun to go back to school next week and tell the guys I watched two chicks mud wrestle, make out, and then have a wet T-shirt contest." He ducked as Kennedy tried to swat him with her wet towel. "Wouldn't have had to tell them it was my sister. Ouch!" Carson caught him on the arm with her towel, and she and Kennedy exchanged a glance before they both tackled him, getting the remains of mud and water all over him in the process, as his beer went flying and spilled down his shirt. They both grabbed up muddy shoes and socks, smearing those down both his front and backside.

"Mama!" Kennedy poked her head inside the back door. "You need to come hose down Parker."

"Hey!" Parker stood, looking down at the mess they'd made of him and realized Kennedy was right. "Watch your back, Shea. You too, shorty." He threatened both of them, before both women scampered inside the house and closed the back door.

Forty-five minutes later Carson sat at the snack bar in the kitchen, clad in a clean warm sweat suit, her hair damp and gelled back. After showering together, Kennedy had fallen asleep while Carson rubbed her back. Not sleepy at all, Carson had left her to her nap and wandered downstairs to see what was going on. Now she was munching on freshly baked oatmeal butterscotch chip cookies, alternating bites with sips of ice cold milk. "Sorry for the trouble." She glanced sheepishly at Aileen, who was busy putting away sandwich fixings from feeding the children.

"No need to apologize, Carson." She placed a loaf of homemade bread in the bread box and closed it before she removed her apron and took a seat across from her daughter's...lover...she acknowledged. It was strange after so many years to think of her middle child as part of a couple. She picked up a cookie, sniffing the warm, sweet scent before she took a bite. "Been a long time since I watched my daughter play like that."

"What about other holidays?" Carson picked up a second cookie, deciding counting fat grams was pointless over Thanksgiving. "These are sinful, you know." She grinned at Aileen.

"Thank you. Oh, they always play a game of football, but she's not been hosed down since she was in college, I don't believe. She played, but her heart was never really in it. She did it for Parker's kids more than anything." She studied Carson, who looked all of sixteen years old at the moment. "Five years ago my daughter gave up on life, or at least the fun side of it. I assume she's told you about Angela?"

"Yes." Carson waxed sorrowful, remembering the bitter tears Kennedy had shed the night she'd shared her story. "She never got over that, did she?"

"Maybe she has." Aileen watched Carson closely as her statement sunk in. "She's not had an easy time of it since high school. About the time she made peace with her father and forgave him for her Comanche heritage, she told us she was gay." She felt her cheeks redden in shame. "I didn't take it too well, and I know I let her down for a long time. I..." She sighed. "I thought it meant her giving up having a real life, or at least the life I wanted for her. I was ignorant, Carson, and I did everything I could to try to convince her it was just a phase. I wanted her to marry, and have a husband and children, and a house, all the things that to me constituted happiness. And I was so afraid for her."

"Why?" Carson chose not to comment, allowing Aileen to speak freely.

"I was afraid she might be discriminated against, or maybe even physically harmed by bigoted people. I didn't want her on a path that would make her life harder than it had to be. I didn't understand how she could be gay. I felt like I had done something to make her that way. Boys were always buzzing around her from the time she was thirteen, but she was never interested. I saw it, but didn't want to see it. She's such a beautiful girl."

"Yes, she is." Carson's eyes warmed and her voice softened as she spoke.

Aileen could clearly see the love in Carson's eyes, and said a quick silent prayer of gratitude for it. "I finally went down to the university library and read up on homosexuality and came to my senses. I realized that I had to give up my notions of what is normal and what is not, and that Shea is exactly who she was meant to be. It wasn't a choice, and there was nothing I could do to make her be straight. So I sent her off to school in Santa Fe and prayed for her every night."

"And y'all made your peace then?" Carson poured herself another glass of milk.

"It was a gradual process, but yes, for the most part, I let her go. I had to. She had been so unhappy for most of high school, but in college and law school, and those first few years in Houston, she blossomed, or so we thought. We didn't know she was still drinking and taking drugs until Angela died." She looked down, clasping her hands in her lap. "She told us all about her life and how she'd been living. I think Angela was the first thing that had made her happy in a very long time, and that was snatched from her before it ever had a chance to grow. The light went out in her after that night."

"I know," Carson commented quietly.

"Oh, she gave up the drinking and the drugs and she began to build her career and her own law firm. We were so proud of her for that. She has that nice house out there on the lake, and the land, and the horses, and she takes care of Pete. On the surface, she has everything." She paused, taking another bite of cookie.

"But she wasn't happy." Carson felt sad, knowing the lonely life Kennedy had been living before they met. "Neither was I." She swiped away a tear. "I know what loneliness is, Mrs. Noc...Aileen. I don't have a family. I'm sure she's told you that."

"Yes, child, Parker did, and you have a family now. I hope you know that." Aileen reached across, clasping Carson's hand. "You're both much too young to be as alone as you were. Here, my daughter, about to be thirty-three next week, and she might as well have been sixty, the way she's been living. It broke my heart, because the one thing I knew she was missing was love. I think she's found that now."

"She has." Carson looked down to hide her tears. "Hey." She looked up, her thoughts derailed. "Did you say she is going to be thirty-three next week?"

"Why, yes. Didn't you know?" Aileen pushed another cookie across to Carson.

"No. Actually, we've been together only a few months. I don't think we ever talked about birthdays. Guess we should. Mine is December 8th, so it's coming up too. What is the exact date of hers?"

"November 29th, next Wednesday." Aileen smiled. "Will

you two still be here then?"

"I think so. I think we'll be getting back from backpacking on Tuesday, and were planning to stay through until Friday." Carson realized she'd have to scramble to make proper birthday plans. "Where's a nice dinner place around here?"

"The Gage Hotel, down in Marathon." Aileen laughed. "It's about the only place, actually, but it is nice. Good food, good wine, and you can get a candlelit table if you want it. Nice rooms, too." She watched Carson blush again.

"Hmm." Carson found her own smile. "I'll have to make some plans between now and then. Oh, gosh. I need to get her a gift."

"I think you already have." Aileen patted her hand. "Carson, I didn't finish what I wanted to say to you. I made peace with my daughter's sexual orientation several years ago. All I've wanted for her since then is for her to be happy. When she looks at you, I see joy on her face I haven't seen in years. She adores you."

Carson blushed and looked down. "I adore her too," she spoke softly.

"Oh, I know you do, honey. And I think she's finally found that happiness I wanted so badly for her." She tilted her head, waiting for eye contact, smiling gently when she got it. "I know two months is a short time, but have you two discussed the future?"

"In vague terms, yes." Carson's forehead wrinkled in serious thought. "This is all kind of new to me and she's been very patient. I've never had a girlfriend and never lived with anyone before, at least not as a couple. If you're asking if we've made a long-term commitment, no, we haven't, not in so many words." She looked up, balling her hand into a fist and holding it against her chest. "But I know what I feel inside. I love your daughter with all my heart. That much I can tell you and be sure of."

"I have no doubt, Carson. It's written all over your face." She stood, leaning over, bracing her weight on the counter. "I want to ask of you one thing."

Carson tilted her head curiously. "I'll do my best. What is it?"

"Take care of yourself." She cupped Carson's face briefly and patted her cheek before she stepped back. "She needs you."

"I'll go you one better." Carson smiled, emphasizing her words. "I'll take care of her, too, because I need her every bit as much. In fact, I think I'll go see if she's still asleep."

"All right. She needs to be up in time for dinner, and that will be in another few hours." Aileen watched thoughtfully as Carson disappeared up the stairs.

Carson walked quietly down the hallway, listening intently as she opened the door to Kennedy's room. She heard a few soft whimpers and watched as Kennedy's hands twitched and her body jerked a few times. She mumbled a few incoherent words in a frightened tone, and Carson was at her side in an instant, reaching out to smooth a frown from Kennedy's forehead. "Shh." She carefully lay down next to her, stretching out on her side and stroking the dark head. "Damn. Been a good week since you've had any bad dreams." She bent close, whispering quietly. "It's all right, honey. Everything's going to be all right."

Kennedy's eyes fluttered open in confusion as she gradually became aware of her surroundings. "Oh." She closed them again in relief, her heart still pounding against her chest. She took Carson's hand and slipped it inside the terry robe she still wore, placing it against her chest.

"Oh, honey." Carson leaned across, taking Kennedy into her arms. "Feels like it's going to beat right through your skin."

"I know," Kennedy rasped out, her voice thick with sleep. "I had that dream again, where you were kidnapped, and I couldn't get there in time and you..."

"I died?" Carson kissed her on the cheek. "I assure you I'm very much alive, thanks to you."

"Carson, don't you ever die on me, promise?" Kennedy burrowed into the warm embrace, feeling Carson wrapped around her like a comforting security blanket.

"Funny, I just promised your mother I'd take care of both of us." Carson stroked her head, feeling Kennedy grow still.

"You what?" Her dream forgotten, she pulled away, just enough to see Carson's face.

"I just had a mother-daughter chat, kind of, only it was me and your mother." Carson smiled at the alarm in Kennedy's eyes. "Relax. I didn't share anything private." She swatted Kennedy's butt. "And you failed to tell me your birthday is Wednesday."

"You didn't ask." Kennedy smiled, lifting Carson's sweatshirt and nibbling at her stomach, memories of her lover covered in mud and water spurring her on.

"I know, but now we're here and I didn't get to make any plans for it before we left Austin. Oh..." Warm lips tugged at her navel ring, sending a jolt of pleasure directly to her groin and nipples.

"Plans are way overrated." The sweatshirt came off, followed by the sweatpants. "Spontaneous is pretty good sometimes, don't you think?"

"I...oh..." The lips moved up, and Kennedy circled her breast with light kisses and flicks of her tongue. "Yeah. Spontaneous is good."

"Heh." Kennedy removed her own robe and went to work in earnest.

"SO." CARSON BOUNCED a little as she sat on the end of the bed, her denim-clad legs crossed. "This place we're going tonight, it's one of your old hangouts? 'Cause I really want to see all the places you used to go when you lived here."

"Hmm. Yeah, sort of, keeping in mind I wasn't old enough to drink when I actually lived here. This was more of an early adulthood hangout when I was home from school. Although after I turned eighteen, I could usually get in. If we couldn't get in, we did our share of hanging outside places like this one, begging people to buy us beer." Kennedy turned, tucking a long-sleeved powder blue button-down into her faded jeans, which were ripped at the knees, with frayed bottoms. The edge of a white ribbed tank top peeked out above three un-buttoned buttons, and she wore her nickel-plated black cowboy boots and a matching black tooled-leather belt, which she cinched up with its plain silver buckle.

"Have you changed much since back then?" Carson swung her legs over the edge of the mattress and reached down, tugging on her own black cowboy boots.

"Well, maybe a few tiny lines and I weigh a little more." Kennedy considered, looking in the mirror as she raked her fingers back through her hair to order it. "The hair's the biggest change."

"How so?" Carson stood, smoothing down the front of a soft black suede shirt that was tucked neatly into the waistband of her jeans. The shirt had fringe on the sleeves and along the yoke, along with a few silver studs. She also tugged a woven black belt through her belt loops and smiled as Kennedy moved in to buckle it up.

"My hair was long and straight, down to my waist, until I started interviewing for clerkships after my first year of law school." She gave Carson's hip a pat. "I'm usually unbuckling those for you." She winked and smiled before she turned back to the dresser, grabbing up her wallet and tucking it into her back pocket, snapping a shiny trucker chain to a belt loop to ward off pickpockets. "You got a chain too, or do you want me to carry your ID and cash for you?"

"It was down to your waist? Wow." Carson tried to picture it. "Um, I think I packed my chain." She rummaged around in her overnight bag. "Yeah. Here it is." She quickly snapped it onto her wallet and they were ready to go.

"Harley or 4Runner?" They made their way down the stairs and outside, pulling on their leather jackets against a slight chill as they stopped on the porch.

"Are you nuts? Harley of course." Carson took her hand and impatiently dragged her back to the barn.

"All right, but it'll be cold." It was a clear, crisp night with a hint of winter in the air, though it was almost a month away.

"Nah." Carson practically skipped along, swinging their arms. "You'll be cold. I'll be behind you. You're my wind block."

"Oh, fine. Glad I'm good for something." Kennedy rolled her eyes, but smiled. They reached the barn and donned their helmets, along with the chaps, and soon they were off, racing down the narrow highway under a starlit sky. The moon was rising, splashing a pale glow across the land, accentuating the many dips and hills that led up to the taller mountains in the distance and lending a ghostly quality to the vast landscape.

In no time the town was behind them, and they veered off the main highway onto an even narrower road with no marker. It zigzagged several times and Carson held on, feeling Kennedy's body leaning into the turns, balancing the bike. She wished there were a way to mute the engine's noise so she could hear the sounds of the night creatures she knew they were missing, especially the coyotes they had heard the first night they were there.

Almost too soon, a cluster of red, white, and blue lights appeared up ahead, and gradually a long, low building took shape, along with a parking lot full of cars, trucks, bikes, and even a few big rigs, off at the far edge of the property. As they drew closer, several neon beer signs grew clear, hanging from inside the windows. Up on a pole was another sign with the words "Armadillo Flats" in red scrolled lights, along with a whimsical lighted gray armadillo wearing a cowboy hat and holding a tall mug of beer.

Kennedy swung into the parking lot and pulled into a row of motorcycles. As she cut the engine, raucous honky-tonk music poured from the open doorway, along with the sound of shattering glass, followed by a long string of colorful profanity. As they removed their chaps and helmets and stowed them away, a large man stumbled through the front door of the bar, aided by a forceful shove from an even larger man, apparently a bouncer. "Get on out of here, ya drunk bastard!"

"Ah'm shottaly tober...shottaly shober...ahhh!" The first man waved an exasperated hand and teetered on the bottom step, then extended his leg in an exaggerated fashion and weaved toward the cars. He spotted the two women and paused, readjusting his direction, and with great effort, moved toward them, only losing his balance twice in the process.

"Trouble," Kennedy mumbled under her breath, placing herself between Carson and the man. Six feet away she could smell the whiskey on his breath and could see his unfocused brown eyes, along with a very red nose and a heavy dark five o'clock shadow.

"Ladies." He attempted to tilt his hat and dropped it. "Dang it!" He bent over, trying several times before he managed to pick it up again, slapping it back on his head in a lopsided manner. "Can I offer you a drink?" He hiccupped, and produced a leather-covered flask from his jacket pocket. "Shack Zaniels...errr. Zhack Daniels?" He took a healthy swig of the whiskey and held it out toward them.

"No, thank you." Kennedy edged around, trying to head toward the front door.

"Then can you point me to ma truck? Can't seem to find it." He wobbled, and suddenly his world began to spin and his face turned pasty white. Then green.

"Let's get inside. This is gonna get really ugly." Kennedy grabbed Carson's hand and ran for the door, entering the bar just as the sounds of retching reached their ears.

The bouncer had been watching the entire exchange from the doorway, and he grinned broadly at them, one gold front tooth glinting in the low lighting. He nodded graciously to the two women. "Ladies, welcome to Armadillo Flats. Mosey on up to the bar and tell old Bill back there your first drink's on Tiny. I'll take care of him if he tries to come back in here."

"Um...thanks, Tiny." Even from her 5 feet 11 inches, Kennedy had to crane her neck to look up at the man, who was easily three times her size in girth as well. "Carson." She placed a hand in the small of Carson's back, steering her through the crowd to the plain bar, pulling up two padded vinyl and chrome bar stools and checking them carefully for grime or beer before they sat down. She ordered up a longneck Mexican beer for Carson and a bottle of root beer for herself.

She smiled as the drinks were delivered. The root beer came in a dark brown bottle, and looked enough like a regular beer to keep ignorant cowboys from giving her grief about not having a 'real' drink, and insisting on buying her one. She took a sip, her eyes scanning the entire room, taking in the local color she'd all but forgotten since her years in Austin. "Been a long time since I've been in here."

"Yeah?" Carson sat back on her stool, leaning against the bar and propping one elbow up on it. "See anyone you know?"

"A few, yes." She casually draped one arm across the bar behind Carson, not quite touching her shoulders. "Place hasn't changed much, although I don't remember Tiny. Bill, I do, vaguely. I think he was a few years behind me in school."

"So what did you used to do here?" Carson cringed at an off-note from some yodeling singer blaring from the jukebox.

"Drink beer, score pot, cruise chicks, and raise hell." Kennedy's face was sober as yet another layer of her life was peeled back for Carson's scrutiny.

"Cr...cruise chicks?" Carson looked around the bar, which fairly oozed with testosterone.

"Not like I had Gaby & Mo's to work with here." She gestured toward two girls who were dancing together. "Funny thing, two girls can dance together and no one thinks much of it, because we've been doing it since like second grade. But if two guys were to dance together in here, they'd be run out of town on a rail."

"But how did you figure out which girls were interested?" Carson's brows knit in confusion as she studied the various women in the place.

"Little things." Kennedy leaned closer. "Eye contact, partly. Body language. How close they'd get when I'd talk to them, stuff like that. Sometimes if I was fairly certain of the interest, I'd ask them to dance. Nothing too slow or romantic or anything like that, but usually, the signals sent off dancing would be enough to seal the deal."

"What deal?" They had had a discussion about the past before and she knew Kennedy had not done a lot of sleeping around.

"Sometimes I could get them to go out back to my truck and make out for a while." She looked down for a moment, until she felt a gentle touch to her thigh.

"It's all right, honey. You had to learn somewhere, right?" She resisted the urge to give Kennedy a quick kiss.

"Yeah, I guess so." Kennedy managed a small smile. "It was easier once I got to Santa Fe, but this place, especially the summer after my senior year of high school, I could sneak in. Not like they checked ID much. But that summer, I'd come out to my parents and I was so curious, trying to figure it all out."

"Bet you broke some hearts." Carson leaned back slightly, until Kennedy's arm across the bar was touching her back.

"Yeah. Didn't mean to. I was like a wild thing. I wanted so badly to know what it was like to be with a girl, but I was so afraid. I did a lot of making out before I ever got brave enough to go any further." She glanced around, noting pairs of mostly male eyes admiring them, along with a few pairs of female ones. "A few of the older women I hooked up with couldn't figure out why I wouldn't go all the way with them, because for them it was no big deal."

"But it was to you?" Carson almost whispered. This was something they hadn't discussed, and she prodded carefully.

"I didn't want to lose my virginity in my pickup truck to a one-night stand." Kennedy spoke softly. "I was realistic enough to think that I might not be able to hold out for true love, but I at least wanted to have some sort of relationship or feelings for the person I had my first time with. So when I finally did..."

"Shhh." Carson covered her lips with her fingers. "Not here, please. I would like to hear about it, but not here, in this place."

"All right. It'll keep 'til later." She brushed a kiss across the fingers. "Lord." Her eyes warmed as they wandered over Carson. "I have got to remember to be cautious in here, and that is going to be so hard to do, because you look beautiful, and that shirt is so nice and soft, and the lights look really nice in your hair."

"Thank you. You look pretty hot yourself." Carson sat closer still, smiling as Kennedy finally placed her arm snugly around her shoulders. "We can dance though, can't we? I mean at least some of the faster songs."

"Absolutely." She scowled at a young man as he started to approach Carson, and she unconsciously dropped her hand possessively around Carson's shoulder. Her face remained stony, and she watched him visibly swallow before he thought better and moved on. "Mine," she snarled, a bare whisper that even Carson couldn't make out.

Carson tapped one foot against the crossbar on her stool in time to the music and drained her beer bottle to half-full. She considered ordering a tequila shot and decided to wait a while. She was about to ask her partner to dance, when a tall thin man approached them, his skin much too pale for someone who lived in the West Texas sun. His light brown hair fell haphazardly across his forehead, and his face bore a somewhat haughty expression. "Shea Nocona." He bellied up to the bar, getting way too far inside Kennedy's personal space, to Carson's eye.

"Hello, Rick." Kennedy didn't smile, and Carson could feel a slight tension in the arm at her back. Kennedy sat up straighter, her jaw muscles also tensing, as she turned slightly, but not fully, toward the man. "Long time."

"Too long." He gave Carson the once-over and dismissed her, turning his attention completely toward Kennedy. "You home for the holidays?"

"We're home for the holidays and a little backpacking. Then back to Austin." She set her empty root beer bottle down accepting a fresh one that magically appeared from Bill behind the bar. "Thanks." She nodded at him, smiling briefly.

"You need a little recreational addition for your backpacking trip?" He spoke low, leaning ever closer into her space, hovering almost in her ear. "I've got quite a selection out in my truck."

"No, thanks." Kennedy leaned back away from him slightly, almost, but not quite, pressing against Carson in the process. "I'm not into that anymore."

"Not even a few little hits?" He moved around, taking a sudden interest in Carson. "Your friend going with you? Maybe she'd like something?"

"No." Kennedy swung further toward Carson, placing one boot on the sidepiece that supported the legs on Carson's barstool. "She wouldn't."

"Maybe she can speak for herself." His humor was gone. "I've got some primo weed out back, little lady. Some Ex. Even a little coke. What do you say?"

"No, thank you." Carson also sat up taller, feeling Kennedy's arm curl tightly against her shoulders.

"Man, you are so not like your brother." He sneered at her in distain. "I'd heard you'd become a dyke and a totally uptight do-gooder. Guess I heard right."

Kennedy stood so swiftly her barstool almost toppled over. ""What do you mean by that?"

"Dyke?" He laughed cruelly. "Maybe you and your little friend can go outside and give me a show, because I know you know what it means."

"No." She brushed off the insult. "What do you mean about my brother?"

"He's been in here every night since he got home. This is the first night I haven't seen him, come to think of it." He looked around quickly, as if to confirm his statement. "Too bad. He's been my biggest customer this week. Guess he's doing all right for himself back in Austin, huh?"

The rage rose up so fast there was no stopping it and before she had time to think, she'd slammed him against the wall, one arm twisted behind his back between his body and the wall, one forearm across his throat, and one threatening knee in his groin. "Stay away from my brother." She pressed harder, watching his face turn red as his Adam's apple was constricted. He coughed, unable to speak, and started to struggle. "Don't move, unless you want to get to know this knee even better." He stopped fighting her and made a choking noise. "You sell so much as another gram of anything to Pete and I will come find you, and you'll wish I'd killed you by the time I'm done. Understand?"

She cautiously released him as he nodded. She was bigger than him and packed with a lot more muscle. He shook his arm, and grasped his neck, trying to make the choking sensation go away. "Careful there, Shea. You might start to squeak when you walk."

She rolled her eyes. "You sold him something last night?" He hesitated and she moved toward him. "Yes or no. Just tell me, because I'll find out anyway when I get home."

"Yeah." He nodded, looking over her shoulder to where Carson stood, her body rigid with apprehension. "Bag of pot."

"Just pot?" Her eyes narrowed, snapping with anger.

"What do you think? He is your brother, after all." He straightened his shirt collar in a dignified manner. "You're a damned hypocrite, Shea. You know that? Are we finished?"

"For now." She turned her back on him and strode back to the bar, feeling her insides shake. "Bastard," she muttered, picking up her root beer and gulping down most of the cold, frothy liquid, watching her hand tremble slightly as she set it back down. She felt someone watching her and turned to her right. "Oh, good lord. I should've known where there is Frick, Frack wouldn't be too far behind."

"Shea." A much more attractive man tilted his head at her, a smug smile on his face. A sandy-colored moustache twitched in amusement, and his ruddy complexion was much more in keeping with the desert sun and wind.

"Not funny, Tom." She leaned back against the bar. "You two haven't changed at all in the fifteen years since I left this place. Isn't it about time you earned an honest wage instead of selling crap to innocent kids? I'm half a mind to turn you both in to the sheriff."

"I wouldn't if I were you." The smile disappeared and his face grew icy cold. "Word of warning, Shea. You go on back to your rich-bitch world in Austin and stay out of our business. You'd be just like us if you hadn't left, and you know it." He stalked away from them, gabbing Rick by the elbow before they made a speedy exit outside.

Kennedy sat down, resting her forearms on her legs as her head hung down. She played with the fringe in the rips at her knees until two hands appeared in her line of sight, resting gently on her thighs. One hand came up, cupping her face and tilting it up. "You wouldn't be like them."

"That's the thing." She answered painfully. "I would."

"No, you wouldn't." Carson resisted the urge to yell at her for reinforcement.

"You can't know that." Kennedy swallowed, willing Carson to contradict her.

"I can too." Carson clasped one hand over her heart. "I know, in here. Come on." She enfolded a warm hand with one of her own. "Let's get out of here."

"Where do you want to go?" Kennedy allowed herself to be led across the floor and out the door, edging through the growing crowd. Another pair of unseen eyes watched them leave, and Pete slipped from the shadows in the corner as his sister exited the bar.

Kennedy took a deep breath of the cold fresh air, glad to be out of the smoke and the noise.

"Anywhere." Carson fished in Kennedy's jacket pocket, finding the bike keys.

"I'm sorry I brought you here." Kennedy shoved her hands in her pockets, dragging her feet in a dejected manner as they walked toward the bike.

"I'm not." Carson tucked a hand in her elbow. "Now you know who was selling drugs to Pete. What are you going to do about it?"

"Have a talk with Pete first. Then another with Parker." She shook her head in frustration, feeling a growing internal warmth she suspected was residual anger and adrenaline. "We'll most likely turn them in. I don't think I can just let this go, even if they did used to be my friends."

Carson merely nodded, feeling way out of her element and unsure of what to say. They reached the bike, re-donned their chaps, and took off. The cold air felt good after the heat and chaos of the bar and Kennedy flipped her visor up, enjoying the wind full in her face. As they neared the main highway she blinked, trying to clear a sudden blurring of the stars overhead and the lines in the road.

She shook it off and turned onto the highway, revving the engine and laughing giddily, as a feeling of euphoria slowly came over her. The blurriness returned and the bike wove, crossing the line before she managed to right it. She felt Carson's arms almost squeeze the life out of her and she laughed harder, feeling prickling heat all over her skin.

"Kennedy, stop the bike, please!" Carson yelled in her ear, and she automatically obeyed, slowing and pulling to a stop. She braced one leg, swinging the other over the saddle as Carson jumped off first. She tried a couple times before she got the kickstand locked in place and let go of the bike.

"Oh, my lord." She laughed again, watching the moon blur and dance a little in her vision. The warmth grew, flooding her system, and she unzipped her jacket, ripping it off and tossing it across the bike saddle, along with her helmet.

"Honey, what's going on?" Carson took off her helmet and warily approached her, having watched the little display from a safe distance away.

"Those bastards." Kennedy draped one arm across Carson's shoulders in a sloppy manner, pulling her close as she brushed a kiss across her head.

"You're sweating." Carson dabbed damp beads from Kennedy's upper lip, then swiped a hand across her forehead. "And you have a fever. Honey, are you sick?"

"Noooooo." Kennedy giggled and hugged her again. "Those bastards must've put Ex in my root beer." She felt dizzy and leaned on Carson for support. "How do you feel about pushing the bike home?"

Carson looked down the lonely stretch of road, spotting a solitary light way off in the distance. Her heart was beating wildly with fear and she took deep breaths to calm herself. She had no experience with Ecstasy or any other drugs, and fervently hoped whatever it did wasn't too serious. "You may feel hot, but you'll catch cold if you don't put this back on." She grabbed up Kennedy's jacket and helped her put it back on. "How far is home?"

"Too far." Kennedy tried to gather her wits. "Let's push it over behind some trees off the road out of sight and we can come back for it in the morning."

"All right." Carson guided her back to the Harley and realized Kennedy was in no shape to try to hold it up. "You get the kickstand up and then get out of my way, okay?"

"Okay." Kennedy hugged her again and complied. "Oooo." She ran a finger along Carson's soft faded jeans at the back of her leg, between the chap's straps. "Your jeans...they're glowing a little bit."

"Whatever you say, honey, now move." She braced herself, her arm muscles bulging along with her thighs as she pushed the heavy bike across the field a ways and into a grove of trees. "Kickstand help, please." Her arms were starting to shake as Kennedy came bounding to her side like an eager puppy, quickly helping her get the bike parked.

"Okay, stud." Carson placed a hand on each of Kennedy's shoulders, forcing her to concentrate and listen. "Before you're too far gone, what does Ecstasy do to you, and how do I take care of you until it wears off?"

"Oh." Kennedy laughed. "Makes me kind of silly."

"No kidding," Carson deadpanned, raking her fingers back through sweaty locks. "And obviously makes your body temperature go up. What else?"

"Lights look amazing." She looked up at the moon. "And makes me get all kind of huggy and stuff."

"Okay. What do I need to do for you?" She wrapped a supportive arm around Kennedy's waist, guiding her back to the road and the long walk home. She wanted to berate herself for not keeping a better eye on their drinks during Kennedy's confrontation with Rick, but there was no time for it now. She could kick herself later. "Come on, honey. Tell me exactly what to do to get you through this."

"Need one of the lollipops in Mama's candy jar, soon as we get home." She stumbled a little and grabbed Carson with both arms, steadying herself.

"Lollipops? Why? Does it make stuff taste better too?" Carson could feel the heat radiating off her. "Honey, walk slowly, okay. I don't know what this is doing to you inside, but I'm guessing we don't need to do anything to raise your blood pressure."

"Yes. But I need lollipops, because in a little while I'll probably start grinding my teeth." As if they had a mind of their own, her teeth did grind together, her jaw clenching as the drug began to take full effect. "Oh, god." She laughed lightly. "I feel so good and so bad all at the same time."

"If I told you to stay here and not go anywhere, can I trust you not to move?" Carson stopped, facing her and bracketing her hips with her hands. "I could go get Parker to come pick you up."

"Noooo." Kennedy pulled her into a hug, enjoying the contact greatly. "Not Parker. I'd never be able to explain this to him."

"I could explain for you." Kennedy's hands were wandering up and down her back, before they wandered lower, over her butt. "Not here, okay? No high blood pressure, remember?"

"But you feel so good." Kennedy pouted but let go as they began to walk again. "I think it's only three more miles. We can make it."

"Okay, let's see how far we get." Carson steered them to the other side of the road, so they'd be walking against any oncoming cars. A hand slid down her back and into her back pocket as Kennedy giggled again. She sighed. It was going to be a very long three miles.

"THESE BOOTS WEREN'T made for walking," Carson muttered, almost humming the tune as she spoke. Her feet were killing her and she wondered if she'd be in any shape for hiking the next day, then realized it was a moot question, since Kennedy most likely wasn't going to be up for it either. She estimated they were still a mile from Big Star Lodge and she had no idea what time it was. Her watch did not have fluorescent dials or numbers, and she whipped out her cell phone, pressing a button on it to check the time, a habit she'd gotten into since Kennedy had bought it for her. "Damn." She clicked the phone shut and shoved it back in her pocket. "I keep forgetting there's no freaking cell reception out here. I wish we were back in Austin. Much more vacation just might kill me."

"Ooo. Pretty." Kennedy spied a car coming toward them way off in the distance, the headlights putting on a special show that only she could see. She leaned more heavily on Carson and nuzzled her hair. "God, you smell really good." She laughed, then frowned as Carson gently attempted to push some of her weight off. "Don't you love me?"

"Of course I love you, honey." She gave Kennedy a quick kiss on the cheek. "Just getting a little tired is all."

"I feel grreeaaattt." Kennedy let go of her, weaving into the road as the car drew closer.

Carson grabbed her arm and pulled her back to safety. She sighed in utter relief as the vehicle passed them a safe distance away. Headlights loomed from behind them and she turned, recognizing Pete's truck. She started to wave as he pulled over and put the truck in park, shut off the country music blaring from the radio, then hopped out. "What the hell?"

"Long story. Just take us back to the house, please." Carson nudged Kennedy toward the back of the extended-cab truck, opening the door and helping her inside. Kennedy giggled and curled up on the back seat, drawing her legs up under her.

"Oh my god." Pete came closer and peered in after her. "She's drunk. Saint Shea the mighty has finally fallen. Guess she'll have less room to talk after this." He laughed for a split second before Carson grabbed the collar of his jacket, jerking him closer until she could see his eyes.

"She's not drunk." She shook his jacket, crumpling a handful of leather in her fist.

"She is too." He tried to pull away and struggled as Carson gave him another forceful tug, then let go, shoving him back against the truck. "What the hell is wrong with you?" He eyed her warily, then thought better of it and opened the passenger door for her.

"You have no idea." She gritted her teeth and resisted the urge to slap him. "You have no fucking idea, so just get in and take us home, and then go get stoned or drunk, or whatever the hell you want to do."

"Okay." He held up both hands in supplication. He couldn't recall ever hearing Carson use the f-word, and he closed the door after her. He got back in the truck and headed toward the house. The clock on the dash showed it was a little past midnight and Carson remained silent next to him. Other than the occasional glance toward the back seat, she looked straight ahead, warring with her own anger for the short drive.

From the back seat, Kennedy pressed her nose against the window, then rolled it down and stuck her head out, tilting it back and watching the colorful stars go by overhead. "Weeeeeee!"

"If she's not drunk, then—"

"Save it!" Carson snapped and held up a hand. "Just don't go there right now."

"I don't feel so good." Kennedy wailed, her head snapping back inside the cab, just as they turned into the driveway.

"Hold on, honey." They rolled to a stop and Carson jumped out, tugging the back door open as Kennedy stumbled out, landing on her knees and doubling over, wrapping both arms around her stomach. She couldn't decide if she was going to throw up or pass out, and she looked up in despair.

"I feel dizzy." Her voice trembled, and her entire body was shaking.

Pete shook his head at the display. "Carson, welcome to the Shea I grew up with. My earliest memories are of Mama and Pa dragging her upstairs drunk, stoned, or both. She put them through hell and me too in the process."

She managed to get Kennedy to crawl out of the way of the truck, then turned, leaning back in the window. "If you hold her in such disdain, why are you following in her footsteps?" She looked up for a moment, gathering her thoughts. "Go on or come in, your choice. I've got to take care of her and I don't have time to explain what happened tonight, but trust me when I tell you it isn't what it looks like."

"Whatever." Pete waited for her to step away, then backed up a bit and turned around, gunning the engine as he headed back for the highway, making a turn in the direction of Armadillo Flats.

The house was dark inside, but Carson managed to get Kennedy up to the third floor with a minimum of noise. She said a silent prayer of thanks that the master bedroom was on the opposite end of the hall from Kennedy's room, and a second thanks for the small nightlights that were plugged in at intervals all along the lower part of the hallway wall. She got Kennedy undressed and into a T-shirt and helped her into bed.

"I c-c-can't st-st-stop shaking." Kennedy's jaw clenched and she ground her teeth a few times, her heart racing with fear. "I'm so thirsty." She reached out, clutching at Carson's arm.

Kennedy looked up at Carson, her expression breaking Carson's heart. Kennedy was terrified and completely confused, that much was obvious. "I'm going to go get you some water, and some Sprite, and crackers, and those lollipops you wanted. I'll be right back, I promise." She smoothed sweaty bangs out of frightened eyes and tried to keep from crying herself, watching a few tears squeeze out and trickle down Kennedy's cheeks.

"Don't leave me." Her grip was feeble around Carson's wrist, and she could feel the tremors as Kennedy continued to shake.

"Honey." Carson leaned over, kissing her on the forehead. "I have to go long enough to get some things to make you feel better, but I promise you I won't be gone long." *I hope,* she added silently. She wasn't completely familiar with the kitchen downstairs and realized she had no idea where crackers or the candy jar were. She got up, forcing herself to turn her back on the sniffles she heard coming from the bed.

Kennedy watched her, as the room spun and her stomach twisted painfully. A shiver ran through her and her jaw clenched before she began grinding her teeth in earnest. "No, please," she begged as Carson walked out the door. She'd done something very bad, and this time Carson was leaving her, she was certain. She rolled over and began to cry.

As Carson entered the hallway, she debated for only a moment before she hesitantly knocked on Parker's bedroom door. She waited, listening, and almost re-thought her actions, when a dazed Katie opened the door a crack. "Carson? Sugar, what's wrong?"

"Can I talk to Parker for a minute?" She heard muffled noise from inside the darkened room and Parker's head appeared above Katie's. "I'm sorry to bother you, but I need some help."

"What's wrong?" Parker tugged a T-shirt over his head. "Where's Shea?"

"She's sick, sort of." Carson bit her lower lip. "I need to get some things for her, but I don't know where they are, and I don't want to leave her for too long."

"Sick?" Parker stepped into the hallway. "Wow. She never gets sick. What do you need?"

"Water, crackers, Sprite, a thermometer, and..." She released a puff of air. "...a handful of lollipops from the candy jar. She said she wanted them."

"Lollipops?" Parker glanced from Katie back to Carson. "Carson, is she...?" He searched her eyes. "Ex?"

"Yeah, I think so. Long story." Carson looked down, wrapping her arms around herself. "Someone drugged her root beer. I...I should've been watching out for us better. It just never occurred to me..."

"Damn." Parker's face clouded with anger. "Okay. I know what to do. Go on back in there. Katie, sweetheart, can you go get the thermometer from the bathroom, and a basin of water and a rag? I'll go downstairs and get the other stuff. Carson, go into her top desk drawer and I think you'll find her old sports mouth guard. It'll be better than lollipops, plus it won't hurt her to fall asleep with it in. I'll be back up as fast as I can, and you need to tell me exactly what happened tonight."

"Can...can I wait and let her tell you?" Carson looked like she was about to cry, and Katie edged around Parker, draping an arm over her shoulders.

"Of course it can wait, sugar." She glared at Parker and nodded toward the stairs. He took the hint and went down to the kitchen. "Go on in there, hon. She needs you. I'll be there just as quick as I can."

"Thanks." Carson shuffled back into the room, finding Kennedy curled up in a ball in the middle of the bed on top of the covers. She was still sniffling and shaking, and Carson turned on a small desk lamp, then grabbed a handful of tissue as she yanked the top desk drawer open, finding the mouthpiece right where Parker said it would be.

"You came back," Kennedy rasped. "Stay. I won't be bad again, I promise."

"Aw, honey, you haven't been bad. Just hang on a few more minutes." She sat down on the bed, sliding over until she was next to Kennedy. She wiped the tears off Kennedy's face and urged her under the covers, tucking the sheet and blanket over her up to her waist. Her T-shirt was already damp with sweat, and she moaned, grabbing at her stomach with one hand.

"Hurts." Her teeth ground together and Carson winced at the sound.

"Here." She brushed a finger over Kennedy's lips. "Open up for me, please?" Kennedy was too confused to protest and she complied, as Carson slipped the mouthpiece in. "Bite down. It'll make you feel better."

Kennedy closed her mouth around the piece, then crept closer, resting her cheek against Carson's leg. She rubbed the denim with one shaking hand, her eyes rolling upward to confirm that it was indeed Carson she was curled up with. "Mmmph."

"Shhh." Carson stroked her head. "Don't try to talk." She looked up as Katie entered the room and placed a basin on the desktop, then approached with a wet rag and the thermometer. "I'm afraid she'll bite it in two if we try to put that in her mouth."

"Not going to take it orally." Katie stopped at the foot of the bed and studied the thermometer in the low light. She looked up as she heard Carson make a bit of a strangled noise.

"Um..." Carson tried to articulate her thoughts. "I think she would kill me tomorrow if she were to find out we..."

"Oh. Oh, no, hon. We aren't going to go there. Trust me. I wouldn't want to face her tomorrow either if we did. We can use her armpit." Katie handed over a damp, cool rag and Carson placed it across Kennedy's forehead. "Shea, sugar, I need to pull your shirt up just a little bit." She drew the covers back, got the T-shirt over one arm, and put the thermometer in place, then pulled the covers back up.

Parker came in while they were waiting and placed a pitcher of water, a bottle of Sprite, a cup, a straw, and a box of saltines on the nightstand. "Damn." His sister's brain was obviously a million miles away. "Do you know who did this?"

"Yeah." Carson looked up, keeping one hand on Kennedy's head. "Some guys she knew back in high school, I think. Her system... I'm worried about her, Parker. She doesn't even drink caffeine, only drinks maybe a glass of wine or a beer every few weeks. Never takes anything stronger than ibuprofen. She doesn't eat hardly any junk food even. Her body isn't used to dealing with stuff like this."

"I've a mind to kill them, after I find out who they are." Parker paced back and forth at the foot of the bed. "One hit of Ex won't kill her, provided they didn't give her too much, and it doesn't look like they did. But you're right. She may feel a little sick before it works its way through her system."

Katie retrieved the thermometer and looked at it. "Ninety-nine degrees, so same as a hundred in her mouth. A little high, but nothing to get too worried about. Get some water and Sprite in her if you can. Best we can do is let her sleep it off. And get some sleep yourself, sugar." She stood, placing the thermometer on the desk.

"We'll talk in the morning, okay?" Parker watched Carson nod and followed Katie, turning as they reached the doorway. "If you need anything, don't hesitate, Carson."

"Thanks." She managed a small smile. "Parker, don't tell your folks just yet. I have a feeling she's going to feel pretty bad about this in the morning, even though she didn't do it on purpose."

"Okay. Get some sleep. She may be flying for a little while yet, judging from her eyes, but she doesn't look like she's going anywhere. I think if you stay with her, she'll stay put. Good night." He closed the door behind him.

"Night." Carson tugged her boots off, wriggling her sore feet in relief, and quickly shucked the rest of her clothing, trading them for a baseball-style shirt. She crawled up on the bed and over to the nightstand, pouring some cold Sprite into the cup and placing the straw in it. With a bit of fuss, she got Kennedy to sip most of it slowly.

"Thank you," Kennedy finally croaked, trying to focus on Carson's face. Carson started to push the mouthpiece against her lips, and she poked at it with her tongue, holding off for a moment. "I...scared..." She was still shaking a little bit, though not as much as before. "Can't think much right now. Don't leave me again, please?"

"It's okay." Carson cupped her face. "I'm not going anywhere. I'll be right here with you all night. I promise. Nothing bad is going to happen to you. I won't let it." She cringed internally at her own words. She'd already let something bad happen, hadn't she?

"Hold me?" Kennedy curled around her outstretched legs, resting her head in Carson's lap.

"Always." Carson urged the mouth guard back between her teeth, then settled back against a stack of propped up pillows. She stroked Kennedy's head, feeling the tremors against her leg as her body fought the effects of the drug. Whatever euphoria Kennedy had been feeling seemed to have disappeared when she stuck her head out the window, replaced by fear, tremors, and a slight bit of nausea, though she hadn't actually thrown up.

Carson was a little less worried since Parker and Katie didn't seem overly concerned, and she figured Parker must have had some personal experience with Ecstasy, judging from his reaction. Mostly, she was angry. Boiling mad, to be precise. Angry with Pete and doubly angry with Rick and Tom. Yeah. That was their names. She could picture their smug faces and she wanted to smash them in with her bare fists.

She was even angrier with herself for turning her back on their drinks. What if they had put something more dangerous in the drink, like heroin or something? Or what if they had put something in both their drinks? They could have died out there

on the road. She found herself shaking in a manner similar to
Kennedy the more she thought about it. They could have died
regardless. She remembered the bike weaving and her heart
leaping into her throat in the split second before Kennedy had
pulled over.

The rage bubbled up as she realized how carelessly the two
men had played with their lives. She wanted to make them hurt,
wanted to torture them, and it wasn't too difficult to imagine just
shooting the both of them. It frightened her how easy it was to
picture herself pulling the trigger, and she bit back a bitter taste
in her throat. With a trembling hand, she poured another cup of
Sprite and gulped it down herself, feeling relief as it slid down
her throat and hit her stomach. It was close to 1:00 a.m., and
though her body was weary to the bone, her mind wouldn't shut
down.

She looked down, focusing on Kennedy, who appeared to be
dozing fitfully, her body jerking from time to time. She was still
sweating, and Carson debated getting her a fresh shirt. Still,
Kennedy did seem to be sleeping a little and she wasn't
completely soaked through yet, so she decided to let it go for a
while longer. Gradually, Carson's head lolled back and she fell
into troubled sleep, her arms wrapped loosely around Kennedy's
body.

Around 4:00 a.m. Carson bolted upright and looked at the
clock, turning her head from side to side as the vertebrae popped
painfully. Her neck and back ached from falling asleep sitting
up, and her mouth tasted like fuzz. She heard Pete stumbling
around in the hallway and realized that was what had woken
her. She heard him drop something and curse, and deduced he
was most likely drunk. She shook her head in disgust and
slipped out of bed, digging through Kennedy's bag for a dry T-
shirt.

Kennedy was awake, silently watching Carson's every
movement, and she sat partway up as Carson helped her change
shirts. "Thank you," she whispered, sucking gratefully at the
straw as Carson offered her another cup of Sprite. "S...sorry."
She looked down. "Can't remember everything, but I know I..."

"No worries." Carson leaned over, silencing her with a
quick kiss. "Go back to sleep. We can talk in the morning. I'll be
back in a minute, all right?"

"Where?" Kennedy shifted, rolling onto her side.

"Bathroom." Carson kissed her again on the head. "Be right
back." She slipped outside and went down the hallway, quickly
taking care of business and also brushing her teeth. "Ugh." She
peered in the mirror at her bloodshot eyes and the dark circles

under them. "At least my teeth don't feel like they're wearing little socks anymore." She located some mouthwash and used it for good measure, swirling the minty liquid around for a long time before she spit it out. She looked in the mirror again. "After this is all over, I may just join her on the teetotaling side of the fence."

She padded back down the hallway and into the room, turned off the light, and slid under the covers next to Kennedy, who immediately snuggled up to her. "Niffst," Kennedy lisped out around the mouth guard.

"Good night to you too, honey." Carson rubbed the strong back, glad to feel that her shirt was still dry.

"Lumpf yogh." Kennedy's hand curled over Carson's hip.

"I love you, too." She kissed Kennedy's forehead. "Sleep now. Hopefully we'll both feel better next time we wake up."

Chapter
Four

IT WAS NOT quite dawn when Kennedy woke up. She squinted at the clock and groaned silently. Her body felt vaguely like it used to after a hard day of rodeo bull riding...the days the bull won, that is. A headache was edging its way past her temples, though it wasn't the pounding throbbing sensation she'd feared she might wake with. Her mouth felt like cotton, her tongue was swollen, and her eyes felt like sandpaper.

Gradually, she realized she was sprawled across Carson, whose arms were wrapped loosely around her, with her hands resting flat against her back. Very slowly, she untangled herself, quickly tucking a pillow in Carson's arms. Carson immediately snuggled up with the pillow, hugging it tightly and making Kennedy smile. The smile rapidly disappeared as bits and pieces of the night began coming back to her.

"I never wanted you to see that side of me," she whispered, reaching out and pushing soft bangs aside, smoothing a slight frown with her fingertips. All she'd wanted to do was take her girlfriend out for a drink at an old hangout, and Carson had wanted so badly to see it, trying so hard to understand everything about her. "Maybe you understood a little more than you bargained for, huh?"

Slowly, she sat up, tugging at the constricting T-shirt. She'd gotten used to sleeping naked the past few months and the stretchy material draped over her body felt strange. It was such a peaceful, comforting thing to fall asleep and wake up wrapped around Carson, and to feel her skin against her own.

The tall pitcher of water called to her like a siren, and she got up and stumbled around the bed to the nightstand. She peered into it and with no further thought, picked it up and gulped down half the contents, drinking directly from the pitcher. Immediately she could feel the headache starting to ease and wondered if it was from dehydration as much as from the aftermath of the Ex.

Ex.

She'd done it quite a bit in the past, although pot had been her drug of choice. She'd tried cocaine a few times, but feared getting hooked. During law school, a guy at a party had tricked her into shooting heroin once, telling her it was coke. As further enticement, he'd opened up a fresh, unused syringe, ensuring she wouldn't be sharing someone else's needle. Before, she had only snorted coke and had agreed mostly out of curiosity as to how shooting it would be different. She'd known what it was the minute it hit her system, a very different sensation than coke, and it terrified her, even as it sent peace rushing through her veins. A few days later she'd tracked him down and beaten him almost senseless. After that night, she swore off all recreational drugs except pot.

It had taken losing Angela to make her walk away from drugs completely and alcohol only in the rarest of circumstances. Now she felt dirty and violated. After years of clean living, in one night someone had polluted her system with the vile chemicals against her will. A part of her wanted to run and run until she was certain she'd sweated it all out, but running was a very bad idea at present, given how her head felt, and her feet, after the long walk home.

She looked at Carson, the guilt rushing over her and hitting her in the gut. Carson knew about the drinking and the pot. Those could be attributed to typical college kid stupidity. Now Carson knew she'd done Ex, too. How could she ever tell her about the cocaine or heroin, and if she did, would Carson see her differently? Lose respect for her? Think of her as some reformed druggie? It's what she was, after all, wasn't it?

She felt sick and had to stay very still for a moment, lest the water she'd consumed come back up. Once the nausea subsided, something akin to panic rose up, and she bolted from the room, rushing down the hall to the bathroom, where she stripped off her clothing and stepped into a hot shower. She had the water as hot as she could stand, scrubbing her skin until it was red and trying to steam the drugs out of her pores. She stood under the water for a long time, feeling it pour over her head and beat against her face, streaming over her body. She tried to imagine the drugs washing down the drain with it.

Finally she turned off the water and dried off, wrapping up in a clean robe. It smelled like spring rain from her mother's fabric softener, the scent a little too strong after the sensory overload from the night before. Still, the soft terry was comforting and she hugged herself as she stood in front of the mirror, finally clearing a spot in the steam-covered glass to reveal her very tired face that needed a lot more sleep.

She wasn't sleepy, and she stood there for a long time, trying to decide what to do. There was Pete to deal with, a Harley to retrieve, and two drug dealers she'd just as soon kill as look at. She knew what she had to do about them. She just wasn't sure when or how to go about it, whether to turn them in right away, or wait until after the backpacking trip.

Oh, god. She sat down on the toilet lid and buried her face in her hands. They were supposed to leave for the park in a few hours, and she could barely propel her own body forward at present, much less carry forty pounds on her back. She knew she'd been in the bathroom a long time, judging by the morning light that filtered in through the shade over the one small window. She should get up and go somewhere else, but couldn't bring herself to move. A soft knock at the door made her look up and she cocked her head, listening.

"Kennedy?"

She sighed. She recognized the voice, and besides, there was only one person in the house who called her by that name. One person who saw her for who she was now, not who she'd been back then. To Carson, she was a lover, a best friend, a successful lawyer...hell, even a hero, although she didn't believe that one. There was no 'Shea' in Carson's world. No redneck, hell-raising, pot-smoking loser. At least until last night. Her eyes stung and she squeezed them shut as a few tears escaped.

"Come in," she rasped, watching the knob turn.

Carson stepped carefully into the small room, squinting through the few wisps of steam that still lingered in the air. It felt like a sauna, it was so warm. "Honey?" She moved closer until she could see Kennedy's shining eyes. "How're you feeling?"

"I...I..." Kennedy reached out, knowing Carson would catch her. Somehow they ended up on the floor on the rug, curled up next to the side of the tub.

Carson held her, feeling her shake with silent sobs. "Shhh." She stroked her wet head, rocking her a little bit. "Let it all out."

"S...so...sorry," she gasped out.

"For what?" Carson kissed her head, still holding on tightly.

"That you had to see what you saw last night." Kennedy hiccupped, her face hidden against Carson's T-shirt.

"Me too." Carson's voice was low and even. "Because I went to a really ugly place." Carson gently pried Kennedy's fist from her T-shirt, curling her own hand around it. "Those guys who drugged you— I wanted to kill them. I think I still do."

Kennedy's heart sank, and she drew a deep breath. She'd

disappointed the one person who mattered most. What's more, her kind-hearted lover now wanted to kill someone, all because of her. So much for being a hero. She forced herself not to start crying again. Carson didn't need more of her tears on top of everything else. Shaking slightly, she sat up and pushed back, unable to meet Carson's eyes. Only once in her life had she felt lower, and Carson knew all about that time as well.

"Honey, I know you feel like crap, but there's something you need to know." Carson frowned at the distance in her eyes. "I don't know if you remember or not, but Pete picked us up last night and took us the rest of the way home. He thought you were drunk. I couldn't make him believe otherwise. I'm sorry. I couldn't walk any farther, and you kept trying to walk out into the road, and I was just so tired..." she trailed off. "I'm sorry," she stated simply, clasping her hands in her lap.

"Pete." Kennedy sighed. "How can I draw a hard line with him after that? Rick and Tom were right, you know. Kind of hypocritical for me to be jumping my brother for doing the exact same things I was doing at his age."

"It's not the same," Carson insisted. "It isn't."

"Isn't it?" Kennedy huffed an unhappy little puff of air. "You don't know the half of it." Her eyes flicked over Carson, whose own eyes lowered sadly at the biting words. "Sorry. That was uncalled for. I...just. Dammit!" She stood and wrapped her arms around herself. "I don't feel good, Carson. I'm not myself this morning. Maybe you'd be better off without me for the rest of the day."

"No." Carson stood and placed both hands on her shoulders, resisting the urge to try to shake some sense into her. "I'm going to stay right here with you and take care of you and help you get to feeling better."

"Um..." Kennedy looked down at her feet, which were pruney and still ached. "About backpacking..."

"Tomorrow." Carson's voice was decisive and Kennedy was glad of it. "Right now, why don't you go crawl back under the covers while I go get us a tray of breakfast and bring it back up? You think you could eat a little something?"

"I probably need to try." Kennedy reluctantly let go, wiping her robe sleeve across her face and scrubbing her eyes. "Sorry for losing it like that."

"No. Don't be sorry." Carson cradled her face with both hands. She looked down for a moment, gathering her thoughts. Kennedy needed her to be strong. Her own guilt would have to be pushed aside for a little while longer. "Let's get you back in bed and get some food in your stomach."

She stopped. There was one more thing that had to be said, for the moment. "I know you think you have no right to tell Pete what to do. And that might've been true before last night."

"But..."

"No, you listen to me," Carson cut her off angrily. "You did drugs. I get it. And chased women, and drank, and raised hell, and got tossed in jail. I know all of that. But you could have died last night. By overdose or by motorcycle wreck. All because two guys wanted to teach you a lesson, at least that's what I believe they were doing. Why else would they slip you something you didn't want, that they didn't even get paid for? You made it clear to them they weren't to deal to your brother, and they in turn made it clear they wanted you out of their business. And like it or not, that is all tied to Pete. That's what makes this different." Carson began to shake. The realization she could have lost Kennedy causing the anger to rise all over again.

Kennedy stared at her in stunned silence for a long moment. The knowledge that Carson could have died as well slammed into her gut like a sledgehammer and she gasped, a soft sobbing noise. A mixture of guilt and anger swirled through her veins, making her head hurt all over again. There was so much she wanted to say, but all she could do was nod and pull Carson close to her, burying her face into her hair. "You're right," she finally whispered. "I'm so sorry, Carson, you're absolutely right. Okay." She stood and straightened her posture. "Hard line it is with Pete, no matter what."

"I..." Carson mentally kicked herself. "I didn't mean to try to tell you what to do," she stammered.

"I know." Kennedy kissed her forehead. "But you did offer me some much-needed clarity." She closed her eyes, wishing all the ugliness she was feeling would just disappear. She'd been so self-absorbed in her worries about someone giving her drugs and what that had done to her body, she'd failed to see the much bigger picture. Selfishness was a particularly nasty thing, and she felt the shame all over again.

KENNEDY SHOVED THE door open and stormed into Pete's bedroom. She'd slept a few more hours, kept down her breakfast, consumed a large amount of orange juice, and was feeling much better than she'd expected to, at least physically. She marched over to his jacket and yanked it off the back of the desk chair, rummaging through the pockets, waking him with curses muttered under her breath.

"Hey!" He sat up, throwing the covers back. Carson was

leaning in the doorway and almost averted her eyes before she realized he had on long flannel pajama bottoms. "Shea!" He leaped to his feet, swaying for a moment as blood rushed to his head from the sudden movement. "What the hell do you think you're doing? This is my room and my stuff."

As he advanced toward her, she located the bag of pot and held it up. "By the time I get back to Austin, be moved out." She crossed her arms, her stance wide.

"What!?" He stopped in dumbfounded shock. "I saw you last night. You were in worse shape than I was when I got home, you damned hypocrite. At least I never killed anyone while I was drunk. Mama and Pa never had to come haul me out of county jail either. You have no right—"

Carson attacked him so fast he had no time to react, and they both landed on the floor with her on top of him, her fists pounding his chest. "You shut up! Your friends almost got us killed last night." She shook with rage and drew back a fist, aiming for his face, when a gentle hand closed firmly over it and she was lifted bodily off him and dumped on the bed. "Kennedy! He—"

"I know." Kennedy placed herself between her brother and her fuming lover. "Pete." She sighed. "The things I did in the past will always be with me. No one is more ashamed of that than I am. But I'm not going to sit passively by and watch you make the same mistakes and use me as an excuse for it."

"All I'm doing is drinking and smoking a little pot." He sat up, his posture rigid and his face hard and angry. "I'm not hurting anyone, and now you're kicking me out. Who are you to do that?"

She sat down on the bed, aware of Carson at her back. "You may think you're not hurting anyone, but the fact is, because of what you're doing, Carson and I could have died last night." She watched his face twitch a little, but he remained silent. "I ran into Rick and Tom at Armadillo Flats. They told me they've been dealing to you, and I threatened them with the sheriff. One of them, I think Tom, slipped some Ex into my drink when we weren't looking. I almost wrecked the bike on the way home."

"Maybe you should've stayed out of my business." He stood up, retrieving a T-shirt from his bag. "If you wouldn't have gone nosing around asking about me, then nothing would've happened."

"It wasn't like that," Carson interrupted. "They tried to sell us drugs and they mentioned selling to you in the process. Maybe you should pick your friends more carefully."

"Maybe you should stay out of family matters that are none

of your concern." He turned his back on them and pulled the T-shirt over his head, then bent over to pick up a pair of socks from the floor. "If you weren't here, y'all wouldn't have been in that bar, now would you? Shea isn't the one who drinks and goes to bars." He heard a rustle and turned back around just as Carson fled from the room.

"Carson!" Kennedy stood, torn between going after her and finishing the conversation. She headed for the door and stopped. "I meant what I said. Be gone from the garage apartment by the time I get home next weekend. Don't bother trying to pick up the horses, the dogs, or the cats. I already called the stables and the kennel and told them you no longer have rights to do so. Don't try to go in the house, either. Valerie and Serena are meeting a locksmith today to change the locks and re-code the alarm system. They'll be keeping an eye on the house and the boats until I get home. Vandalize anything, and I'll call the police myself."

His face flushed dark red and he clenched his fists at his side, resisting the urge to go at her full force. "How am I supposed to get by next semester?"

"That's your problem, but you might start by saving your drug and beer money for groceries and rent." She took another step before he spoke again.

"What am I supposed to tell Mama and Pa about all of this?" he whined.

"I don't much care what you tell them." She paused for a moment. "And you ever talk to Carson that way again, it will be me tackling you instead of her. I'm sorry it's come to this, really I am. But I can't let you keep living with me and supporting you if you're going to hurt the people I love. She doesn't deserve that."

She slammed the door and took off down the hallway for the stairs, taking them down as fast as she could. She stopped when she reached the first floor, looking around and spotting only her father in the kitchen. "Where's Carson?"

"She ran out the back door to the barn." He placed a pitcher of iced tea on the counter. "What happened? She was crying and we didn't see you coming after her. Did you two have a fight?"

"No. She and Pete had a fight." She reached for the back door, but Joseph stopped her. "Pa, I have to go talk to her. Her feelings are really hurt."

"Your mother already went after her." He took her hand a led her to the snack bar.

"But I have to — "

"No, you don't." He gave her a gentle push. "Your mother is a wise woman. Sit, and tell me what's going on. I could hear you and your brother yelling all the way down here, although I couldn't make out the words. I'm glad our guests are down in the park for the day."

"Sorry." She raked her fingers back through her hair and accepted a glass of tea, wondering suspiciously if they weren't being tag-teamed. "It was a really bad night last night, Pa. I'm not sure if I'm doing the right thing, and I promised I'd talk to you if I needed help with Pete."

"Then talk to me, Shea." He took a seat across from her. "I don't like to see you all fighting and never did. I've heard Pete coming in late every night since he's been home, or early, to be accurate. I'm no fool. I know you children. Know what all you were up to in high school. I'm not blind, either. He's going to his old haunts and seeing his old friends. You used to do the same thing for many years whenever you came home. We've known your brother drinks a lot for quite some time and assumed you knew that as well. What's changed?"

Her shoulders slumped and she looked into her glass, swirling it and listening to the ice cubes clink against the sides before she looked up. "I just threw him out of the garage apartment in Austin."

"Go on." He leaned on the counter on his forearms. "I'm all ears."

THE BARN WAS warm and quiet, save for the occasional nickering of the horses and the low, constant clucking of the chickens. The faint sounds drifted up into the loft, and Carson scooted back further in the corner, sinking into the hay and curling up in a ball. Rage had given way to exhaustion and sadness, and the nagging guilt that she should have been watching Kennedy's back in the bar. She sniffled and found a tissue in her jeans pocket.

Then there were Pete's words to Kennedy about Angela. She knew they were spoken in anger, but damned if they hadn't cut to the bone. She could only imagine how Kennedy had felt, if it hurt her that badly. She wanted to slug him as hard as she could. She'd watched Kennedy make slow but steady progress in getting rid of her guilt over Angela's death and was afraid Pete's verbal tirade would set her back.

And then there were Pete's words to Carson. Maybe she was nosing in where she didn't belong. She was probably wrong to have jumped him like she did. Maybe she shouldn't even have been there, and let Kennedy handle the situation one on one. She'd merely asked if she wanted support and Kennedy had seemed to want her with her. What if she really hadn't? Pete probably felt ganged up on. If she hadn't been there, maybe he wouldn't have said the things he did to Kennedy.

He was right, she had to admit. None of it would have happened if they hadn't gone to the bar, and she was the one who pressed for a visit to Armadillo Flats, wanting to see one of Kennedy's old hangouts. It certainly wasn't Kennedy's style anymore. Maybe she should have spent more time getting to know the woman who existed now, not the girl from the past. Maybe she shouldn't have come to Alpine at all.

She sniffled again and blew her nose, wishing she were back in Austin. Or maybe even Dallas. Her old apartment with just two cats sounded less lonely than her present circumstances. A rustling noise caught her attention and she turned as Aileen's head appeared at the top of the ladder leading up to the loft. "Mind if I join you?" She walked gingerly across the loft floor and plopped down next to Carson in the soft pile of hay.

"No." Carson sat up, drawing her knees up to her chest and wrapping her arms around her legs. "Sorry for my little scene in there."

"No need to apologize, child. My daughter can be rather difficult to deal with at times."

"That's not—"

"So can my son," Aileen cut her off. "They don't really know each other. Shea was twelve when he was born, and Parker fourteen. He barely remembers living in the same house with Parker. He was only six when Shea left for Santa Fe. It was almost like having two separate families, and Pete is an only child, as far as his outlook. He had us to himself for most of his growing up years."

"I never really thought about it like that." Carson suddenly realized that she didn't often see Kennedy and Pete have any truly meaningful conversation, unless discussing the grocery list or exercising the horses counted. "I'm an only child myself. I don't have much experience in sibling rivalry."

"What I have is a youngest child who thinks he's an only, and a middle one who was the baby until she was twelve. Not a nice combination at times." Aileen smiled in a bemused manner. "I could hear them yelling from the pantry a while ago. I almost came up there, but when I reached the second floor, I heard them scrapping overhead, rolling around on the floor, and decided I'd just let them duke it out."

"Um..." Carson rubbed the side of her neck and ducked her head. "That was Pete and me."

"Really?" Aileen appraised her daughter's companion with a

new eye. Carson wasn't tall, but seemed solid enough. "Who won?"

"Nobody, in this situation." Carson covered her face and scrubbed her eyes, then rested her chin in her hands. "He said some things to Kennedy I just couldn't tolerate and I jumped him. It was pretty stupid."

So her self-sufficient daughter had found a protector. Interesting. "You don't strike me as the violent type. Must've deserved it, whatever he said."

"He..." She stopped, unsure of exactly what Kennedy planned to tell her parents about Pete. She knew she planned to tell them about her drink being drugged, but she hesitated, wondering if Kennedy would want to tell her mother herself. "I..." She searched Aileen's confused face, hoping to find a way out.

"Carson. I'm going back in the house when I'm through talking to you, and I plan to sit my children down and knock their heads together, unless you give me a good reason not to." She patted Carson's arm. "What happened?"

"Some bad things happened last night." Carson picked up a straw and twirled it in her fingers, watching it disturb the dust motes dancing in the light from the loft window. "We went to Armadillo Flats."

"A place that should be torched, far as I'm concerned." Aileen was seething, her tone very familiar. "Go on."

"We ran into some guys Kennedy knew in high school. They tried to sell us some drugs." Carson pursed her lips inward, trying to figure out what to say next.

"You know all about that, I know." Aileen looked up at the ceiling for a moment. "My daughter gave us fits for most of her teens. We've talked about that. Pete was just a toddler when we first started having real trouble with her. There were so many nights I know he heard us yelling at her and her yelling back. I always wondered if that did any lasting damage to him."

"Guess I never thought about that either," Carson offered, hoping Aileen would talk for a while.

"We picked her up from the sheriff's office on several occasions." Aileen's voice grew soft. "We'd get a phone call, usually in the middle of the night. He'd picked her up drunk, or just out wandering late at night when we thought she was in her room asleep. Joseph would go after her and bring her home, and I'd light into her when they got here. They never arrested her, technically. She was an honor student and Joseph is well-respected around town. But she deserved to be, and I always tried to make her understand just how serious her behavior was.

I didn't understand at the time why she was acting out the way she did. I didn't understand what a hard time she had been given at school all those years for looking different. She hit puberty about the time Pete was conceived, and I think maybe, looking back, I wasn't there for her after that like I should have been, and neither was her father. Her father and I were so busy running the lodge, and him creating and selling his artwork. We had five mouths to feed and it wasn't a real easy time for us back then."

"I don't think she holds any hard feelings now." Carson touched Aileen's shoulder. "She speaks quite fondly of both of you."

"That's good to hear." Maybe they'd done all right, after all. "So Shea was offered drugs last night. She turned them down. That's a no-brainer. What happened after that? Knowing her, she didn't even drink anything alcoholic, am I right?"

"Yeah. It's just that she and the other guy, Rick was his name, he kept pushing, even after she turned him down. He said some things, and kind of hit me up too, and she lost it." She grew silent, remembering Kennedy shoving Rick against the wall, the other patrons quickly giving them space. The bouncer had let it go, too. Had made no move to break them up. Sure of her details, she continued. "There was another guy there, Tom. I didn't even know he and Rick were there together. While Kennedy and Rick were arguing, we think Tom slipped some Ecstasy into her drink."

"What?" Aileen barked angrily. "We should call the sheriff. Those guys should be arrested."

"It's kind of complicated." Carson took a deep breath. They had discussed it. How to tell the sheriff what had happened without getting Pete arrested in the process. "Anyway, we didn't know about the Ecstasy until it started taking effect on the way home. We were on the bike and had to pull over because she couldn't drive it properly. Kept weaving and her vision kept blurring."

"So they could have killed you and my baby? Is that what you're telling me?" Aileen stood, brushing straw off her legs with an agitated motion.

"Yeah," Carson's voice was small. "And I feel like it's all my fault. I should've kept an eye on our drinks. Maybe if I'd done a better job of that, she wouldn't have spent all night sick, and maybe Pete and I wouldn't have fought. I feel like I've made a horrible mess of things. I know better. It's one of the rules anymore. Never turn your back on your drink in a bar." She sniffled and covered her face again, wiping at her eyes with the back of her hand.

"Oh, honey." Aileen sat back down, tentatively rubbing Carson's back. "None of it is your fault."

"I was the one who wanted to go there in the first place. Kennedy would have been happy to watch a movie in the family room. If she had died last night because of me not watching her back, I don't think I could ever forgive myself. Those guys..." Carson began to cry in earnest and felt Aileen draw her into a hug.

"This is a small town, Carson. No one thinks about things like that here." She continued to rub Carson's back. Parker had told her about Carson's history, and she wondered if the girl had had any mothering in a very long time. "I can promise you my daughter would have warned you if she'd thought it was a concern. That bar may be rowdy, and much as I hate it, for the most part it's just a bunch of drunken locals who have nothing better to do on the weekend. They aren't people any of us would normally ever have reason to fear."

"But those guys — "

"Stop it, now. Don't go blaming yourself, child. You told me you didn't know Rick and Tom were together, correct?" She felt Carson still for a second, and nod. "Then how could you have known you needed to keep an eye on him?"

"I...I didn't. It's just that in Austin, or Dallas, I would never have let that happen." Her body heaved with a final sob and she took a deep breath before she looked up, digging for the tissue in her pocket again. "Sorry. I must look a mess. I wanted to kill them last night. I can't bear the thought of losing her."

"Believe me. I want to kill them too, right now. They put my baby's life in danger and yours too. And knowing my daughter, she feels the same way about them putting you at risk as well." She tilted Carson's chin up. "Now, tell me what this has to do with Pete."

"I..." Carson looked at her in panic. "...I can't. Not without — "

"Because they're his dealers." Kennedy climbed the rest of the way up the ladder to join them. "When I threatened them and told them to leave him alone, they retaliated with the Ex. They were trying to send me a message to back off." She crawled up next to her mother, settling into a spot where she could see Carson's face too, as she spoke. She'd heard her crying when she entered the barn and had waited as long as she could stand before climbing up that ladder. Carson's face was blotchy, but otherwise, she looked like she was past crying, at least for the moment.

Aileen shook her head. "I didn't know he was doing drugs,

too. The drinking, I've known about since he was in high school. What...what's he doing?"

"Only pot, far as I know." She decided not to mention the bag Parker was going to have tested, or Tom's comments, which made it fairly obvious the bag contained something more. "Where's Parker?" Her thoughts did a U-turn.

"He took Katie and the children horseback riding." She peered out the window. "Headed down toward the park. So...that's why telling the sheriff about Rick and Tom is complicated?"

"Yeah, because it could get Pete arrested in the process." Kennedy leaned back against the wall and drew her legs up, her arms resting loosely on her knees. "I thought I might wait until he gets back to Austin, but I think I have to turn those guys in, eventually, Mama. If we'd died on the road last night, they'd be facing manslaughter charges, at the very least. I think they need to understand that."

"And I think you're right, but how are you going to protect your brother?" she questioned gently.

"I'm not." She regarded her mother warily. "Mama, I just kicked him out of the garage apartment. Told him to be out by the time I get home. I talked to Pa right before I came out here and he agrees with me. Said if Pete can't make it in school financially this semester, he can move back here, but he'll have to get a job if he does, and stay clean as well."

"I see." Aileen grew thoughtful. "There's no other way?"

"No. I don't think so." Kennedy steeled herself, knowing her mother was in the unfortunate position of being between two warring children. "I told him a few days ago if he brought drugs home, he couldn't live under my roof anymore. It puts my law license in peril if he was to get caught there, plus after what he said to Carson today, I might've kicked him out anyway."

"What did he say?" Aileen tilted her head, looking back and forth from her daughter to Carson.

"Kennedy, it's all right. I don't..." Carson pulled away from Aileen and sat up, crossing her legs.

"It's not all right." Kennedy's features scrunched up in anger. "You're a part of my life now. I won't let him make you feel like an outsider." She turned toward her mother. "He told Carson to stay out of our family business and tried to blame her for what happened. I can't let him treat her like that."

"And you shouldn't. Anyone my children choose to share their lives with is family, as far as I'm concerned," Aileen agreed with her, missing the look of utter panic that flashed over Kennedy's face, before she got it under control. As for Carson, it appeared she was on the verge of bursting into tears all over again. And Kennedy could only hope they were good tears this time.

"I guess I need to go have a talk with him. Maybe I can talk some sense into him, although it never worked with you or Parker. Seems like my children are all bound and determined to learn things the hard way." Aileen watched her daughter flinch slightly and regretted her words. "Shea, I am so proud of you...of who you've become. Don't misunderstand me. I'm just frustrated with Pete, and frustrated with myself that I didn't know what he was up to. I was hoping to get by without having to go down this road a third time. There may not be enough henna left in the store to hide the gray hairs by the time this one is settled. Now, I think you two need to talk. Am I right, Carson?"

"Yeah." Carson looked down, feeling Kennedy's questioning gaze almost as a physical thing.

"Then I'll be on my way." She kissed her daughter's head, and impulsively, turned and kissed Carson's as well. "I think you two need to quit beating yourselves up." She disappeared down the ladder, hearing the crunch of Kennedy's knees as she crawled across the hay, closing the space between her and Carson.

"You okay?" She settled her arms around Carson, who immediately snuggled up, wrapping her own arms around Kennedy's middle.

"No." She rubbed Kennedy's stomach, slipping her hand beneath the oversized sweatshirt she was wearing, seeking warm skin. "I keep feeling like I should've kept an eye on our drinks last night. Every time I think about that bike and how I thought we might tip over." She shivered.

"Listen to me. This was not your fault. Last night, that had to be pretty scary for you." She brushed her hand over Carson's head. "I blame Tom. I didn't even see him there, and if I had, I never in a million years would've thought he was capable of that. I'm angry that what he did could've killed you. Could've killed both of us."

"I'm sorry I took off from Pete's room like that. I kept thinking about everything and wondering if maybe I was in your way up there." Kennedy continued with the gentle touches, looking down at their outstretched legs, which had somehow gotten tangled together.

"I wanted you there. I..." she stopped, thinking about her mother's words. Did it frighten Carson, to basically be referred to as her spouse? She switched gears, hoping to deflect any of that fear. "Carson, about what Mama said, about family..."

"You know, she made me feel really good talking to me and all." Carson rested her head on Kennedy's shoulder. "It's been a long time since I was able to talk with my mother. It was kind of nice to have that perspective on things. I love your family. I...I wish, that as long as you and I are together, that it would be okay if I do talk with her like that from time to time." She looked up, searching Kennedy's face.

Was it okay? Was she ready for Carson to grow close to a mother she was at odds with for years? She examined her feelings carefully, realizing that for Carson, who had lost so much, there was only one answer. Finally, she squeezed Carson more tightly and smiled, pressing their bodies close together. "More than okay."

She took Carson's hand, holding it up and placing her own against it, noting their relative sizes. Her hand was quite a bit bigger and her wrists more thick and corded. Carson's were by no means delicate, though. They were strong and capable, even if they were smaller. She brought Carson's hand to her lips and kissed the back of it before closing her own over it and drawing it between their bodies against her chest. "No more beating yourself up over this, okay?"

Carson nodded, ducking her head and brushing her lips over their entwined fingers. "I'll try." Inside, she still felt unsettled, wondering if she had stepped on familial toes, despite reassurances to the contrary.

Kennedy tweaked her nose, making her smile, then wrapped her legs around Carson, holding her in a playful vise. She traced her face with her fingertips and kissed her closed eyelids. "Mama said something else, about spending lives together and all. I know we've not been together for a real long time, but I just want you to know that the part of my life I've spent with you has been the best part." She hugged Carson and felt her shaking, and looked down to see fresh tears spilling down her cheeks. "Hey, what's wrong?" Carson opened her eyes, the gray irises shining vividly against her pale features and the golden hay.

"Nothing. Can...can I tell you something and not scare you away?" She cupped Kennedy's face, trailing her hand back through her hair and feeling her head nod. "You've come to mean everything to me. I just wanted you to know that." She drew in a shuddering breath. "I love you," she whispered against Kennedy's lips as they met.

They spent several moments that way, exchanging kisses and gentle touches, until at last Kennedy drew back and pulled Carson against her once more, kissing her forehead. "What do you say we go on our backpacking trip in the morning and try to forget all the mess with Pete for a little while? Just you and me and a tent under the stars, and no worries until we get back."

"Does the tent have a mesh roof we can open up and see the stars from our sleeping bag?" She nuzzled the sweatshirt, rubbing her face against the soft fabric and drawing in the scent of their dryer sheets, along with Kennedy's own distinct musky sweetness.

"You bet." She kissed Carson again, running one hand down her side and behind her denim-clad leg, pulling her even closer.

"You're on then." They hugged each other tightly, just enjoying the warmth and the silence for a while. Carson almost drifted off, her body relaxing completely, and she forced herself to open her eyes. "Hey, you." She touched the end of Kennedy's nose. "Why don't we go finish packing up our backpacks, eat an early dinner, and get turned in early tonight?"

"So we can get some sleep before the trip?" her voice teased, along with her hands.

"Eventually." Carson flashed her a sexy grin and laughed lightly. Kennedy growled in her ear, a purring, tickling sound, and she laughed harder as they reluctantly parted and made their way down the ladder and back into the house.

KENNEDY SAT ON the top step of the back porch, surrounded by dogs, none of which she had grown up with, but all of which knew her as the human with doggie treats in her pockets. "Hey, now." She tilted her face up, receiving sloppy kisses to both sides of her jaw line. The dachshund and the terrier were both trying to scramble into her lap, pawing each other in the process. "There's enough for all of you. Back off."

She dug in her down vest pocket, retrieving a handful of small dog biscuits. She got rid of two of them by tossing treats in opposite directions, well away from the porch steps. Talia's littermate, Sheba, and Pecos, the German Shepherd, ended up in an affectionate wrestling match, with plenty of nips and tail-wagging, along with happy doggie yips and barks that rang out across the back lot, breaking through a rare foggy morning.

She ruffled Sheba's head and snuck her a treat without making her work for it. The dog planted a wet swipe across Kennedy's nose, and she made a face. "Bleckh." Encouraged by the noise, Sheba did it again, and suddenly all three big dogs descended, snuffing her pockets for the hidden biscuits, finally forcing her onto her back on the porch as she tried to shove them off. "Hey! No squishing me now. Not fun."

"That's not what you said last night." Carson stepped from inside the kitchen doorway, where she'd been watching and smiling as Kennedy's more child-like side came out to play.

"Auggh." Kennedy finally managed to sit up. "You, darlin', can squish me any time you want." She winked. "Especially if you do what you did last nimphh..."

"Hush." Carson bent over her from behind, covering her mouth and kissing the top of her head. "Your folks might hear."

"You started it." Kennedy reached up and grabbed her, pulling her over and dumping her on her back on the porch before she straddled her on her hands and knees. "Besides, nothing they haven't done before, I'd wager." Her eyes twinkled and she leaned in, stealing a kiss. "Hey!" Kennedy raised up on her knees, turning around and glaring at Rosie, the Rottie-Mastiff. "She poked me in the butt."

"Aww. I don't blame her. It's such a cute butt." Carson reached up, grabbing handfuls of said body part. From there she ran her hands down the back of Kennedy's legs and then back up again, massaging her behind and hearing a little gurgle of pleasure.

"Mmm." Kennedy descended again, kissing her more thoroughly than before, almost forgetting they were on the back porch in broad daylight. "Don't rub the lamp unless you want the genie to come out and play."

"Is the genie ready to go backpacking?" Carson's hands were still wandering, quite with a mind of their own.

"Much more of that and the genie is going to ditch backpacking and take you back upstairs for the rest of the week." Kennedy captured her hands, stilling them and kissing each one in turn before she released them.

"Nope." Carson sat up, pushing Kennedy along with her. "I've been looking forward to this for too long." She watched full lips purse into an all-out pout. "Not that a week in bed with you doesn't sound delicious." She kissed her again for emphasis. "How about three nights sharing a sleeping bag? And maybe a night or two at that spa down there near the park when we're done?"

"Ooo. That sounds like heaven." Kennedy stood, tugging Carson to her feet. "Unfortunately, this time of year we probably should've booked a room early if we wanted to do that."

"Oh, well." Carson's eyes were thoughtful. "Maybe they'll have a cancellation."

"We can always check when we come back off the trail." She ambled to the end of the porch, hefting up a full backpack. "Let me get these out to the 4Runner and we'll be on our way."

"I can carry mine." Carson picked up the pack next to it. "Might as well get used to it if I'm going to be carrying it for four days."

The back door opened and Parker stepped out. "You two taking off?" They'd said their goodbyes to the children the night before, as well as Katie, who was upstairs getting them ready for the drive back to Odessa. "Looks like it'll be a nice day after this fog burns off." He sipped from a steaming mug of coffee. "Been some strange weather this weekend."

"You know what they say. Don't like the weather in Texas, just wait a few minutes and it'll change. Be back in a second. Don't go anywhere." Kennedy made her way down the steps and across the yard to the carport, where she stowed her pack in the truck and took Carson's, who was right behind her. She closed the hatch and draped an arm across Carson's shoulders, guiding her back to join Parker.

"Katie coming down to say goodbye again?" Carson shoved her hands in her pockets.

"Probably not. The kids always get fussy when they realize we're leaving this place. They love it here, plus it means they have to go back to school tomorrow, and that means some homework tonight when we get back." Parker leaned against the side of the house, crossing his boots at the ankles. "She's trying to gather up all their toys and clothes, and make sure they're all dressed and fed before we hit the road."

"Pete?" Kennedy looked down, kicking at a knot in the wood with the toe of her hiking boot.

"Still asleep." Parker studied his sister's posture, a picture of dejection. "Shea, you did the right thing. Everyone agrees on that except Pete. But you can't expect him to be happy about it. He's probably going to be angry at you for a long time to come."

"If not forever." She finally looked up, her brother's face reflecting her emotions. "I just hate this, and I really hate having to go to the sheriff at the end of the week."

"Why not get it over with now?" He frowned. It wasn't like his take-action sister to procrastinate.

"I...just need a few days to clear my head first." She looked down. "Yesterday was a really tough day. I haven't felt like that in...years. Still don't feel quite myself. The Ex and all..." She worried her lower lip, tugging at it with two fingers. "Much as I'd like to kick Pete's ass all the way back to Austin, he is our brother. I want to think about how to go to the sheriff with as little damage to Pete as possible."

Her tone was defeated, and Parker recognized it as his sister's way of working through extreme guilt feelings. It was all too familiar, the slight slump to her usually tall posture, the flatness in her voice, and the pain in the depths of her eyes, if he looked close enough. "I can come back up and go with you if you'd like," he offered.

"No. You aren't a witness. Carson will be with me, and Pa may go with us as well, to see what he can do about helping me get them to lay off Pete." She snorted. "Not that he'll have the good grace to be appreciative."

"Go on, and enjoy your trip down in the park. Pete'll be back in Austin by the time you get back and maybe there will be a few days' peace here before you go back yourself." He looked up, past them, watching the Sunday morning sun warring with the fog. The dogs were still nosing around, occasionally snuffing Kennedy's now-empty pockets, and out in the corral the two mustangs were frolicking, kicking up their heels like young colts in the crisp morning air. "You got enough layers in those bags? Gets cold at night up there."

"Aren't going to need layers at night." Kennedy smirked. "We're zipping our bags together."

"Oh." Parker's cheeks colored a little. "Guess that'll be even better."

"Hell of a lot better." Kennedy chuckled, feeling Carson's questioning gaze. She leaned over and whispered in Carson's ear, and watched it turn bright pink. "...best way to stay warm," she finished a little louder.

"Didn't realize that." Carson raked her fingers back through her hair and looked down, smiling just a little bit, despite her embarrassment. It was different than what she'd grown up with. Being an only child had offered a great deal of privacy and a certain air of properness in a lot of her dealings with her parents. She'd watched Kennedy's family, especially Kennedy, Parker, and Katie, and was amazed at the total lack of privacy, lack of boundaries, and the banter among them, some of it frankly ribald in nature. It was warm and funny, and at times she felt like an outsider, until one of them would draw her in, and before she knew it, she found herself right in the thick of things with the rest of them.

It was comfortable most of the time, and she'd quickly come to love Kennedy's family, and the big warm circle of love she felt there. At the same time, she was overwhelmed at times and was looking forward to some time alone with her lover. She was unused to being under one roof with that many people, and definitely not used to things as simple as waiting in line for the bathroom, or learning that he who did early morning dishes duty was relieved of all further chores for the day. Even with only two guests in the lodge, the presence of Kennedy's entire family created a lot of extra work, so morning dishes was a coveted job.

Joseph had clued her in on that one, and they'd shared dish duty a few mornings, conspiring to go prop their feet up while the others got the more mundane jobs of cleaning rooms and bathrooms, preparing meals, taking care of the guests' needs, or doing the piles of laundry the lodge created. She marveled at how much work it was and wondered how Joseph and Aileen managed when it was just the two of them, especially if they had a full slate of guests. It gave her a new understanding and appreciation of just how hard the couple had worked for most of their lives, both to stay together, and to make a living for their family in such a beautiful place.

It showed in how Kennedy conducted her own affairs: the carefully chosen lakefront acreage she lived on, the dogtrot house with its special little comforts like jets in the tubs, the boats, the inviting rustic furniture, and the eye-appealing artwork. Her kitchen was full of healthful food and her beds bore soft, warm linens. Looking around, Kennedy had re-created in Austin much of what she had grown up with, with the added bonus of the lake to play on and enjoy in the evenings as they sat on the back porch, a porch much like the one they were standing on at present.

There was easy affection between her and her family, save for Pete's current problems, and Joseph and Aileen were obviously still very much in love with each other. Despite Kennedy's troubled teens, Carson deduced it was that example of love and support that had won out, and she knew it was Joseph's direct support of Kennedy that had pulled her through those dark days after Angela died. He was an intelligent man and bore a sensitivity that allowed him to easily see inside people's hearts and minds. She'd spent a little time wandering through the lodge and his studio, looking at his paintings and the beauty he'd transferred from his mind's eye to canvas.

She saw so much of him and his treatment of Aileen in Kennedy, down to the solicitous unconditional love Kennedy showered on Carson every day. She was living out the example set by her father, and Carson had come to realize that Kennedy was every bit as capable of that same lifetime love and commitment her parents shared. Suddenly it hit her that Kennedy most likely was looking for exactly that kind of relationship, and wanted it with her. Moreover, along with her mother's fiery passion, she'd inherited her father's steadfast patience. Kennedy was waiting. She knew it. Waiting for a sign that Carson wanted the same things she did. If Carson wanted all

of what she saw before her, it was hers. All she had to do was
make up her mind and make it clear to Kennedy that her
commitment was just as strong.

Well. That was something to think about on the hiking trail,
now wasn't it?

"Carson? Carson." Kennedy shook her a little, and she
looked around sheepishly, realizing she'd missed an entire
conversation.

"Oh. Sorry." She rubbed her eyes. "I zoned out there for a
minute. Probably need some caffeine for the road. Give me a
minute." She patted Kennedy's shoulder and ducked inside the
house, appearing again with a travel mug full of Aileen's fresh-
brewed coffee, along with a Tupperware container of warm just-
baked orange-iced sweet rolls Aileen had pushed into her hands.
The older woman followed her out the door, stopping in the
doorway to take in the morning.

"You two have fun, and be careful." Aileen studied her
daughter, whose gaze was all over her shorter companion, her
expression warming and softening as Carson approached her at
the end of the porch and held up a bite of sweet roll. Kennedy
nipped it up with a playful snap of her teeth, laughing as Carson
bumped hips with her and said something Aileen couldn't
understand. "Don't mind me, I'm only your mother," she spoke
up, smiling as her daughter looked up with a brilliant smile of
her own gracing her lips.

"Oh. Mama." Kennedy's smile remained, and she blushed,
briefly lowering her eyes. She looked back up in a completely
unguarded moment, knowing her emotions were written all over
her face. "Sorry. I got distracted by this evil woman tempting me
with bad sugary food."

"Oh, like I had to force you to eat it." Carson held up
another bite and Kennedy took it as well. "Uh-huh. Hey!"
Kennedy nipped her fingers in the process, raising one saucy
eyebrow as she chewed the bite of roll. "You're the evil one, not
me."

"I'd have to agree with you on that one, Carson." Aileen
joined the circle.

"Me too." Parker grinned. "Sorry, Sis. She made that killer
guacamole the other night. Have to stay on her good side."

"Fine." Kennedy crossed her arms in mock hurt. "Maybe I'll
lose your butt on the trail."

"No, you won't." Carson nudged her, standing on tiptoe and
whispering something that made Kennedy blush from her roots
to her open flannel shirt collar.

"Uncle." She covered her face, feeling the heat. "Guess we

should get going. Um..." She looked up to knowing grins on her mother's and brother's faces. "What?"

"Nothing, nothing at all." Parker rolled his eyes and whistled a little under his breath. "Have fun, Shea. Seriously." He smiled at her. "Time enough to worry about everything else when you get back."

"True." She turned and pecked her mother on the cheek. "Bye, Mama. When Pa surfaces from his paint-induced haze in the studio, tell him I'm filing my plan with the Visitor Center at Panther Junction, in the event y'all need to find us for any reason."

"Bye, Aileen. See you on Wednesday." Carson hugged her and Parker in turn. "Give Katie my love, and have a safe drive home."

"All right. Get going, you two." Aileen shooed them off the porch. "Stick to the trails."

"Mama..."

"I mean it, Kennedy Shea. There've been cats spotted down there recently, even out in the daytime." She shook a finger at them for emphasis. "Trails. Are we clear?"

"Clear," Kennedy mumbled.

"Cats?" Carson took her hand as they walked to the truck.

"Mountain lions." She keyed the lock and held Carson's door open, giving her a hand up into the passenger seat.

The door closed and Carson found her seatbelt. Mountain lions. Seems there would be lots of things to think about on the trail.

Back on the porch, Parker waved with his free hand, cradling his mug with the other. "I'm staying until they get back, Mama. Katie and I already talked about it. She's going to drive back with the kids and come back and get me next weekend."

"Oh?" Aileen wiped her hands on her apron, watching as the two women drove away. "You see it too, I take it?"

"I see a lot of things." Parker sipped thoughtfully at the fragrant brew. "For one thing, Shea's trying to handle this thing with Pete all on her own. Well, I'm not going to let her."

"You don't know how relieved I am to hear that," Aileen fretted. "I know her. She's reached a point in life where she feels protective of me and your father. For some reason, she has to be strong around us. Maybe she's trying to make up for the past, but I don't think she'll ever lean on us again like she did in her twenties. You...you'll always be her big brother. She's been calling on you for help since she broke her arm in kindergarten."

"True." Parker smiled briefly in memory of carrying a sister who was almost as big as he was from the playground jungle gym to the nurse's office of their elementary school.

"What else do you see?" She tucked a hand in the crook of his elbow.

"She hasn't been this fragile since Angela died." He smiled sadly. "My sister is head over heels in love, and she's terrified it's not reciprocated."

"Oh, it most assuredly is." Aileen nodded vigorously. "If they'll both quit blaming themselves for what happened at Armadillo Flats, they just might figure it out."

"Yep." He turned, leaning in the doorway. "They're either going to pull it together on this hiking trip, or fall apart."

"Yep," Aileen echoed him. "I just hope and pray it's pull together. My baby girl's been broken too many times."

"All the more reason I feel like I need to stay," he answered softly.

TRUE TO PARKER'S prediction, it was a gorgeous cloudless day once the fog burned off. "Is the sky really that blue? Does that color really exist naturally?" Carson looked up at the most beautiful shade of vivid blue she'd ever seen. She thought about that for a moment and turned, stepping across the path and forcing Kennedy to stop in her tracks. Carson pulled her lover's sunglasses up and peered into her eyes for a long moment. Almost the most vivid.

"What?" Kennedy tilted her head to one side in confusion.

The shades dropped back into place. "Guess it does exist naturally." Carson grinned and turned again as they continued to follow the Oak Canyon trail from the main basin area of Big Bend. "Where are we headed again?"

Kennedy chuckled and hunched her shoulders, shifting the weight of her backpack just a little. "I figured since you've never been here, we'd do some of the main attractions first, like hike up Emory Peak this morning and then head on down to one of the campsites on the South Rim Trail to camp tonight. Then hike back out tomorrow and take Panther Pass past Casa Grande, hike up there and then through the Pine Canyon Trail and camp for the night there tomorrow night. Then hike back to the truck and drive down to either Santa Elena Canyon or Mariscal Canyon and hike along the river for the last couple of days."

"Cool!" Carson was finding the pack easier to tote than she'd expected. It had been a few years since she'd been backpacking, but the packs really were designed to distribute the weight well, and the straps could be adjusted so the weight was mostly on her hips, rather than her shoulders and back. The area they were in was wooded with both evergreen and deciduous trees, and the recent rain had coaxed forth brightly-colored flowers. It was an oasis in the middle of the desert. The leaves were turning, and in the occasional open areas on the trail, they could look out for miles over a visual feast of color.

"There's an awesome view at the top of both Emory and Casa Grande, and a few surprises along the way too." Kennedy stepped a little closer to her partner. Most of the time they could walk side by side, although in a few spots they were forced to go single file. She usually let Carson lead, mostly so she could watch her partner's muscular calves in action. They had matching walking sticks they'd picked up in the gift shop at the basin, each one carved with desert and western etchings, and the tops of the handles wrapped in soft suede leather, along with braided rawhide wrist straps.

"What kinds of surprises?" Carson sucked from her water bottle. One of the first rules of desert hiking, or any hiking for that matter, was to drink early and often. If you were thirsty, you were already dehydrated, and the arid climate didn't allow for mistakes with water. In addition to carrying two gallons of water each, they had a tiny filtration system with them, for use with the creeks along the way.

"Just some nice things to see and some nice views." A chipmunk skittered across the path almost under Kennedy's feet, and she did a little dance to avoid tripping over it. "Damn." She kicked at an acorn the rodent dropped, and it ran back out, picking up the lost booty. It stood on its haunches and scolded her, chittering away for a bit. "Hey!" She shooed at it, watching it scamper to a safer distance. "You're the one that nearly tripped me. Be glad I didn't stomp on your little hide. Or your dinner." It scolded her again before dropping to all-fours and disappearing into the undergrowth.

Carson was laughing so hard she had to stop walking for a moment. "Oh, my god." Her sides hurt from laughing against the restraining pack straps. "That was too funny. Do you think it understood you?"

"Nah. It's just a furry rodent, Carson." She looked back over her shoulder anyway to see if the critter was following them.

"I don't know." Carson smiled. "After seeing that commercial for auto insurance, I got to thinking about all the times squirrels have run in front of my car or in front of me while I'm jogging. Makes me wonder if there isn't some underground animal conspiracy against humans. That Town Lake trail back in Austin is downright dangerous some days."

"Yeah, but more from horny male ducks in mating season

than from squirrels, at least in my personal experience."
Kennedy felt her dignity slide back into place. "That, or bat
guano if you're standing in the wrong place during nightly
migration."

"Ewww." Carson wrinkled her nose.

"Speaking of." Kennedy knelt down on the trail. "Take a
look at this."

"Kennedy, I wanted to observe nature out here, but a pile of
poop wasn't what I had in mind." She wrinkled her nose again
and leaned cautiously over Kennedy's shoulder.

"No. Look. See those bits of fur there?" She picked up a stick
and poked at it.

"Yeah. So?" Carson backed away, uncertain what was in
store.

"This is cat scat. A mountain lion was right here on the trail
in the last day or so, most likely last night." She stood, tossing
the stick into the brush. "Pretty close to the basin. Little too close
for my tastes. We need to be extra careful with our food and
toiletries tonight, not just for bears, but for cats, too. I have a
feeling they're starting to get used to seeing humans around. Not
a good thing. They don't need to start thinking of campsites as
good places to find food."

"How do you know it's not bear poop?" Carson stepped well
around the little pile.

"Too small an offering, and there weren't any berries mixed
in." She laughed lightly at the face Carson made. "Need to be
careful of them too, although I'd rather have a bear in camp than
a mountain lion. Guess Mama was right about sticking to the
trails. Not too much danger in broad daylight, at any rate."

They walked on in silence, choosing to listen to the sounds
of nature all around them as they hiked. The birds were out in
full force, with several mockingbirds singing their hearts out in
praise of the bright sunny day. Small, unidentified creatures
made tiny rustling noises in the growth just off the path, and
Carson spotted more than a few lizards and squirrels.

At last they reached the base of Emory Peak and began the
long, steep climb to the summit. Halfway up they stopped for a
break and took off the backpacks, leaning them against a tree
just off the trail. A broad, flat rock invited, and they sat on the
edge, drinking water and looking out over a colorful expanse of
green and yellow leaves. "It's just gorgeous here." Carson dug a
protein bar out of her pocket, unwrapping it and breaking it in
half. "Want some?"

"Yeah, thanks." Kennedy munched on the bar, sliding closer
until their legs were touching. They were both in shorts, having

shucked their jeans at the base when they realized how warm the afternoon promised to be. They were still wearing flannel shirts over their T-shirts, but soon the sun would force those off as well, to be shoved in their packs or tied around their waists. "Ooo. A full-leg shave." She traced the bare skin just above Carson's knee.

"Yeah, I figured I might not get to shave again for three days, so I should do a thorough job." She smiled, feeling goose bumps follow her lover's fingertips.

"Your legs are hairless, sweetheart. I swear you really are as smooth as a baby's bottom." She let her hand still, resting on Carson's leg.

"Nah, it's just blonde and fine and you can't see it real well." She finished off her bar and carefully folded up the wrapper, sticking it in her pocket. The bars were a lot tastier than most healthy bars. Kennedy had turned her on to them, explaining her own trial and error process in finding something palatable that wasn't loaded with fat and sugar. Living with a vegetarian had proven to be an interesting challenge. Most days she was perfectly happy and willing to eat the same foods Kennedy did, and was surprised at how much variety there was to be had without meat.

Still, there were times when she simply needed a good old cheeseburger or a steak. Kennedy was fine with that, and if they cooked it at home, she cooked something for herself that was comparable, like a veggie burger. If they went out, she could always get a loaded baked potato, minus the bacon bits, of course. Like so many other aspects of their limited experience together, they were learning to compromise in ways that made both of them happy.

She studied the long, lean body next to her, enjoying the dappled sunlight playing against reddish-brown skin. Kennedy was muscular and long, built a lot like a swimmer or a distance runner, although she packed a little more muscle. If she were shorter, she might have easily passed for a gymnast. She had almost no fat on her, though, and Carson worried about what would happen if Kennedy were ever sick for more than a day or so. Her reserves were slim to none. She reached out, running her own hand down Kennedy's arm, and then her thigh, squeezing her knee when she reached it.

Kennedy captured her hand, raising it and kissing it. "You ready to head for the top? The view is worth the climb."

Carson's eyes roamed lazily from Kennedy's hiking boots to the top of her head. "There are a few views worth the climb around here." She smiled and leaned over, kissing her charmed lover on the lips.

"Or we could just go pitch camp now." She stood, offering Carson a hand up.

"Nope. You said this is a must do in Big Bend, so let's go conquer it, honey. Plenty of time for sleeping bag Olympics after the sun goes down." She hopped off the rock and back onto the trail, feeling Kennedy's hands on her shoulders as they went to their packs and put them back on.

"Count on it," Kennedy purred into her ear as they started on up the trail. It was steep and narrow and covered in loose soil and gravel in many spots. Most hikers on the trail allowed a prudent amount of distance between groups, in case of any sliding falls, but occasionally younger Boy Scout types would go barreling past them, yelling enough to send any small animals running for the nearest shelter. "Have to put up with that this close to the basin. Once we get out on the South Rim, and especially in Pine Canyon tomorrow, we'll lose a lot of the riffraff."

"Good." Carson used both hands on her walking stick to heft herself up and over a smallish ledge in the middle of the path. "I like my wildlife to be furry and on four legs."

"I'm sure you'll get to see something larger than a squirrel before this trip is over. I can't think of a time yet when I've been up here that I didn't see deer, coyote, and the occasional fox. Javelina and jackrabbit, too. Bears, more rarely. Cats almost never." She followed Carson up, taking the ledge with ease in two steps of her long legs.

"Javelina?" Carson stopped and turned halfway around. "I'm having an *Old Yeller* moment here. Do I need to be on the lookout for trees to climb, just in case?"

"Nah. I wouldn't go out of my way to provoke them, but as long as you keep a respectful distance, they aren't quite the piranhas they were made out to be in the movie." She stepped in next to Carson, sharing the narrow path, their shoulders almost touching. "Main thing I'd be worried about are those cats. If you see one of them, don't run, no matter how much instinct tells you to. You want to stay still and see if they will go away on their own, and if not, walk away slowly and don't turn your back on them."

"Hmm. Hope I don't see one of those." Carson looked around, trying to spot any creatures in the trees around them. She drew in a deep breath, the scent of the place reminding her very much of some of the spots they'd hiked just west of Austin. The foliage was, in fact, quite similar, especially in the more open areas where there was abundant mesquite and various types of cactus. Less familiar was the occasional agave plant, and she secretly wondered if she could snip some and try to figure out how to make tequila with it.

As they neared the summit, speech grew scarce in favor of breathing. Both women lost their footing a few times, though neither one actually fell down. The walking sticks and having each other to lean on made a big difference. Finally, they reached the top and Kennedy located a lookout area with a clear view for miles.

"Oh my gosh." Carson surveyed the horizon. "Is that Mexico?" She pointed to an area past a sliver she assumed was the Rio Grande River.

"Yeah." Kennedy pointed in the same direction. "See that brownish haze way off in the distance?"

"Yeah. Reminds me of Dallas on ozone action alert days." She shaded her face with her hand. "What is that, dust? We're too far away from a city for it to be—"

"No, you were right the first time. It's pollution from factories built just a little ways over the border." Kennedy found a spot to dump their packs, helping Carson out of hers. "A gift from NAFTA. Greedy Americans taking advantage of the more lax Mexican environmental laws."

"That's terrible." Carson shrugged her shoulders up and down, then whimpered as Kennedy took the hint and started massaging them. "What about the park? Does it hurt things here?"

"Absolutely." Kennedy dug into a vicious knot at the base of her neck, slowly working the tight muscle loose. "It affects the plants and animals alike; it can even affect the weather. Man, you're tight. Your pack too heavy?"

"Not really. Guess I'm just not used to all of this after being a lazy bum for the past month. Come on, let's sit for a while before we go back down." She found a section of rock jutting out where they could stretch out some. Kennedy sat back against a smooth section of rock wall and Carson snuggled up between her legs, leaning back and sighing in contentment as long arms wrapped around her. "Can we camp here?" She closed her eyes, enjoying the contact and the sunlight.

"No. I signed us up for one of the spots on the South Rim, but you'll be glad of it in the morning." She nuzzled Carson's hair before resting her chin on her head. "The sunrise view over there is killer."

"Ooo. Can I take coffee?" She felt a little shiver as Kennedy took a few tentative nips at the side of her neck.

"Absolutely, and thank god for those coffee bags you found

at the store. I was trying to figure out where to fit a camping coffee pot in my pack. Those bags saved weight and space." She continued to nibble at Carson's skin, just enjoying snuggling out under the trees. No one else was around, giving them the privacy to be a couple with no curious eyes.

"You would've carried a coffee pot up here just for me?" Carson had found a box of coffee bags at the grocery store, used just like tea bags. Combined with a packet of instant hot chocolate, she had mocha java to look forward to along with their instant packets of oatmeal for breakfast.

"You bet. I thought about trying to carry a bottle of red wine up here, since it doesn't need to be chilled, but decided it might be too much weight in the pack." She switched sides, feeling Carson relax more against her. She reached up, checking the wicked knot in her neck, smiling when she felt it was almost completely gone.

"Confession time." Carson glanced over her shoulder. "I snuck a little flask of tequila into my pack. I knew it was one of the few hard liquors you like, plus we only need a shot or two, so lots less space and weight."

"Aren't you clever?" She pulled Carson's T-shirt aside at the neck, continuing her exploration, slowly kissing her way along a mostly-exposed shoulder.

"Do you know how much I want to get naked with you right now?" Carson mumbled, turning her head and finding Kennedy's lips, sampling them for a long while. They pulled back, and Carson settled in her arms again, Kennedy's cheek pressed against the side of her head. "Do you realize we've made love almost every day since I moved to Austin?"

The question came out of the blue, and Kennedy thought about her answer for a few moments. "Is that a bad thing?" She finally responded, hoping fervently it wasn't.

"No. Just...different, for me at any rate. I guess I was just wondering...oh, I don't know what I'm wondering. It's all still pretty new to me. But you knew that." She smiled, squeezing Kennedy's arms against her in reassurance. "It's a good kind of new and different. Just..."

"You're wondering if it's normal?" Kennedy hazarded a guess.

"Mmm. Kind of, I suppose." She turned a little bit in Kennedy's arms, doing a little nibbling of her own.

"Well, ooo, that's nice." Kennedy's thoughts were derailed. "Okay, where was I? Um...I think lots of couples, especially in a new relationship, tend to be pretty physical. You and I, we built up to sex pretty slowly, and I think maybe things kind of exploded for us, once we reached that point. There isn't really any 'normal,' I don't think. Just whatever a couple is comfortable with. Does it make you uncomfortable to be doing it as often as we do?"

"No." Carson kissed along her jaw line. "I just hoped you didn't think I was some kind of nympho or something. Seems like there are times when I can't keep my hands off of you. I probably initiate it at least as often as you do."

"Heh." Kennedy's eyes twinkled at her in amusement. "If you are a nympho, please don't go changing for me." She tweaked Carson's nose. "Seriously, I've thought no such thing. It's been real nice, getting to know you on that level. I think after the holidays, and especially after you get settled into a job, we might slow down a little bit." She shrugged slightly. "I dunno. I guess maybe some couples make love every day even after it isn't new anymore. Maybe it's a lifetime thing for some of them."

"I think I'd like that." Carson snuggled up against her. "I like lying in your arms afterward, and falling asleep. It's so peaceful. Or waking up and starting the day feeling so very loved by you. Like I said, it's a nice new and different."

"Well, the point is, whatever is right for us is right for us, sweetheart. As long as you feel good about how we're doing things right now, that's what matters." She kissed Carson again, running her hand up and down her bare lower leg, feeling Carson respond to her. "I think I could get naked with you right now, too, but not a good place. I'd hate to shock any unsuspecting Boy Scouts."

"Do you ever think about doing anything really wild?" Carson ran her fingertip along Kennedy's forearm. "I know on our trip to Mexico, we came pretty close to having a top deck experience on the boat."

"Mmm. Yeah, but I think I'd had a few too many fruity drinks with cute little umbrellas and plastic animals on the rim. Not really my style and I was really glad later we took it to our cabin. In a sleeping bag in a tent is about as outdoors as I'd like to go at this point, unless we're alone on our own boat back home. Al fresco sex sounds fun in theory, but dirt, rocks, spiders, and ants tend to make the reality of it a whole lot less appealing."

"But do you think you'll ever get bored and want to try something different?" Carson frowned, not quite sure she wanted to know the answer.

"I'll never get bored with you." Kennedy cupped her cheek, tilting her face up. "As for trying something different, I love what we do together, because it comes from a place of our love and respect for each other. I don't need wild and kinky, sweetheart. Do I have some fantasies I haven't shared yet? Oh, you bet. And in time, I will, and maybe we'll try them, and maybe we won't." She kissed her passionately, her expression very serious as they surfaced for air. "But don't go worrying you're going to wake up one morning in shackles with me wielding a crop. I promise you that is not in my fantasies."

"Oh. I wasn't worried about that, per se. I think I feel like you do." Carson searched her eyes. "I meant it. I like that idea of the couples who stay in love and continue to express that on the physical level. I..." She swallowed. "I like the idea of waking up in your arms every morning." It was all she could bring herself to say at the moment, but it was enough as she saw the tiny light dawning in Kennedy's eyes.

"I like that idea too." She hugged Carson tightly. "Very much." Kennedy closed her eyes, her mind spinning. Was Carson saying what she thought she was saying? She squeezed her closer, holding on as if for dear life. They needed to have a more decisive talk on the subject. Sometime soon, after she got her courage up.

Chapter Five

THEY PITCHED THE tent in the last hour of sunlight, finding a secluded site reached by a narrow footpath off the main South Rim Trail. It was on a bluff, surrounded by trees on three sides, overlooking a vast vista on the south side with an unrestricted view that was clear well into Mexico. They were far enough around to the southeast that they couldn't see the sun setting, although they could observe the changing colors of the sky, which gradually turned from pale blue, to gorgeous burnt orange and fiery red. As the sun dropped, so did the temperature, and both women shed shorts for long leggings and fleece tops before they made camp.

It was a tiny tent designed specifically for backpacking, and was barely wide enough for the two sleeping bags, even when they were zipped together. Kennedy made quick work of emptying all food products and toiletries from their backpacks, storing them in the thick iron bear box that was bolted into cement several yards from the tent. The packs themselves she stowed in the small vestibule at the front of the tent, after taking out the miniature backpacking stove.

No bigger than a teapot, the butane stove had two parts, the fuel vessel and a folding burner that clamped onto the top. She placed their one cooking pot on the burner and emptied a packet of freeze-dried vegetarian chili inside, mixing it with the appropriate amount of water from one of their water bottles. She lit the stove and stood, arranging the few logs in the eating area so they were close to the stove. No campfires were allowed in the park because the dry climate, the trees, and fires were a recipe for disaster.

Kennedy turned the flame down low and moved near the edge of the bluff where Carson stood, drinking in the remaining warmth of the sun. "Hey." Kennedy wrapped her arms around her from behind, kissing her on the side of her neck. "Gorgeous, huh?"

"Yeah." Carson soaked up the bright display of color. "It's amazing. Almost unreal."

"Desert dust helps give the light that rich color." Kennedy relaxed, feeling Carson's arms against her own, squeezing her closer. "Dinner's on and should be ready in about fifteen minutes or so."

"I can smell the spices. Smells good." Carson sniffed the air. "Ooo. And pine. Lord, it's just about perfect here. Think the park would let us build a cabin right on this spot?"

"Um, that would be a 'no'." Kennedy smiled. "Nice thought, though. That would sure be a nice sight to see every night."

They stood in silence until it was dusky and the sounds of night creatures began to replace those of the day. Somewhere off in the trees, an owl hooted and a light wind rustled the leaves overhead. Something slivered through the brush at the edge of the campsite, scaring up something else which skittered off in the opposite direction. Way off in the distance, a lone coyote howled and was quickly joined by its companions in an impromptu song to the rising moon.

They returned to the logs and sat near the stove, taking turns stirring the chili until it bubbled just a little. Kennedy removed it from the burner and turned off the stove before she took up their community spork, their one eating utensil. She dished up a bite of the chili and blew on it, then offered it over to Carson, who sniffed it and took it cautiously into her mouth. "Mmm. That's really good. More, please." She opened her mouth in expectation and received a quick kiss in response. "Ooo. More of that too, please."

Kennedy laughed and took a bite herself before offering her more chili. "I'll give you all of the latter you want."

"Dessert." Carson winked, and they continued to take turns eating from the pan until the chili was gone. "That was quite tasty." She smacked her lips and patted her belly, leaning back against the log and stretching lazily. It was peaceful there, and she was pleasantly tired, glad to have gotten some much-needed exercise in such a beautiful place. Her back and shoulders ached slightly and her feet were weary, but overall, she felt good.

"Yeah. Freeze-dried food just keeps improving. Come a long way from the stuff the army used to eat." Kennedy rinsed out the pan, carefully wiping it clean, before she filled it again and turned on the stove. "We can have some hot chocolate. I brought the packets that have the little marshmallows mixed in with the instant chocolate."

"Cool. I'll go get it." Carson trotted over to the bear box, working the bear-proof latch and fishing around in the fanny pack of food that they had detached from one of the backpacks. Soon they were curled up against one of the logs, legs stretched out as they snuggled together, drinking chocolate from two tin camping mugs and looking up at the stars.

"Big dipper." Kennedy pointed up over the treetops. "And there's the little one."

"And the North Star." Carson pointed along with her. "Lot more stars here, even than what we see at home."

"Yeah. Too much light there, even all that way outside Austin." And there was that word home again, setting Kennedy's emotions spinning like a top. She decided to let them spin and sipped at her chocolate, enjoying the warmth of the beverage sliding down her throat and the warmth of Carson's body snuggled up against her. "Might get down in the 40's tonight. Maybe even the 30's."

"I've got you to keep me warm." Carson finished off her chocolate and almost swiped her upper lip, laughing in surprise instead when Kennedy reached over and did it for her, following up with a light brush of her lips. "You sure you got it all?"

"Maybe not." Kennedy smiled and gulped down the rest of her own drink before she tossed the mug aside and circled Carson with both arms, tilting her back against the log before giving her lips a more serious and thorough exploration. "Mmm." She stretched out a little more, draping one leg across her lover's, feeling their bodies begin to move together.

Kennedy lowered the zipper on Carson's fleece top and slipped one hand inside, stroking the thin silk long underwear top she had on beneath and feeling Carson's ribs expand suddenly at the contact, along with the warm puff of air against her own neck. The material was soft and smooth and she explored further, feeling a nipple harden against her fingertips. Her own heartbeat picked up in response and she left Carson's lips, nibbling down her neck to her pulse point, nipping at it and tracing the curve of her collarbone with her tongue.

"More," Carson whispered, as Kennedy's hand dropped down, tugging the silk free from her waistband and finding warm skin. Her other hand followed, lifting the silk most of the way up. She slid down, teasing her lover with her lips, starting at her navel ring and working her way up to first one breast and then the other. Carson gasped, arching into her, her hands combing back through Kennedy's hair. "Oh, god." She hissed at the sensual contact, frantically seeking more as she tried to wrap herself around her partner, feeling Kennedy's hips beginning to rock against her.

Kennedy came up for air, her breathing erratic, and she

cradled Carson's face, kissing her forehead and then her lips, getting lost in another long kiss. Slowly, she pulled back, smiling at the pale light spilling across lover's face. "Why don't you go get undressed and crawl into the sleeping bag, while I clean up these mugs and secure the bear box for the night?"

"Best idea you've had since the hot chocolate." Carson kissed her again and felt Kennedy pull her to her feet. "Hurry." She ran her hand up Kennedy's stomach, ending at the side of one breast, then sauntered to the tent and disappeared inside.

"Whew!" Kennedy threw her head back and looked up at the blanket of stars, feeling her pulse race. She drew in a long, deep breath and shook her head to clear it, then knelt down, using as little of their precious water as possible to rinse the mugs. She looked all around the area where they had eaten, searching with her flashlight, making sure there was nothing left out to tempt any bears or other hungry creatures. Once the box was securely closed, she gave the site one last once-over, then swaggered over to the tent, feeling the heat at the thought of what was inside.

"Carson?" She unzipped the mesh inner door and crawled inside, turning and zipping closed the outer vestibule, then the middle solid nylon closure, and then re-zipped the mesh door. "Carson?" She crept the short distance across the narrow space and tilted her head, listening. Heavy breathing greeted her ears. "I'll be damned." She smiled and quickly divested herself of her own clothing.

She slipped into the sleeping bag, zipping them both inside it. Curling against Carson's back, she braced herself on her forearm while she leaned over. They had unzipped the solid top of the tent, clipping it back and leaving only the mesh top between them and the stars overhead. In the faint light it was clear that Carson was fast asleep, a victim of several miles of hiking and a full stomach, exhaustion winning out over lust. "Guess we don't make love every night after all," Kennedy whispered. She bent down and kissed Carson on the cheek, then lay down, pulling her tightly against her. "Sweet dreams, love."

She lay back down and closed her eyes, sighing in utter contentment at the sensation of their naked bodies pressed together. Carson mumbled in her sleep, a happy little sound escaping her lips as her hand unconsciously found Kennedy's against her stomach and covered it. Unexpected joy welled up inside and Kennedy blinked a few times at the sudden sting of tears in her eyes. It was all out of proportion to the simple gesture as she buried her face into Carson's hair, inhaling her sweet scent. It was a perfect moment, and she lay awake for a while, unwilling to surrender it over to sleep.

THE MOON ROSE, shining down into the little glade and dusting the tent in silvery light. A whispering breeze made music with the leaves overhead and rustled through the undergrowth, sending small dried bits of debris tumbling across the open campsite. At the edge of the trees, a large furry creature snuffled the air, sorting out the various scents wafting on the wind. The human scent was more than familiar, and the odd smell of the nylon tent. Butane odor lingered near some logs that always gave hope of leftover tidbits.

The animal lumbered into the clearing, nose twitching, lips slightly parted, releasing heavy breaths that occasionally morphed into snorty, curious, growly sounds. Long claws rasped across the dirt and rocks, and heavy paws trampled leaves and grass underfoot. He thoroughly searched the area where they had shared dinner, knocking aside logs and smelling teasing hints of food, but finding none.

Inside the tent, Kennedy awoke, sensing something was amiss. She sat up and cocked her head to one side, closing her eyes and concentrating.

There. A congested heavy breathing sound gave it away and she smiled a little, just as the first rattle of the bear box reached her ears. Carson stirred and rolled over, frowning as she realized Kennedy was sitting up. "What's wrong?" She sat up.

"Shhh." Kennedy raised a finger to her lips. "Bear," she whispered directly into Carson's ear. Carson's eyes grew wide as saucers, but she remained silent. Another rattle sounded across the clearing along with a frustrated roar, and Kennedy found herself with a lap full of lover. She stifled a laugh and hugged Carson instead. "It's okay." The words were almost inaudible. "Stay put."

She quietly removed Carson from her lap and slithered to the front of the tent. Inch by inch, she opened the mesh door and the outer door and crept forward into the cramped vestibule, where she opened it just enough to peek outside. Painted in moonlight was the biggest black bear she'd ever seen. He was wrestling with the iron bear box, which was now making a constant metal clanking noise. Both big paws braced the sides of the box, and he was butting it with his head, howling out his frustration. She shook with silent chuckles and motioned Carson forward.

Cautiously, Carson joined her and looked out, ducking her head under Kennedy's arm. She felt safe there and sat back on her heels, watching the show. The moon dusted his thick coat with bluish highlights, and glinted off sharp canines whenever he growled. Finally, utterly thwarted in his mission, he stood on his hind legs, let out a ferocious roar, and dropped back down to all-fours before ambling out of the clearing away from the bluff, toward the footpath that led to the main trail.

After several silent minutes Kennedy re-zipped the tent doors, and they crawled back into the sleeping bag. "Is he gone?" Carson whispered, clinging to Kennedy in a face-to-face death grip.

"Yeah." She reached up and untied the rolled-back tent roof, snapping it into place. "Just in case he comes back and decides to check us out." She settled back down, automatically taking Carson into her arms again. They cuddled together quietly as her hands stroked slowly up and down a smooth, soft back, calming her slightly dazed lover. "You okay?"

"Yeah." Carson snuggled up tighter. "I've never seen one quite so close up. He was a big guy, wasn't he?"

"Biggest I've seen." She continued rubbing Carson's back, one hand sliding up and massaging the base of her neck. "Need to report him to the base tomorrow, just so folks can be made aware. Typical bear behavior though. He looked for food, found nothing, and moved on. Harmless as long as he's not provoked."

"Oh my gosh." Carson grew still. "I faced that bear completely naked. I can't believe I did that."

Kennedy burst out laughing. "Sweetheart, if he'd come after us, clothing wouldn't have stopped him."

"Yeah, but if I'm going to die by bear attack, I'd like to be found with my clothes on." She gave in to her own laughter as Kennedy lightly ran her fingertips up both sides in a half-tickling, half-sensual motion. It felt good, and she returned the touches as their legs tangled together and their lips met for a lengthy exchange. "I fell asleep on you, didn't I?" She buried her face into warm, musky-scented skin, nuzzling and kissing a few spots in the process. "Sorry about that."

"Yeah, but that's okay." Kennedy rolled them over until they were spooning tightly. "We were both pretty wiped out. It was really nice holding you while you slept." She tightened her grip, pressing her stomach against Carson's back.

Carson reached down, grasping a hand and lifting it. She kissed the knuckles several times, before she tucked it between her breasts, curling her own hand over it. "This feels right, doesn't it?"

Soft kisses at the nape of her neck were her answer. "Nothing has ever felt more right," Kennedy whispered. There was so much more to be said, but she wasn't sure she wanted to say it in the middle of the night in a sleeping bag in the woods. Instead, she curled around her lover, feeling both of them breathing, and her own heart beating in her chest. Beneath her fist, Carson's heart beat along with her, and she fell into dreamless sleep.

CARSON STIRRED AND sat up, scrubbing at her eyes with her fists. It was still full dark, only the breeze rustling the leaves disturbing the silence. Next to her, Kennedy whimpered and clutched at her, mumbling unhappily. "Not again," Carson whispered. "Thought we had whipped these."

She lay partway down, resting on her forearm and reaching across, stroking Kennedy's head. She continued to mutter in her sleep, frowning and tossing about in restless agitation. "No. Carson, no."

Carson sighed. "Honey, it's okay." She wished there were a way to make the dreams subside without waking Kennedy, who desperately needed sleep after the past few days. "I'm right here."

"Sorry." Kennedy was still asleep, but the apology came out an agonized cry that broke Carson's heart. She slid closer, curling up against Kennedy, hoping it would calm her. The long arms wrapped around her like a vise and she groaned, her breathing cut short.

"Honey." She squirmed out of the embrace, and immediately Kennedy began to toss again. "Guess it's time to wake you." She touched Kennedy's head again, sifting the long hair through her fingers, before she gently grasped Kennedy's shoulder and shook it. "Honey."

"Agghhh!" Kennedy flew to a sitting position. She looked around, getting her bearings, and then moaned heavily, dropping her head into her hands.

"Here." Carson pushed a water bottle into her line of sight, and she grasped it, sucking it empty.

"Ugh." She took a deep breath and threw her head back, looking up.

"You wanna talk about it?" Carson took the bottle and set it aside, slipping over until their legs were touching.

"No," Kennedy answered unconvincingly. She glanced at Carson, her expression a mixture of pain and curiosity. "S'all right."

"Same old, same old?" Carson persisted.

"No." This one had been a new nightmare, one that left her alone in a very different way. "No. It wasn't."

"Oh." Carson crossed her legs and drew them up, wrapping her arms around them. "Okay." There it was again, that uncomfortable silence. She hated it. Hated treading on it, and especially hated trying to get across it. It was new territory, and she realized woefully she didn't have the tools to break through the walls Kennedy was very capable of raising if she chose to.

It hurt and made her weary and she laid back down, sadly rolling over, her back to Kennedy. It was all too much, and she stifled a sob, catching it right before it escaped. There she was, in a tent barely big enough for two, and she felt almost as alone as she had in the barn loft the day before. She shivered, her body visibly shaking, and a long presence curled around her from behind.

"Carson?" Kennedy tentatively touched her arm and felt it go rigid. "It was just a nightmare."

"I know." Carson kept her back turned, offering no encouragement. She felt Kennedy pull away and sighed. It was going to be a very long time until dawn. "If it was just a nightmare," she whispered sadly, "then why can't you talk about it?"

"Because this one might be true." Kennedy lay there, mere inches from her lover. It might as well have been a canyon, and she teetered there on the edge, hoping there was a bridge.

"What do you mean?" Carson rolled over, facing her, and they both simply looked into each other's eyes for a long moment. She reached out again, stroking Kennedy's head and watching her eyes close. "Talk to me, please?"

"I never wanted to disappoint you, especially like that," she whispered.

"What are you talking about?" Carson cupped her face, her thumb brushing across a wet cheek.

"But you said..." Kennedy opened her eyes, more tears trickling across her face. "You said I sent you to a really ugly place."

It took a moment before clarity smacked Carson between the eyes. "Oh, god. I never meant..." She scooted closer. "No. You didn't send me to the ugly place. Rick and Tom did."

"You aren't disappointed with me?" Kennedy reached across, touching Carson's arm hopefully, grateful when she didn't pull away.

"No." She leaned closer and pecked Kennedy's lips, then her nose, then her forehead. "Why would I be?"

"You saw me high." Kennedy sniffled. "Not a pretty sight."

"Honey, you didn't get high on purpose. Tom did that to you," Carson soothed. "That wasn't your fault. You said you didn't blame me for it, right?" Kennedy nodded. "Well, I certainly don't blame you for it either. It's a very bad thing, which happened to both of us. Obviously, we're both still processing it."

"I guess." Kennedy flopped on her back. "But you wondered if I wanted to smoke when I showed you the pot. I did drugs in the past, Carson. I can't change that. It will always be a part of me."

"Oh, Kennedy." Carson sighed. "I didn't really think that. You were being so secretive, and all of a sudden you whipped it out and said you'd kept it. For a split second, I was confused until you explained yourself. I can't take that back either. I didn't do drugs. I don't know what that's like and I don't have a frame of experience to put that in."

"I've done some really bad things, things I haven't told you about yet." She rested her head on Carson's shoulder, and felt her fingers raking through her hair. "I guess I'm afraid someday you're going to finally learn something about me that will send you packing."

"Short of revealing you were a teenage serial killer, there's almost nothing you could tell me that would change the way I feel about you," she spoke into Kennedy's ear, feeling her breathing against her. "I love who you are now. I love who you were, because that person became who you are now. Everything happens as it's supposed to. I really believe that. Whatever horrible things you think you did, I can't help but think that maybe someday you're going to use those experiences to help someone else."

"Carson, I haven't even begun to tell you everything about my past." Her voice was timid, almost like a child's.

"I sure hope not." Carson sat up a little, re-settling Kennedy against her. "We've only been together for about three months. I'd hate to think I've learned everything there is to know about you already. Look, honey, we just chose different paths to grow up is all, right? There was a heck of a lot more to do in Dallas. I imagine if I'd grown up out here, I might have done exactly what you did. It must have gotten a little..."

"Boring?" Kennedy supplied. "You bet. But not all the kids out here did drugs."

"But a lot of them did, obviously. I'm sorry you had such a hard time of it back then." The soft words brushed over Kennedy, Carson's breath warm against her face. "And I'm very glad you survived it in one piece. Maybe you were meant to go through everything you did back then so you could help Pete today. I'm not going to judge you for your past, honey. Maybe you had to go through all of that to become who you are today."

"I had to meet you to become who I am today," Kennedy

answered quietly. "Your opinion is worth everything."

"Then you listen to me." The low, firm voice rumbled against Kennedy's ear. "You did not disappoint me in this. I was terrified, not because of what you were doing, but at the thought that we — that you — could have died out there on the road. Those two guys almost got us killed and that pisses me off. You think you had to meet me to learn to live again?" Kennedy nodded. "Well, that goes both ways. I just started living again, and I'll be damned if two redneck punks are going to take that away from me."

"God." Kennedy's world righted itself just a little. She rolled to her back and pulled Carson against her, wrapping her arms around her and settling back in a position they had gotten used to in three short months. "I feel like such an idiot. I've spent two days thinking — "

"Shhh." Carson touched her lips. "It's been a tough time, and it's not over. No more kicking ourselves over this. All we can do is move forward."

"I'll do my best." Kennedy nuzzled her head.

"That's all I'd ever ask." Carson closed her eyes, feeling the exhaustion creep back over her. Soon, they were both fast asleep.

THE BAREST HINT of gray pre-dawn light fell across two sleepy figures sitting on the edge of the bluff, wrapped up together in a blanket, awaiting the rising sun. Carson sipped at her coffee and hot chocolate mixture, while Kennedy took her chocolate straight up. After the middle of the night heart-to-heart, neither woman had really had enough sleep. Kennedy felt like she had been run over by a truck and her neck was stiff. She dreaded carrying the pack and wondered if they could bypass the climb up Casa Grande and go directly on to Pine Canyon after they reported the bear at the basin.

"Kennedy?" Carson turned a bit in the blanket. "You said Pine Canyon is beautiful, right?"

"Yeah." Kennedy shifted, trying to find her energy. She felt a bit out of sorts, unsure of where the negative emotions were coming from. "It is."

"And you said Emory Peak is higher than Casa Grande." Carson cupped her mug in both hands, inhaling the fragrant steam.

"Uh-huh." Kennedy suddenly found her missing energy and smiled as she guessed where the conversation was headed. "That's true."

"What if we skip Casa Grande and go directly to Pine

Canyon? Take it easy today?" She took another sip of the coffee, sighing as it warmed her, and she felt her brain cells begin to kick into gear.

"I think I love you." Kennedy smiled warmly, tilting her head and kissing her cheek. "And I think that's a great idea. And it'll give us more time to enjoy the surprise I wanna show you in the canyon."

"Can't wait." Carson returned the kiss. "Ooo." She gazed across the wide-open space before them. "Oh my god, that's gorgeous."

Pink and purple sun rays fanned across the sky overhead, while below them were billowing clouds, puffed up like pale coral-tinted cotton balls, completely obscuring the ground below. The sky gradually lightened from navy to royal, to bright pale blue as the sun burst over the horizon, popping through the clouds. The valley below was covered in ground fog, but there, up on their private bluff, the clouds provided a rare sight, and they both reveled in it.

"Looks like you could just launch yourself out there and land on them, doesn't it?" Kennedy set her mug down and grabbed the edges of the blanket, wrapping it around both of them and pulling Carson back against her.

"Yeah, all nice and soft." She turned, tilting her head up and sharing a kiss. They were both already dressed for hiking, and their packs were ready to go after a pre-dawn meal of instant oatmeal. "So we go report the big bad bear and then go enjoy the canyon?"

"That's the plan, Stan." Kennedy helped her up and they stood for a long moment in a warm hug inside the blanket, neither woman inclined to move too quickly. "One surprise for today and another one for tomorrow."

"Oh, I can't wait!" Carson did a happy little shimmy against her, laughing as Kennedy nipped her ear. "Hey." Her eyes grew serious and she reached up, touching Kennedy's face. "Thanks for not shutting me out last night. I know that's hard for you sometimes. But that tent, it was feeling mighty small for a few minutes there."

"I hate what those guys did to us. We survived, and then I...I almost let them take you from me anyway. My own stupid fear." She tilted Carson's chin up, and a gentle thumb brushed across the side of Carson's face. She swallowed in reflex. "My entire world was in that tent," Kennedy whispered, her eyes catching the sunlight, a fiercely protective spark that reached out, warming Carson all over.

"You..." Carson hugged her tightly, absorbing the closeness.

"You make me feel so much..." She released a trembling sigh, feeling the hug returned two-fold. "Sometimes I can't..."

"Is it too much?" The hesitation behind the question was evident as Kennedy braced herself in the event she was told to back off, to give her space, to give her time to think—all the things she'd heard before the move to Austin and in the weeks since they'd lived together. Maybe she'd misread the signals. Maybe she was fooling herself to think that this was more than just a little bit of fun for Carson. And it was fun, wasn't it? They enjoyed so many of the same things and laughed together often, and things in the bedroom were incredible. Maybe that was enough. Maybe 'I love you' didn't carry the same weight with Carson as it did with her. "If it is, I can...just tell me, Carson. I don't want to smother you. I..." A thumb brushed gently across her lips, silencing her.

"No. It's not too much." Carson searched startled eyes, watching them soften in understanding. "Not anymore." She balled up a fist, pressing it against Kennedy's chest. "What I was trying to say is, I feel so much with you, and sometimes I can't seem to tell you what I'm feeling. Does that make sense?"

"Perfect sense." Her own voice sounded far away, overshadowed by the rush of blood in her ears, a relieved sensation flooding her system. "Sometimes I feel the same way." They hugged again, both women sighing in unison. And sometimes, Kennedy reflected, words weren't necessary. The urge to talk it out, to settle things once and for all, would win out soon enough, making at least a few well-chosen words necessary. That was no longer such a frightening prospect. Maybe, just maybe, she already knew what the answer would be.

THEY MADE LEISURELY time traversing the Lost Mine Trail, the first trail leading through Pine Canyon. Just off trail, sometimes heard and sometimes seen, was a babbling brook, fuller than usual after the recent rains. It added an extra layer of peacefulness to the early morning hike, its musical sound blending with an abundance of twittering birds. Technically, per maps, the Lost Mine Trail ended abruptly and a trek through the woods was required to reach Pine Canyon Trail, but so many campers had made the hike that a faint path was visible at the end of Lost Mine.

"First part of the surprise coming up in about thirty more minutes." Kennedy smiled, turning back toward Carson, who was a few feet behind her on the very narrow path. Off through the trees they caught an occasional glimpse of Lost Mine Peak.

At 7,535 feet, it was taller than Casa Grande, but shorter than Emory by almost 300 feet. The area they were in was heavily wooded and much more secluded than the more well-traveled trails from the previous day.

"First part?" Carson hustled until she was as close as she could get without bumping into Kennedy. "There's more than one surprise today?"

"Yeah." A self-satisfied grin flashed back at her. "I just remembered a really cool place we may be able to camp tonight, if you're feeling adventurous."

"Honey, no offense, but if tonight brings any more adventure than last night, I'll be ready to go check into the nearest hotel." She thought about that for a moment and hooked one finger through a utility strap dangling from the bottom of Kennedy's pack. "Well, we might finish at least one adventure that we didn't last night, but other than that, I'd like to actually sleep tonight."

"Oh, I think we can arrange for both of those, although I don't always have control over things like bears." Kennedy stepped carefully onto a log, checking the other side for hidden snakes before she stepped over. "Clear."

Carson did a little jump over the log behind her, crunching in some leaves on landing and frightening a large lizard, that ran up the nearest tree, his neck puffing in and out as he breathed out his fear. "Oh." She stopped to study it. It was green, with a bit of pale yellow stripe down its side, and beady black eyes. "Sorry, little guy. Didn't mean to stir things up." She glanced ahead where Kennedy had already made several yards on her and turned, trudging on. "Hey, thought we were taking it easy today."

The taller woman slowed down, waiting for Carson to catch up. "I keep forgetting about these long legs."

"Funny, there are days I can't stop thinking about them." Carson batted her eyelashes, pleased at the blush her comment produced.

They pressed on, enjoying the sun and shadows that painted the path in interesting chunky stripes and a light breeze that held the temperature at a pleasant level, neither hot nor cold. The clouds had burned off again, just like the day before, and the sky was crystal clear blue. They'd applied liberal coats of sunscreen to their arms, legs, and faces, and every now and then Carson caught a whiff of Kennedy's skin, mixed with coconut. It made her mouth water.

It was amazing, this physical attraction they shared. She knew the driving force behind it was a strong bond of love. It was a love they were still learning to express on several levels, but that pure animal attraction never ceased to catch her by surprise. Truth be told, she had worried for a while that maybe they were focused too much on that aspect of their relationship, but they had taken the time to become friends before they ever took that last big leap. She smiled though, remembering just how hard it had been to wait on a few occasions. Now she was glad they had. When they did come together, it was an expression of love. Not that lust didn't have its place, but given past experience, lust without love was unsatisfying in the end, she'd learned, and usually died a quick death.

This...her eyes fell on those long, strong, brown legs, watching the muscles shift as Kennedy walked. Walking really wasn't a good description for it. When Kennedy moved she swaggered with a smooth, sexy, confident stride that did more than just cover ground. Those legs conquered their territory. *Mmm.* She shook her head. They'd sure conquered her a few times.

No, this was something that just kept growing stronger with each passing day. She'd not experienced this level of desire in the past with anyone. It had taken a while to not be embarrassed by just how powerful it was at times. She'd be reading, or puttering around the house, or sitting at her computer, and Kennedy would catch her eye, and...boom...she wanted her so badly there was nothing to do but satisfy that need.

But not all their touching was sexual in nature, and that, she acknowledged, was reassuring. They touched each other quite often, just while talking or curled up on the couch reading the paper together and especially at night as they fell asleep talking. Kennedy, especially, had seemed to need the affirmation of tactile contact after they'd gotten Carson's things moved in. It was a way for her to make sure Carson was there, and alive, and okay, in the aftermath of her kidnapping. Carson was more than willing to indulge that, allowing Kennedy to cuddle up with her whenever she needed to. Now it had just become habit to make physical contact with each other often, even if it was nothing more than one of them propping a foot in the other one's lap while one played on a laptop and the other napped or read a book.

It was nice, and something she'd come to realize she didn't want to live without. She looked up, to find Kennedy standing in the middle of the path, hands on her hips, staring at her. "What?"

"Just wondering where you'd gone off to." She chuckled. "I called your name like four times. We need to hike off trail here and down to the creek. What were you thinking about anyway?"

Carson opened her mouth and then closed it. A sheepish smile tugged at her lips. What to say? She glanced down a bit, her gaze lingering at thigh level. "Your legs."

"Still?" Kennedy tossed her arms up in mock exasperation.

"You started it." Carson closed the distance, reaching out and touching one of the very tempting legs.

"I can finish it, too." She waggled her eyebrows, moving closer and draping her forearms on Carson's shoulders. She teased her with her eyes for a moment, allowing her gaze to drift from her head down to T-shirt covered curves and back up to a perfectly shaped mouth. Slowly she ducked her head, meeting those lips in a willing exchange, and for a while the birds, and the brook, and the wind faded away. She purred, deepening the kiss as she felt Carson's fingertips trailing along the sides of her legs just below the hem of her shorts. "Come on, before I forget something important, like my name." She pulled back, taking Carson's hand and leading her off trail through the trees, down a gentle slope toward the water.

Carson realized the trickling swishing sound of the water had given way to something more pounding and steady, and she gasped as they reached the creek and hiked around a bend to behold a breathtaking sight. "Oh. Wow." A waterfall, at least 200 feet high, tumbled from between two high bluffs, crashing into a pool that spread out, joining the creek farther down past the bluffs. It was narrow and the sun sparkled off it, painting dancing rainbows in the spray below. "So this is why you told me to wear my swimsuit underneath today?"

"Yep." Kennedy looked around, spotting what she had hoped was still there: a large flat rock in the sun on the falls side, about two feet off the ground and just big enough for two people to sunbathe on. "Water is a tad cold this time of year though, so it might be good enough just to get some sun for a while."

"No way." Carson followed her over a log bridge to the other side and to the rock where they divested themselves of their packs. Carson made quick work of stripping off boots, socks, shorts, and T-shirt as well. "This may be the closest thing I get to a bath for two more days. I'm going in there for a few minutes, just to get clean."

"All right, but you've been warned." Kennedy fumbled at her own clothing, distracted by her partner's cute muscular form, clad in a tiny navy blue bikini. It amounted to four triangles of material held together with string, and spaghetti straps that tied around her neck. Kennedy was wearing a more athletic purple bikini with a high-cut bottom and a racer-back top that could double as a very stylish sports bra.

Kennedy shook her head and forced herself to turn long enough to fold their clothes and set them at the edge of the rock. Next she pulled out the camping blanket, making a softer place to lie in the sun and spread it over the rock, placing their hiking boots at each corner to keep it from blowing up. Lunch would consist of sandwiches and apples they'd picked up in the shop next to the ranger station after reporting the bear, a nice break from trail mix and protein bars.

"Yeow!" Carson shrieked as she entered the water. It was icy, so cold it made her feet hurt. *Okay.* She looked down and groaned. She'd made it in up to her ankles. *I can do this.* She gritted her teeth and quickly waded in deeper until the water was up to the tops of her thighs. "Oh...my...lord. It's cold!" She yelled to the smirking figure sitting on the rock.

"Told ya." Kennedy stretched out, extending one leg and leaning back on her elbows, enjoying the show.

"All right, but you just remember that tonight when I'm all nice and clean, and you're not." Carson splashed some water in her direction. "If you join me we can get clean together."

"I can take a sponge bath without actually getting in," Kennedy retorted. "And without freezing my ass off."

"Fine." Carson turned her back on her, walking a little farther in. She was beginning to get used to the temperature. Either that or she was simply growing numb. She looked down at her swimsuit top and grinned wickedly. "I'll just bathe here all alone," she called over her shoulder. She reached up and untied her top, slowly removing it with her back turned. She bunched it up in her fist and looked back over her shoulder again, grinning when she realized she had Kennedy's undivided attention. She turned, just long enough to fling the top onto the bank, and then turned her back again. "Have it your way."

Carson's voice lilted over toward the rock as Kennedy glanced first at the bit of navy material that had landed a few feet away and then at the muscular back and the nice rounded suit-covered curves below it. She groaned. "I am so whipped," she spoke aloud for the benefit of a small nearby rabbit. "Lord, I am such a dog, come to think of it." She pushed herself off the rock, smiling when she realized Carson knew she was coming in, but wasn't going to turn around. She removed her own top and braced herself as she entered the water, oblivious to the cold liquid, intent on one goal.

Kennedy stopped just short of her, close enough to touch her with her hands, without closing the distance. She squeezed Carson's shoulders and moved a little closer, almost touching, and leaned over, her lips brushing against a soft earlobe. "You are pure evil." She ran her hands down solid arms and around to a flat stomach, finally allowing their bodies to touch.

Carson gasped in surprise as two hardened nipples pressed against her skin just above her shoulder blades. She tilted her head up and back just as Kennedy's hands came up, closing over her breasts and cupping them, holding them in her palms. She closed her eyes, resting her head back against Kennedy's shoulder, opening her mouth as hungry lips sought her out. Kennedy's hands began to move, teasing her, before they slid down again, turning her around and grasping her hips, lifting her up until she was wrapped around the impossibly long body.

Kennedy held her close, breathing in her scent, feeling the combination of warm sun, Carson's even warmer body, and the cold water washing around them. She pulled back and laughed mischievously as she quickly took them into deeper, much colder water. Freezing, as a matter of fact, but it felt good to play, and the outrage on Carson's face was worth being completely covered in goose bumps.

"Oww!" Carson beat at her back in reflex. "I'm evil? Oh, I think you're the evil one, Miz Nocona. Oh, lord, but that's cold." They were in to their armpits, much nearer the falls, cold water rushing all around them.

"You said you wanted to get clean." Kennedy's eyes twinkled in feigned innocence. She held Carson securely. "Take a breath, sweetheart."

With that, she dunked them both under, coming back up as Carson shrieked in her ear. "Put me down!" She kicked at Kennedy's behind with her heels, her legs still wrapped around her.

"You sure about that?" Kennedy chuckled, letting go and watching Carson drop in, the water coming up to just under her nose. Carson's eyes popped open in surprise then narrowed, and she could just make out the wicked grin below the surface of the water. "Uh-oh." Too late. She yelped as lips and teeth closed around a very sensitive body part, nipping at her. "Hey! You bit my nipple!" She knew it was just a little nip, something Carson had done several times in the past, but the cold water heightened the sensation, a half-pleasurable, half-painful experience. She couldn't decide if she should put a stop to it or beg for more.

Laughing, Carson made the decision for her and launched herself out of the water and back into her arms, wrapping around her again, her weight settling around Kennedy's hips. Both women were rapidly forgetting about the cold. "Sometimes my height is just right." Carson sought out her lover's lips again, spending a goodly amount of time exploring them until they finally admitted it really was freezing, and decided to leave the water in favor of the warm sunny rock back on shore.

A while later after lunch, they were both stretched out on the rock, Carson using a sweatshirt for a pillow and Kennedy using Carson's stomach. They'd put their tops back on, as sunburn on some body parts just wasn't much fun, and were enjoying an afternoon's respite of complete lethargy. They'd both dozed on and off, allowing the warm sun to soak into their bones and darken tans that still lingered from summer.

Carson was awake after a pleasant nap, but quite unwilling to move. One arm was draped across Kennedy's stomach, and she absently combed the fingers of her other hand through the long hair spilling across her own chest and stomach. She could feel the lungs under her arm rising and falling in deep, even breaths, and occasionally Kennedy's eyelids fluttered, chasing dreams. "Good girl," she praised her sleeping lover. "No more nightmares allowed, you hear me?"

Kennedy stirred a little, smacking her lips in her sleep, before she settled back down, folding her hands across her stomach and Carson's arm, pinning it in place. Carson smiled, her eyes drifting lovingly over the curves and angles of the long body. Nearby, a couple of blue jays picked at their leftover sandwich crusts, fussing at each other and stealing the same tidbit back and forth several times before one of them got the upper hand and flew up into the trees with his prize. She watched him teetering on a narrow branch and sighed, drawing in the scent of pine, the canyon's namesake.

She couldn't remember the last time she'd felt so peaceful. It was a balm to her soul, the solitude, the sun, the constant pattering of the falls and the close presence of her lover. Even Kennedy's steady breathing and heartbeat served to lull her into deeper contentment, and she gave into her body's craving, indulging in another nap.

Napping turned to dreaming, and she found herself floating on the clouds from sunrise. She felt total serenity there, a weightless, happy sensation, and the sun warmed her skin all over. She tried swimming in the clouds, bouncing along, when suddenly one of them folded over her and little cloud fingers reached out, tickling her stomach. She giggled and swatted at them, but they only moved to another spot. She laughed some more, and gasped as one of the clouds kissed her lower belly, and then licked it before it wrapped around her navel stud, giving it a tug. "Hey!"

Her eyes popped open, and she sat partway up, spying a

guilty face bent over her belly. "You." She swatted at the dark head. Kennedy grinned at her and licked her way up Carson's midline with tiny flicks of her tongue.

"Couldn't resist. Been watching you sleep in this bit of scrap you call a swimsuit." Kennedy continued on her quest toward her lips. "I was good for thirty whole minutes before I caved in."

"In that case, you're forgiven." Carson returned the kiss at a leisurely pace. "Besides, that was a nice way to wake up. You got some sun." She trailed a fingertip across Kennedy's chest. "I like this purple suit. Looks really nice with your skin and eyes. Would make a nice picture."

"Thanks." Kennedy smiled and ducked her head at the compliment. "I haven't worn this one for you yet, have I?"

"Nope." Carson fished around in her nearby pack. "How many swimsuits do you have, anyway?"

"Not sure." Kennedy curled up on her side, propping her head on an upraised hand. "A good dozen. I'm on the lake a lot in the summer, and I like to swim for exercise sometimes, so...um...Carson, what are you doing?"

A click of a shutter and Carson sat up, crossing her legs. "Taking your picture, 'cause you're so freaking gorgeous." Another snap. "Please. I haven't taken many photos of you."

"No, you haven't." Kennedy eyed the fancy digital camera and nodded in approval. "Nice. I didn't even know you had that." She stretched out, indulging her lover in a few saucy poses. The sun felt good, she was rested, and it wasn't much farther to their camping spot. They could take their time getting there. It occurred to her they hadn't seen another person since early morning, and her thoughts took a turn down a more risqué path. "You want something a little more artsy?"

"Like wha...oh. Yeah. That works." Her stomach clenched in reflex as Kennedy removed her top, and then her bottoms, and stretched out fully on the rock, stomach down, her arms crossed in front of her and her chin resting on her folded hands. The dip of her lower back and the curve of her backside, followed by long lean legs, provided a visual feast for the camera, not to mention the photographer.

Kennedy listened while Carson took a few shots of her in profile, and then turned her head, laying her cheek down on her arms and facing Carson. "How's that?" She flashed a smile, noting the flush to Carson's face. Her own skin was starting to heat up and she suspected it was more than just the changing angle of the sun.

"Really nice," Carson answered softly, moving a little closer. "Can...can I?" She crawled up on the rock. "Roll over on your back for me."

Kennedy complied, allowing her hair to fan out above her head. She crossed her arms over her chest, looking up as Carson straddled her hips, camera still trained on her. She smiled for a few shots, then allowed her eyes to speak for her, her expression one of unmistakable desire.

It was tough to concentrate while being consumed by those eyes. "Can you...just..." Carson reached down, grasping her arms and unfolding them. Kennedy continued to gaze into her eyes as one arm stretched out in a leisurely curve over her head, and she covered a breast with one hand, exposing the other for the lens. "Beautiful," Carson breathed out, snapping a few more shots, and resisting the urge to reach out and touch all that tempting flesh.

"That thing have a timer?" Kennedy reached down, untying the bathing suit strings at Carson's hips.

"Um..." Teasing fingers tickled up her thighs. "Did you ask me something?" The camera was taken from her hands and Kennedy pulled her forward, kissing her while she untied her top and tossed it aside.

"Can you set the camera on timer?" Kennedy flicked at an earlobe with the tip of her tongue, feeling warm breath against her neck.

"Oh, yeah, you mean you want...us?" Carson glanced from the camera to their partially joined bodies.

"Yeah, just a nice little shot of us curled up together." Kennedy patted her bare behind.

"Okay, let me..." Carson got up, the swimsuit bottom falling the rest of the way away before Kennedy discretely scooped it up and tossed it to join its top. Looking around, Carson propped the camera up on one of their backpacks and knelt down, focusing it back on the rock where Kennedy had curled up on her side, drawing Carson in on sheer magnetism. She hurried back over to the rock and curled up in the curve of the long body, almost forgetting for a moment what they were doing. She crooked her leg to keep from exposing too much of her lower body, and Kennedy wrapped a long arm around her, covering her breasts.

"Nice," Kennedy whispered as they gazed into the lens and heard the snap. "One more?"

"Sure." Carson slid out of her embrace and trotted over, resetting the timer. She rejoined her and resumed their spooning position.

Kennedy grinned and slid her knee between Carson's legs from behind and cupped a breast with one hand, leaving one exposed. She cradled Carson's head back a little and kissed her, just as they heard the snap of the timer. "No more pictures." She nibbled at the back of Carson's neck, teasing her breast with one hand until she heard a low moan of pleasure. "Roll on your stomach for me, please?" Kennedy sucked a sensitive earlobe and licked at the soft skin behind it. "Please?"

Carson shivered in anticipation at the request and complied, stretching out and resting her forehead against her folded arms. Strong hands massaged her back and she moaned again. "God, that feels good," she moaned, enjoying the touch, a combination of relaxing kneading and light teasing traces of Kennedy's fingertips.

"You have the most beautiful back." Kennedy bent over, her lips following her fingers in a lazy path down Carson's back. Her fingers trailed lower, scratching lightly over her ass, followed by those lips, kissing delicately at tender baby-soft skin.

It was the most erotic experience of Carson's life, sending an instant jolt of desire between her legs. "Oh, sweet Jesus." She bit her lower lip. A gentle hand lifted her hips, placing her folded sweatshirt beneath her lower belly, exposing her and increasing her desire. "Oh, yeah." Insistent fingers teased her inner thighs, urging one leg up into a bent position.

"Is this okay?" Carson nodded in mute pleasure, and Kennedy continued with the light stroking as she kissed her way back up the smooth, muscular back, nuzzling her face into the crook of Carson's neck as she stretched out beside her. The stroking became much more intimate, and Carson turned her head, welcoming a long, soulful kiss.

Kennedy felt her lover's body reacting and heard the little whimpers coming from the back of her throat. She rolled over, pressing against Carson's side and nibbling at her back, her fingers seeking the source of Carson's pleasure, playing her until Carson cried out, her hips rolling up against her until Kennedy sought out her lips once more, pulling her into her arms and kissing her soundly, rubbing her back in circles until she finally came back down.

Carson panted against her, seeking contact everywhere, her hands wandering as she tasted Kennedy's chest and then moved lower, smiling as Kennedy's lungs puffed out in surprise. Carson rolled to her back bringing Kennedy with her and sliding her knee between her legs. Her hands trailed slowly up Kennedy's thighs and braced her hips, guiding her, feeling all that sinewy power over her as Kennedy sought her own release, grinding against Carson's upper thigh. Carson reached up, squeezing a breast while her other hand continued to guide Kennedy, feeling strong hips rocking against her. "Giddy up, cowgirl." She laughed lightly as her hands slipped around to Kennedy's backside, squeezing her ass. Judging by the unguarded pleasure on her face, Kennedy was very close, and Carson pressed into her, matching her rhythm, speaking in low, sultry tones until Kennedy finally cried out, collapsing into her embrace and burying her face into Carson's shoulder.

"Wow," Kennedy breathed weakly. "I don't think I can move." She rolled to her side, pulling Carson to her and kissing her for a long while, as their hands stroked up and down each other's back.

"I think we scared off the wildlife," Carson joked. She crawled up against her lover, feeling a light kiss to her head. Against her ear, Kennedy's heartbeat was starting to slow, and she rubbed Kennedy's belly, feeling her breathing return to normal.

A giddy laugh escaped Kennedy's lips, and she wrapped a hand around the back of Carson's head, combing her fingers through short, wavy locks. "Whoa." Her body was still twitching a little bit from time to time and she felt pleasantly discombobulated. "I think I lost most of my brain cells."

"Is that good?" Carson returned the touches, brushing Kennedy's hair back, revealing more of her beautiful face.

"That, sweetheart, was some mighty fine mind-blowing sex." She touched the tip of her nose. "Or at least that is the more polite term for it." She drew in a long breath and released it in a huff. "God, that felt good." She wriggled all over, the energy still swirling around inside.

Carson looked rather pleased with herself, her hands still wandering lazily against her skin. "Yeah, it did." She cocked her head to one side. "What's the impolite term for it?"

"That you fmphhh my brains out." She nipped at the firm hand that clamped over her mouth.

"Shhh. Never mind." Carson cautiously held her hand near full lips, just in case. "I do not need to hear I did that to you. It might make my head explode. I'm a good girl."

"You sure were." Kennedy flashed a sexy grin at her. "Does that bother you?"

"No." She snuggled up, feeling a strong arm pulling her close. "I'm just not used to anyone getting that kind of pleasure from me." She trailed a fingertip up Kennedy's cleavage. "Lots of times in the past it wouldn't have mattered much what other body was involved."

"I made you feel that way?" Kennedy started to sit up, but was firmly pushed back down.

"No. Oh, no no no." Carson quickly kissed her in reassurance. "The last guy I dated. He...it just was kind of icky sometimes."

"Sweetheart, I'm sorry." Kennedy hugged her tightly. "You wanna talk about it?"

"Not right now." Carson nuzzled her skin, inhaling her scent and imprinting it in her mind. "I just shared something really fantastic with you and I don't want to ruin it. Sometime I will, though." She sighed inwardly. How could she explain it to Kennedy, anyway? That someone could make you feel completely ugly and totally destroy your self-confidence, while they were supposed to be making love to you? *Hell,* she mused. Knowing Kennedy, she'd probably go hunt him down and kick his ass. She smiled, deciding that might not be such a bad thing.

"All right." Kennedy frowned, picturing ways to torture whoever had made Carson feel 'icky' during love-making. Drawing and quartering seemed like a good choice. The frown deepened and her mind wandered along those lines until she felt a gentle touch to her face. "Huh?"

"Honey, you growled." Carson smoothed a hand across her brow. "You okay?"

"Yeah, I'm fine." She found a smile. "Sorry. I got distracted." She glanced down along their still-naked bodies. "What do you say we take another quick dunk in the water and go find a spot to camp in before we get some really embarrassing sunburn?"

"Good idea." Carson patted her hip and rose up, stretching lazily.

A short while later they crossed the bridge for the last half of their hike.

Chapter
Six

THEY HIKED OFF trail along the creek which eventually fed into the Pine Canyon trail. Kennedy debated their campsite choice. She'd filed a plan with the basin for them to camp at one of the official Pine Canyon campsites. No one would be checking up on that most likely, because it would require a ranger to hike in and start doing headcounts at the campsites, which almost never happened. Although, she considered, if her family needed to find them, they wouldn't be in the area they were supposed to be if she did what she wanted to do.

Ah, well. She smiled. They'd be hiking back to the basin in the morning to get the truck to drive down to the river area anyway. Not like anything that arose before then could really be handled anyway. "We need to cross the creek again next chance we get." She used her walking stick to poke a pile of leaves before stepping through them. "Seems like there's a dead tree that goes across up here that we can use.

"Um...how wide a dead tree?" Carson studied the flowing stream nearby. It wasn't a raging river, but she had no desire to get back into the cold water, especially fully-clothed with a heavy pack on her back. "Can we walk across?"

"Might have to scoot across on our bellies." Kennedy grinned and waited.

"With forty pounds on my back? I don't think so." Carson caught up to her, tugging at her pack from behind. "Honey, I am not a monkey."

"Coulda fooled me." Kennedy made monkey noises and received a swat to her behind for it. "Heh." She stopped and turned. "I was just kidding. Actually, I think there's a bridge we can use to cross."

"That wasn't funny." Carson pouted, slapping her on the arm for good measure.

All mirth disappeared and Kennedy looked down at the red mark on her arm. "Sorry." She turned and hiked on in silence, her playful mood shattered.

Carson watched her and sighed. She looked at her watch and heard her stomach rumble. "Honey." She caught up again. "I'm sorry too. I don't know where that came from." She rubbed the arm she'd slapped. "I think I'm tired and hungry mostly. And PMSing a bit."

"Oh." Kennedy winced. "Means I probably am too." Their cycles had quickly synced since living together which made for three weeks of bliss per month and one of hell at times. At least, she reflected, they weren't on different schedules, making for perhaps two weeks of hell a month. "At least it's usually better when I realize that's what's going on."

"Me too." Carson took her hand, twining their fingers. "Sorry I hit you."

"Didn't hurt nearly as much as your words did." Kennedy squeezed her hand to remove the sting of her own words. "Just wasn't expecting that considering how well we've been getting along today, and talking things out last night."

"We almost always get along." Carson looked up at the strong profile, smiling when Kennedy looked at her, her expression softening to one of complete adoration.

"We do, don't we?" Kennedy tilted her head, studying a slightly sunburned face. "You know, I actually expected us to fight a lot more than we do, all things considered."

"Why?" Carson laughed lightly. "Couldn't possibly be because we're two stubborn, independent, strong-willed women who've both been on our own for a long time, could it?"

Kennedy burst out laughing. "Luckily we are learning to talk it out. And we're both able to act like grown-ups." She squeezed Carson's hand again. "That's probably our saving grace at times."

"That and a large dose of the good kind of hormones." Carson smiled cheekily. Makeup sex, she'd discovered, had its merits, although she'd rather not have to go through the circumstances that led up to it.

"Oh, definitely. You remember our first fight?" She glanced over at the sheepish face next to her, her own emotions matching it. "That damned seatbelt argument after that guy stalked us at the fair?" Carson nodded in silence and Kennedy continued. "I wanted to make love with you so badly that night."

"Yeah, I did too, but I'm glad our first time wasn't the result of a fight." She felt Kennedy move closer, pecking her on the head before they continued on in silence.

The afternoon had been gorgeous and the shadows were starting to lengthen between the trees. It was already growing

cooler, and they stopped once to pull on flannel shirts over their
T-shirts. There was indeed a bridge, and soon Kennedy led them
well off-trail, through the trees and around the back side of a
ridge. They made a sharp turn and continued on until they
entered a box canyon with high rock bluffs and many more tall
trees. An eagle glided from one bluff, soaring up and across to
the other side, taking Carson's breath away.

After an hour or so they neared the end of the canyon, and
Carson could distinctly hear the falls again, although they were
nowhere to be seen. "Have we gone in a circle?" She looked
around trying to locate the source of the water. She could smell
damp rock and rich well-watered soil, along with the heavy
scent of pine and cedar.

"Not exactly, com'ere." Kennedy all but ran, the pack
making running more of a chore than she cared for, but her pace
picked up and she impatiently forced herself to slow enough for
Carson to keep up. She led them between a crack in the bluff into
a cave of sorts that was narrow and flat and cool. "Look."

She led Carson toward the back and around a corner where
daylight streamed in through the back side of the falls, which
were pouring down beyond an opening at the back of the cave.
"Oh, wow! This is amazing." Carson inched toward the opening,
a ledge that jutted out about a hundred feet over the pool below,
but was hidden and several feet back from the waterfall. "No
wild animals in here, I take it?"

"Never has been that I know of." Kennedy turned in a circle
looking around. "It's a pretty simple little place with no alcoves
or shelves or anything an animal could use to hide from enemies.
The walls are smooth and it's not real warm, especially in
winter." She kicked at the cave floor. "It has good, soft dirt. We
can pitch the tent in here or, if you're up for it, just toss our
sleeping bags and thermarests down here without the tent." Her
eyes glinted, hinting at what she hoped Carson would answer.

"Let's be adventurous." Carson dropped her pack against
the wall. "Hey, is that a fire ring over there?"

"Yeah." Kennedy dug out her bedding, arranging it on the
ground and waiting for Carson, so they could zip the bags
together. "Another little guilty secret. There's no foliage in here
to catch fire and no way a ranger could spot smoke. And with
both ends open, the smoke doesn't build up either, so, yes,
sweetheart, we can build a campfire tonight in here if you'd
like."

"Ooo. I'd like very much." The ring was between their
sleeping bags and the front of the cave. They could see the
waterfall from where they would sleep and Carson decided it

was the most perfect camping spot she'd ever known. "Wish we had stuff to make s'mores."

"Heheh." Kennedy retrieved a bag from a side pocket of her pack. "As you wish. One small box of graham crackers, two Hershey bars, and a baggie of marshmallows, coming up, my dear."

"But how..."

"We can build fires down in the area where we'll be tomorrow night, so I brought these for then. We can get more at the store before we drive down there tomorrow." She finished zipping their bags together. "I'll go hunt us some firewood if you'll dig out our dinner stuff."

"Works for me." Carson gave her a little pat on the hip as she stood and passed by, then turned to their bags, locating her flashlight first. "Here." She handed it to Kennedy. "I'll find yours while I'm digging for the cooking pot."

"Thanks." Kennedy ruffled her head and left her alone to begin dinner preparation. She found the pan, their spork, the tin cups, and the packet of vegetarian spaghetti that was that night's offering. "Wine would've been nice," she reflected and dug out her flask of tequila instead, as well as packets of hot chocolate to go with the s'mores. There wasn't much to prep until the fire was built, so she stood, wandering idly around the cave, finding herself near the falls.

She sat down cross-legged watching the water drop past her, the remaining sun sparkling off the spray. It was an utterly peaceful place and she sighed, wishing she could fully indulge in that peace. There was a lot to think about, and judging from the direction of conversations they'd had, a big talk was fast approaching. She acknowledged she was no longer overwhelmed at the prospect of living with a lover. It had been nice waking up together, sharing breakfast, and coming together again in the evening to discuss their day. Kennedy worked long hours at times, leaving Carson to settle into life in Austin at her own pace.

The house had never been cleaner, the laundry was kept up and she usually began preparing dinner as soon as Kennedy called to tell her she was on the way home. They typically finished up dinner prep together and then went out on the back porch swing to share a glass of wine or hot chocolate while they talked and watched the sun set over the lake. A few times they went for an evening horseback ride, and about once a week they took dinner out on the sailboat and shared it on the lake. Most evenings they watched TV, rented movies, read, played board games, or simply went to bed early. She smiled at that. No matter what time they went to bed they usually found time for lovemaking, sometimes in the morning, but most often at night when they could take their time.

Her eyes wandered over to the sleeping bags and a little shiver of anticipation chased down her spine. "Lord," she spoke aloud to the waterfall. "Not like we didn't just go at it three hours ago."

No, she sighed a little. Living with Kennedy had been more fantastic than she could possibly have imagined, and Kennedy had gone out of her way to make it a pleasant experience for her. She'd start searching for a job after the holidays, and then they'd settle into a more normal routine. And there, she acknowledged, was maybe the last remaining core of her fear. She'd seen her parents live a life that would have bored her to tears and that was something she didn't want.

"Drat." She tossed a pebble into the water. She wanted the home and the nice life, and the love most of all, and maybe even kids. The thought of sharing life with another person was very appealing. She just didn't want that life to become boring and predictable. She snorted. "As if." Nothing about their relationship had been boring thus far. "Hell, maybe we need a little dose of boring from time to time, come to think of it."

There was no question that she was in love with Kennedy. "Just..." She pursed her lips inward. "Do I want to spend the rest of my life with her?"

Something niggled at the back of her mind and she turned the question around. "Do I want to spend the rest of my life without her?" It hit her with startling clarity. The thought of life without Kennedy was physically painful, a cold, lonely knot that settled in her gut before she shook it off.

"Absolutely not." She smiled, a happy little giddy rush of energy coursing through her body. It was so easy, really, if she thought about it the other way around. But did one broach the word "forever" after being with someone for two months? That part she wasn't sure of and decided that it wasn't something she had to figure out all in one night.

She loved Kennedy and she wanted to make a life with her. That was enough for now.

"And speaking of...." She stood and stretched. "Let's see if she needs some help with wood gathering."

DUSK SETTLED THROUGH the woods as Kennedy made her way back to the cave with a stack of logs in her arms. She had a camping hatchet and had hacked up a few larger chunks of wood and made a sizeable pile just outside the cave door, adding to it with each trip back until she was satisfied she had enough to keep a fire burning all night if they wanted. Along with the larger logs, she had found some kindling and a bit of dry undergrowth to use as tinder.

As she drew closer to the cave she looked up, spying the first star of the evening shining brightly through the tops of the pine trees which were blackened in silhouette against the dark blue sky. She stopped and closed her eyes tightly. "Star light, star bright, first star I see tonight. I wish I may, I wish I might, have the wish I wish tonight." She opened her eyes and the star twinkled at her, almost like a wink. "I am sure I imagined that." Shaking her head at herself she continued on. It had been a long time since she wished on a star, or kissed a necklace clasp, or tossed a penny into a fountain. Her birthday was coming up in a few days. Maybe when she blew out the candles on her cake...

"Just stop it," she chastised herself aloud. "Carson loves you. That's good enough for now." Her heart hurt. It wasn't enough. "Damn it." She stopped again and stood there, just breathing, clutching the wood against her body, feeling a tangle of emotions washing around inside. "Never wanted anything until I met her."

Liar.

"All right," she continued the argument with herself. So she had wanted many things: a successful career, and a nice house, and the respect of her peers. She'd gained all that and then some. Hell, she'd even made a few good friends along the way. It had been empty and it had taken a while to admit to herself she wanted love. She wanted a lover, a life partner no less, and a family, and all the things her parents had, and Parker had. She'd shoved all those dreams deep down inside, certain she wasn't meant to have them. All that had surfaced in a whirlwind of emotion the night Carson literally came dancing into her arms. Having Carson in her life made her want things she'd never dared dream of.

Carson held her heart in her hands and had the ability to make those dreams come true, or shatter them with a single word. And that, she admitted, was what she was afraid of, to gather every bit of her courage and be shot down. She wasn't quite ready to face that possibility just yet.

Things were really good between them and she was loath to ruin it. "Well," she spoke to a pair of squirrels. "This is a beautiful night, isn't it? Guess I'd best get back to the girl and commence with a little spooning by the fire, eh?"

Her boots crunched faintly in the undergrowth and she

frowned, hearing the snap of a twig back in the woods and a shuffling that was amiss and out of sync with her own footsteps. She turned and looked back into the shadows, seeing nothing. She shivered in reflex and kept walking, picking up her pace. Finally she arrived at the cave and dropped the last armload onto the woodpile. A loud crunching noise sounded behind her, and she spun around.

On the edge of the trees was white, wispy vapor. She squinted. "It can't be." Very carefully, she sat down on a low boulder just outside the cave entrance waiting to see what would happen. Slowly, the vapor took shape and stepped out from the other side of the grove.

Well. Her heart stopped for a moment. It was the white buck, her spiritual guardian. Her mind spun. Two appearances in as many months. Why was he back? Her sight turned inward, thinking about all her insecurities and her desires concerning Carson. "What are you trying to tell me?" she whispered.

"Hey, I thought you might like your fleece shirt, so I... Oh." Carson's jaw dropped as she stepped outside the cave and she carefully climbed in behind Kennedy on the boulder, bracketing her with her legs and resting her chin over her shoulder. "Wow," her voice was barely audible in Kennedy's ear.

"You can see him?" Kennedy whispered in surprise, turning her head just the slightest bit.

"Of course I can," she whispered back. "He's stunning, isn't he?"

"Shhh." Kennedy's heart beat double time, for a different reason, as the buck drew closer. He was stately, his rack of antlers like great bare tree branches. Wise, dark liquid eyes bore into them as he glided silently into the clearing a mere ten yards from them, the pale moonlight spilling down, shimmering off his hide in silvery patterns.

She felt Carson's arms tighten around her waist, and she covered her hands with her own. They were breathing in rhythm, she realized, and Carson's heart beat against her back in time with her own heartbeat. The legs against her thighs pressed inward and warm breath trickled past her neck into her flannel shirt collar, warming her all over. She couldn't tell where Carson began and she ended, so close was the body wrapped around her and the emotions that flowed thickly between them. It brought tears to her eyes and she heard Carson sniffle at the same time.

The buck stood there for what seemed a lifetime before he turned, fading ghost-like into the trees and disappearing from sight. They sat in complete silence for a while longer, both of them processing what they felt.

"You really saw him?" Kennedy didn't turn right away, still feeling the current between them and the warm body blanketed around her.

"Why do you keep asking that?" Carson nuzzled her neck, drawing in her scent and feeling her skin tingle in reaction. She was having a hard time concentrating on anything but warm skin and a body that felt vibrantly alive in her arms. She wanted to crawl inside all that energy and wondered, vaguely, if that were possible.

"Because..." Kennedy slowly turned to the side, draping one leg over Carson's. "It isn't supposed to happen that way. I...he's my spiritual guardian. It's a very private thing. I've never heard of anyone..."

"Whoa." Carson drew in a breath. "That...*that* was the buck you told me about? It just didn't occur to me that... Really?"

"Yeah. Really." Kennedy turned fully, sitting in the space between Carson's legs, her own long legs draped over Carson's in an upraised fashion, wrapped loosely around Carson's waist. "I've never heard of two people seeing a spiritual guardian at the same time. I'll have to ask Pa about it when we get home and find out if it means anything."

"Did...did you feel...?" Carson stopped, gathering her thoughts. "That was pretty intense for me. Was it...?"

"For me too." She took Carson's hands into her own, chaffing them and drawing them up before she pressed her lips against each of them in turn. "I could feel you, all mixed up inside me, if that makes sense. Mixed up in a good way, I mean."

"Yeah, that's what I felt too." Carson could still feel it, something drawing them together and binding them so tightly that nothing could ever rend it. Every fear she had dissipated, and their eyes locked in an understanding they couldn't yet voice.

Carson smiled almost shyly, pale lashes fluttering in the low light, and Kennedy drew her close, hugging her tightly and rocking back and forth. "I'm never letting go of you," she whispered.

"Good, 'cause I'm never letting go of you, either." Carson felt the sharp intake of breath and kissed a warm cheek.

It felt so good, Kennedy wanted to cry. It wasn't exactly a proposal, but it was so close to a promise that when the time came she no longer needed to fear the answer. They remained locked together until the moon rose, then they grabbed an armload of wood each and moved back inside for the warmth of the fire, and the greater warmth of each other.

"WHAT IS IT about the sound of water that's so relaxing?" Carson casually flipped her marshmallow, toasting it to a pale golden brown before squishing it against her Hershey bar and covering it with graham crackers. She took a bite, chewing slowly, relishing the sweet treat. "Mmm. Thanks for bringing these. Camping isn't complete without s'mores by the fire."

"You're welcome." Kennedy savored her own dessert, secretly admitting that Carson was having an effect on her Spartan eating habits. She smiled, wondering if she'd be eating cheeseburgers and fries before all was said and done. "Gives me an excuse to be bad."

"You..." Carson nudged her shoulder. "...have no problem being bad without my help, thank you very much."

"Me?" Kennedy pointed a finger at her own chest, feigning innocence. "I'm a good girl." She finished off her s'more, brushing the crumbs from her hands. "You've corrupted me, utterly and completely."

Carson snuggled up even closer, finding her lips and savoring them, along with the faint hint of chocolate and marshmallow that lingered there. "Glad to be of service, ma'am. Speaking of corrupting, I believe you were going to tell me about your first time sometime."

"Oh." It took Kennedy off guard and she sat back, raising her knees and wrapping her arms around them in thought. "All right. If you'll tell me about Mr. Icky afterward."

"Um. Sure." Carson mimicked her pose, briefly eyeing the untouched tequila flask and wondering if some fortification might be in order. Maybe. She turned her full attention on Kennedy. "So...you said you wanted to at least have some feelings for the person, right?"

"Yeah." Kennedy looked down, studying her fingernails with great interest. "I made it through that last summer before college untouched, so to speak." She smiled. "Pa and Mama and I packed up my footlocker and headed up to Santa Fe, where they got me settled into the dorm. Then we went out to dinner and after that they headed out to spend some time in Chaco Canyon."

Chaco had come up in conversation often enough that Carson decided they needed to visit there together someday. It was where she'd developed a keen interest in all things Native American. Her eyes roamed over Kennedy and she chuckled internally. There was one Native American artifact that stood out above all the others. "And you began to explore Santa Fe?"

"Yeah. I met my roommate, Holly, a girl from Albuquerque who was an art major. We hit it off after she saw a few of Pa's pieces. He'd given me a couple of small matted paintings to hang on the wall above my bed. It was so strange being in a place so open and different from how I'd grown up." She paused, taking a healthy swig from her water bottle.

"So she was your first?" Carson accepted the water as it was handed across, wetting her own dry lips.

"No, she was straight but not narrow." Kennedy smiled. "Took a while before I came out to her, but she was pretty key in setting me on the path to enlightenment. She was the one who found out there was a gay and lesbian student group on campus, and took me walking by the coffee shop where they were meeting one evening. Shoved me through the door and left me there."

"That's cool. I wish I'd been clued in enough when I was in college. UT had so much to offer." Carson fiddled with her charm bracelet, the one Kennedy had given her in Dallas. She wore it nearly all the time, stopping at odd moments to eye the little key that fit the heart charm Kennedy wore on a chain inside her shirt.

"Yeah, she was real cool. So. I started going to the meetings and they had a few socials. Some of the girls told me about some parties they had once a month in town. They moved around from place to place. They weren't just students. Quite a few locals went to them too. The age range was pretty broad. It was nice, though. I got to know several older couples that way and saw what it was like to be in a long-term relationship with another woman. Some of them had been together twenty-five years or more."

Carson looked up, their eyes locking for a long moment. "I've not known any couples like that." She smiled warmly. "But it's nice to know there are couples like that out there. Kind of encouraging, huh?"

Kennedy swallowed, her smile matching Carson's. "Very encouraging." She reached out, tracing Carson's knee with her finger while she spoke. "Anyway, these weren't like Dallas or Houston parties. A lot of earthy spiritual types live in Santa Fe, so we had poetry readings and sometimes sat around while one girl played the guitar and we sang. Sometimes a few of us would go out back and smoke a little weed. I met this woman at one of the parties near the end of my first semester—Andrea—Andie. She was twenty-four, had long, honey-blonde hair and big brown eyes. A few inches shorter than me. She was a high school art teacher. Seems like I'm always mixed up with blondes and artists." She grinned.

"Ooo. An older woman." Carson laughed lightly. "And. So?"

"So...that's about it." Kennedy teased her.

"Um. Okay." Carson looked down, unsure if it would be prying to ask for more details.

"Kidding." Kennedy tickled her knee before she resumed stroking it. "We started hanging out. We went on a lot of hikes, went skiing a couple of times, and shared several bottles of wine over a few weeks. We were a little slow on the uptake, but eventually admitted we were attracted to each other. My spring break coincided with hers, so we took off for a condo at one of the nearby ski resorts. Didn't get much skiing done, but by the end of the week she'd taught me some very nice things."

"Were you in love with her?" Carson grabbed her hand, twining their fingers.

"No. Puppy love, maybe. She was more a lesbian mentor than anything. We parted as very good friends at the end of that year and still saw each other off and on until I graduated and left Santa Fe. I lost track of her after I moved to Houston, but last I heard, she was permanently partnered." She shook her head. "I felt bad for her. She couldn't be out because of her job. Made it tough for her to have a partner, much less have children with one. She wanted kids. I hope she got to have them."

"Do...do you want kids?" It popped out before Carson could stop herself, and her heart leaped into her throat as she looked up.

"Yeah. I guess I do." It was scary, treading on ground that might be a deal breaker, and Kennedy could hear a rushing in her ears as she continued. "It's what I grew up with. Knuckleheads or no, I love my brothers, and I love Parker's kids. Family is pretty important to me, especially considering how much I screwed up growing up. No matter how bad I was, or what I did, my family was always there for me. And I like kids."

"You're great with Parker's kids." Carson squeezed her hand. "How many of them do you want?"

"I think two at least." She rubbed the back of Carson's hand with her thumb. "Do you want kids?"

"I do. It's just..." She took a deep breath. "I don't want to give birth to them. It's not so much a fear of pain or pregnancy. Well, it's partly that. But I wasn't supposed to be born. My mother had a lot of problems and my father was a preemie. I don't have the best genes for childbirth." She peered timidly up. "How do you feel about that? About bearing children?"

"Never got that far in the plans." Kennedy shifted until her hands covered Carson's knees, her own legs crossed in front of her. "You...you don't have to get pregnant. And neither do I. Sometimes, I think there are an awful lot of kids out there who need a home, ya know? Kinda figured maybe there was a kid or two out there I could love every bit a much as if I gave birth to them."

"I have no doubt of that." Carson covered Kennedy's hands, lifting them and kissing the palm of each one in turn. "I did a lot of babysitting in my teens. There were a couple kids I could easily have loved like my own."

Their eyes met silently, another hurdle jumped. Kennedy felt her heart slow down to a somewhat normal rate and she looked around, spotting a smooth spot against the cave wall behind Carson, but still near the fire. She crept over and leaned against it, stretching out her legs, as she pulled Carson against her. "So. Mr. Icky?"

"Mr. Icky." Carson sighed heavily. "Have I mentioned you're the only good relationship choice I've ever made?"

"You've hinted at it a few times, yes." Carson had been with three men before they had met and no women. Two of the men, Kennedy got the impression she'd only slept with once. "So was Mr. Icky a long-term thing?"

"Longest term I ever had, about five months." Carson suddenly felt very small. "Ray had been married twice. We met at a wedding. He was only five years older than me but had been around the block a few times. Anyway, I was warned about him, but he was a hunk and I was at a point where I needed a boost to my self-esteem. I couldn't believe he was interested in me. He had done some body building competitions in his early twenties and he still had most of that. He was nice to look at, at any rate."

"Ah, your very own boy toy." Kennedy ruffled her head.

"Yeah, kinda." Carson managed a small smile. "Unfortunately that was about all he had going for him, but it took a while to figure that out. He was cheap. I thought it was romantic at first, him wanting to cook dinner all the time, but when I realized we had only been out to dinner once, on our first date, it got kind of old. Especially since I was almost always dessert. We didn't go do things together. We'd cook dinner and then we'd go to bed. It was the first time I'd been in what I considered to be an adult relationship. The whole sleeping over thing and all."

Kennedy listened intently and quickly calculated how many times they'd been on real dates. She breathed an internal sigh of relief when she determined they'd been out on a date at least once a week since they'd met. Not to mention a week in Mexico together. "So that's kind of icky, but I'm taking it there's more to it than that."

"Yeah. I found out both of his ex-wives had been strippers

when he met them and that he had always dated strippers. That was intimidating enough. I mean, come on." She gestured down at herself. "I try to take care of myself, but this squatty body is not exactly what I'd picture in an exotic dance club, you know?"

"Oh, darlin'" Kennedy playfully leered at her. "You're the hottest body on earth in my book."

"Thanks." Carson swallowed. "Could have used some of that ego-boosting back then. He apparently was trying to clean up his image and chose me because he thought I was wholesome. He was always judging what I wore and would get mad if I wore anything out in public he thought was too provocative. We didn't go out other than to go to the store or something, and then it was fine if I was with him. He was all into me being dressed in short shorts and skirts, but if I was leaving to go home or out somewhere without him, he wanted me covered from neck to feet."

"Typical jerk who wants a trophy on his arm but gets pissed at the trophy if someone else looks." Kennedy picked up one of the sticks from the nearby kindling pile, doodling in the cave floor dirt while she listened.

"Yeah, I guess. No matter what he thought he wanted me to be—some girl next door type—in the bedroom he never let me forget about those strippers, or that I wasn't as sexy or hot as they were. I felt so inadequate. He wanted me to be all wild in bed, but he was the first guy I'd ever slept with more than once. He..." She sighed, lowering her head. "He wouldn't—take care of me when he was done. He'd get angry if I hadn't climaxed when he had and he'd roll over and go to sleep. So, I finally started faking it to make him happy."

"Bastard." Kennedy felt the rage rise up, and the stick snapped in her hand. "Where does he live?"

"Dallas." Carson patted her leg. "Down, honey. There's a little bit more. He...was..." She stopped, burying her face in her hands. "Why is this so hard?"

"Sweetheart, you don't have to tell me if you don't want to." Kennedy pulled her even closer, kissing the top of her head.

"No. I think you need to understand this part of my past because it's really all I had before you." She grabbed the flask, uncapping it and taking a swallow, feeling the amber liquid burn its way to her stomach. "He kept pushing me to do things I wasn't comfortable with, but I wouldn't give in. The last night I stayed with him there was this small framed naked picture of one of his exes. He'd set it up in a cubbyhole in the headboard. Anyway, I didn't notice it until after we'd... I realized he'd been looking at her the entire time. He made some comment about me not being a real woman and maybe I should see what one looked like. I didn't see him anymore after that, but I felt really bad about myself for a long time. I figured maybe there really was something wrong with me."

"No one should treat you that way. No one." Kennedy's face grew dark with rage and she flung the remains of the stick into the fire. "If I ever meet him, I just might go Lorena Bobbitt on his ass. If I don't kill him first."

"Kennedy?" She shook her fuming lover a little. "Honey, he's in the past. No sense in killing him, okay?"

"But he deserves to be dead." Kennedy beat the cave floor with a fist and turned, taking Carson in both arms and hugging her with all her might. "There's nothing wrong with you. My lord, far from it."

"You've gone a long way in building my self-esteem in that regard." Carson hugged her back, nuzzling her face against her neck. "You make me feel beautiful."

"You *are* beautiful." Kennedy kissed her head again, continuing to hold her close. "When I walked in that conference room that day we met, I was smitten from the get-go. I saw you with your cousin at lunch that day. Thought he was your boyfriend and I was so disappointed."

"I didn't know that." Carson smiled. "Good thing you were behind me to catch me at The Round-Up when my Cotton-eyed Joe line decided to play crack the whip instead."

"You fell in my arms, and I had to think real hard about setting you back on your feet." Kennedy smiled, the firelight glowing in her face, and then grew serious. "Somehow, I think we would've met one way or the other."

"I think so too." Carson studied her features at close range, taking in the high cheekbones, the sun-kissed skin, and eyes that shone back at her, full of love. She thought about Ray and it seemed like another lifetime. She let go, releasing one more thread of doubt, that little voice that told her she would never have a successful relationship, that she wasn't good enough, that she couldn't satisfy.

And just believed.

Those eyes crinkled and warmed, Kennedy's gaze falling on her and making her smile, right before Kennedy ducked her head, seeking her out, nibbling her lips and deepening the kiss as they slowly undressed each other. The warmth of the fire and the cool cave air mixed with incendiary touches, heating Carson's skin and sending pleasant chills skittering across it at the same time.

And then the cave spun as she was scooped up and carried

the short distance to their sleeping bags. She let go again, feeling Kennedy's touch, and hearing her voice, those eyes meeting her gaze and holding it, wordlessly conveying a desire that set her body on fire, and took her breath away. Kennedy was fully with her, loving her, whispering in her ear and slowly stroking every inch of her skin, not letting up, their bodies joining in a dance of a different sort. Carson reached out, eagerly returning touch for touch as they crashed over the edge, the nearby waterfall echoing the sensations.

They lay together wordlessly for a long while, Carson tracing circles on her lover's stomach, while Kennedy rubbed her back in kind. The fire crackled warmly, pushing back a light, cold breeze that trickled in from the front of the cave. Carson snuggled up, pecking a bare shoulder several times before resting her head against it, enjoying the sound of the rushing water and the sensation of Kennedy's arms wrapped around her, their legs still tangled together. "Seeing that buck this afternoon was pretty awesome."

"That's the third time I've seen him." Her fingers played along Carson's spine, searching idly for knots to massage, and finding only completely relaxed muscles. She smiled and kissed Carson's forehead. "Saw him that first time when I went on my vision quest. Saw him again when we hiked Enchanted Rock."

"What?" Carson sat partway up. "You told me about the vision quest then, but failed to mention that second sighting, Miz Nocona."

"It surprised me. I never expected to see him there. I needed time to process it some." She smiled sheepishly. "He showed up when I was trying to figure out how to ask you to move to Austin. And then you up and asked if it would be okay if you moved there. It...it was like he was trying to tell me something, maybe about you. A spiritual guide is just that — a guide to help you figure out the right path."

"So what does it mean if we saw him together?" Carson kissed the upper curve of a breast, feeling Kennedy's silent chuckle as Carson followed it with a light warm breath over her skin in a sensuous tickle.

"Do that again and I'm not going to be able to form a coherent thought." She shifted, rolling to her side and running her hand up and down Carson's hip. "That's why I want to talk to Pa, to see if he knows if that has ever happened before. Most of us, we don't talk much about our vision quests. Pa and the rest of my family, they don't even know about the buck, and I don't know what their guides are either. It's a very personal thing."

"I think I'd like to go on a vision quest sometime." Carson

returned the gentle touches as they talked. "Do you have to be Native American to do that?"

"Dunno, but you could always do it anyway. It's pretty tough, though. No food for a few days, and the smoking part might be difficult for you." She smiled, cupping Carson's face. "I could go on one with you. It wouldn't be quite the same, but we could just be quiet and meditate together. Maybe we could find something to substitute for smoking like maybe a sweat lodge or something."

"Ooo. Get all sweaty with you? I am so there." Carson moved closer still, as the touches grew more insistent and they came together again. A pair of warm lips worked their way slowly down her body, pausing for a long while at her belly and navel ring before moving lower. She thought fuzzily that something was vaguely familiar, a sense of déjà vu...the cave, the fire, and the waterfall, and the long lean body hovering over her on the bedroll. Then she quit thinking altogether, her body rising up and meeting Kennedy, joining her on a very different kind of quest.

Much later Kennedy lay awake with Carson soundly asleep in her arms, snuggled down inside the sleeping bags. The fire was still burning, though it was mostly red hot coals, and the falls sang a lullaby to her, the babbling water covering her in a blanket of peace. Carson stirred in her arms and she stroked the pale head, soothing her until she was still again. "This, sweetheart..." she whispered quietly, hoping the words might sink in through her lover's dreams. "...this can be that one good relationship you've been looking for, if you'll let it be. If you'll have me, I promise I'll never let you forget just how much you're loved."

Outside the cave, way over the mountains, the clouds rolled in, and off in the distance Kennedy heard the crack of thunder. She frowned. It wasn't supposed to rain. Ah, well, she reasoned. There were a lot worse things than spending a rainy day together in the cave. She slowly drifted off, a smile twitching at her lips as the falls and Carson's breathing drew her into pleasant dreams.

KENNEDY STIRRED, GRADUALLY waking up in the darkness. It felt like early morning, but she had no real way of knowing for certain without checking her watch which was tucked safely into a pouch in her pack across the cave. She breathed in deeply, taking in the scent of damp rock, wet foliage, and Carson's skin, along with the cottony smell of the sleeping bags. She remembered the earlier thunder and wondered if it was raining. The roaring sound of the falls precluded hearing any rain that might be falling.

The air was chilly against an exposed shoulder and she looked around, realizing the fire had burned down completely. It was almost eerily dark, and she could just make out the shape of Carson's body, the bedding around them, and a bit of the wall next to them. She reached out from beneath the warm nest, locating her flashlight and then slowly slipped out of the bag, careful not to disturb Carson. She walked a bit toward the fire ring and switched on the light, holding it low to the ground so as not to illuminate the entire chamber and wake up Carson.

Kneeling down next to the stone ring, she made a fresh stack of logs, tucking in some of the smaller sticks and pushing a good amount of the tinder beneath all of it before she located a match and set the fire ablaze. She watched it build and grow, the flames licking at the dry tinder and quickly devouring it while the sticks slowly caught fire as well, and finally some of the logs began to burn.

Soon the cave walls were bathed in warm light, shadows dancing all along the top near the ceiling. She could see Carson now, her head poking out of the covers, resting on a curled up arm. She could just make out the slightest rise and fall of the bedding with her breathing, and she took a long moment to simply drink in the sight, finding a great comfort in it. It seemed so familiar, although she knew they'd never camped together before, much less slept in a cave. It felt almost homey and she tucked that away to ponder later. Satisfied the fire would keep burning for a while, she made her way toward the front of the cave.

As she approached it she did indeed hear the patter of a hard steady rain, and drew in the rich scent of wet soil and bruised leaves. She flipped off the flashlight and stood in the entry, her eyes slowly adjusting to the darkness. There were several trees nearby, but above them she caught the occasional flash of lightning, and heard the rumble of faint thunder somewhere over the mountaintops beyond the trees. It felt primal, standing there in the darkness, naked, watching the rain fall, and without much thought, she set down her flashlight and stepped out into the deluge, shivering as it poured over her skin.

It felt good and it was a bit insane, and there was no real explanation for why she did it. She threw her head back, her hair falling against her shoulder blades before it was quickly plastered to her skin. She wasn't sure how much time passed, but realized she was cold and should really think about going back inside. Her next thought was that she had no towel. "Well, that was one of my stupider moments." She padded back into the cave, shaking herself, feeling the water pooling off her skin and dripping onto the cave floor. She felt invigorated and her skin was already warming back to its normal temperature.

Their packs were on the far side of the fire and she unzipped hers, locating a sweatshirt she could use to dry off. As she stood, she heard Carson stir across the fire, along with an unintelligible murmur. The murmuring turned into an audible yawn and she smiled, imagining Carson stretching. "Hey," she whispered, just loud enough to be heard if she were awake.

"I must be dreaming," Carson's voice was husky with sleep.

"Why do you say that?" Kennedy chuckled, rubbing the sweatshirt down her arms and across her body.

"Because there's a gorgeous, wet, naked woman standing in the firelight. She looks like you, but last time I checked you were dry and in this sleeping bag with me." She rolled over, propping her head on her hand and enjoying the show.

"I got up to build the fire back up." Kennedy bent over, drying her legs.

"And this explains why you're all wet how, exactly?" Carson asked sleepily, another yawn making her jaw pop.

"It's raining." Kennedy finished drying off and laid the sweatshirt out near the fire to dry. "I went out and stood in it."

"Why?" Carson lifted the edge of the bag as Kennedy approached, her form silhouetted from behind in warm gold and red light. Carson's eyes drifted appreciatively over her, the affection evident on her face.

"Because I could." She crawled into the bedding, snuggling up and pulling Carson close. "Mmm. You're warm."

"And you're nuts." She kissed her briefly on the lips. "But I like you that way. What time is it, anyway?"

"Forgot to check, but it doesn't matter. It's raining and we're not going anywhere for a while, so you get to sleep in this morning." She nuzzled Carson's head, sighing in utter contentment as her warmth and scent completely enveloped her.

"Have I mentioned I love you?" Carson located a shoulder, nipping it lightly before she kissed the spot, then wrapped herself around the long body, effectively trapping Kennedy.

"Feels wonderful." Kennedy drifted pleasantly between wakefulness and sleep.

Carson tucked her head against Kennedy's chest, her heart under her ear. Long arms held her securely, one hand against her back and another cradling her hip. She was pretty much sprawled on top of her lover, something she rarely did while awake, but a position they often ended up in once they fell asleep. The closeness felt so good it brought tears to her eyes and she sniffled, one tear tracking down her nose and landing on Kennedy's skin.

She'd read of being immersed in someone and had sometimes wondered what that felt like. Now she understood. All her senses took in the moment. Kennedy's breathing filled her ears, her warmth mingled with her own, and in the low firelight she could just make out the curve of a shoulder. Her fresh rain-cleansed skin smelled sweet, and Carson poked out just the tip of her tongue, tasting the hint of salt on that skin before she pecked the spot and closed her eyes. She briefly wondered if it were possible to burst from happiness. She sniffled again, and felt long arms pull her in even tighter, pulling her up until her head was tucked under Kennedy's chin.

"You wanna tell me why you're crying?" Kennedy's voice surprised her and she jumped just a little.

"Because I'm so happy?" Carson felt a pair of lips brush across the top of her head.

"And you say I'm nuts." Kennedy's chest shook with a silent chuckle. "Sweet dreams, love." She kissed her head again and turned just a little, settling them both deeply into the bedding as they drifted away on the music of a crackling fire and roaring water.

"THIS HAS GOT to be the most decadent breakfast I've ever had." Carson accepted a bite of oatmeal, hand-fed at close range from their spork.

"More decadent than when we went to Fredericksburg?" Kennedy nibbled a suddenly-pink earlobe.

"Yeah, only because that was indoors in a bed, naked with you. This is outdoors in a cave, naked with you." She took another bite, enjoying the apple-cinnamon flavor as it washed over her tongue.

"Ah. I see." Kennedy took a bite of her own, finishing off the double portion of instant grain before she set it aside for Carson's chocolate and coffee mix. She'd decided to try it herself and took a tentative sip. "Whoa. That's pretty good." She gulped down two more healthy swallows before Carson took it from her.

"Careful there, stud. You're hyper enough without too much caffeine in your veins. Don't want to have to tie you down to keep you from flying off." She sipped at the mixture in utter enjoyment.

"Tie me down?" Kennedy growled in her ear. "That has possibilities."

"You're incorrigible." Carson patted a bare stomach. They were sitting up by the fire, propped against the wall, wrapped up together in their joined sleeping bags. A light mist was falling outside, but the sun was already promising to peek through the clouds, and they'd decided to go forward with plans to drive down to the border and hike along the river for the next two days.

"Insatiable, when it comes to you," Kennedy corrected her, a sexy smile gracing her lips.

Carson kissed her soundly, pulling back only a few inches, her breathing still irregular.

Kennedy could feel the breath lingering in the air between them, the softness where their skin brushed together, and the shared body heat they generated beneath the thick down covering. She slowly pulled Carson into a long hug, rocking them back and forth as the blanket gradually slipped down, pooling around them. "Guess we should get dressed and get moving, huh?" She made no move to pull apart, however, feeling Carson's long blissful sigh against her neck.

"Or we could sit here like this for four or five days." Carson tightened her grip, the contrast of warmth between them and the cold at her back causing interesting chills to run down her spine. "But yeah, we probably should get going if we plan to do any hiking today."

"All right." Kennedy released her, taking her hands and holding them for a moment. "This is kind of a magical place, isn't it?" She looked around them, taking in the sun that was indeed creeping past the falls and illuminating the cave floor in pale light.

"I think..." Carson squeezed her hands and looked down, drawing in a breath. She looked up, putting the force of her emotion into her expression. "I think we brought the magic here." She leaned in for another brief kiss. "And I think we take that with us, wherever we go."

Kennedy slowly absorbed her words. Something had changed in the cave yet again, bringing them closer still. The buck flashed through her mind and the almost electric current that had flowed between them since they first made camp. Words whispered in the darkness, in the warmth of an embrace washed over her memory, warming her from the inside out. "We are quite a team, aren't we?"

"The best." Carson rose, pulling Kennedy up with her, stretching and feeling her spine pop in the process.

They dressed and packed up their belongings, and carefully doused the remains of their breakfast fire before they made their way back to the cave entrance. They lingered there, looking back into its depths, hearing the faint sound of the falls as it echoed back toward them. "We should come back here every year." Kennedy bent down, picking up a bit of smooth quartzy-looking rock and pocketing it. She found another and handed it off to Carson.

"It's a date, then. Same time, every year." Carson pocketed the rock and reached out, twining their fingers as they hiked out of the canyon for the long trek back to the 4Runner.

STEAM ROSE ALL around them, along with a strong tangy mineral scent that wafted up and away on a light breeze. Carson ducked under the water and stood, rivulets running down her body. "You are evil." She shook her head and reached up, swiping the water from her eyes. "You could've told me that 'Hot Springs' really meant hot springs before I dunked myself in that ice water yesterday."

"Would've spoiled the surprise." Kennedy handed her a towel as she emerged from the natural warm baths on the southeastern edge of the park. "Besides, you seemed to rather enjoy that there cold bath, if I recall." She exaggerated her Texas drawl, winking at her lover as they both moved to the 4Runner to remove their swimsuits and re-don hiking clothes.

"I did," Carson admitted. "But this is absolutely heavenly. We need to come back here tomorrow evening after we finish our hike."

"Absolutely." Kennedy crawled into the truck and quickly slipped into shorts and a T-shirt, tying her flannel shirt around her waist for easy access. She ran her fingers through damp locks and left them down to dry for a while.

They'd enjoyed a bumpy ride over unfinished roads and the truck was covered in dust. It had even seeped inside the vehicle, coating the dashboard in a fine layer, and Kennedy made a mental note to have it detailed when they got back to Austin. "We have a couple of choices here." She unfolded a map on the back seat, waiting for Carson to join her.

The blonde crawled into the truck, still clad in yet another tiny bikini. Kennedy's eyes roamed over her in appreciation, her hand coming to rest on a smooth thigh. "So, what are our choices?" Carson peered down at the map.

"We can make camp near here and hike in toward Mariscal Canyon, or we can drive down closer to Solis Landing and start hiking back to camp up near here. Either way means making a round trip back to the truck at some point, either this afternoon or tomorrow, depending on where we camp." She idly stroked Carson's knee, smiling as she leaned closer.

"How about park here, near La Clocha and hike in with our packs? If we're tired, we can make camp at Solis Landing. If not, we can hike back and make camp at La Clocha." She traced the trail along the Rio Grande River, pointing out the two spots.

"Works for me." Kennedy folded up the map. "You know, if we commit to hiking in and hiking back, we can make camp first and break out the fanny packs, and hike without so much weight on our backs. We'll make better time and be a heck of a lot more comfortable."

"Ooo. Now there's a plan." Carson scrambled out of the bikini, digging around in the back of the truck for her clothing.

"Good thing I got the limo tint on these windows." Kennedy thumped the thick dark glass. "I'd hate to have to bail you out of the county jail for public nudity."

Carson rolled her eyes and turned. "Honey, half the people in those springs were nude."

"Yeah, but your body is a lethal weapon." Kennedy slid closer. "One look and people would be dropping all over the place. Running into trees. Banging into boulders. Falling off cliffs. Place would be a mess."

"If you're trying to flatter me, it's working." Carson sidled up, grabbing her around the neck and pulling her close for a lingering kiss. She felt Kennedy's hands slide up her bare back and grew limp, as Kennedy gently massaged all up and down her spine. "Mmm. That feels divine."

"You feel divine." Kennedy stole one more kiss, then handed Carson her shorts and T-shirt. "Get dressed, before I get undressed." With a gentle swat to her bare behind, she exited the truck and moved around back to make sure their packs were ready.

They drove into the La Clocha campground and found a secluded spot to pitch their tent, effectively staking out the area for themselves. Kennedy stowed the main packs in the back of the 4Runner, and they buckled on the detachable fanny packs, making sure they had the essentials needed for a long day hike. "Let's make sure we take a few extra things, just in case."

"In case what?" Carson dug around in her pack, making sure she had sunscreen and extra trail bars.

"In case something happens and we take longer to get back than expected. It's a long hike in and back. Wanna make sure we have the water purifier, enough trail bars to make a meal, and that flint and striker thing you bought at that Scarborough Faire festival up in Dallas. Might come in handy if we did need to build a fire for anything." She checked her pack, finding all the mentioned items.

"Well, heck. If we end up stuck for too long, this might come in handy." Carson pulled out the tequila flask and tucked it into her pack. "Maybe we can cram a sleeping bag in here," she teased Kennedy, receiving a scowl in return. "Honey, I'm just kidding." She patted Kennedy's cheek. "I'm glad you think of stuff like that. Makes me feel safe knowing you're looking out for us."

Kennedy smiled, obviously placated, and reached out, twitching Carson's pack into place. "You ready?"

"You bet." She held out a hand, looking up as Kennedy's hand slid into it and they took off down the trail together.

The path meandered in and out of wooded areas, taking them along the bank of the Rio Grande River. The water was high due to all the recent rain and as they came out into an open sunny area a raft passed by below on the water, carrying four people. It bore the logo of a local rafting tour company, and they stopped to watch as it floated past on the swift current.

"That looks like fun." Carson stood near the edge, observing the party until they were out of sight. "Can we try that sometime?"

"It is, and we can." Kennedy pulled her back a prudent distance. "Careful. Bank can crumble underneath you in some places. I'd hate to have to go fishing you out."

"You've been rafting down there?" Carson dug out her ball cap, in deference to the now cloudless sky.

"Not down there. Been rafting up in Colorado, though." She frowned, squinting into the trees behind them. "But we could try it here sometime, if you'd like."

"What's wrong?" Carson followed her gaze.

"Nothing." She turned back toward the trail ahead of them. "Thought I saw something, but I think it was just a jackrabbit."

"Oh." They twined hands and moved on, following the trail until they reached the end of the wooded area. The landscape opened up before them, a mass of red and brown and pale rock rising up in peaks on the Mexico side of the river, and dropping down into the river valley before it rose up again at a gradual slope on the U.S. side. Off in the distance they could see Talley Mountain to the north and Mariscal Mountain to the southwest.

"Wow. Gorgeous." Carson studied the high peaks across the river and felt suddenly very small. "Bet it would be easy to get lost up in there."

"Or easy to hide." Kennedy turned in a slow circle, taking in the sunny topography. "Pretty wild country out here, that's for sure."

They hiked on in silence, simply enjoying the amazing vista all around them. Studying the countryside, Kennedy stole surreptitious glances at Carson. November had been a long month, in some ways. They'd slowly adjusted to living together in Austin. In other ways, time had flown. So much had changed so quickly it was easy to forget everything that had happened to them in October.

Now, looking at Carson's face, she seemed to be doing better, the dark circles and tiny lines that had formed around her eyes in the days following her kidnapping starting to fade. For a while, she'd carried so much tension in her neck and shoulders that she almost appeared to be in pain when she moved. Kennedy had spent long hours massaging knots out of muscles strung tight as piano wire. A month of catching up on sleep, eating healthy meals, and having no real responsibilities had also gone a long way in erasing more stress than any one person should have to endure.

Kennedy had come to love the life they were beginning to make together. It was amazing how easy it had been to welcome Carson into what had been a very solitary world, for the most part. She saw Pete every few days, but their conversations were pretty sparse. She thought about her younger brother, wondering if he had gotten moved out of the apartment in Austin. She regretted having to draw a hard line with him, but acknowledged that sending a strong message would hopefully knock some sense into him before it was too late.

"What do you suppose Pete is up to right now?" Carson squeezed her hand as they walked.

"Read my mind." She squeezed back. "Knowing him, he's found some frat brother to take him in. Doubt he moved into their house, though. They charge way too much to live there." She kicked at a rock in the path, and then another, aiming and hitting larger rocks with them. "I'll be curious as to what Parker's lab buddy finds in that bag of pot, though."

"I never got the attraction to drugs." Carson tread cautiously onto what was obviously a touchy subject.

"They make you feel good," Kennedy replied. "Getting high. Going mellow. Nicotine. Alcohol. All of it, in small doses, gives you a rush. Problem is, you're poisoning yourself at the same time, and it starts taking more and more of it to get the same effect. I still wonder how many brain cells I destroyed before I finally came to my senses. Pot stays with you. It settles into your fatty tissues and hangs around for a while."

"You don't have much fatty tissue." Carson gave her a playful pinch on the waistline.

"Hey!" Kennedy caught the naughty hand and held it. "Yeah, but it settles in the fatty tissues of your brain. I'm just glad I never got hooked on acid. That stuff is bad news. Can sneak up on you and give you a bad trip months after you've used it. This latest round with the Ex, it pisses me off. I've not touched anything, Carson, anything illegal, in five years. I worked so hard to leave that behind me, and so hard to cleanse my system of all the garbage. I...I felt violated the next morning."

"Oh, honey." Carson squeezed her hand. She hadn't even considered that side of things. "I'm so sorry. Makes me want to hurt those guys." She frowned. "But I bet, as healthy as you are and as you live, you've probably already worked most of it out of your system."

"I hope so," Kennedy groused. "All drugs, really, even legal ones, I'm pretty cautious about using them unless I'm really in bad shape."

"I noticed a couple of ibuprofen can knock you out," Carson agreed. "Not to mention what just one beer or glass of wine does."

"Look who's talking, Miss dance on the bar after one drink." Kennedy teased, watching Carson's hackles rise in indignation.

"Only time I got tipsy was in Mexico and I did not dance on any bars," Carson huffed. "Did I?"

Her expression was so cute that Kennedy burst out laughing. "No, sweetheart. The only place you did any truly dirty dancing was alone with me in our cabin on the boat. But you and I are both pretty lightweight when it comes to anything much stronger than caffeine. Even caffeine makes me shake."

"So I noticed. You were bouncing down the trail this morning after drinking that mocha coffee." Kennedy's hand dropped down to Carson's behind, slipping into her shorts pocket.

"I was not bouncing because of coffee." She stroked a firm butt cheek before removing her hand. "I was in a really good mood."

"I see." Carson blushed, remembering the night in the cave. "Last night was really nice. It felt...primal. I think that's a good word for it."

"I felt really close to you." Kennedy draped an arm across her shoulders. "Still do. I think we need to try to have a weekend away together every month, if we can. Even if we just drive out to the bed and breakfast in Fredericksburg. Or maybe even if we just hole up at home and don't do anything but have a relaxing time with no chores other than taking care of the animals."

"I can go for that." Carson smiled up at her. "Maybe we can

spend some time out on the lake on the sailboat, just lazing around."

"That would work too." A breeze lifted her hair, and Kennedy reached up, tucking it behind her ears. Up ahead she spotted another raft and steered them closer to the riverbank to watch.

It drifted closer, but there was no laughter or shouting, like the raft they had seen earlier. This one was old and patched, and loaded with over a dozen people, women and children, all packed into it. The occupants were silent, and as they came close enough to take shape, appeared frightened. Furtively, they glanced up at the two women standing high above them and two oarsmen re-doubled their efforts, pulling with the water to pass them as quickly as possible.

"Illegals." Kennedy finally commented after they'd passed. "I'm surprised they're passing along the park border, though. Bet they missed some drop-off point farther up river and now they have to get past the park before they can bail out."

"Really?" Carson had heard of Mexican immigrants crossing the border illegally since she was a child, but it was the first time she had actually witnessed such an action in progress. "You mean they just float along and get away with it?"

"Right now they're on the river. They're not doing anything wrong until they cross over to this side and get out." She gestured out toward the vastness of Mexico before them. "Miles and miles of nothing. And even when you finally reach something, it's a poor existence. To them the river is the borderline between wealth and poverty."

"Should we turn them in?" Carson knew many of Kennedy's clients were undocumented workers, a subject they hadn't discussed very much.

"We could, but it wouldn't do much good. By the time we hike back to civilization they'll be long gone. Would probably be tough to find them." She turned toward Carson, drawing her over to a rock beneath a rise that provided some shade. "I kind of hate to turn them in. They take jobs no one else will take. What I try to do is work with them when I find them. Help them get green cards and apply for citizenship. I help them get whatever benefits are available to them. Most of them are sending their meager wages back home to Mexico, supporting probably ten other family members they left behind."

"I can't imagine living like that." Carson dug out a trail bar, unwrapping it and breaking it in half to share. "I remember seeing those huts in the Mexican countryside. Couldn't figure out what those people were living on. Seeing the kids there brought tears to my eyes. They had no life, and did not appear to have much of a future either."

"They don't." Kennedy munched on the trail bar, looking down river as the raft turned into a tiny dot before it disappeared around a bend and out of sight. She drew one leg up, wrapping her arms around her leg and resting her chin on her knee. "Hot today, isn't it?"

"Too hot for November, that's for certain." November 28th. She made a mental note to wake her partner up with a nice birthday gift the next morning. "How long do you think it'll take us to drive back out of the park tomorrow, after we finish hiking?"

"Not long. Why?" A tanned face turned toward her, a tiny smile playing at full lips.

"Birthday girls should not ask so many questions." Carson leaned over and kissed her. She smiled against Kennedy's mouth as the kiss became heated and they spent a long moment indulging in each other.

"I've got all I could ever want or need right here with me." Kennedy looked down, tracing the worn lines on the rock with her fingertip.

"Well then," Carson's voice caught, thick with emotion. "Maybe you'll get exactly that tomorrow, birthday girl." Their eyes met and lingered, so close to saying things that wouldn't wait much longer. "Uh-oh." Carson suddenly stood, moving toward the river.

"More of 'em." Kennedy watched another full raft draw near, almost a carbon copy of the one that had passed them earlier. "Wonder if they're all part of the same group?"

"Bet they are." Carson shaded her face with her hand, watching as they passed below them, the river lightly tossing the raft from side to side. She turned, and jumped as a loud, cracking, explosive noise rang out behind her. Before she could turn back Kennedy landed on top of her, knocking her to the ground and covering her up. "What was that?"

"Gunshot." Kennedy's voice was strained, her breath in short puffs against the back of Carson's neck.

"They're shooting at us?" Her voice squeaked, partly from fear, and partly from bearing Kennedy's weight.

"Yeah." The long body slowly slid off her and Kennedy hugged the ground next to her.

"You're certain that was a gunshot?" Carson stayed on her belly, turning her head to see if she could still see the raft.

"Yep." The strain in Kennedy's voice became pronounced. "Carson. They got me."

Carson felt it then. A warm, sticky wetness soaking through the back of her T-shirt where Kennedy had laid only a few moments before. "They...they shot you? Oh my god, Kennedy." She started to sit up, only to be pushed back down.

Kennedy cried out softly from the pain of the effort. Fire lanced through her left shoulder and into her arm, shooting darts across her chest and back as well. "Need to crawl away from the bank. Come on."

"But...you're bleeding." Carson could see the growing red stain now, as she rose up a bit, peering at her back. "Kennedy, we need to get you to a hospital. We can't just—"

"Shhh." Kennedy reached out with her right hand, cupping Carson's face. "We will, but first we need to get away from this bank and see what kind of damage they did. Help me get back to the rock, please? I think the raft is far away enough now that we can stand. Just get me to shade and we'll take a look."

"All right." Carson stood, her legs shaking, as she helped Kennedy up. As they got to their feet another shot rang out and Kennedy screamed in agony, crumpling to the ground and holding her leg, as blood ran down it between her fingers. "Kennedy!" Carson dropped with her, her mind spinning as she looked around. "What the hell?"

Kennedy sobbed in pain, slowly lifting her hand to see blood running down the front of her leg from a wound to her upper thigh. It pooled on the ground beneath her, staining the pale yellow rock dark crimson. Just as quickly, she realized she'd been facing the river when she was shot in the back. "Neither shot came from the river." She grimaced, forcing back the edges of a blackout. "Came from the other direction." She glanced toward the uneven terrain that rose up from the river valley on the U.S. side. "Someone up there is shooting at us."

Chapter
Seven

"WE'RE TOO EXPOSED here." Kennedy inched forward toward the rock they'd been sitting on earlier. The pain was incredible and spots danced in her vision. She felt dizzy and her stomach twisted with waves of nausea. "I...god it hurts." She gritted her teeth and kept inching along.

"Kennedy. Honey..." Carson scrambled after her, watching the trail of blood left behind as she moved along the ground. "Take it easy." Another shot rang out and Carson yelled in surprise as it ricocheted off a nearby cactus, much too close for comfort. "All right, let's move, then." She placed an arm around Kennedy's waist, helping her along until they were in the shelter of the rock.

"Aughhh." Kennedy groaned and shifted to her back. Her leg was covered in blood, and her T-shirt sleeve was soaked as well. "Get the first aid kit out."

Carson quickly removed both their fanny packs and untied the sweatshirt from around her own waist, tucking it beneath Kennedy's head. Despite her deeply-tanned face, a gray paleness was creeping beneath the surface. Her expression was a tad vacant, and her jaw was set, tense with pain. "Need to stop the bleeding." She removed Kennedy's flannel shirt, untying it and retying it above the leg wound. "Honey, I need to pour some water over this and clean it up enough to see what's going on."

Kennedy nodded silently in compliance and looked down, clamping her jaw shut as Carson uncapped a water bottle and cool water ran over her leg. She didn't think she could hurt any more, but discovered that wasn't true. It was like digging into the wound with a knife, and she whimpered, tears leaking from the corner of her eyes.

"Sorry, honey." Carson gently wiped the blood and water away. She breathed a sigh of relief. "Looks like the bullet just grazed your leg here. Lots of blood, but no bullet hole. Just...a really deep scrape-looking cut. It's already starting to slow. The bleeding is, I mean." The gash ran along her outer thigh from front to back, right below the edge of her shorts. The hem was soaked in more blood and her leg shook slightly, twitching as Carson gently probed the muscle.

"Tighten the shirt a little bit, just in case." Kennedy's breathing was shallow, her voice hoarse with the effort of containing the screams her body desperately wanted to release.

Carson moved, rising up slightly, and another shot whizzed past her head. She dropped to the ground and felt a hand clamp over her mouth, Kennedy's right one. "I know," she whispered as the hand was removed. "Need to keep quiet so they can't track us too much." She quickly re-tied the knot in the shirt and wrapped her leg in gauze, then looked up toward Kennedy's shoulder injury. It was obvious the wound was at the back, and equally obvious there was no exit injury in front, as far as she could tell. "Honey, you need to roll over on your side so I can check this one out."

"Get your pocket knife and cut the shirt away if you have to." Kennedy rolled over, bracing herself, hearing the snick as Carson unzipped her pack, and the slight click of the knife as she opened it.

Carson started with the soaked sleeve, slicing up toward her shoulder until she had cut clear through the neckline. She slowly peeled the front down to reveal a relatively clean sports bra. She carefully cut the bra strap and pulled it down. "No injury in front. Honey, your shirt is stuck to your skin in the back. If I pull it down, it'll hurt. Kennedy, I don't know if I can..."

"You can." Kennedy closed her mouth, determined not to scream, focusing instead on a lizard that sat a few feet away on the rock, its black beady eyes watching her warily and its tongue darting out, testing the air. She felt the tug at the material, followed by something akin to fire. If someone had pressed a live coal against her skin, she figured it couldn't have been much worse. Her body jerked in pain, but she remained quiet otherwise, closing her eyes as tears squeezed out of them.

"Oh." Carson drew in a breath. The back of the sports bra and most of Kennedy's shoulder blade were covered in blood, and a fresh seepage continued to pour slowly from a large ugly bullet hole just below the top of her shoulder. "I...I think the bullet's still in there. You're still bleeding. Should I try to clean it?"

She leaned over for an answer and saw tears streaming down Kennedy's face. "Oh, honey." She swiped them away, hearing one sob of pain. "Can I...?" She shifted, getting Kennedy's head into her lap, feeling her right hand curl around

Carson's calf, squeezing it for all she was worth.

"Just pour water over it for now. We need to figure out a way to get away from here before we do much else." She braced herself again, trying not to move as the cold water lanced through her. "Cover it with one of those large waterproof bandages."

"It's still bleeding pretty good." Carson tore open the bandage and dabbed around the edges of the injured skin, trying to clean off a big enough spot to apply it. "Don't think the bandage will last for long."

"S'okay." Kennedy shook her head slightly as beads of sweat broke out on her forehead. "If we crawl along below this rock, we can stay out of sight for a bit, at least until we get close to that little rock ridge over there." She gestured with her right hand. "Tree line's too far away, but if we can drop down below the edge of the riverbank, maybe we can get away from them."

Carson took both fanny packs, belting one above the other. She glanced over at Kennedy, who was watching, a grim, determined expression planted bravely on her face. The fact that there was no protest at her carrying both packs told her exactly how much pain she was in. She tied her sweatshirt back around her waist, and got around behind the longer body, determined to place herself between Kennedy and whoever was up there above them. "You ready to crawl?"

"No, but let's go." It hurt like hell, and every time she moved her left arm or leg, pain shot through her entire body, forcing tiny puffed whimpers from her lungs. She felt Carson's hand at her back, comforting her more than anything. Crawling slowly over rocks, brush, and the occasional bug, they gradually reached the ridge, the one spot they would be exposed until they could get behind it.

"How do you want to do this?" Carson placed a hand at Kennedy's back, feeling her lungs heave with the effort of breathing.

"You go over first and be ready to pull me if I can't make it." Kennedy turned as much as she could. Despite the exertion, Carson's face was pale, her features fearful. "Go on. You can do it."

Carson touched her face once, and then leaped forward, staying low to the ground. As Kennedy moved behind her, another shot glanced off the ridge a few feet away. She reached out, grabbing handfuls of Kennedy's clothing, pulling her behind the ridge with her. She heard a cry of pain and rolled over, allowing Kennedy's head to rest against her stomach for a moment. She automatically combed her fingers through sweaty locks, then traced a high cheekbone with her fingertips. "Sorry."

"No," Kennedy croaked out, trying to catch her breath. "You did good, but we need to keep moving. I figure they must be pretty far away or they would've caught up to us by now."

Carson casually slipped her hand beneath Kennedy's back. She was careful not to press against her injury, but could feel fresh warm blood seeping through the tattered remains of her shirt. She pressed her lips together tightly, trying hard not to cry. Kennedy's pallor had increased and she could see an artery just below the surface of her skin, at her neck. It quivered erratically, beating much too fast. She reached down, just below her breast, feeling her heart pounding against her hand. "How are you doing?"

"Me?" Kennedy grimaced. "I'm doing fine."

"Liar." Carson sniffled once, drawing in a deep breath to try to calm herself.

Kennedy laughed lightly, stopping when it hurt too much. "Sweetheart, we've still got to get to the river. You ready for that?"

"I am," Carson answered with as much determination as she could muster. "But I can't stand watching you hurt."

"Don't have a choice. We can't stay here." Kennedy shifted, forcing herself not to react as daggers shot down her leg. "Look, let's get to the riverbank and regroup, all right?"

"All right. But let's go slow." Carson stroked her head and carefully moved, helping Kennedy get to her stomach for the long crawl ahead. It was hot and her throat was parched. She could only imagine what Kennedy was going through. She felt like a big baby, unable to buck up like she should. How could she be there for Kennedy if she couldn't even pull herself together? She sniffled, warm tears tracking down her cheeks as they slowly reached the bank and slipped over the side into some blessed shade.

It was cooler there, a breeze drifting up from the water's surface. A large bird lofted overhead in a lazy circle, too high to determine if it was an eagle, a hawk, or a buzzard. Carson shivered at the prospect of buzzards and frowned, her determination renewed. Neither she nor Kennedy was going to become buzzard bait, not if she could do anything to stop it. "Now what?"

"We keep going down river, back toward camp." Kennedy closed her eyes, feeling her heartbeat in her ears. "Need some water, please." A water bottle reached her lips and she sucked at it. Even swallowing hurt and she could feel both wounds still bleeding. Looking down, she could see blood around the edges of the gauze Carson had tied over her leg. She dared not think about how much blood she'd lost, or how much she was still losing.

"Honey, we can't crawl all the way back to camp. It would take days." Carson cradled her head in her lap, resting back against the red and brown dirt.

"You could hike out for help." Kennedy found her hand and clasped it to her chest. "I could hide away somewhere until you get back."

"I can't leave you." Carson shook her head violently. "I won't. We just have to figure out something else."

"All right." Kennedy's head felt light again and she swallowed several times, blinking to clear her vision. "Let the river work for us."

"Huh?" Carson stared down at the brownish-blue flow. It was swift, but not so fast that it would pull a person under if they had a life preserver. Unfortunately they had nothing but their fanny packs, and those would only add weight, not help the situation.

"We find us a good solid branch and hang on. Let the water carry us downstream back toward camp." Kennedy looked around, spotting a thick growth of brush down by the water. "Something from there might work. Think you can pull a big branch loose from there?"

"Need to get us down there first." Carson looked up at the edge of the bank, afraid that at any moment their shooters would appear and they'd have nowhere to hide. "Honey, can you belly-crawl down there and get out of sight while I work? I can help you get down there."

"Let's go." Kennedy shifted and they mostly slid down the scree that coated the side of the bank. Rock slivers nicked sensitive skin, and both women were covered in scrapes by the time they stopped beside the water. Carson braced a booted foot at the base of a long branch and gradually twisted it, working it a bit. Finally, she stomped on it with all her weight and it snapped. It was mostly dead wood, much easier than if it had been fresh and green.

"Will this do?" She dragged it around for Kennedy's perusal. Bloodshot eyes gazed at it and she nodded. "Kennedy." Carson knelt down next to her. "You've got to be able to hang on once we get in the water. Can you do that?"

"I've got one good arm. Sure." She lifted said arm, wiggling her fingers in proof. "We've got no choice."

Carson looked worriedly up at the bank. She sensed they were running out of time and she nodded once, committing herself to getting them to safety. "All right. Let's do this thing then."

Kennedy managed to sit up, sliding along on her behind to the very edge of the water. Carson went in first, dragging the branch with her, helping Kennedy get her right arm wrapped firmly around it. She wrapped herself around Kennedy, bracketing her with both her own arms to help her keep a hold. With all her might she pushed away from the river bottom, kicking until suddenly the water picked them up and they were floating downstream. She briefly prayed there were no water moccasins in the river, and rolled on her back, holding Kennedy against her, between her body and the branch. "Hold on, honey. I'll try to keep a watch out for help."

Kennedy laid back, her head against Carson's shoulder. The water was incredibly cold, but it felt good, numbing some of the pain in her leg and arm. Truth be told, she was barely hanging on to the branch, her body weak as a newborn colt. She closed her eyes for a moment, feeling the warm body behind her, and giving up her trust that Carson would take care of her.

They floated along, the current quickly carrying them away from the danger zone. As they rounded a bend, Carson looked up and saw two figures standing on the bank not too far from where they had gotten into the water. They were two far away for her to make out facial features, or even determine gender. She could see them gesturing, obviously angry, and she figured they must have been pretty far away to take that long to get to them. She shuddered as another shot rang out. She had no idea if they were within range and she quickly ducked down, pulling both of them as much under the branch as she could without going completely below the surface.

In a few more minutes they rounded the bend and were no longer in sight. She breathed a sigh of relief and surfaced again, hearing Kennedy groan at the movement. "Sorry, honey." She pulled her closer, turning enough to keep an eye on where they were going. She had no idea how far they had hiked that afternoon, and judging from the angle of the sun, they only had a few more hours of daylight.

Now Carson had time to feel the cold, and fervently hoped she would be able to tell where to try to pull out of the water. She looked up and saw the beginnings of trees way up ahead on one side, and realized they had a very long way to go to get back to La Clocha. She also realized that their shooters might have a vehicle and be expecting them there if they had followed them out.

Carson thought about that. When they left La Clocha, theirs

was the only tent pitched. What if no one else showed up to camp for the night? It was remote there, not the most popular area of the park by a long shot. Worse, what if they arrived at camp only to be greeted by the very people trying to kill them? She suddenly realized she didn't know who was a friend and who was an enemy. She couldn't flag anyone down on the bank lest she accidentally drew the attention of the ones they were trying to escape.

So.

What to do? It was late afternoon and the sun was beginning to sink lower. Already partially in shadows, the water was getting colder. She guessed it to still be several miles back to La Clocha. The river was moving, but not fast enough. She weighed her options and sighed, angling them toward the Mexican side of the river. As if in answer to a prayer, she spotted what appeared to be a cave, or at least a deep alcove in the tall rock walls and she kicked toward shore, hoping to land so they wouldn't have to travel far to reach it.

"What's going on?" Kennedy had drifted in and out of awareness, her body shivering as a fever set in, her system trying to fight the foreign object imbedded in her shoulder.

"Shhh. I'm getting us to shelter. We can't go back to camp tonight, honey. It's too far and too dangerous." Carson reached shallower water and found her footing, helping Kennedy float for as long as possible.

Her mind was too addled to argue and Kennedy merely accepted the answer, stumbling ashore supported by Carson's body and arms. She managed to stay on her feet, limping in whatever direction Carson led her. She fuzzily realized it was the best decision. She couldn't last much longer in the cold water, and she had no strength left for walking, much less swimming.

At last they began a short climb up to the area Carson had spotted. It was indeed a deep alcove, not quite a cave, but it was sheltered overhead and on three sides. Carson guided her far back into the shelter, helping her lay back against the back wall. Their clothes were soaked, and Carson quickly removed the fanny packs and her sweatshirt, once again placing the soaked garment behind Kennedy's head. She also removed as much wet clothing as she could, until Kennedy was in her underwear and ruined sports bra. She was shivering, goose bumps dancing along her skin, and her teeth chattered.

"Hold on. I need to build us a fire." Carson stumbled out of the cave, blindly gathering every bit of brush she could and dragging it back to the cave. She looked around, choosing a spot toward the back and behind part of the rock wall, hoping the wall would hide the flames from outside observers once darkness set in. Carefully, she made a ring of rocks and built up the wood and twigs before locating the flint and striker, grateful she had it, since it wasn't affected by water. After several strikes, a spark hit the tinder and she blew on it softly, sheltering it with her hands, smiling as it began to grow.

"Kennedy, honey, let's get you over here by the fire." She helped her move over a few feet, and rested back against the wall, with Kennedy's head in her lap. "Guess we need to give your wounds a proper cleaning, huh?"

"N...n...need..." Kennedy's teeth chattered and she reached for the fanny pack nearest her, crying out softly at the pain of stretching her body.

"Be still." Carson stroked her head. "What do you need?"

"Gotta sterilize it." Kennedy gestured toward the pack. "Pour some tequila on it."

"That would hurt like hell." Carson's voice was incredulous. "Kennedy, I can't do that."

"You can." Kennedy's voice was weak and she coughed, clearing some water from her sinuses. "I'll drink some of it first, just enough to take some of the edge off."

Carson buried her face in her hands, which trembled at the prospect. She felt a touch to her leg, Kennedy's right hand caressing her skin. "I'm afraid I'll make it worse."

"You won't. It's alcohol. Put some of that antiseptic cream in it after you clean it, then re-bandage it." Weak fingers tugged at Carson's leather belt. "Now. Get me drunk and make me burn." She managed a small chuckle.

Carson choked out a laugh, which turned into a sob, and she wiped her hand across her eyes. "I hate hurting you."

Kennedy reached up feebly, touching her face. "I trust you, sweetheart. You have to do this. Can't risk infection. Fever..." her voice trailed off and she shivered, her skin clammy from lack of clothing.

Carson found the flask and cream, and propped Kennedy up, getting a few shots of the amber liquid into her, reserving the rest for the task ahead. She watched as Kennedy's eyes became quite glazed. Kennedy giggled once and then whimpered as pain shot into her arm, her good hand squeezing Carson's leg as she rolled over onto her stomach. The tequila was doing its job, but she wasn't nearly as out of it as she wished she could be.

Carson took a few breaths and peeled back the bandage, watching fresh blood flow from the bullet hole. She set the precious bandage aside to re-use, and poured the tequila over the wound, hearing a muffled scream. "I'm so sorry I have to hurt you like this," she whispered. Kennedy was shaking continually, sweat beading up all over her skin as she applied more tequila. Carson used the antiseptic cream, filling the wound, and then covered it, carefully pressing the adhesive edges of the bandage against raw, red, skin. "Almost done, honey."

Kennedy could barely breathe, the pain was so great. She buried her face against Carson's lap. Fire raced across her back, stabbing pain radiating all over her body. At last she faintly heard Carson say "all done." And she relaxed, rolling on her side, her head still in Carson's lap.

Carson's face was covered with tears, as was her own. She carefully gathered Kennedy up, cradling her as they both cried. "Don't ever make me do that again," Carson sobbed out.

"Clean my leg, then it'll be over." She shifted again. "Come on. One splash of tequila and some more cream and we're done."

Carson sniffled and quickly took care of her, flinching in sympathy when Kennedy did, the alcohol setting her leg on fire. "Here. I think I've got one bit of dry gauze here in the middle of this roll." She cut away the wet material, and did indeed have just enough dry left to wrap the leg a couple of times. She moved away long enough to lay all their clothing and everything in the fanny packs out by the fire to dry, stripping down to her underwear as well. She was thankful it wasn't as cool as the day before, though she feared what the night might bring.

She wrapped up in Kennedy's long wet flannel shirt and put her boots back on long enough to go out one more time and gather as much dry brush and fire building material as she could find, piling all of it near their chosen sleeping spot. The sun was setting, and the temperature was starting to drop. It was going to be a long night and she trudged back into the alcove, settling back and getting Kennedy situated so she was lying back against her, as much of their bodies in contact as possible. The fire was warm and she salvaged a couple of damp trail bars, ripping one open with her teeth, unwilling to let go of Kennedy with one hand.

"Time?" A sedate voice drifted up, and Kennedy gazed dazedly into the firelight.

"Sundown." Carson leaned over, kissing her forehead. "Drink." She held up the water bottle and Kennedy obeyed, sucking down a healthy portion of water.

"Cold." Kennedy shivered, trying to curl into the body under her.

"I know." Carson wrapped herself around her as much as she could. "Better?"

"Yeah." Kennedy squinted, her focus not quite on target. "Love you," she crooned, still slightly tipsy.

"I love you too." Carson blinked away fresh tears. "You hungry?" She held up a trail bar.

Kennedy turned green at the smell and pushed it away. "No. Just...tired. Hurts."

"Sleep now, if you can." At least one of them should get some rest, Carson reasoned, and it wasn't going to be her. "We'll figure out what to do next in the morning."

Her system overrun with pain and alcohol, Kennedy moved lazily, rolling a bit until she was resting on her right side, her body still stretched out against Carson. She laid her head back against Carson's chest and closed her eyes. Her head was throbbing, as were her shoulder and leg. She knew she had a fever and that she was probably not completely coherent.

Kennedy heard a rustling noise and looked toward the opening of the alcove. Carson moved beneath her and they both gasped as the white buck appeared in the entryway, stopping and staring at both of them for a very long moment before he seemingly faded from view. "Did you see him?" Her voice drifted upward.

"Yeah." Carson's heart beat faster. Maybe it was a sign. A good one, she hoped. She looked around, reaching for some more brush to feed the fire, when something in the very back of the alcove caught her eye. "Hang on." She slipped out from under Kennedy and crept back on all fours, the roof overhead too low for her to stand. It was a tarp, rolled up and tied with twine, resting against the back wall, half hidden behind a rock.

She unrolled it and studied it. It was a bit musty-smelling and dusty, but otherwise in good shape, not ridden with any bugs and without so much as even one hole. She looked up and out into the night, wondering if it had been there all along and the buck had come by to point it out to her, or if it had somehow magically appeared. "Thank you, sweet Jesus. Or whoever provided this," she hastily added.

It wasn't a sleeping bag, but it was a layer against the chill. She crawled back over to Kennedy, situating them as before, and then drew the tarp over them, sneezing as the dusty smell reached her nostrils. Dust she could live with a lot more easily than hypothermia. She felt Kennedy finally begin to relax and quit shivering, and after a long while felt the even breathing of sleep.

Carson looked around. They had a fire, food, water, and

now a blanket. She sighed unhappily, comparing the current cave to the one from the night before. Her thoughts turned sober as she remembered that someone out there wanted one or both of them dead. Who was it, and why? Drunken rednecks who decided to shoot at human beings? Or someone who had actually tracked them from who knew where? She relaxed back against the rock as much as she dared, determined to keep watch until dawn.

"WHERE'D THEY GO?" Rick sat partway up from his perch behind a large live oak tree. He shaded his face, peering toward the riverbank.

"Considering Shea isn't walking, not far." Tom stood, brushing red dust off his jeans. "Let's go take a look."

"I knew you wanted to scare them, but holy crap, this sure went down differently than I figured it would." Rick retrieved a pack of cigarettes from his shirt pocket, tapping it against his palm before he opened it and pulled one out, cupping it with one hand while he lit it. Smoke trailed up around his head, drifting over the tree branches.

"Yeah, well believe me, it didn't turn out how I expected it to, either. What a fucking mess." Tom followed suit, briefly eyeing one joint he had hidden in his pack next to the legal tobacco. There would be time for that later, after they hiked back out. The sun was sinking, casting long shadows over the tops of the hills, making strange patterns on the dips and curves of the landscape below. A chill ran down his spine and he looked around, then cautiously slid down the steep slope to the edge of the river, making sure to stay hidden behind the ridge between them and the higher outcroppings above them.

Rick came tripping down to join him and both their mouths dropped open. Down river they spied Carson and Kennedy and their tree branch, floating swiftly away on the current. "I'll be damned." Tom spat out a wad of tobacco, watching it land in some brush below the edge of the riverbank. "Get back before they see us." He tugged Rick away from the bank.

"We'll never find them, not unless they go back to their camp." Rick tossed his ball cap to the ground in disgust. "And this was just starting to be fun."

Tom resisted the urge to slap him upside the head. "I think they've been scared enough, and luckily, I don't think they've seen us. Could get us in a whole lot more trouble than we ever bargained for if they did. This has turned into a damned cluster fuck, you idiot."

"This was your idea!" Rick stepped back, mindful of Tom's larger size, but he wasn't quick enough. A large fist picked him up by the shirt collar, twisting it tightly around his neck, as Tom's face contorted in rage.

"Nothing happened here today, you got me? Nothing!" He shook Rick and let him go, watching as he fell to the ground in a coughing fit.

"Damn, man." Rick rubbed his throat. "I'm on your side here. No worries." He waved a plaintive hand in the air.

"One word to anybody and you'll regret it." Tom kicked savagely at a rock, watching it roll and tumble down into the water.

Rick stood up, picking up his hat and gathering his dignity about him. "Let's get out of here. This place is starting to give me the heebie jeebies."

"Lucky you didn't get your fool head blown off." Tom snorted and took off down the trail, occasionally looking back up and over his shoulder toward the hills. "It'll be dark before we get back to the road."

"We planning on waiting for them at their campsite?" Rick caught up with him but stayed out of reach.

"No. We are going to go back to town, get cleaned up, and go to Armadillo Flats." Tom's eyes rolled. "Are you stupid? You saw the blood. Shea's hurt bad. Last thing we need is to be seen anywhere near their tent or their truck. We weren't here today. Do you get that?"

"I get it," Rick muttered. They were too out in the open for his tastes and he unconsciously hunched over, tucking his hands into his pockets. His sweat-soaked shirt was sticking to his back, and he could feel the sunburn at the back of his neck. He pulled his ball cap further down over his forehead and kept his head down, wishing they were closer to the trees.

They neared a rise on the trail and a shot rang out, sending both men scrambling for cover. "What the hell?" Tom belly-crawled to the riverbank and eased over the side, with Rick following quickly behind him. His head poked up just enough to take a quick look around before he ducked down again. "Dammit!" He squinted, just making out Carson and Kennedy again, as they slipped around a bend out of sight.

"Now what?" Rick hunkered down well below the bank's edge, rolling over and grimacing as he inadvertently sat on a small spiny cactus.

"Somebody else wants those bitches out of the way. Let's lay low and just hope they don't want us out of the way as well. Come on." He nodded toward the water. "Best we hike from down here for a while. And hope like hell none of those damned touring companies come along with people able to ID us."

"What about Pete?" Rick followed him down nearer the water. "He's waiting for us back at their campsite. How do you think he'll react when he finds out his sister's been shot?" A dragonfly darted in his face and Rick swatted at it, almost tumbling into the water in the process.

"Not a word to him about this. As far as he's concerned, we just tell him we had a little chat with Shea and came to an understanding." Tom's eyes narrowed. "Understood?"

"Buh..."

"Understood?" Tom whipped out his hunting knife, brandishing it around in an arc for Rick's benefit. "I don't care if the first he knows about this is when they drag his sister's dead body out of the river. He ain't gonna hear about it from us, you got me?"

"Whatever you say, man." Hiking was difficult with legs that felt like Jell-O. "I just wanna go home and forget today ever happened."

"That would be a very good idea." Tom tucked the knife back into his boot and picked up his pace, racing with the sun to reach civilization.

"CARSON?" A HOARSE voice carried feebly in the light of shimmering coals.

"Right here, honey." Carson stroked Kennedy's head, trailing her fingertips across a warm forehead.

"Cold." Kennedy coughed and cried out as the motion pulled at her shoulder.

"Here." Carson pulled the tarp more snuggly around them, cursing at the ruined bottle of ibuprofen she'd found in her fanny pack. The pills were mush, drowning in brown river water. "Is that better?"

"Yeah." Kennedy shivered, her teeth chattering before she clamped her jaw firmly shut.

"Just a second." Carson eased out from beneath the covering and crept over by the fire, adding some brush to it and stoking it until it lit up, filling the small space with warm light. She felt their clothing, sighing with relief when her fingers met with dry material. "Thank you for dry desert air." She gathered up everything and quickly helped Kennedy into her shorts and Carson's own T-shirt and sweatshirt, placing the over-sized flannel shirt over all of it. The T-shirt and sweatshirt were a little big on Carson, and blessedly fit Kennedy without squeezing against her injured shoulder.

It was getting cooler outside and Carson donned her own shorts and the remains of Kennedy's T-shirt. She got both of them into their socks as well, and crawled back under the tarp, arranging herself so that she was once again wrapped around her partner, Kennedy lying back against her under the musty canvas. Carson's arms were covered in goose bumps, but under cover it wasn't quite so bad, and Kennedy's apparent fever unfortunately added to the warmth.

"What about you?" Kennedy stroked a bare forearm with her right hand. "You need to put on one of these shirts."

"I'm fine." Carson pulled her closer and felt around for the water bottle. "You need to stay hydrated."

"Yeah." She sucked at the spout, a small measure of relief flooding her system as the cool liquid slid down her parched throat. "Maybe that'll help replace some of the blood I lost." Her vision was a little blurred and she blinked, Carson's face coming into better focus. "You think I lost very much?"

"No," Carson lied. "Hot-blooded as you are, you had plenty to spare, stud."

Kennedy produced a brief, pained chuckle and reached up, touching her face. "Don't feel much like a stud right now." Her thumb brushed Carson's cheek. "Some birthday, huh?"

"Might have to celebrate it a little late." A few tears trickled down her cheeks and Kennedy caught them, swiping them away.

"Every minute with you is a celebration." Kennedy forced herself to focus and look up, trying to project the depth of the love she felt. "My last day on earth, I want to spend it in your arms." She felt light-headed and closed her eyes again, snuggling up as she felt Carson pull her closer, until her head was against Carson's shoulder. "If I died right now, I'd die happy."

"Don't you go talking like that." Carson's chest felt so tight she couldn't breathe for a very long moment. "No dying allowed. Not now. Not next week. Not fifty years from now. You are going to grow to be old and gray, you hear me?" She was shaking and felt Kennedy's grip tighten around her forearm. She looked down, watching several expressions flit across Kennedy's fevered face.

"That'll take a long time." Kennedy smiled, pushing the pain aside. "You've seen Pa. Not much gray there yet. It's in our genes."

"You'll be beautiful with gray hair." Carson stroked the hair in question, pushing sweaty bangs off her forehead.

"So will you." She closed her eyes again, soaking in the

comforting touch. The ground was a little less hard beneath her legs and the cold somehow a little less so. Kennedy concentrated on Carson's warmth against her body, and the gentle sound of her breathing. She rolled a little, until her ear was against Carson's chest. She was rewarded with the sound of a firm, steady heartbeat, and she reached up until she could feel it as well.

"Ah, but that will be a long time too." One hand covered Kennedy's. "Blondes don't show their gray until they have a whole lot of it."

"So you really think I'm going to live to be old and gray, huh?" Kennedy tilted her head up and opened her eyes, focusing on Carson's face, so close in the firelight.

"I know you will." Carson found a smile and almost lost it as Kennedy reached up, touching her lips for a brief second, before she eased her hand back down beneath the tarp, coming to rest on her arm again.

"If I do. If I survive this...." Kennedy swallowed, a motion visible even in the low light. "Will you promise to hang around and grow old with me?" Sad, earnest eyes locked with Carson's as she brushed her thumb against the baby-fine hair on Carson's forearm.

A very soft, sad, little happy yelp escaped, almost like a puppy whimpering, and Carson blinked, scattering tears down her cheeks. "I promise." She leaned over, kissing Kennedy's forehead.

"Good." Kennedy's eyes drifted closed and she groaned a little, as an odd jabbing sensation stabbed through her shoulder. A slight smile lingered, though, and she felt Carson resume stroking her head. "Gotta go out for a little while now. Tired."

"Sleep, honey. I'll be right here when you wake up." Kennedy's breathing deepened and the fire crackled, sending sparks shooting and drifting up into the darkness. Way off, a coyote howled, and Carson gazed steadily beyond the alcove's entrance, pondering her options to get help.

SHE WAS FLOATING down river on a raft. It was warm and sunny and the water babbled merrily, carrying her along at a comfortable pace. Kennedy lay on the raft across from her, wearing a swimsuit that was probably illegal in a dozen states, and a come-hither smile that made Carson want to crawl over and wrap herself around all that smooth skin covering an incredibly long, lean body.

Carson smiled and cat-stalked across the raft. Just as she

reached her, Kennedy rose up, with the sun shining behind her, creating mahogany highlights in her hair. As she stood, a cracking noise rang out and Kennedy dropped to the raft, covered in blood.

No. Carson tried to scream and couldn't.

She jerked awake, her heart pounding in her chest, and her T-shirt drenched with sweat. She shivered, both from cold and dampness, and from the lingering tendrils of the dream. She looked down and remembered that at least part of it—the bad part—wasn't a dream at all. Kennedy was resting against her, her right side tucked up against Carson's stomach and legs, keeping her weight off her left arm and leg. "Damn." Carson scrubbed her eyes with her fists, then stared into the inky blackness. The fire had died down, but she was loath to crawl from under the tarp to build it back up.

Kennedy appeared to be resting peacefully. A little too peacefully. Fear clutched at Carson's throat, almost closing it, and she delicately placed her hand just below Kennedy's nose, not touching her, but close enough to feel shallow breathing against her skin. She sighed in relief and then frowned. The part of her outside the tarp was cold, but underneath it was blazing warm.

She carefully pulled aside the collar on Kennedy's flannel shirt and felt the skin at the back of her neck. She was burning up and her skin was dry. Her hand drifted lower to feel fresh wet warmth soaking through the three shirts. "Honey, not good," she whispered. Kennedy stirred and mumbled, almost as if she heard her, and she reached out with her left hand, crying out in her sleep in pain. The hand came to rest on Carson's knee.

"Carson?" Her voice was that of a frightened child, and even in the darkness, her confusion was evident.

"Right here." She touched Kennedy's forehead, pushing her bangs aside. Her head was warm too, and Carson reached over, locating their water bottle. "Drink."

Kennedy sucked feebly at the water, as if it were taking great effort. "Where are we?" She pushed the bottle away, yelping again as pain shot from her shoulder down her arm.

"Same place." Carson stroked her hair. "Just waiting for dawn so I can figure out what to do."

"Do about what?" Kennedy shifted. "Ouch." She grew still. "Hurts all over."

"I know." Carson forced herself to speak calmly, realizing Kennedy didn't remember everything that had happened to them. "Honey, you remember getting shot?"

"Shot?" Kennedy rolled over a little bit, so she could see

Carson better, but weariness overcame her, and she closed her eyes. She remained silent for so long that Carson had decided she either didn't remember or had fallen back asleep. "Oh yeah, shot." Her eyes fluttered open again. "You took care of me."

"Yeah." She sniffled and felt Kennedy's fingertips against her leg under the blanket, and then her hand curled around Carson's thigh, a comforting gesture that made her release a tiny relieved laugh, along with a few more sniffles. It was absurd that she was the one being comforted.

"It's okay, Carson." Kennedy's voice bore more clarity, and she continued stroking her leg. "We're gonna be okay. You're doing real good."

"I should probably check your shoulder since you're awake. Make sure it's doing okay." The distraction of purpose, of something to do, drove back a dam that had threatened to break since Kennedy was first shot. She knew at some point she'd probably lose that battle, but as long as she could stay focused on the next step, it was easier. Carson found the flashlight and folded back the tarp. Kennedy immediately shivered as the cool air washed over her very warm body.

"Fever?" Kennedy swallowed, her throat suddenly dry again.

"Yeah, I think so." Carson carefully got the sweatshirt up and over the injured shoulder, and then unbuttoned the flannel shirt, sliding it down enough to peel the T-shirt underneath it up. She shined the light at the wound. Blood was seeping from it, but not as heavy a flow as she had thought, given the soaked shirts.

"Hurts." Kennedy felt gentle fingers trail across her back below the wound. "Feels like it's bleeding."

"A little bit." Carson pressed the water bottle to her lips again. "Drink."

This time Kennedy drank much more vigorously, realizing she was probably dehydrated from fever. Her brain felt fuzzy, and around the points of severe pain at her shoulder and leg were concentric circles of more dull pain that radiated out and gradually dissipated. She was freezing inside, and doing her best to hide it, since there was not much Carson could do about it, except..."Fire?"

"Oh, yeah." Carson carefully slid out from beneath Kennedy and crawled over to the fire ring, building up the pile of tinder and brush. She got a small blaze burning again and scrambled back over, pulling the tarp back over them as Kennedy lay down, this time with her head in Carson's lap. "Better?"

"Yeah," she lied. She was so cold that the fire couldn't touch her. There was no more clothing to be had. "Maybe if we both get completely under here we can get really warm."

They got rearranged, with Carson lying fully horizontal at last, her head resting against the daypack, while Kennedy lay on her stomach with her body draped on top of Carson, her head against her shoulder. Carson tucked the tarp around them and felt their shared body heat begin to warm the thin layer of air beneath the covering.

"Mmm." Kennedy's eyes closed. "You sleep too. Fire will keep the critters away."

Carson waited, feeling Kennedy drift off. The utter solitude of their situation pressed in on her, and at that moment, she felt as if they were a million miles from civilization. It was dark and cold, and somewhere out there, someone wanted them dead. The fire might keep the four-footed predators away, but it was the two-footed ones she was worried about.

Carson was weary, a lack of sleep, lack of proper food, and the extreme stress and physical exertion all combining to make her entire body feel like a lead weight. She had to stay awake, and thoughts of Starbucks flitted through her mind. A hot mocha latte sounded like heaven, both for the warmth and the caffeine. Her coffee bags were back in the truck, along with the mug to drink the coffee from.

It was easy to imagine monsters at the edge of the alcove. The shadows thrown by rocks and brush were becoming bears and wolves to her tired imagination. She shook her head to clear it and forced herself to sit up just a little bit, lest she did fall asleep. Sleep wasn't an option until they were somewhere safe. A great yawn almost popped her jaw out of joint, and she groaned, feeling like an old woman.

She'd already fallen asleep once, she realized, remembering the raft nightmare. A raft. Her mind wrapped around that idea. Maybe she could find enough branches to pull something crude together and float them out of the wilderness to safety. She hoped that somewhere a ranger was making rounds and they would be missed. Though she wasn't sure how much good it would do, since no one knew which direction they'd hiked out from their tent site. Still...if they were missed, hopefully they'd be looked for.

One of the shadows at the edge of the alcove took shape and moved closer and her heart leaped into her throat. She couldn't scream, couldn't move, paralyzed and waiting. The white buck appeared, standing there, the fire painting his hide shining silver. Liquid dark eyes sparkled back at her. She looked down. Kennedy was fast asleep. Looking back up, she swallowed.

"You appearing to me without her knowing it now?" Carson frowned. "She'll freak if I tell her about that. I don't know if I did the right thing, pulling us out of the river. But I don't think we would have survived staying in much longer, and walking didn't seem like an option." Tears sprang into her eyes, and she shook her head and sniffled. "This tarp was a relief and all, but she's talking to me about dying." She sniffled again, swiping the back of her hand across her eyes. "If you really are supposed to protect her, she could sure use it right about now. I could, too. I can't lose her, do you understand that? She's become my life." Surprisingly, the buck didn't move as she spoke, but merely stood there, studying her, his eyes boring into her with the wisdom of the ages. She knew she was awake. She could feel every scrape, every tired muscle, every achy joint in her body.

"Please?" she begged. The buck stepped away and lowered his head once before he turned and faded into the shadows. Carson wondered if that was his way of saying yes. Overwhelmed and weary, she closed her eyes for as long as she dared, sending out a little prayer that God, or the Great Spirit, or someone, would look over them and see them safely home.

"GREAT!" TOM CIRCLED the truck, kicking a completely flat tire. "That's just great." He turned, facing Rick, who was leaning against the side of the pickup, nursing a cold beer. "You want to tell me again how it is the spare tire is missing?"

"Not missing," Rick drawled between sips. "You just kicked it. That is the spare. Had a flat last week. Just hadn't gotten around to getting a new one yet." He tilted the can back and felt it slapped out of his hand. "Hey!" He stepped aside a little, out of Tom's reach. "That was only half-empty." He watched remorsefully as the pale amber beverage foamed out of the can and was quickly soaked up by the parched desert soil.

"You managed to pack a cooler of beer, but not a spare tire?" Tom snorted in disgust and glanced westward toward the setting sun. They had taken one of the unimproved back roads between La Clocha and Sierra San Vicente, where they'd seen Kennedy and Carson, so as not to be seen on any of the main park roads. The road had proven to be dried in deep ruts after the recent rains, and somehow they'd blown the tire there in the middle of nowhere.

"Well..." Rick opened the door to the extended cab and reached inside, digging through the ice chest for two more beers. He tossed one to Tom, who caught it and opened it, downing half of it in a few gulps. "We walking on out tonight and catching a ride at Rio Grande Village?"

"No, you idiot." Tom sneered at him, wondering how Rick had survived childhood. "It's too far. We're going to sleep here tonight, and then we'll have to hike the back road all the way in tomorrow. We'll pretend we came hiking in from the other direction, and we're gonna call Doug and see if he'll come get us."

"What about my truck?" Rick whined.

"We'll get Doug to bring you a tire, but we'll have to drive the long way around to come fix it and hope no one goes nosing down this road looking for those bitches between now and then. I hate sleeping in that truck. It's too damned cramped inside."

"We don't have to sleep in the truck. Got a tent and sleeping bags," Rick offered. "Got all my camping gear behind the front seat."

Tom shook his head. "You got beer and camping gear but no spare tire." He finished his beer and crumpled the can in his fist. "Figures. Okay..." He looked around. "We can't risk camping at La Clocha, and that's the closest site, so let's see if we can find a spot hidden in the trees down there. No fires, got me?"

"Got you. I'm not stupid." Rick missed Tom's rolled eyes as he ducked into the truck and pulled out his camping equipment.

"Let's set up camp and then you go get Pete and drag him up here. Not a word, though. In case you have any ideas to the contrary." Tom grabbed the tent from behind the front seat.

"Dammit it, man, how many times do I have to say I get it?" Rick grumbled. Soon they had pitched the small tent in a shady spot. "I'll go get Pete."

"Better hurry. Be dark soon." Tom lit a cigarette, drawing deeply from it and exhaling through his nose. He contemplated his joint, but decided he wasn't in the mood to share.

"Water's almost gone." Rick crawled back in the tent and came back out with a small water filtration device. "I'm going to take a leak and then head down to the creek and filter us some more before I head out."

"Fine. Go on. You gotta be good for something." Tom waved him off and sneered as soon as he was out of sight, pulling out the joint after all, lighting it and drawing the smoke into his lungs with pleasure. It would be gone before Rick would be back.

Rick trampled sullenly through the trees, mumbling under his breath. "'Gotta be good for something'." He mimicked Tom's voice as he shoved branches aside, walking almost blindly in his anger. "Treats me like I'm stupid all the time. I've half a mind to walk out of here tonight with Pete and leave him to die of thirst. Would serve him right." He moved on and shortly reached the creek, where he skidded down the slippery embankment and bent down, carefully filling the bottle with fresh, clean water.

A rustling noise sounded up stream and he stopped, growing completely still, then he slowly and silently crept behind a rock, listening. He heard nothing else but birds and the babble of the stream, and finally resumed his task. "I'll have the willies from this day for a while, I do believe." He finished filling the bottle and started making his way back to camp.

It was almost dark, and he regretted not bringing a flashlight. "It'll be a damned long walk to get Pete. Hope the rattlers are all burrowed in for the night." He watched the ground carefully, making slow progress in the dimming light. He stopped about fifty yards back from the campsite, set the water down, and stepped behind a large tree to take care of business. As he was zipping up, the crack of a gunshot rang out and his heart leaped into his throat. A second shot shattered the night air and he automatically dropped down on his belly, mindless of critters.

The shots had come from the direction of the campsite, and he listened intently, barely breathing, and hoping his gray sweatshirt was dark enough to blend into the dusk. Slowly he belly-crawled toward camp, a few feet at a time, stopping at intervals to listen. His own breathing sounded loud to his ears, the fear making hearing difficult.

Finally, several yards from the campsite, he heard two male voices, speaking low. He grew completely still, determined to spend the night right where he was if necessary.

"You sure that one's dead?" A gravelly voice carried through the air to Rick's hiding place. He couldn't see the campsite at all and hoped he could trust his ears to tell him if anyone started walking his way.

"Yeah." A higher voice answered. The accent was definitely not from West Texas, or Texas at all, for that matter, and Rick tried to place it. "Thought there were two of them."

"So did I."

Rick heard a rustling and realized they were digging through the tent.

"Where d'ya think he is?" High voice grew closer and Rick quit breathing completely.

"Beats the hell out of me." Gravel voice also grew closer, and Rick realized if he looked up at all, he'd probably see the two men, who sounded as if they were standing only a few feet away just at the edge of the trees.

"Do'ya think he'll be back tonight?" High voice started to move farther away.

"Looks like camp was pitched for more than one, so, yeah, maybe we should wait for him. I don't like him being out there." Gravel voice followed high voice.

"You sure they saw us?" High voice sounded tired.

"I'm not sure, no, but we can't take any chances." Gravel voice grew muffled, and Rick heard the sound of the tent being unzipped, followed by the jingle of the truck keys. "Let's wait in that beat up piece of shit truck. I've had enough of this stinkin' fresh air for one day. Hell, it'll make a good hiding place."

Rick waited, listening as the men walked uphill to the truck. It was a fair walk, but finally he heard the slam of the doors and he released a long breath, realizing his insides were shaking. Carefully, he turned and belly-crawled back to the creek. It took a long time, but at last he felt safe enough to stand.

He thought about everything Tom had said.

Tom was dead.

He snorted. "Who's the smart guy now?"

Tom had said they should avoid the ranger stations and being seen in the area because of Shea and her friend being shot at. But now someone had shot Tom. It seemed reasonable to Rick that he and Pete could hike to the ranger station and get help. They could get a ride home and he could sleep in his own bed.

Yeah.

He took off toward the river, avoiding the trails in favor of the tree line. In a half hour he reached the other campsite, where Pete was pacing in agitation, the growing darkness magnifying every sound. He looked up as Rick approached.

"Where in the hell have you been?" he yelled.

"Shhh." Rick trotted over. "Quiet."

"Why? And where's Tom?" Pete looked expectantly down the trail past Rick.

"Tom's dead," Rick answered quietly. "And we need to get out of here."

"What?" The blood in Pete's veins turned to ice water and he had to sit down. He sank slowly to the truck running board. "I told you my sister was a piece of work." He shook his head. "You mean Shea killed him? What in the hell did y'all do to them, anyway? I though you were just going to give 'em a scare."

"We didn't do a damned thing to them," Rick spat out, forgetting his own admonition to be quiet. "Everything went wrong, man. Everything. There's a couple of guys out there looking for me, I think. They killed Tom. We have to get out of here. Now!"

"Where's Shea and Carson?" Pete eyed him warily.

"We need to talk." Rick started down the trail. "But we need to get out of here. Come on." He waved at a dumbstruck Pete, who stood and just stared at him for a long moment before taking off after him.

THE PALE FINGERS of dawn crept inside the alcove, reaching out and touching two miserable figures huddled together beneath the musty tarp. The fire had burned completely out and there was precious little left with which to restart it. Carson lifted the water bottle and tipped it up, taking only a few swallows as she realized it was almost empty.

Kennedy stirred, slowly opening her bloodshot eyes as she tried to remember where they were. She moved and winced, yelping as the motion pulled at her very stiff shoulder. "Ouch." She felt Carson's hand on her head, stroking her hair, and she closed her eyes, soaking in the comfort. "Feel like a big baby."

"You're still warm." Carson felt like she'd been run over by a truck, her back and neck muscles screaming in protest at sleeping on the hard rock in a partially upright position for most of the night. What little bit of that time she'd actually slept was debatable. "Honey, not good to have a fever this long."

"Fever?" Most of the night was a forgotten blur and Kennedy frowned, trying to pull the pieces of her memory together. "Must've been pretty out of it."

"Eh." Carson extended her legs, trying to stretch without jostling her. "Not too bad, considering. I've got to figure out how to get us out of here. I've been hoping they'd find our empty campsite and the truck and come looking for us."

"If the rangers have been doing their jobs." Kennedy's throat was parched and she looked around, spying the water bottle still in Carson's hand. "Can I have some of that?"

"All of it." Carson held it up and waited until Kennedy emptied it. "I'm going down and filter us some more and see what it looks like out there. Maybe see if there's any sign of anyone looking for us."

"What side of the river are we on?" A thought settled uneasily into Kennedy's head and she rolled to her back a little bit more, careful not to put any pressure against her left shoulder. "Mexico or U.S.?"

"Mexico." She looked down, reading the troubled expression on Kennedy's face. "Why?"

"Sweetheart, they won't come looking for us here." Kennedy tried to sit up and managed to get propped partway, resting on her right forearm. "No jurisdiction."

"So we're on our own to get home?" Carson's shoulders

slumped, and she closed her eyes at the sting of tears, determined not to make things worse than they already were. She covered her face with her hands and released a long, trembling breath. "Thought getting us out of that river was the best thing. Maybe it was the worst."

"You did what you had to, Carson." Kennedy forced herself further up, gritting her teeth to hide the pain of the small effort involved. "I was so cold. And so were you. And those guys..." She shifted, leaning against the rock behind them. "There were two of them, right?"

"Yeah." Carson uncovered her face, swiping at one eye and catching the moisture that threatened to leak out and spill over. "They were too far away to really tell anything more. Could've been girls. Or one of each."

"Just can't figure out who would've been after us." Kennedy extended her legs out cautiously, pain shooting down the left one from the spot where the bullet had grazed her. She reached over and carefully pulled back the tarp, then worried at the gauze with her right hand, bending in an awkward position to reach it. "Ouch." She slipped the bandage down and studied the wound.

To her still-addled brain, it didn't look as bad as the day before, if she recalled, scabbed over nicely with no signs of infection, although there was still a fair amount of swelling and she could tell just from looking there would be a nasty scar when it healed. "Looks like these legs are gonna be a little worse for wear. Might not be as loveable as they were before," she halfway joked, glancing sideways at Carson.

Carson touched the tanned face, urging eye contact. "You listen to me." Her voice was no-nonsense earnest. "I don't care about all that. It's not what matters to me. Fifty years from now, you'll still be just as beautiful to me as you are right now. You...you..." Her head dropped down, and her chest rose up and down with a great, shuddering sigh. "You scared me last night. Talking about dying and all that. I...just don't you go dying on me anytime soon. I've been through enough death in this lifetime. One more will kill me. So...just...don't."

Dying? Kennedy was stunned. "I don't remember much of last night," she confessed. Not entirely true. She did remember one moment with vivid clarity – one that basically amounted to a very convoluted proposal of marriage. Ah, well. Time to discuss that one later. First things first. "I was in so much pain from that very first shot. I...I'm sorry. Carson." She reviewed her lover's words and mentally kicked herself. *Her parents. Oh, god.* Carson's head was still ducked, and she tilted her own head, seeing a tear drip down and land on Carson's leg. "Oh, sweetheart." Grateful Carson was to her right, she pulled her close, until her head was resting on Kennedy's shoulder.

The dam finally burst and Carson began to sob, her body shaking as all the fear and worry of the past eighteen hours came rushing to the surface. "How...how am I going to get us out of here?" She sobbed some more, sniffling as she tried to get her emotions under control. "I can't carry you. I can't swim us both across the river. Your leg...how far could you walk? And the fever. And people out there shooting at us. And we have almost no food..." She felt a kiss to the top of her head and sniffled as the tears began to abate. "I'm scared. I know I need to be strong for us, but damn it, honey, I'm scared and I don't have any answers. None."

"Shhh." Kennedy ignored the pain and rocked them both a little bit, feeling the shaking body she held begin to grow still. "One step at a time. Can you go get us some water?"

"Yeah." Soulful eyes peeked up and a few more tears trickled down Carson's cheeks. Kennedy leaned over and gently kissed them away.

"We still got some trail bars?" She kissed Carson's forehead for good measure, feeling her nod. "Then we have breakfast. Get us some water, and then we'll talk about our next move, okay?"

"Okay." Nibbling her lower lip, Carson got up, taking the water bottle and filter with her, and exited the alcove.

"Be careful." Kennedy thought about the shooters. "Keep your head down." Carson nodded and Kennedy watched her go, waiting a few minutes and gathering her courage. Cursing, she pushed herself up, one slow inch at a time, until she was on her knees. It hurt like hell, darts of pain stabbing her all up and down her back and leg, and she shook from both fever and pain. She forced herself to stand, shedding a few tears of her own as she tried to rest her weight on the injured leg. "I couldn't just go and skin my knees like a normal person, could I?" She hobbled forward a few steps, stopping as vertigo threatened to take her down. "No. I had to go and get myself shot. Whoa..." She wobbled and waited, making herself look at the wall directly in front of her. "Must've lost more blood than I thought." She took a few more steps, still feeling light-headed. "Or maybe my blood sugar is way off. Or maybe I'm burning up."

"Kennedy?" Carson's voice called from outside. "It's...oh." She entered the alcove, spotting her now-standing lover. "Hey. Can you walk?"

"We'll find out." Kennedy managed a few more steps to meet her halfway. She absently accepted the full water bottle, drinking for a long moment and trying to draw up reserves of strength. She handed the bottle back over and draped her right arm across Carson's shoulders, as together they hobbled to the entrance of their little sanctuary. Staring eastward, Kennedy shaded her eyes against the rising sun and squinted. "Let's get ready and do this thing."

"You think if we can get near the closest part of the camping area, maybe someone will see us from across the river?" Carson peered up at her hopefully. "How far do you think that is?"

"Mmm. Four miles, maybe?" She tested her leg, standing on both feet. Four yards seemed impossible to traverse without excruciating pain, let alone four miles. "Piece of cake."

Carson could see the tense jaw line and a body so stiff it made her hurt just looking at her. Even Kennedy's words were measured, as if she was forcing herself to speak normally, holding in any noise that might give away her suffering. There was no point in calling her on the 'piece of cake' comment. They couldn't stay where they were for much longer. "Let's eat some trail bars first, honey. Fortify ourselves a little bit."

"Carson, if I sit down, I may not get up again today, so if you don't mind..." She gestured toward their things, still lying beside the cold fire ring. "We can eat while we hike out."

"Okay. Let me get the packs together." She started for their belongings and felt Kennedy's hand on her shoulder, and turned.

"Just get everything you can in one pack. We can replace the other. No sense in you carrying two of them when you're going to have to help me as well." She leaned back against the wall, closing her eyes as another wave of dizziness washed over her. The rustling of nylon reached her ears, along with the snick of a zipper opening and closing a few times. She heard a muffled curse followed by a mumbled 'stupid, stupid, stupid,' and raised an eyebrow, waiting to see if any help was needed. Instead she heard a frustrated breath, followed by more rustling, then light footsteps as Carson approached, carrying her boots.

"Let me get these on you." Carson stooped down, helping Kennedy into her socks and the sturdy hiking boots. She tugged at the laces and rested her hand on a trembling left calf, feeling the tension in the leg. She looked up at a face contorted in pain. "Sorry." She finished up and stood. "Found these hidden in an inner pocket of your pack." She held out a bottle of perfectly-dry ibuprofen. "Didn't know there was another pocket in there, waterproof at that – guess I missed it last night. All that pain." She peered sorrowfully at Kennedy, observing a slight bit of light returning to her tired eyes.

"Forgot about them myself." Kennedy picked out four of the tablets, popping them in her mouth and swallowing them all at once with a long swig of the cool water. "Probably a good thing. Might've used them all up last night, and they're going to come in handy today, I think."

"Will you be okay to walk?" Carson frowned, safely pocketing the precious bottle of drugs in a zippered pocket of her shorts.

"Yeah. Got no choice." She reached out her right hand and watched Carson's slip into it, giving her a little tug until their bodies came into contact. They stood that way for a long moment, hugging each other as if for dear life, Kennedy's cheek resting against the top of Carson's head.

"Happy birthday," Carson whispered rather unhappily.

"Hey..." Kennedy's breath brushed across Carson's hair, warming her scalp. "You're here with me. That makes it happy in my book, any day."

"I had such a nice day planned..." a sad voice trailed off.

"Day's not over yet." Kennedy pushed resolutely away from the wall, resting her hand on Carson's shoulder. "Let me know if I put too much weight on you."

"Okay." Carson dug in her pocket and pulled out a trail bar, ripping it open with her teeth and breaking it in half, holding a piece up for Kennedy. She watched the tan face turn ashen for a moment. "Not settling well?"

"Nope. And I don't want the ibuprofen to come back up." They were moving downhill toward the river, and each step on her left leg was excruciating. She suspected the twisting sensation in her stomach had more to do with pain than illness. "Maybe in a little while I'll try again." She felt weak, her limbs rubbery as she lifted one foot at a time. The thought of hiking four miles in hope of finding a ranger and rescue was daunting. The thought that if they didn't find one they might have to walk all the way to Rio Grande Village was enough to make her cry if she thought about it too hard, so she didn't.

"You need to keep your strength up." Carson took a bite of the bar, glad for the tiny bits of chocolate chip mixed in with granola and raisins. It was something small to be thankful for, but she focused in on it, allowing the chocolaty taste to linger on her tongue before she swallowed.

"Throwing up would make me feel decidedly weaker than I already do, sweetheart." She draped her arm fully across Carson's shoulders, her hope fading as she realized there was no even terrain to be had for as far as she could see. "Don't worry," she said to herself as much as to Carson. "We'll be fine."

They walked on in silence, Kennedy due to physical misery and Carson's of a more emotional variety. The sun was already warm, beating down on them. The sweatshirt and flannel shirt were both shoved into the pack, leaving Kennedy in Carson's snug T-shirt, and Carson in the tattered remains of Kennedy's blood-stained and torn one. Her black sports bra peeked out where the shirt had been cut, and she could feel the sun warm on her skin. At least, she reflected, their sun screen was still intact, and she stopped once, spreading it over both of them, careful to avoid Kennedy's leg injury.

"How's the shoulder?" She capped the lotion and zipped it back into the daypack, then peered at Kennedy's back, spotting fresh bright red stains mixed with the dried brown ones on her shirt. "You're still bleeding, honey."

"Hurts, but at least I don't have to walk on it. I'll be fine." She thought about that as they continued to maneuver over rough loose shale and scrubby desert flora. It felt like a crater had been dug out of her shoulder. A sling might have been prudent, but just the thought of anything rubbing against the wound made her hurt. As long as she was certain nothing was broken, she preferred to keep the arm loose.

"Hey." Carson's voice caught her attention. "What's that?"

Something large floated by on the river a little way below them. Something large and dark green. "Stay put." Carson scrambled down the bank to the edge of the water, watching as the object went on past. "A raft! Empty!" She ran downstream a ways, but the water carried it too swiftly for her to keep up. After giving brief chase, she gave up and climbed back up to Kennedy's side. "Damn."

That about summed things up. Kennedy hugged her to her right side just a little before they moved on. "Wonder how it got away?" she ventured.

"'Cause I wasn't fast enough." The utter dejection was evident, earning her another side-hug.

"No, I mean from whoever had it upriver." She looked downstream, but the raft was already a dot on the water. "No way anyone could've caught that. Nice try, though."

"Maybe someone tied off last night and didn't do a good enough job of it." Carson finished off her half of the trail bar, stowing the other away in hope Kennedy would want it later. She drank from the water bottle and held it up for Kennedy to do the same.

Kennedy swallowed, still feeling dizzy and nauseous. "Probably so." She forced herself to keep moving, though the urge to simply lay down right there on the spot was almost overwhelming. Her leg continued to hurt with each step, and the sun was soaking through the T-shirt, making her wounds itch and throb at the same time. She glanced at her watch. It was 8:00 a.m. They'd probably traveled a quarter mile, and it had taken half an hour. She did some mental mathematics and sighed.

Four miles was going to take eight hours at that pace, assuming she didn't collapse first.

Chapter
Eight

THE PHONE RANG incessantly and Aileen let it go, her arms elbow-deep in dishwater. Crystal was a pain to clean, but two of their guests, a couple celebrating their anniversary, had requested the romance package for the weekend, which included mimosas, coffee, and heart-shaped muffins for breakfast, delivered to their room each morning. Along with the mimosas, Aileen always insisted on providing her fine crystal champagne flutes. She snorted. In actuality, the heart-shaped muffins were more difficult than cleaning crystal stemware. If she didn't pop them out of the muffin tin just right they often crumbled which was the reason she always made more than necessary. Besides, she and Joseph could always share the leftovers.

She cocked her head to the side, listening as the answering machine picked up, and a woman's West Texas drawl twanged in her ear. "Carson Garret? Hello?" The voice paused, then continued, "It's two o'clock and we expected you for check-in around noon. We'll of course hold the room until eight p.m., but since you requested the early arrival, we were just double-checking on your whereabouts. If you get this message, give us a call..."

The voice droned on, leaving a callback number. Aileen frowned. The number wasn't the one for the Gage Hotel, as she had that one memorized, often setting up dinner reservations for her guests. She couldn't place the number, other than the area code was local, and she wondered, with some amusement, what Carson had planned for her daughter's birthday and realized Carson had been forced to leave their phone number with whatever hotel was calling, given the sporadic cell service in the area. She shook her head, knowing full-well that keeping to a schedule on a backpacking trip was a crapshoot at best and wondered if the two girls were having fun and what might have held them up on the trail.

She liked Carson, and especially liked the effect she was

having on her often serious loner of a daughter. Shea hadn't been quite so much of a loner in high school, although Aileen had despaired of her ever finding friends that didn't constantly land her in hot water. It had taken a long time to figure out that, along with embarrassment at her heritage, her daughter had simply been bored as a teenager. The public schools of Brewster County had been sadly lacking in anything that remotely resembled intellectual challenge for someone of Shea's capabilities.

Her first clue should have been when she found her daughter sprawled in a corner of the upstairs den, pouring over an old set of encyclopedias at the tender age of four. Not just looking at the pictures, but reading, and doing a fairly credible job of it at that. She'd scrimped and saved and purchased a newer set of the books, ones that actually included the space exploration program and presidents beyond Harry Truman. She'd saved the set, wrapping it up and putting it under the Christmas tree the next year. When Shea opened it, all the other presents under the tree went forgotten for well over an hour as she flitted from book to book, looking at the pictures and casting adoring glances at her parents for such a treasure of a gift.

As time went by those adoring glances had been fewer and further between, and at times she had wistfully wished for the days when a five-year-old Shea could be won over with something as simple as an ice cream cone, or as complex as a set of books. *Ah, well*, she mused. After all was said and done, her daughter had turned out better than she'd ever hoped or dreamed. And at last it seemed that one missing puzzle piece had slipped into place as she observed Carson's steady and sure presence in Shea's life and the light in her daughter's eyes when she caught her watching Carson unaware.

There was love there, no doubt, on both sides and she fervently hoped this one would be a keeper. Wasn't it what every parent ultimately hoped for his or her children? The happiness that can only come from sharing your life with someone else? It didn't matter anymore that Carson didn't come in the package Aileen had dreamed of for her daughter for so long, and she chuckled at herself, realizing that gender hadn't even crossed her mind when she'd first scrutinized Shea's companion. For a long while she'd accepted the fact that if Shea ever brought someone home, it would be a girl. She'd gotten right past the exterior and looked inside the woman, seeing all the qualities she could hope for in a life partner for any of her children.

The phone rang again, and she released a frustrated breath as she finished rinsing the last glass and set it in the drain rack next to the sink. The answering machine picked up again and another female voice called out, this time for her daughter. "This is Keena Smothers. I'm the game warden down here at the Rio Grande Village ranger station. I'm looking for Miss Kennedy Shea Nocona. We found her 4Runner sitting down by La Clocha in the park, but near as we can tell no one camped here last night. We need to find her and ask her a few questions. We've got a big mess down here, so if someone could have her..."

Aileen dropped the dishrag and rushed to the phone, drying her hands on her apron as she ran. She grabbed the receiver, her hand shaking. "Hello? This is Kennedy's mother. What do you mean no one camped there?"

"Near as we can tell, no one did, ma'am. Two backpacks are in the back with sleeping bags still rolled up. Been that way since I made rounds at 7:00 a.m. this morning. No signs any fires were built or that any tents were pitched there, unless maybe they slept in the truck." The ranger took a breath, switching gears as she found herself talking to a human being after all. "We're just trying to find her."

"She and a friend are backpacking in the park." Aileen's heart skipped a beat. "Much as my daughter loves camping, only torrential rains would have driven her to sleep in the truck. You said there's a mess. What's going on? You need to find her for some reason other than your head count?"

"Weellll," Ranger Smothers drawled. "Yeah. Pretty much everything's gone to hell in a hand basket down here."

"What do you mean by that?" Aileen's knuckles turned white as she gripped the phone. "My daughter...I take it you haven't seen her anywhere down there? Just a minute..." She covered the phone with one hand. "Joseph!" Her voice bellowed in a tone that had brought her husband running on many occasions over the years. She heard his footsteps on the basement stairs and uncovered the phone.

"Ma'am, there's been a homicide in the park not far from her truck. I probably shouldn't say much more than that, but the victim was male, so it's not your daughter. We're just trying to find her to see if she saw or heard anything...tie up our loose ends...just routine stuff." She huffed and continued. "Damned pot-smoking hippie involved, most likely. Found a tiny bit of a joint near the body. Lab's already confirmed it."

Joseph reached Aileen's side, her worry obvious from across the room. "What's going on?"

"I'm talking with a park ranger. Shea and Carson are missing. They didn't sleep at their campsite last night." She turned her attention back to the ranger on the phone. "There's been a murder down there, too."

"What? Are they all right?" Joseph resisted the urge to take the phone from her. "Don't hang up. I want to talk to them when you're finished."

"They can't find them." She handed off the phone. "Here, you take it. I'm going to go change so we can drive down there."

Joseph took the phone and introduced himself, listening as the ranger repeated her story. "But there's no sign of my daughter at all?" he asked as she finished.

"Not yet." She hesitated. "Mr. Nocona, it doesn't make sense, unless she and her friend headed out hiking before sunup. We haven't found anyone else in the area at all, other than two hikers that came into Rio Grande Village station in the wee hours of the morning and called a friend to give them a ride out, but they said they'd come in the opposite direction of the crime scene. Looked like they'd been hiking all night, the numbskulls. Now I need to find them for questioning as well. Got my hands full down here."

"Called a friend? Were they local?" Joseph, unlike his more high-strung wife, had the presence of mind to take notes as they talked. "You get names?"

"Yeah, they were...let me see..." Joseph heard the rattle of shuffling paper and waited, tapping his pen impatiently against his notepad. "One of them was Richard Wolden. Yeah, definitely a local, because I've seen him around the park before. Let me flip through my notes and see if I got the other one."

The sound of rustling paper reached Joseph's ears, and at the same time his hackles rose. "Rick Wolden? Listen. My daughter... She was planning to turn him into the sheriff after her backpacking trip. She'll have a fit for me jumping the gun, but she thinks he and a friend of his drugged her drink out at Armadillo Flats earlier this week. You found the other one?"

"Yep. Guy named Peta..." She trailed off and there was deadly silence on the other end of the line. "Say, his last name is Nocona, too. He related to you? A buddy picked them up, but I didn't get his name."

Something pricked at the back of Joseph's mind. It was an uneasy feeling he'd come to associate with his gut instinct, something that rarely failed him. "He's my son." He sighed wearily. "Don't you worry, ma'am. I'll be hauling him in to talk to you just as soon as I find him."

"Thank you, sir. It's all just routine," she responded gravely. "You and your wife coming down here?"

"We're leaving right now." He spotted Aileen coming down the stairs in her jeans and hiking boots. "Be there soon as we can."

"All right sir, I'll be here."

Joseph heard the click as she hung up and he turned to face his wife, debating telling her about Rick and Pete's presence in the park. "Have you heard from Pete today? I thought he headed back to Austin."

"No." Aileen's brows rose at the seeming randomness of the question. "Why?"

"Honey." Joseph held the door for her as they went out to their own truck. "He and Rick Wolden were down in the park last night near the same area as Shea's truck."

Aileen's face grew pale. "You think they were up to something? Surely you don't think he...?"

"No, but it's a little too strange to my liking. Let's get down there. Maybe by the time we get there, Shea and Carson will have turned up."

"Hey, where are y'all going?" Parker emerged from the stables with a basket of eggs in hand.

"Down to the park. Shea and Carson are missing." Joseph squeezed Aileen's hand, and then closed the truck door.

"What!" Parker trotted toward the truck, leaving the eggs on the porch as he passed it. "Let me in, I'm going with you."

"No." Joseph clasped his shoulder. "I need you to go find your brother. I don't think he's left for Austin yet."

"Huh?" Their eyes met and locked. "Oh."

"Son, be careful." Joseph went around to his own side, climbing in and starting the engine. "There's been a murder down there. A man was killed. I'm not sure I know my youngest son anymore."

"You be careful too, Pa." Parker backed away, giving him room to pull out. In short order Joseph was breaking the speed limit, headed south for the park.

THE SUN SHONE down from directly overhead, casting unseasonably warm rays on the desert valley below. Two exhausted sweaty figures sat in the shade of the canyon wall, listening to the water rush by below. They had made slow progress, but the woods were growing closer.

"Honey, try to eat some of this trail bar, if you can." Carson held up half of her lunch, watching as two tired eyes opened and peered at her mournfully. Kennedy was in so much pain it made Carson hurt watching her.

"Be a waste. Just gonna come back up." Kennedy shifted and winced silently, looking down at her leg. The bandage was spotted with fresh blood, and from the pain in her shoulder, she suspected it was in similar condition. "Check my shoulder, will ya? See what's going on."

"You hurting? I mean any worse than you were?" She stood on her knees, sliding around as Kennedy presented her back to her. "Oh."

"Oh, what?" She felt the shirt being lifted and gasped as the cotton tugged at her wound. "Ouch. Careful. I think..."

There was a large bloody spot directly over the wound, and Carson carefully got the shirt the rest of the way up and saw fresh seepage. The entire shoulder blade was swollen and an angry red color. "Heat's probably bad for it."

"Walking two miles over rough terrain's probably bad for it too." The shirt slid back down, sticking to her sweaty back. "My head hurts so bad it feels like it's going to explode."

"Need more ibuprofen?" Carson unzipped her shorts pocket and pulled out the precious bottle of painkillers. "Been four hours."

"Yeah." Kennedy sat back and gratefully accepted the handful of gel caps, as Carson held the water bottle to her lips. She sucked at it slowly, wondering if pills and water would both stay down. After she swallowed she remained still, resting back against the rock on her right side, waiting for her insides to start doing the tango. Her stomach only fluttered a little, then settled down. "Carson, maybe you should go on without me. You could cover the last two miles a lot faster, maybe get the truck and drive it back to this side of the trees and I could get across the river to it somehow, or if there's rangers nearby, you can bring back help."

"And if those guys are around and start shooting at you? Then what?"

"I'll duck." Kennedy laughed quietly. "Sweetheart, I can find a place to hide for a while. Just get me a bottle of water and leave the drugs, and I'll be fine."

"I'm scared to leave you." Carson knew it was the right thing to do, logically, but nightmares of finding Kennedy dead upon return tugged at her. She looked at Kennedy's face. It was tense with pain, even her jaw was clenched, and her entire body was unnaturally stiff. "God, you're hurting so much, it makes me hurt, too."

"Then go. Please. I honestly don't think I can go on. My vision's gone blurry from the headache. It might be a migraine setting in. And the more I walk the more I'm going to bleed, and I don't have much blood to spare." She took Carson's hand and brought it to her lips. "Go on, Wonder Woman, and finish saving my life."

"I..." Carson's jaw clamped shut. She managed a smile, patting Kennedy's cheek as she released her hand. "Just returning a favor. Here..." She picked up the water bottle. "Let me get you a refill so you'll have a full supply. You need to keep drinking as much as you can."

"I know." She watched as Carson got up and picked her way down to the embankment. Soon she was out of sight, having scrambled down a short drop off to the water's edge. Kennedy closed her eyes again. Feeling dizzy sitting down was a bad sign. Being thirsty despite drinking water was, too. Despite the heat she was chilled and suspected her fever had risen. For a fleeting moment she contemplated her own death, and just as quickly shoved it aside. She had way too much to live for. "Get the water and hurry for help, sweetheart."

Carson stepped gingerly along the water's edge, searching for a spot she could kneel in without falling in. The space between the higher embankment and the water was fairly narrow, steep, and uneven, and she wasn't sure how quickly it got deep. She pushed back some shrubbery and stepped through it, finding a likely place to get the water, when a bit of unnatural color caught her eye.

She looked up and spotted a patch of dark green peeking through some dead brown brush that hung out over the river. The water washed by and the green bobbed up and down and shifted, and she could just make out their runaway raft from earlier, caught there by some miracle. "Whoa!" She tossed the water bottle aside and took off, oblivious to rocks and cactus, reaching a point where she had no choice but to wade in.

The current was swift, but as she tested her footing, the water was only calf-deep. She trudged through the water, making one careful step at a time so as not to fall, praying she didn't stir the water any more and dislodge her treasure. She came to the brush and reached through, grabbing some rope that was looped around a branch, holding the raft in place. She worked her way around to the other side and found herself in waist-deep current that threatened to knock her off her feet.

"Dammit!" She painstakingly got the raft loose and examined it. It was old and patched in a few places, but hadn't taken in any water, and there was even one paddle lying in the bottom. "I hope I have a few more miracles left today." She looked skyward for a moment, then began tugging it upstream, making her movement even more difficult. As she reached the spot where she had tossed the water bottle, she tripped over something under the water and fell to her hands and knees, her chin just above the surface, but the rope was still in her hand.

She got up and pulled the raft onto the bank, tying it securely to the shrub she'd so recently plowed through. A warm trickling sensation made her leg itch, and she looked down. Both knees were bleeding from whatever she'd hit on the river bottom. "I am *not* pouring tequila on those," she mumbled as she climbed back up the embankment.

Kennedy heard her approach and opened one eye. "What happened?" The other eye popped open. "You get in a fight with a fish?"

"No. I found us a way out of here if we can get you down that bank. Come on." She knelt down, getting an arm around Kennedy and helping her to her feet.

"Where's the water?" The world spun and Kennedy grabbed Carson's shoulder hard with her right hand.

"Plenty of it in the river. I'll filter some and refill both bottles after we get down there." She felt Kennedy practically slumped against her and stopped, patting her stomach lightly. "Honey, give me all you've got here and then you'll be able to rest for the rest of the way. I found that raft down there."

"Really?" Carson's voice sounded far away, as if they were speaking through tin cans and string. Kennedy's brain was fuzzy and everything looked spotted as her head continued to pound. Her field of vision had narrowed, a sure sign she was suffering a migraine on top of everything else. She hadn't packed her migraine meds, as she hadn't had one in a few months.

As they reached the embankment, Carson helped her ease down on her behind. "What's the best way for you to do this?" Carson sat down next to her, holding her hand.

"Roll over and slide down on my stomach. If I do it facing forward I might scrape my shoulder, and I think that might kill me right now." She rolled to her side. "If you can get down there and kind of catch me, break my fall..."

"Sure." Carson jumped down and held her breath as Kennedy slid down, bits of red and brown dirt coming loose and crumbling beneath her. She was almost as tall as the bank, and landed on her feet, wobbling slightly until Carson steadied her, then got her seated while she re-filled the water bottles, watching as the cool liquid filtered through the purification system. "Okay." She stood and placed the bottles in the compartments in the pack designed for that purpose. "Your cruise ship awaits, my lady."

Kennedy chuckled a little and stood, hobbling over near the water's edge, while Carson got the raft into the water, leaving the rope tied to the shrub just in case. Kennedy got to the raft and more or less fell in gracelessly, although she managed to land on her right side. "Oof." She simply lay back for a moment, feeling the coolness of the water through the raft bottom. It made her chills worse, but it felt good against the wound on her shoulder.

"We're off!" Carson untied the rope and hopped in, picking up the paddle and steering them toward the center of the river. "Will I know where to pull in to the other side?" There was no answer and she turned. "Kennedy?"

"I'm here. Just feeling a little queasy. Have to keep my eyes closed because if I look up at the sky it makes it worse. When we get past the woods tap me on the foot and I'll sit up and help you find the pull in at Rio Grande Village." She folded her hands over her stomach, hoping she might nap for what would probably be a relatively short trip.

"Okay. You just rest and leave the driving to me." The motion felt good after their slow progress and the breeze created from moving along the cool river was heavenly against her parched, sunburned skin. As they passed the brush where the raft had been tangled, she could swear she saw a bit of a white blur that lingered for a moment, then vanished into nothing.

THE WATER WAS rough out in the middle and hadn't gone down much, leading Carson to believe there had been more rain up river. Ahead of her the woods grew slowly but steadily closer, while high, rocky desert cliffs quickly faded behind her. She had to continually switch sides with the one paddle, pulling hard to keep the raft from hurling back to shore. It was a good size, long enough for Kennedy to stretch completely out with a few feet to spare at each end. Unfortunately it was wide enough that she had to lean and reach, stretching from side to side with her entire body, each time she switched sides with the paddle.

It was hard work, and she barely had time to look back to see how Kennedy was faring. She felt a hand curl around her thigh and spared a glance at her lover. Her features had softened just a little, and she appeared to be sleeping. It was a relief, whether it was induced by excess ibuprofen or sheer exhaustion. Kennedy had been in so much pain by the time they got into the raft.

Carson still felt residual anxiety at how close she'd come to having to leave her behind. It was entirely possible there were still dangerous people out there, presumably after them. She decided it was fortuitous they had ended up on the Mexican side of the river for a while. Perhaps the men shooting at them had given up and left. She kept watching the shoreline, especially on the Texas side of the river, looking for any sign of humanity, either friend or foe.

Alone with her thoughts, the anger had time to simmer and boil to the surface. Someone had shot Kennedy. Luckily they were either a bad aim or had not intended to kill her. She shuddered and felt dizzy for a moment, as she fought back a wave of pure terror. They still weren't out of danger. Kennedy's condition was still very fragile and exposure to the sun wasn't making it better.

She wanted to kill the shooter. She couldn't remember ever wanting to kill anyone before until that weekend, not even Nick Giovani, the man who had drugged and kidnapped her only a few months before. Tom drugging Kennedy's drink and someone shooting at her, that was different. They had almost taken away something very precious, when she'd only just found it.

Love, Carson had learned, was hard to find and even more difficult to keep. Compatible as they were, she and Kennedy had learned that being in love was easy, but maintaining a relationship was a lot of work. The reward was well worth the effort, as she gradually found herself slipping into a place that was invigorating and comforting all at the same time. She awoke each morning feeling wondrously alive like she never had before and slept each night in a bed of infinite peace. Being in Kennedy's arms could set her senses on fire, or calm them beyond measure.

It was a gift she didn't intend to give up anytime soon.

As they neared the woods her back and arms were starting to ache with the effort of fighting the river, and she was glad of the swift current. They reached the tree line, and she began studying the shore in earnest for a good place to pull in.

"Should we pull in at La Clocha and go to the truck?" She touched Kennedy's foot lightly, wishing she didn't have to wake her.

"No." Kennedy gasped. "We need to go on to Rio Grande Village." She gripped the side of the raft for stability as her head spun for a moment. "How many ibuprofens did I take a while ago?"

"Four, I think. Maybe five. And four earlier this morning." Carson frowned, trying to watch the river ahead of them and Kennedy behind her at the same time. "Honey, you probably shouldn't take any more for a while."

"I know." Kennedy winced as she tried to lay with no pressure on her shoulder. "We should be coming up on La Clocha pretty quick here, fast as we're moving."

Carson studied the shoreline. "I think I see some color

through the trees, maybe a vehicle. Tough to tell."

"Good. The village isn't that much farther and there's a ranger station there. Probably gonna need to get a helicopter in." She lay back down, dizzy from the swift rocking motion of the river.

"Helicopter? Why...oh. Of course." It was over fifty miles to the nearest hospital in Alpine. A helicopter would be much faster than sending an ambulance a hundred miles round trip. "They'd better take me with you." She gulped at a lump that formed in her throat.

"They will." Kennedy reached out, touching her leg. "Gonna need you." She managed a small smile. "May need you to help me remember my own damned name and address for the paper work. Least I've got my insurance card in the pack."

Carson lifted the paddle long enough to make sure the pack was indeed within reach. She frowned as she spotted a compartment next to her. It was some sort of pocket in the side of the raft that was snapped closed. Curiously, she unsnapped it, careful to keep one eye on the water at the same time. She reached in and drew out a bundle of plastic garbage bag material wrapped in several rounds of twine. It was heavy and beneath the thin plastic surface was an odd rough texture. Unable to deal with it, she set it aside to inspect once they came ashore.

They cleared the trees and reached more open countryside again. She sighed with relief. The village was close, according to the map, if she was remembering correctly. She looked back at Kennedy, who was lying very still, save the soft rise and fall of her chest as she breathed. Her right arm was slung across her eyes, but even so, her face was a study in pain. "Migraine?" she asked quietly.

"Oh, yeah," a raspy voice answered.

"I'm so sorry, honey." She paddled harder. "I imagine this will go down as the suckiest birthday ever."

"No." Kennedy shifted, uncovering her face for a moment and touching Carson's leg again. "It's the best one. I got the best gift I could ever want this year." Her thumb brushed across the soft skin of Carson's calf before she closed her eyes again, this time with a full smile gracing her lips. "The very best."

Carson sniffled as her vision cleared and she felt dampness on her cheeks. "Yeah," she whispered softly. "Me too."

AILEEN PACED BACK and forth near the 4Runner, waiting while Ranger Smothers dealt with the investigation team. Inside the truck were both backpacks and a cooler with food inside, including a bottle of champagne. "Hope they get to have their celebration." She closed the cooler lid and crossed her arms over her chest, looking lost.

She walked over to Joseph, who was leaning against a tree nearby surveying the chaos. They watched as a body bag was toted down the trail from them and loaded into the back of the county coroner's SUV, which drove away. "Come here," Joseph beckoned to Aileen, holding out his arm.

She buried herself in his embrace, pressing her face against the clean sun-scented cotton of his work shirt. "I swore I wasn't going to cry unless there was something to cry about." She sniffled and felt a handkerchief pressed into her hand. "Thank you. You always were prepared."

Joseph kissed her forehead and hugged her close. "They're going to be fine."

"You're certain?" She blew her nose and stuffed the handkerchief in her jeans pocket.

"I am." He stroked her head, watching as Smothers approached them. "Our daughter knows how to survive in the outdoors."

"But that man was shot. What if the killer is still in the park?" Aileen fretted.

"Ma'am. Sir." Smothers reached them, pushing her wide-brimmed hat back so she could see them better. "We've got some search parties organized and headed this way from the main park headquarters, and there's a helicopter on its way from Fort Stockton to do an aerial search. With the murder, things have gotten a bit confusing. Any footprints they might have made aren't around anymore. We did find a set of fresh tire tracks near the victim's tent, but we lost them a ways up on the back road. Common truck tire tread. It'll be tough to determine what vehicle they came from, although we did cast a plaster of them."

"Thank you." Joseph nodded at her. "I know you're doing your best. If I know my daughter, they probably hiked up river through the woods. Shea likes trees, if that will help your search any."

"It will. I..." Her government-issue two-way radio went off, and static buzzed for a moment before she picked it up. "Hold on." She gestured at Aileen and Joseph. "Come again?" She made an adjustment to a couple of knobs. "This is Keena. I didn't hear you the first time."

"I said we have a couple of dead bodies here. Female. They..." More static crackled across the air waves, cutting off whatever was being said.

"Damn," Smothers muttered, glancing at Aileen and Joseph,

wishing they hadn't heard. "I'm just going to move over there and take this. I'll be..."

"No. Stay." Joseph held out a hand. "I'd like to hear, if you don't mind."

"All right." She could see the tension in his face and watched as Aileen buried hers in his shirt once again, her shoulder shaking as she cried silently. She held the radio out a bit and moved the knobs around again. "Don't move," she barked into the device. "I can't hear you very well. We have a bad connection. Now. Start from the beginning. Who are you, where are you, and please describe the victims."

"This is Phil Ozborne," a voice sputtered across the airwaves. "I've got two female bodies here. Found them behind a rock covered by branches. I'm a little ways off the Mariscal Canyon Trail, near Talley campground."

"Too far to be them." Joseph continued to stroke Aileen's head. "They couldn't have hiked that far from here." Privately, he acknowledged if they'd hiked all night it was possible, but there was no sense in worrying her any more than she already was.

"Describe them." Smothers' voice conveyed barely contained patience.

"Both look to be in their late-twenties to early thirties, one's tall, and one's short...probably a little over five feet, while the taller one is close to six. One's got long hair and one short..."

Aileen gasped and looked up, covering her mouth in horror. "No," she whispered fiercely. Joseph merely held her tighter, his own features gone pale.

"Let's see," Ozborne continued. "Both Hispanic, black hair and dark brown eyes, the both of them."

Aileen's knees buckled as blood rushed from her head. "Thank God." She almost collapsed, sitting down quickly on the hard-packed ground, taking Joseph with her. "Thank God," she repeated and sobbed anew, this time with tears of joy streaming down her face. "I'm sorry for their families," she sniffled, "but I can't help myself." She struggled for composure. "It's not them."

Smothers breathed a sigh of relief. "Any apparent cause of death?"

"It's the strangest thing," Ozborne sputtered, static starting to build again. "Their skin is kind of grayish and they're white around the mouths. One of them looks like she's vomited on herself. But no obvious wounds or anything like that. I would've thought maybe rattler bite, but there's no fang marks anywhere I can see."

"All right." Smothers pulled out a notepad from her hip

pocket, jotting down a few items while she talked. "Bag 'em as soon as you can and get 'em to the coroner's office. I swear that man will earn his keep today."

"Roger that." Ozborne's voice came through clear. "Over and out."

"Phil." Smothers' voice grew soft. "You be careful out there. We've got a killer on the loose."

"Will do, ma'am." The radio went silent and Smothers clipped it back on her belt. "Sorry about that." She knelt down next to Aileen, touching her on the knee. "Do you need some water or something? Maybe we should go on down to the station at Rio Grande Village. It's air conditioned and you'd have a comfortable place to sit."

"I'd like to help the search teams," Joseph started emphatically. "I know my daughter better than almost anyone."

"Sir, we really advise against that." She gentled her voice. "That close to the situation, folks tend to make careless mistakes and get themselves hurt or lost. Besides, when we find them, they'll probably need you and you wouldn't want to be out on the trail somewhere where you might not be able to get to them quickly."

"We'll see." He helped Aileen up. "But maybe we could go down there and freshen up a bit and grab some sandwiches before we decide. How does that sound, sweetheart?"

"I'm not hungry," Aileen answered weakly. Her equilibrium was slowly returning and she still felt a little light-headed.

Joseph supported her as they made their way to their truck. They were soon tooling along the rough backcountry road, with Smothers following behind in a beat-up jeep. Overhead the sun continued to beat down, parching the land in unseasonable warmth.

THE RAFT BOBBED and rocked as Carson guided it around some floating debris and branches in the water. She was exhausted, and her heart continually jumped into her throat, almost as if she could feel the two men from the day before watching her. They were well past the wooded area, so she knew logically that was impossible. Still, she kept hunching her shoulders, a part of her expecting to hear gunshot. She suspected that sound would stay with her for a long time to come. Remembering her dream from the night before, she shivered.

"I think we're getting closer." Carson looked behind her briefly. Kennedy was still stretched out with her eyes closed. A sheen of sweat dotted her forehead and she was shaking just a little, a slight tremor evident in her hands. "Honey, hold on for me." Carson shoved the paddle hard into the water, doubling her effort, willing them to move even faster. She looked down at Kennedy's bandaged leg, noting a fresh seepage of blood there. The bandage was fast becoming soaked again. "Damn." She bit her lower lip and snorted a soft breath through her nose.

"I'm holding," a weak voice finally responded. "Just feeling kinda dizzy. Not that I wasn't feeling dizzy before."

Carson's ears perked up as she heard a rumbling, vibrating noise and looked up to spot a helicopter overhead. "Oh," she gasped quietly. "I hope our shooters aren't flyers as well." She decided to take a gamble and held up her oar for a moment, waving it wildly back and forth over her head.

The copter dipped lower until she could see a man sitting in the open side door waving back at her. She waved back before dropping the oar back into the water. The chopper drew even closer, a little to the side and overhead. "Ma'am, follow us and we'll guide you toward the landing at the Village up ahead," a loudspeaker blared, shattering their relative peace. Carson lifted her oar once more in acknowledgement as the chopper sped ahead and stayed just a little bit in front and above them.

After a few minutes it began to veer left and Carson followed, her arms screaming with her efforts. The current was rough and very swift, and just when she thought she wouldn't make it, the chopper dropped a line into the raft, its end looped through a clamp hook. She grabbed it and hooked it through a loop at the front of the raft and sat back, breathing hard as they were towed the last several yards toward the landing. The chopper pulled them in, then set down on the ground a little ways away.

Carson got up on her knees and grabbed at a dock, looping the rope around a post and tying it securely. "Help is on the way." She touched Kennedy's face for a second before she scrambled out of the raft and onto the dock, her legs so rubbery she wasn't certain she could walk. Two medics leaped from the helicopter and ran toward her, meeting her halfway. "My partner." She gestured toward the raft. "She's been shot in the shoulder and leg. Lost a lot of blood. We need a hospital, quick."

"How about you?" One medic stopped, giving her a brief visual once-over, while the other continued on toward the raft. "Looks like you've been hurt." He noted the blood on her shirt.

"I'm fine. Not my blood here. Just take care of her, please. She's hurt pretty bad, I think." She hovered behind the medics, anxiously watching as they lifted Kennedy from the raft and got her onto the dock. Carson knelt on the opposite side from the medics, holding Kennedy's hand, as one of the medics got her situated on a stretcher. As they stood and began carrying her up to the helicopter, two familiar figures came racing out of the ranger station, and Carson headed for them, practically bowling Aileen over as she caught up to her and engulfed her in a hug. "I've never been so glad to see anyone in my life," she gasped, and looked up. "She's been shot. Two men, I think. We spent the night in a cave. I...did the best I could."

"I'm sure you did." Joseph patted her cheek, feeling Carson's anguish. "She'll be fine. She has a lot to live for." He gently moved past her to where the two medics were transporting his daughter. She appeared to be quite limp and he frowned. He quickened his pace and reached her just as they approached the helicopter.

"Pa?" Kennedy smiled weakly for him. She'd felt every jolt during the short trip from the dock and wondered if it would be too much to ask them to knock her out for the flight.

"Right here, my cha-nawoonit ecka-peta." He grasped her hand, noting the bandage around her leg. "What happened?"

"Got in the way of a couple of bullets." She winced as she rolled toward him a bit.

"A couple?" He reached out, touching her forehead and taking Aileen's hand as she caught up to them.

"My baby." Aileen also touched her head, smoothing back tangled hair and trying not to cry in her daughter's presence. "What happened?"

"I'm a little fuzzy right now, Mama, but I have a bullet in my shoulder and one grazed my leg." She swallowed down a wave of nausea, growing dizzy again. "Carson took good care of me though."

"I have no doubt." Joseph had a lot of questions, including asking if her brother was involved, but they would have to wait. Kennedy's face was ashen, her voice weak and hoarse. He hadn't missed the tattered and blood-stained T-shirt Carson was wearing, one that was too big to be hers. "You're going to be just fine." He smiled reassuringly.

"Yeah." Kennedy managed to smile back. "After rodeo, skateboarding, and hell-raising in high school, what's a few bullets, huh?"

Joseph chuckled and Aileen smiled and then choked up, as the tears finally escaped. Joseph hugged her against his side, still holding Kennedy's hand.

"I'll be fine, Mama." Kennedy smiled again, and then grimaced as they strapped her into the helicopter, jostling her shoulder in the process. "I'll be eating birthday cake and ice cream by dinner time."

"Frozen yogurt and carob cake," Aileen's voice cracked. "I know how you are."

"See," Kennedy crooned. "Now I have to be well by dinner."

They finished getting her settled while Joseph and Aileen continued to talk softly with her. Carson had stood quietly to the side, but as the medics moved aside to prepare for the flight, she scrambled in behind Kennedy. The medic frowned. "Ma'am, you need to leave now. Only a close family member is allowed to ride with her to the hospital, and we don't have room for all of you, only one."

"Oh." Carson looked down, her voice going soft. "But I promised her I'd go with her." She looked up and spotted Joseph's sympathetic face, followed by Aileen's.

"She is my daughter's next of kin." Joseph reached in and grabbed her hand, squeezing it. "You take her with you. My wife and I will be along as quickly as we can."

"You take good care of my baby." Aileen leaned in, hugging Carson again. She leaned in again herself, just long enough to touch her daughter's arm. "Baby, we'll be at the hospital as fast as we can."

"I'll probably be all better by the time you get there," Kennedy croaked.

"But, sir." The medic studied Carson, whose pale features stood out in stark contrast to their patient's. "I really think you or your wife—"

"Either she goes or I don't," Kennedy piped up. "Now let's get moving while I still have blood left inside my body."

"All right." The medic waited for Joseph and Aileen to step back, then closed the door with a solid slam. The chopper lifted off and the park quickly fell away behind them as they sped toward Alpine.

THE WAITING ROOM was relatively quiet, a relief to Carson's ears after the constant thrum of the helicopter blades during the flight to the hospital. She sat in a corner with a clipboard propped against her knee, meticulously copying down Kennedy's insurance and other information on the emergency room admission sheet. Kennedy, of course, had insisted she could fill out her own paperwork, even as they were wheeling her into the emergency room.

Carson snorted softly and shook her head. "Stubborn..." She looked up as a nurse approached her with a second clipboard.

"Ma'am, when you finish that one for your friend, we need

you to fill this one out so we can get you admitted too." She smiled and set the board down in the chair next to Carson, placing another pen with it, just in case.

"But I don't need admitting." Carson picked the board up and held it out.

"Medic insisted when they brought you in. Said you've been lost out in the park and they just pulled both of you from the river an hour ago." She gently but firmly gave the board a little push back in Carson's direction.

"No, really." Carson gritted her teeth in a fake smile. "I'm fine."

"Ma'am, I'm just following orders, and after all you've been through..."

"Look." Carson set Kennedy's info aside and scooted forward in the chair, pulling the edges of her shorts legs up a little bit. "We were only out there for a day and a night, and I stayed well hydrated the entire time. Even had a full bottle of sunscreen. I'm not the one who got shot. I'm hungry and I've got two skinned knees." She indicated her legs. "If I can get a cheeseburger and a couple of Band-Aids, I'll be fine. What I need..." She blew a puff of air upward in frustration, riffling her bangs. "What I need is to go be with Kennedy. I know she's hurting. If I can just be with her..."

"The medics said her parents are on their way. I'm sure one of them can sit with her while we take a look at you." She wasn't smiling this time, her brown eyes gazing steadily at Carson in a stubborn standoff.

Carson stood, placing her hands on her hips. "I am not going to just sit in here while my partner is in there alone and maybe scared. She's been shot, for crying out loud! If I need to talk to those medics, tell me where to find them..." She glanced at the woman's name badge. "...Myra. It'll take her parents close to an hour to get here anyway. Please."

Myra sighed in defeat. "Hold on." She disappeared, and Carson hastily finished filling out Kennedy's information. She sat forward, her weight partially braced on her hands on each side of her body, her entire stance one of intensely stressed unhappiness. After a long few minutes, Myra reappeared with a blood pressure cuff and a stethoscope.

"They already did that to me once in the helicopter." Carson crossed her arms and sat back.

"Humor me, and after that I'll take you to see your...partner." Myra stood rooted in place waiting for her decision.

Had she used that term? Carson ran their conversation

through her mind again. She had. Hmm. "Okay." She looked up meekly and held out her arm. She hated blood pressure cuffs almost as much as she hated needles. It was over quickly enough and she relaxed, waiting quietly while Myra made some notes on her otherwise blank chart.

"Hang on another minute." The nurse fished two large Band-Aids out of her pocket along with a sterile alcohol pad packet, which she ripped open as she knelt down. She made quick work of Carson's knees, watching as Carson flinched slightly when the alcohol stung her tender skin. After an application of antiseptic cream, followed by the bandages, Myra gave her a little pat on her calf and stood. "Come on. Your blood pressure is on the low side of normal, and you're too darned feisty to be in too bad of shape. But this is a rain check. Once your partner is settled into a room, it's your turn, got me?"

Carson started to protest, but her jaws snapped close with a click as the nurse shook a warning finger at her. "Oh, okay." She stood and followed her out of the waiting room into the hallway. A security guard approached them and held out a white paper bag.

"This what you ordered?" He handed the bag to Myra, who promptly handed it to Carson.

"Ask her." She nodded in Carson's direction.

Carson frowned and took the bag, which bore a bright Sonic logo. She peeked inside to find a..."Cheeseburger. And curly fries." She dug further. "And a vanilla shake." She felt embarrassed at her earlier outburst. "Thank you. How much do I owe?" She started to fish out her wallet, only to feel Myra's hand on her arm.

"It'll be on your bill." She gave Carson's sleeve a tug. "Come on. I think I can find you a clean pair of scrubs to replace that shirt. I know the ripped look is in nowadays, but I don't think that's exactly what the fashion magazines have in mind."

In short order Carson was standing dressed in pale blue scrubs, with her nose pressed to the glass window of the emergency room. She sucked anxiously at the straw in the thick shake, in between bites of the tasteless cheeseburger. She was starving, but felt a little guilty, given that Kennedy was currently lying stomach down while three unidentified medical personnel hovered over her. Carson fervently hoped the one poking at Kennedy's shoulder with an evil-looking metal instrument was a doctor.

She winced in sympathy as she noticed that while Kennedy lay almost perfectly still, one nervous big toe was working away, wiggling in what she assumed was pain. "Hold on, honey," she whispered, fogging the glass. "Well, that was stupid." She reached up, clearing the space so she could see again. She finished half the burger and began tackling the fries, when Nurse Myra wandered by, depositing a bottle of Gatorade on the floor at her feet.

"When you finish the fries, finish that, please." She forced a frown, trying to mask the smile that twitched at her lips. "I figured you for the blue frost flavor, was I right?"

"Yeah." Carson nudged the bottle with the toe of her hiking boot. "I'm a bit partial to blue. Thanks."

"Uh-huh." The nurse shook her head in bemusement and moved on.

Carson turned her attention back to the window and the patient on the other side, noting they appeared to be sewing her shoulder up. "Hope they numbed that up for you." She thought about that and decided the wiggling toe might also mean anxiety, rather than pain. The woman sewing up the shoulder moved down to her leg, while another woman moved in and appeared to be placing a large padded bandage over the shoulder wound.

All three medical types moved in and flipped Kennedy. One of them started an IV while the one at her leg worked on the other wound. Finally, after an eternity, the woman who seemed to be in charge came out into the hallway just as Kennedy's parents came rushing around the corner from the direction of the entrance.

"How is she?" Joseph led Aileen by the hand.

The doctor looked from Carson to Kennedy's parents and back, tugging her gloves off as she began to speak. "I'm Dr. Natasha Williams." She shook hands with all three of them in turn. "She has just a touch of infection in the shoulder wound, but a round of antibiotics should take care of that. Her main problem is dehydration and weakness from blood loss, although she didn't need a transfusion. We removed the bullet with no complications and started an IV to get some fluids in her. She can go ahead and eat pretty much whatever she wants to."

"Thank goodness." Some color returned to Aileen's worried features and she hugged Joseph in reflex.

"I'm going to check her into a regular room, and if she behaves, she might get out as early as this evening, tomorrow morning at the latest." The doctor gazed squarely at Carson. "I understand we need to give you the once-over next."

"You go ahead and check me into the same room." Carson felt suddenly compliant. "Then you can examine me. Deal?"

"Deal." Dr. Williams moved on to talk to Aileen and Joseph,

as a smirking Nurse Myra magically appeared just as Kennedy was wheeled out of the room on a rolling stretcher.

"Mama. Pa?" She saw her parents first, then grinned broadly as a very familiar face peered at her from close range. "Sweetheart." The toe was still wiggling away under the light sheet that covered her, and she smiled sheepishly as Carson gave it a tug.

"Toe's liable to fall off if you don't stop." She leaned over and brushed her lips across Kennedy's forehead, oblivious to any onlookers. "Come on. I'm going to be your roommate for a while."

"How's my baby girl?" Aileen stood over her on the other side with Joseph peering over her shoulder.

"Gonna be just fine, Mama. I'm feeling pretty good right now." Her eyes were slightly glazed and her voice was giddy, and Aileen laughed knowingly.

"And you're on some heavy-duty painkillers." She reached out, stroking her daughter's head, arranging her errant bangs.

"That would be correct." Dr. Williams made a quick adjustment to the IV line and stepped back. "Get them settled and I'll be by in a little while."

"Thank you." Joseph shook her hand again, and then they all followed Myra and Kennedy's rolling transport toward a set of double doors leading to the small hospital's only wing of rooms.

THE ROOM WAS mostly quiet, save the light hum of the monitoring equipment Kennedy was hooked up to, and the soft luffing sound of the curtains that hung over the air conditioning vent, which was just under the window. Carson sat propped up in the bed nearer the window, idly watching the day go by outside. It was clear and sunny, and would have been perfect weather for hiking. She sighed heavily and glanced back over at Kennedy, who was fast asleep.

Kennedy's face was relaxed, and her chest rose and fell almost imperceptibly as she breathed. An oxygen line ran to her nostrils, and they had loosely tied down the arm the IV was hooked into to prevent her pulling it loose in her sleep. Her free arm lay next to her body on top of the sheet, her palm up and open toward the ceiling. In addition to a narcotic painkiller, they'd also given her a sleep aid, mixed in with the fluids in the IV bag.

Carson swung her legs over the side of the bed, padding across the floor in her sock-covered feet, stopping as she placed both hands on the edge of Kennedy's bed. She'd endured her own round of poking and prodding and had been declared well, but in need of rest. She'd gotten a bath and had already napped for two hours, having assured Kennedy's parents they would be fine left alone for a while. They had acquiesced and gone home to check on Parker's progress locating Pete.

She looked up at the IV bag and snorted softly. Kennedy kept her system so pure; she could only imagine the happy dance her lover's corpuscles must be doing. "They could've given you a couple of Advil and gotten the same result," she whispered. She reached out, touching Kennedy's open palm with her fingertips. The large tan hand automatically closed around them, and a little smile tugged at Kennedy's lips as she continued to sleep. "That's it. You have some sweet dreams, honey."

Kennedy's hand twitched again, holding onto Carson even more firmly. She murmured a little and continued to smile as she drew Carson's hand up to her chest. "You awake?" Carson held her breath, but got no response. "Didn't think so." She smiled herself, feeling Kennedy's strong heartbeat against her hand. Her eyes blurred, and clear, salty tears trailed down her cheeks. "You scared the hell out of me, you know? I was so afraid when you started talking about dying last night."

She swallowed. "I...I didn't think you really meant it. You're too much of a fighter, but it scared me anyway. I knew you must've been in a lot of pain to talk like that. And that was so frustrating because I couldn't make it better. I felt so helpless." She sniffled. "I...I couldn't do much of anything."

"Are you kidding me?" a hoarse voice rasped, the vibration shooting through Carson's hand against Kennedy's chest. Carson looked up in surprise.

"You're awake." She patted Kennedy gently on the hip with her other hand. "How long?"

"Long enough." Kennedy coughed and her nose twitched at the annoying apparatus wrapped around her septum. "You did everything...everything, for me. I'd be dead if not for you."

"No way." Carson sniffled again and swiped her hand across her eyes. "Please don't make me think about that, okay?" she whispered, touching Kennedy's face.

In her drug-induced fog, Kennedy saw the lingering fear in Carson's eyes, and squeezed her hand, still holding it against her chest. "Can I take this thing out?" She wrinkled her nose, trying to expel the oxygen feed. "I'm pretty sure I can breathe just fine without it."

"Doctor should be back around in a while, I'd imagine. Maybe you should wait." A petulant face scowled at her and Carson reached higher, smoothing a frown from Kennedy's forehead. "How do you feel?"

"Like something's shoved up my nose," Kennedy groused. "Otherwise, I feel like I got shot twice. But I'd feel a lot better if they'd let me go home and sleep in my own bed."

"They said they might let you out tonight if you behave." Carson smiled as the scowl disappeared.

"I can be good." Gaining a small measure of clarity, she looked around and spied the few leftover bites of Sonic burger sitting on a plate on the nightstand. "Hey." She released Carson's hand and grabbed for the burger, dragging it over and onto the bed next to her. "I'm starving." She picked up the treat in eager anticipation as she drew it toward her mouth.

"Hey!" Carson intercepted her, covering her mouth. "That's red meat."

"Donff crurf." Kennedy's brows frowned and she licked Carson's palm, grinning as the hand was removed in reflex. "Now, where was I?"

"Honey, no!" Carson took the burger away as Kennedy's teeth clicked together.

"But I'm hungry." She batted her eyes fetchingly. "Just a little bite, please?"

"And be wearing this burger a few minutes later?" Carson moved it out of reach. "Oh, no. You've not eaten solid food in over twenty-four hours, you just got over a migraine, your system is full of happy pills, and you haven't eaten meat in how long?"

"Five years," Kennedy mumbled under her breath.

"Honey, if you want to venture back into the land of carnivores, I'll welcome you with open arms, but let's start with something a little more simple, like chicken breast." She rested a hand on Kennedy's stomach. "Your tummy wouldn't know what to do with a cheeseburger right now, I'd wager. Besides, it's cold."

"Breast sounds good." She eyed Carson's chest with a cheeky grin, admiring the warm blush that crept up her neck and across her cheeks. "Gotcha." She took Carson's hand and kissed it softly.

"Are you sure you're in pain?" A pleasant chill ran up her spine as Kennedy's warm breath lingered on her skin. "'Cause you're not acting like a woman who's hurt."

"Pain's pretty tolerable right now. Shoulder's achy. And the leg. But the sharp, shooting parts are gone. My head is fuzzy enough I figure they gave me something for it. Am I right?" Her head tilted back as she spotted the IV bag hanging behind her. "Ah. Yep." A thought occurred to her and her head rolled back forward. "Did I need any blood?"

"Nope." Carson saw the relief in Kennedy's eyes. "But yeah, they gave you some pretty good drugs. You slept for almost three hours."

"Really?" She studied the light outside. "Dinner time?" She smiled hopefully as she looked back up.

"Hold on, and let me go see what I can get for you, all right?" Carson slipped off the bed and felt a tug at her scrubs hem. "Yes?" She stopped, leaning against the mattress top on one hand.

Kennedy trailed one finger up and down Carson's forearm. "No Jell-O."

"Okay." Carson smiled. "Any other requests?"

"No cream of wheat and no broth." She thought for a minute. "No nasty fruit drinks."

"Wow, you've got your hospital staples down." Carson captured the wandering finger. "You spent much time in this place?"

"I was on the rodeo team in high school, remember?" She smiled. "You've seen a few of the scars."

"I've seen all of the scars," she corrected her with a wink. "Okay. Let me see what I can find you in the way of real food." She slipped out into the hallway, spotting Nurse Myra. "Hi." She approached her with a bit of trepidation. "You've already done so much for us, but..."

"What do you need, sugar?" Myra tucked a pen behind her ear and lowered a clipboard, giving Carson her full attention.

"She's hungry." She gestured toward the door to their room. "She can have regular food, right?"

"Right." Myra smiled smugly. "Let me guess, she doesn't want hospital food."

"Worse." Carson leaned in closer.

"Worse?"

"She's a vegetarian." Carson snickered.

"Oh." Myra scrunched her face up in thought. "There's that one little granola-looking place down on Main Street. Let me see what I can do and I'll get back with you in thirty, okay?"

"Thank you." Carson turned and spotted Ranger Smothers headed her way. She hadn't yet met the ranger, but easily recognized the uniform. "Trouble," she murmured.

"Not on my watch." Myra gently pushed past her. "Keena, give them until tomorrow, for crying out loud."

"Look, I'm up to my eyeballs in paperwork here." The ranger tilted her hat back. "I've got witnesses to locate, two full shifts of overtime papers to fill out, oh, and let's not forget two separate crime scenes and the county sheriff breathing down my neck over three dead bodies." She saw Carson frown in confusion. "Whoops."

"Way to go, hon." Myra lightly slugged her on the arm.

"I am so tired." Keena covered her face with her hands for a moment.

"Yeah, and you need a bath too," Myra added helpfully. "Why don't you go home, shower, take a nap, change your uniform, and come back in a few hours after these ladies have had a chance to rest a little while longer?"

"You're right." Keena's shoulders hitched back and she stood up taller. "Ma'am, will you and your partner be up for answering a few questions later?"

"Not sure." Carson met her with a steady gaze. "If you want clear answers, you might want to wait until tomorrow. She's higher than a kite right now and starving. Not a good combination."

"You still be in town all day tomorrow?" Keena searched through a folder. "I've got her folks' address down the road in Alpine."

"Um...yeah. Here." Carson pulled out her cell phone. "Give me your number and I'll plug it into my phone and call you in the morning."

"Good luck getting that to work in these parts." Keena chuckled.

"Yeah, I know, but I'll just store the number here and use the Noconas' phone to call you." She paused, waiting as Keena gave her the number.

"You sure you're not headed out of town until after tomorrow?" She closed the folder.

"No. We have business with the sheriff too." Carson frowned. "What did you mean by three dead bodies?"

"We found three bodies in the park last night." Keena treaded lightly. Kennedy and Carson weren't suspects, but they had been in the park at the time of the murder. "Two Hispanic women and one white male. Haven't ID'd them yet."

Carson's scalp prickled and she felt weak all over again. "Were they shot, too?"

"One of them was, yeah." Keena eyed her carefully. "Ma'am, that's really more than I should say until I speak with both of you formally to get your account of what happened. We'll be comparing the bullet that we found in the dead man with the one they took from your partner's shoulder to see if there is a match. Meanwhile, if you can think real hard and remember as much as you can, I'd be most obliged."

"I'll do my best." Carson felt suddenly sick, her mind racing with the thought of what could have happened had their shooters caught up with them. "She may not be so much help. She was out of it a lot once she was shot."

"I understand." Keena stepped back and straightened her hat. "Listen, I'm going to go get that shower. I'll get in touch with you tomorrow."

"And I need to go find her some food." Myra gestured toward the room behind Carson. "You look like you need some more rest."

Lying down sounded awfully appealing all of a sudden. "Yeah, I probably do." Carson thoughtfully watched them disappear. She turned and placed a hand against the door to push it open and paused. "Three dead bodies?" She shivered. "What the hell?"

Chapter
Nine

AILEEN ENTERED THE third floor family room bearing a tray with two tall tumblers full of a soy concoction. Kennedy had insisted both she and Carson needed to build their systems back up, and Carson had surprisingly agreed to whatever she wanted, indicating just how weary she was from their ordeal.

Kennedy had given Aileen very explicit instructions on what they needed in the shakes, necessitating a trip to a health food store in town. Joseph had willingly made the trip, returning with several different canisters containing odd-smelling powdered mixtures. He'd also picked up bottles of vitamins and minerals his daughter had requested, and some oxygen-infused water Kennedy seemed convinced would help rebuild her red blood cells.

They had pulled out the bed part of the leather sleeper sofa and Kennedy was propped up against a pile of pillows, with Carson tucked against her right side. The television was on with the sound turned down, colorful mute cartoon characters running back and forth across the screen. Both women were dozing and Aileen was loath to wake them. She set the tray on a side table and found the television remote, quietly clicking it off.

Just as she turned to leave the room, the downstairs doorbell rang, and a corresponding chime on the hallway wall just outside the door sounded. The occupants of the bed stirred, and Carson sat up, looking around in confusion and spying the tray. "Oh." She turned and saw Aileen. "Thank you."

"You're welcome. Let me go get the door and I'll be back up." She studied Kennedy whose eyes were still closed. "Probably the sheriff and that Ranger Smothers. I'll tell them to come back later."

"Damn," Kennedy grumbled, her eyes fluttering open. "Didn't you already chase them away once today?"

"Twice," Aileen snarled with disapproval. "Once right after breakfast and again after lunch."

"Oh, I forgot to call her," Carson mumbled sleepily.

"Screw 'em. What time is it?" Kennedy frowned. Both she and Carson had slept most of the day, and she fuzzily realized she had no idea how much time had gone by.

"Nearly supper time." Aileen looked out the window at the lengthening shadows. "No sign yet of..." she trailed off.

"Of?" Kennedy raised an eyebrow in question.

"Let me go get rid of the sheriff, then we need to talk." She quickly exited the room, leaving the two younger women watching in mute befuddlement.

"I have a bad feeling about that," Kennedy muttered.

"Given our recent luck, me too," Carson agreed. Kennedy's face fell at her words, but Carson missed it as she picked up a tumbler and sniffed it, and wrinkled her nose. "Good lord. I agreed to drink this?"

"Chock full of protein, vitamins, and minerals." Kennedy tried to buck up, shoving down guilty, conflicted emotions, and shifted, wincing at the pain in her leg and shoulder. "Stuff is gonna heal both of us up quick."

"Honey, do you need more Vicodin? You haven't had any since last night." Carson picked up the bottle of pills, along with a bottle of the super-oxidized water.

"Not taking 'em anymore." She sucked at the straw in the tumbler, holding it carefully in her right hand. Her left arm was held snuggly in a sling against her chest. The bullet had just chipped the underside of her clavicle, and the doctors wanted her to keep it still for a few days. Kennedy had also been packing in the calcium and vitamin D, along with some glucosamine chondroitin and shark cartilage.

"Kennedy, your body has just been through some serious trauma. Don't you think you should take the painkillers for a while? Give yourself some time to relax without tensing up from pain?" Carson shook the bottle, rattling the pills.

"Pain's my friend. Let's me know what my limits are." She poked her chin out stubbornly and took another sip of her shake.

"But the doctor said..."

"Carson." Kennedy blew out a frustrated breath. "I don't want narcotics in my system, and I sure don't want to get dependent on them. End of discussion. Please?"

Realizing where Kennedy's reluctance came from, Carson relented and set the bottle aside. "All right. Just promise me if you get to hurting too much, you'll at least let me know."

"Sure, if you promise not to force feed me those things, if I do." Kennedy's voice was edgy, a testament to pain, boredom, and a slightly-off feeling she had from all the medication she'd had in her system. Heaped on top of it all was a nagging guilt that somehow everything that had happened to them was her fault. After all, it was her drink that was drugged and her they were shooting at.

"I promise." For the time being, Carson brushed off the bad mood and patted a long leg.

Footsteps sounded on the stairs and Aileen returned. "They'll be back in the morning around ten thirty." She moved to the window, watching until the sheriff's car cleared the long driveway and turned toward town. Slowly, she turned back toward the middle of the room and two gravely expectant faces.

"You said we need to talk?" Kennedy cocked her head to the side.

"Yes." Aileen sighed and sat down at the foot of the sofa bed. "Your father is out driving around town looking for Pete. Parker got on a plane yesterday evening and went to Austin to see if he's already back there."

"Sure, he's back there. He's got to pack up his things. He's supposed to be out of the garage apartment by the time I get home." Kennedy frowned.

"No, honey, he's not. Or at least he wasn't at the time you were shot and that man was killed down in the park." Aileen swallowed, wishing her husband were home. He was the one who had always talked with their daughter about the truly difficult things.

"What do you mean?" Carson's voice was so hard and angry that both women jumped in response.

Kennedy reached across, brushing her thumb against Carson's thigh to soothe her. "Yeah, Mama, what do you mean?"

"Shea, listen to me. That night you two were holed up in that cave, Rick Wolden and Pete were down there. Ranger Smothers took both their names when they came hiking into the Rio Grande Village station and called some friend to come pick them up. It was after midnight. We haven't seen him since the morning before that. Until we heard from the ranger, your father and I assumed he was simply angry and took off for Austin without saying goodbye."

Kennedy was dumbstruck, her mind racing to catch up with the conversation. She felt light-headed and closed her eyes. It was a bad idea, as the room began to spin. Wearily, she opened them. "Damn." She felt the bed moving and realized Carson was shaking. "Carson?"

"I..." In a panic, Carson looked up, first at Kennedy and then at Aileen. "Excuse me for a moment." She got up and quietly, but quickly, left the room.

"I need to go after her." Kennedy started to rise and winced as she felt the stitches in her shoulder pull. "Ouch! Dammit!" A firm hand held her gently down.

"I'll go get her in a minute." Aileen held her daughter down with firm words, if not with physical force.

"But, Mama!" Kennedy huffed and sat back, shifting to take some of the weight off her injured side.

"She's overwhelmed, honey. Let her be while I finish up." Aileen's eyes were brimming with tears. "I'm overwhelmed, too. Your father and I were worried sick about you. First the drugged drink at the bar, then you disappeared, and then when they found you, you'd been shot. When I learned Pete might be involved with the goings on at the park. I..." she choked up and hung her head, shaking it. "I don't know what I'll do if he was." She looked up as a tear slipped down her cheek. "He's my baby. And yet I have to agree with what your father said to Parker. I'm not sure I know him anymore."

"I'm not sure I ever did," Kennedy answered quietly. She looked over toward the window where clouds had begun to gather in the sky, painting it a bleak shade of gray that seemed fitting, given the circumstances. "I think you and I both know it's probably no coincidence they were in the park while we were. Whether he's connected to me being shot..." She looked up. "I don't want to think like that, but I can't help it."

"None of us can help it." Aileen grasped her hand and squeezed it, the tears flowing freely down her face. "The drugs." She frowned fiercely. "All my children...and the drugs."

"I'm sorry, Mama." Kennedy began to cry, too. "If I could take it all back—"

"I'm not blaming you," Aileen interrupted her. "I don't even blame myself anymore. At least not like I used to. They bring it over the border and into this county and wave it in the faces of our children. If I could line all of them up and shoot them, I would." She shook her head sadly. "When I saw what it did to you, it broke my heart. This, I don't know what to do with. It's beyond heartbroken. I can forgive almost anything, but if Pete..."

"Don't." Kennedy reached across, touching her shoulder. "Mama, please don't. It's bad enough what we do know."

Aileen nodded her head sadly. "I can't help it. My family is being torn apart." She touched Kennedy's face, then stood up and moved back to the window. "I wish your father would come home."

"Me, too." Kennedy inched to the edge of the bed and painfully swung her legs over the side. "Mama, I have to go find

Carson. It may be your job to be the mother, but it's my job to take care of her."

"Even though you're not sure of her feelings?" Aileen studied her daughter's face, reading the anguish in eyes that could have been her own.

"Doesn't matter." Kennedy smiled sadly. "Because I am sure of mine." Painfully she turned, hobbled out of the room, and made her way down the hall to her bedroom.

She stood in front of the door, gathering her courage, then slowly turned the brass knob and pushed it open. Carson sat in the round alcove, knees drawn up, staring out the window at the coming dusk. Upon closer inspection, Kennedy spied her stuffed horse hugged tightly against Carson's body, cradled in her arms.

"Hey." Kennedy moved inside the room and closed the door, then eased her way over the smooth wooden floor and sat down across from her. It was obvious from the pile of wadded up tissue at Carson's side that she had been crying. Slowly, Carson looked up at her, as fresh tears trickled down her blotched face. "You know, sweetheart, I'd give just about anything if we could go back to Austin and start this trip over again."

"Me, too." Carson's hand drifted up, brushing the tears from Kennedy's cheeks. "You been crying, too, huh?"

"Lots of bad stuff." Kennedy nodded. "Yeah."

"I can't help it. I know he's your brother, but I hate him right now. I couldn't say that in front of your mother." Carson looked down and began to sob quietly.

"Hey." Kennedy moved closer, ignoring the pain shooting up her leg. "Carson." She maneuvered, getting her right arm around her shaking partner. "It's all right."

Carson shook harder. "No, it isn't. Maybe it would've been better for you if I hadn't..." She broke off as more tears fell.

Gentle fingers prodded her chin up, forcing eye contact. "Better if you hadn't what?"

"Nothing but bad stuff has happened to you since you met me." Carson gulped, crying between words. "Why on earth do you stay with me? Surely things would be better for you if we'd never met."

Kennedy grew very still, realizing that some things hurt far worse than being shot. "You can't be serious."

Carson nodded as she continued to cry. "I know you don't blame me for what happened at the bar. I know we've talked about this." She looked up, searching Kennedy's face. "But sometimes, Kennedy, I sit back and wonder what you see in me. I can't help it. Our first date I kept you up half the night crying about my mother. Our second one was interrupted by blackmail photos. Then you had to save me from kidnappers. We still have to give depositions over all of that after the holidays. You move me into your house and I don't even have a job. Then we come here and after we go to a bar I insisted I had to see, all hell breaks loose. You can't even take me home for Thanksgiving without ending up with multiple meetings with the county sheriff. I can't help it. I have to wonder what you can possibly see in me that keeps you hanging around. And to make matters worse, I can't even manage to shove this stuff aside and let you deal with what's most important right now: Pete and your family."

"I am dealing with what's most important right now," Kennedy answered very quietly. "Oh, Carson." She sat back against the opposite window, head tilted up, searching for wisdom. "I'm not good at this. I could sit down and write out a thousand things I love about you." Carson peered up hopefully, and encouraged, Kennedy continued. "Bad stuff happens, and I would've found out Pete was doing drugs, eventually, whether I'd met you or not. We have had a rough ride in three short months, haven't we?"

Carson nodded and grabbed two more tissues from the box on the desk next to them, handing one across to her sniffling partner. "Exactly my point."

"Well, I have a point to make." Kennedy drew in a long, trembling breath. "I love you, Carson. It's the most amazing thing that's ever happened to me, falling in love with you. It's about all that's keeping me sane right now."

"For me, too." Carson dabbed at her eyes. "But I still don't understand how, after everything..."

"Stop it, please?" Kennedy moved close again until her right knee was tucked between Carson's feet. "I don't understand it either." She reached over, stroking fine blonde hair. "A miracle came dancing into my arms in Dallas one night and made me want to live again. There's no explaining miracles, Carson. They're gifts we don't deserve."

"Liar." Carson began to cry all over again and turned, tucking herself against Kennedy's right side. "You are too good at this."

Kennedy released a long sigh of relief. "I know you're still figuring stuff out." She kissed Carson's head, pulling it against her shoulder. "And that's all right. But can I ask of you one thing?"

Wary eyes looked up at her. "All right."

"Will you try very hard to believe that I love you?" She

stroked a tear-stained cheek, feeling Carson press against the palm of her hand. "And that I love having you in my life? I'm afraid if you can't bring yourself to believe those two very basic things, anything else beyond is going to be pretty tough to wade through."

"It's so hard." Carson trembled against her.

"I know." Kennedy's heart ached for her. She understood all too well what it was to guard your heart so carefully, for fear that one more crack would shatter it into a million pieces. While she had lost Angela, Carson had lost her parents, her home, her job, and had a string of bad relationships not so very far behind her. It had been a very hard truth to realize that she couldn't fix those things for Carson. Save her from kidnappers, offer her a home, love her with no strings attached—she could do all those things, but only Carson could dig down inside and find the fortitude within to believe that this time things could work out and that she really could be happy.

"It's not you." Carson sniffled.

"I know that, too." Kennedy kissed her head again. "If I could fix this for you, I would."

"I know." Carson tilted her head up, nuzzling Kennedy's neck and tucking her head beneath her chin. She eased her hand up between the sling and Kennedy's chest, resting it carefully just below her breast. "I'm never going to take this for granted again."

"What's that?" The touch wasn't sexual, that much Kennedy recognized. But there was love there, gentle waves washing over and through her, slowly soothing her frazzled nerves.

"Your heartbeat," Carson whispered.

They sat there silently, shedding a few more tears together, for everything that happened, and everything that didn't. After a while, heavy footsteps sounded in the hallway and someone knocked softly at the door. "Pa," Kennedy whispered. "You all right for him to come in?"

"Yeah," Carson mumbled listlessly, too drained to even sit up, content to remain where she was, head on Kennedy's shoulder.

"Come on in, Pa." Kennedy unconsciously stroked Carson's head, sifting fine hair through her fingers.

"Sorry to disturb you." Joseph entered the almost-dark room and turned on a bedside lamp before he sat down in the desk chair next to them. "I understand your mother told you about Pete?"

"Yeah." Kennedy sighed. "You find him?"

"No." Joseph's posture was tired and his face was drawn,

appearing much older than it had on Thanksgiving morning. "I looked everywhere. Even went by Rick's and Tom's places, but no sign of anyone home either place."

"Parker?" Kennedy asked hopefully.

"No word yet." Joseph studied her, noting her concern each time she peered down at her companion. "Shea, it's entirely possible he's taken off, if—"

"I know." Kennedy interrupted. "Pa, do you think he...?"

"I don't want to, no," he replied wearily. "I didn't raise mistake-proof children, but I'd like to think I did raise them with the morals to avoid calculated harm to others, especially harm to family." He stood slowly, feeling tired to the bone. He looked down, and on impulse touched Carson's cheek. She looked up at him in surprise. "I'm sorry your first visit here has been a bad one, Carson. I hate to see any of my children hurting, and that includes you."

He slipped quietly from the room as Carson buried her face into Kennedy's neck, sobbing silently all over again.

"SHERIFF'S HERE." JOSEPH stood from the fireplace mantle and reluctantly moved toward the front door. Three pairs of resigned eyes followed him.

"Not enough coffee in the world," Carson mumbled, peering mournfully into a nearly empty mug.

"Howdy, Joseph." A tall man in a beige uniform entered the room, with Ranger Smothers right behind him. He looked around, spotting his subjects.

"Howdy, Shea." He took a seat in a recliner across from them, while Smothers sat on the stone hearth. "Ma'am." He nodded at Carson. "Well, well, Shea. Been a long time."

"Yeah," Kennedy groused. "Last time I saw you I believe we were separated by a set of bars."

"That we were." He stretched out his long legs, crossing his boots at the ankles. "I'm sorry about the circumstances this time, but it's dang nice to be questioning you as a witness instead of as a suspect."

Carson choked on a sip of coffee, her ire raised, her eyes shooting daggers in his direction. She glanced sideways at Kennedy, her anger at his words obvious.

Catching a clue, Kennedy shook her head slightly. "It's all right," she whispered. "Carson, this is Sheriff Randall Waters. As you've heard, he and I go back a long way." She played with the straw in a shake, nibbling on it.

"Pleased to meet you." Carson eyed him curiously,

wondering exactly how many times he and Kennedy had crossed paths. "I guess you want to hear what all happened to us, huh?"

"Yes, I do, and I have several questions for you two as well, but why don't you start from the beginning, one at a time?" He sat back and pulled a pen and a notepad from his shirt pocket, flipping it open and giving them an encouraging smile. Ranger Smothers also took notes. Aileen quietly took a seat off to the side and Joseph joined her, taking her hand and twining their fingers.

Carson launched into their story, telling everything she could remember from when they heard the first shot, until they landed at Rio Grande Village. Kennedy added what she remembered, although her recollection wasn't quite as complete as Carson's. As they finished, the sheriff pulled out another notepad and studied it for a moment. "Ma'am." He eyed Carson. "We found something in that raft. I know it wasn't yours from your story, but did you leave anything in there?"

"I...I don't think so." Carson frowned. "What? Oh..." She looked over at Kennedy, who studied her in utter confusion. "Honey, I forgot to tell you about this, but I found something wrapped in plastic in that raft. I meant to tell the rangers about it, but in all the confusion, I forgot. It was like a brick or something."

"Drugs." Kennedy sighed wearily. "Is that what you found?"

"Yeah." His voice grew quiet. "Miss Garret, I need to get your fingerprints, if you don't mind. Shea, I already have yours."

"But. But I didn't..." Carson's voice shook with fear. Surely they didn't think with everything else she'd had time to smuggle drugs on the side? Her heart began to beat faster as she thought about prison, and trials, and losing her paralegal certification. Drug smuggling was a felony, wasn't it? "Kennedy?"

"Ma'am, we don't think you did anything. We've already dusted it for prints and found a few sets. If you touched it, we just want yours so we can eliminate those as suspect." He chewed on the end of his pen, his expression apologetic. "But we do need them."

"Randy." Kennedy scowled at him. "Not funny."

"I'm sorry, Shea. It's routine. You know that. Been dusting a lot of things for prints. It just helps if we have as much information as possible."

"Okay," Carson reluctantly agreed. "Long as you have something to get the ink off my fingers afterward."

"We do. I'll go get the print kit out of the car in a minute."

He studied the notepad. "You know Tom Mackey?"

Kennedy's eyes narrowed. "Yeah. In fact, I need to file a report on him and Rick Wolden. They drugged my drink at Armadillo Flats last Friday night."

"It'll be tough to prosecute Tom." Sheriff Waters watched her reaction carefully.

"Why?" she snapped. "Damn near killed me and Carson here when I tried to drive my bike before I realized what he'd done."

"He's the body we took out of the park near your campsite." The shock on her face told him plainly she had no idea, and Aileen's soft gasp didn't hurt anything.

"Damn." Kennedy hissed softly. "Suspects?"

"Yeah. Matched the bullet to a locally registered rifle. It's Rick Wolden's."

"You think he shot me, too?" She took a breath. "You match the bullet they took out of my shoulder at the hospital?"

"Ballistics is still checking it out, but it appears to be from a different rifle," Smothers jumped in. "Rick though, we found his truck abandoned out on one of the county roads late yesterday. It had one of them teeny spare tires on one rim and had a blown out one in the bed. The rifle was still on the rack and the only prints on it were his. We dusted the entire truck, and only found his prints, Tom's, and another set we haven't matched to anything in our database. Found the usual...beer cans, camping gear, fishing gear, cooler of food. And a fraternity sweatshirt."

"Which fraternity?" Aileen asked quietly, her voice trembling a little, Pete's name as yet unspoken between them.

"Tau Kappa Epsilon. What do they call them boys?"

"Tekes." Kennedy sighed. "Mama?"

"My son is in that fraternity down at The University." Joseph responded sadly. "We'll get him here as soon as possible."

"He's here now. We just arrived from Austin a couple of hours ago." Parker entered the room. "He's turned himself in down at the jail and is sitting in a cell until he can find a lawyer."

"Turned himself in?" Carson's snapped angrily. "So he was involved."

"Not sure to what extent." Parker eased into the group and sat down across from his sister. "He wouldn't talk to me about it. Found him at the garage apartment. He looks terrible. I don't think he's eaten or slept since he left town. All he'd say is that he expected someone would come after him. About the only thing he would tell me is that he didn't shoot anyone and that he was in way over his head."

"Was he a suspect in my shooting?" Kennedy asked incredulously. "He's involved, that much we knew, but my own brother? I can't bring myself to believe..." she trailed off sadly.

"He's not been eliminated, if that's what you're asking." Randall saw the sorrow in her eyes. "I'm sorry, Shea. No one who was near that rifle has been eliminated yet. Plus we have the two other dead girls, and we're still trying to figure out who they might have been trying to meet up with. And that is the most bizarre thing — "

"They died of massive heroin and cocaine overdose," Smothers interjected.

"Is that the twenty-first century version of goofballs?" Kennedy's voice was incredulous. "That's insane."

"It was way more than an accidental overdose," Smothers continued. "The coroner found some burst condoms in their stomachs. We think they were smuggling drugs over from Mexico."

"Smuggling?" Carson frowned. "I don't understand."

"They ingest condoms filled with drugs." Kennedy turned to her, watching comprehension slowly dawn. "They travel somewhere and hope the condoms pass intact, and after they reach their destination. It's real risky."

Carson's face went through several quick expression changes and she finally wrinkled her nose. "Oh. Ick. Why would anyone do that?"

"The drug cartels down in Mexico and South America, they recruit people to do this for them. Get them fake passports and ID's. They can make a ton of money if they have a successful mission," Randall answered. "If not, they die. We see it every now and then, but usually the smugglers that use the condoms fly in, because they want to get where they're going as fast as they can. Coming overland on foot. Haven't had much of that."

"Rick and Tom were dealing." Kennedy glanced over at Smothers. "Maybe they were meeting up with them."

"Maybe. I've got an APB out on Wolden. I'll cancel the one on Peta." Randall closed his notepad and slipped it into a jacket pocket. "Let me go get that print kit and I think we can wrap things up for now."

"And I need to head over to Rick's and search for any other firearms, since I don't need a warrant. I can go in as a game warden. I need to see if any of his match up to the bullet they took out of you." Smothers also stood. "Okay, then I'm on my way."

Smothers shook hands all around, and Waters followed

behind her. "I'll let you know as things progress." He tipped his hat and they left the room.

"Thank you." Aileen went down to see them to the door. It was too much to process, and she welcomed the chance to escape.

"That really all he said?" Kennedy asked bitterly. She didn't need to clarify whom she spoke of.

"I didn't tell him much." Parker looked over, meeting his sister's deeply-hurt gaze. "He was just sitting there in the garage apartment, surrounded by packed boxes. Even the mattress was bare. At first all I told him was that we'd best get back to Alpine because the sheriff had some questions for him. He...um... Damn, this is hard." He got up and began pacing back and forth next to the window. "The first thing he asked was if you were okay."

"How'd he know to ask that?" Kennedy asked quietly.

"I asked him the same thing, Shea, because I hadn't told him a thing about what had happened." He moved over to the fireplace and leaned against the mantle. "He didn't answer at first, until I asked him point blank if he knew who shot you. He swore he didn't know you'd been shot, but it was obvious he did know something had happened to you. He knew he'd been caught and he was in a panic. All he'd say after that was that he didn't shoot anyone, and that he wanted a lawyer before he'd talk."

"So he knew something had happened to Kennedy and he just left?" Carson rose, her hands balled into fists. "Left us out there to die? Didn't go talk to anyone?"

Joseph lowered his face to his hands. "He's not my son anymore. Not if..." He stood and walked over to Kennedy, placing a hand on her head. "I don't know what to believe anymore, Shea." He knelt down, looking from Kennedy to Carson and back.

"I keep going back to one thing he said." Parker sat down. "He did tell me he was in over his head. I got the impression he was afraid, maybe even for his life. He seemed relieved when they locked him up."

"Well, good for him," Carson snapped. "I'm glad he's relieved." It was all too much, and she stood and saw spots, teetering before Parker caught her.

"Hey." He patted her cheek. "You still with us?"

"Yeah," she answered woozily, realizing Kennedy had her good arm beneath her. "Wow. That hasn't happened in a long time."

"I think we need to go rest for a while." Kennedy nodded toward the doorway. "Can you help us, please?"

Both men helped them to Kennedy's room, standing in the doorway as the two women crawled on top of the comforter, snuggling up together. "Thanks, Pa, Parker." Kennedy sighed with resignation. "Give us a while, okay?"

"Okay. But I'll check back in a few hours." Parker disappeared.

"I need to go find your mother, and tell the sheriff the fingerprinting will have to wait." Joseph turned and also disappeared.

"Thanks, y'all, for everything." Kennedy nodded, watching them leave, her heart heavy with more than she thought she could take. Her family was fractured, and under the circumstances, there was very little that could be said. A warm hand came to rest on her belly, sliding beneath her shirt.

"I'm sorry." Carson rubbed the soft skin, feeling the muscles shift beneath it. "I wish I could make it all go away." Silence greeted her ears and she felt Kennedy shaking. Slowly, she rose to see tears streaming down Kennedy's face. "Oh, honey." Carson shifted, rolling to her back and carefully pulling her lover to her, cradling her in her arms.

"My...my own brother..." Kennedy choked out. "Nothing will ever be the same after this." She continued to shake, her tears soaking Carson's shirt. "Nothing. It will tear my family apart." She eased up until her head was on the pillow next to Carson's. "It doesn't matter if he didn't shoot me." She closed her eyes as Carson continued to stroke her hair, pushing it back from her face. "You said it. He obviously knew something had happened to me, and yet he left without a word and didn't even bother to find out if I was alive or dead. And if he knew something happened, it isn't much of a stretch to think he was involved in helping people hurt me, even if he didn't pull the trigger. I don't think there will be any forgiving him at this point, no matter what his story is."

"This is the part where you expect me to tell you to reserve judgment until we hear his story, isn't it?" Kennedy nodded, gazing earnestly back at her. "I wish I could say that, but it's not what I feel, honey. Not this time. I hate to disappoint you in this, but this is one time when I can't take the high road. Because what I'm feeling at this moment is close to homicidal." Carson swallowed. "Jail is a safe place for Pete, because if Parker had brought him home, I don't know what I would have done. I hate him right now more than I've ever hated anyone."

"I don't want you to hate on my behalf," Kennedy answered sadly. It was hypocritical, given their short history. She had her own list of people she hated at the moment, for all the same reasons she knew Carson felt the hatred. Precious things had almost been lost way too many times since they'd met. "But I can't deny you something I feel myself."

"I love you." The words rolled off Carson's lips with a frank simplicity. "That night in the cave, after you fell asleep, I felt so alone. The thought of losing you, just the thought of it, I knew it would rip a hole inside me that nothing could ever fill. There's a part of me that wants to run from this as fast as I can. I think you know that."

Kennedy's eyes filled with tears and she nodded again. "I know," she whispered. "And much as it hurts, for what it's worth, I understand. I...actually, I appreciate your honesty. At least you're not leading me on."

"I'd never lead you on." Carson leaned over and lightly kissed her lips.

"What a mess." Kennedy sighed unhappily. "All I wanted to do was take you home to meet my family and see where I grew up. And you said you wondered why I stay around. I have to tell you, after all this, I wouldn't blame you if you went running for the hills."

"Honey, we live in the hills." Carson laughed lightly, tired of all the ugly emotions. "There is one thing I'm starting to believe."

"Yeah, what's that?" Kennedy rolled carefully to her right side, resting her weight on her upper arm and propping her head on an upraised hand. She fervently hoped Carson might toss her a crumb to believe in. Most of her world was pretty unbelievable at the moment.

"Maybe there really is some force greater than ourselves binding us together." She reached across, rubbing her thumb back and forth against Kennedy's cheek. "There's something I didn't tell you about the cave. You were asleep and I was feeling pretty scared and alone."

"I wanted to stay awake," Kennedy apologized. "I was just so out of it and all. I'm sorry."

"Oh, no, no." Carson continued her attentions, watching Kennedy's throat work as she swallowed. "You needed to rest. But while you were sleeping the buck came back. I was feeling desperate, and I was so angry and afraid I might lose you. I kind of yelled at him and told him if he was really your guardian, you needed all the help you could get. I think he understood me. I halfway wonder if he didn't grant us some kind of magic that night. You seemed a lot better the next morning than you should have."

"He...he appeared to you without me knowing it?"

Kennedy's voice was full of wonder. "Now I really have to talk to Pa about what it all means." She knew what she hoped it meant. She wanted nothing more than for Carson to make up her mind, once and for all, that they shared the lifetime love she herself was so convinced of. "Thank you."

"For what?" Carson pushed her onto her back, hovering over her, her eyes glowing warmly in the semi-darkness provided by the drawn curtains.

"For giving me some hope in the middle of a very hopeless time." She smiled as Carson's thumb eased over, tracing her lips. "Figured I might be all out of miracles by now."

"No." Carson leaned closer. "I think the miracles have just begun." Gently at first, she brushed her lips against Kennedy's, surprised when the injured woman's right arm wrapped around her, pulling her closer. Carson gave into the warm passion, kissing her lover senseless, willing away everything that had happened, if only for a short while. They slowed down gradually, trading several short kisses before Carson moved up, kissing two eyelids and then the tip of Kennedy's nose. "Let's rest, honey. I think we have a tough few days ahead of us."

The even breathing of sleep was her answer. Smiling, she eased over and down, resting her head on Kennedy's right shoulder. "You are my miracle," she whispered to the sleeping woman.

A few hours later, Parker hesitantly knocked at the door.

"Come in," Kennedy called out softly. She looked down at the compact, sleeping body sprawled against her and shrugged. "Not like they don't know about us," she muttered.

"Oh." Parker started to back out when he saw the sleeping woman.

"No, it's okay." Kennedy stroked Carson's head. "She's out. Besides, if we sleep much more, it'll be tough to sleep tonight. Come on in." She patted the mattress next to her.

Parker closed the door and sat down. "She must be really wiped."

"Tough trip." Kennedy met his gaze. "For both of us."

"How are you feeling?" He gestured toward the sling. "That's gotta hurt."

"Mostly a dull ache now." She leaned her head to the side, studying the blue material with a critical eye. "It was pretty bad for a while though, out in that cave. Bad for both of us. I thought I was going to die." She looked down at her sleeping partner. "I think I scared the living daylights out of her."

"I can't imagine." He shook his head. "And I still can't believe Pete just left, knowing you were in trouble."

"Do you believe he didn't know I'd been shot?" Even as she asked, she realized it might be the deal breaker. If he'd left without a word, knowing she'd been shot, she doubted she'd ever be able to forgive him.

"He appeared genuinely surprised enough when I told him that I'm inclined to believe him, yes." He rubbed his temples, warding off a headache. "Still, Shea, it was dark, you hadn't returned to your campsite, and the last he knew, you and Carson were floating down a cold river in November. A rain-swollen river at that. Irresponsible doesn't even begin to describe his actions."

"Accessory to attempted murder comes closer," she corrected him, just a little too sharply. "I've seen so many young guys like him lately. They seemed to have grown up completely selfish, almost like they have no morals or conscience at all. I just never figured him to be one of them." She sighed heavily. "Don't know why I didn't. All he's done since he got to Austin is change majors as often as he can and party. His grades...he gets by with a gentleman's C. The problem is, I've been the closest to that and even I was letting it slide."

"Not your fault, Shea." Parker patted her good leg. "Maybe it's not anyone's fault. You know Mama and Pa didn't raise him to be this way. For all you and I did, we both got our heads on straight, eventually. Despite everything, there was some core inside both of us, of knowing what the right thing is. Maybe Pete has that too, but just hasn't hit bottom yet."

"Maybe," Kennedy mused. "Although this time, I don't think it could have come much closer to the bottom unless Carson or I had died. And that..." She looked down, her hand still stroking Carson's head. "That's what angers me most. If she'd been hurt or killed, I'd be in jail right now for murdering my own brother. Losing her, that would do me in."

Parker studied the sleeping woman who had so effectively laid claim to his sister's heart in a very short period of time. "I know," he spoke quietly. "Before everything happened, were you having a good time?"

"Yeah." She smiled, her eyes far-off for a moment. "A really good time. There was this one moment..." She shook her head, realizing there was no explaining the connection they'd shared during their time in the cave by the waterfall. "Parker, how did you know Katie was the one?"

He smiled, his expression matching his sister's. "I knew because I felt exactly like you do right now."

"Figured." She reached over, touching his arm. "I'm glad you stayed. I know it's probably helped keep Mama and Pa sane."

"I stayed for you, too." He picked up a framed photo of his children from Kennedy's bedside table. "They all look up to you, you know that, don't you?" She reluctantly nodded. "After what happened at Armadillo Flats, I just figured it was a good idea to hang around and keep an eye on things. Least I could do after all you've done for me." He swallowed, feeling choked up for a moment. "My little girl, she idolizes her Auntie Shea."

"Parker, I'm sorry —"

"I'm not," he cut her off. "If she grows up to be just like you, I don't think I could be more proud."

"Hey." She play-slugged his arm, purposefully breaking the mushy mood. "Maybe you'll have another little girl."

"Maybe." He smiled. "Would be nice for Erin to have a sister. Regardless, we're done after this. I promised Katie I'd get snipped after four."

"That's damned noble of you, Parker. Most men would expect the wife to get her tubes tied."

"Yeah." He raked his fingers back through his hair. "It's less invasive for men, though. You need me to deep freeze a few swimmers for you while we're at it?"

She blushed to her roots. "We, um...we actually talked about that while we were hiking."

"Really?" It was Parker's turn to blush. "You discussed my swimmers?"

"No." Kennedy laughed lightly. "We talked about having kids. I think if everything works out, we'll probably end up adopting someday, assuming the legalities work out." She frowned, pondering the offer. "Come to think of it, if you could save a few test tubes for us, I'd be grateful. No telling how things might work out by the time we get to that stage. If we can't adopt, I guess it could come down to her having a kid with you, or me having one with her cousin."

"I never figured you'd want to get pregnant." He cleared his throat. "Not that you won't be a great mom, but..."

"I'm not real keen on the idea, but I do want kids, and I'd do it for her in a heartbeat." She smiled. "Hell, it's only nine months. How bad can it be?"

"Um..." Parker scrubbed the side of his neck. "Speaking as the spouse of a woman who has now been pregnant four times, those will be the longest and yet the shortest nine months of your life. Be glad you've got a supportive partner if you do go down that road. That's all I'm saying."

"Katie's a lucky woman." She looked down at Carson. "And so am I."

"I'm the lucky one," Parker gently corrected her. "Finding

her, having a family... Shea, it makes everything else pale in comparison. I never knew what life was really all about until I met her."

"I understand," she replied quietly. "Because I'd forgotten how to live until I met Carson."

"Well." Parker stood and stretched. "Speaking of, I'd best go call my lovely wife and fill her in. Given the circumstances, it looks like I'll probably be here a few more days."

"Thanks, Parker."

"Hey, I have to be good for something." He smiled and winked and quietly slipped out of the room.

Chapter
Ten

"PA." KENNEDY MADE her way down the stairs to the art studio, looking around and spying her father sitting on a high stool, looking out the ground level windows. "Not getting much done today, huh?"

"No." He turned and faced her. "I've started sketching a dozen times, but all the work is coming out dark and depressing today. Doesn't sell well around these parts." He managed a smile. "Where's Carson?"

"I think she's helping Mama." Kennedy gestured toward the stairs. "Actually, she pretty much nudged me down here. She knew I'd been wanting to talk to you alone."

"Astute," Joseph commented, noting the radiance that permeated his daughter's features when she spoke of her companion. It was amazing to see, given everything that had happened.

"Best thing that ever happened to me," Kennedy replied quietly. "Ranger Smothers called a bit ago. They found Rick Wolden camping down in the park in one of the remote spots and hauled him in."

"I see." Joseph got up and grabbed another stool, gesturing for his daughter to take it. "You need to stay off that leg as much as possible," he chided her. "Is Rick what you wanted to talk to me about?"

"No, not exactly." She looked down. "She said they'd already taken his statement, or at least a general one. He's also looking for an attorney before he'll talk."

"I hope Pete finds a good one," Joseph remarked earnestly. "I know you obviously can't represent him, but I don't suppose you know of anyone around here or in Austin?"

"Maybe." Kennedy brushed him off. "Maybe after I have time to quit wanting to kill him," she added. "Thought you were going to disown him?"

"So did I." Joseph turned, fiddling with some paint brushes

resting in an easel tray next to him. "But he is my son, and I've decided I need to hear what he has to say first."

"Not so easy for me just yet, Pa." She licked her lips. "I hope you can understand why."

"I do." He reached across, carefully laying a hand against her injured shoulder. "So, if you didn't come down here to discuss Pete, what did your lady friend send you down here for?"

She looked up. "Pa, what does it mean if two people see a spiritual guardian at the same time?"

Joseph smiled, welcoming the diversion. "That would depend on the circumstances," he answered slowly. "It's a very rare thing. I heard once of a father and son seeing one at the same time, and shortly thereafter, the father was killed. The elders think the guardian appeared so as to take over the job of watching out for the son. That guardian stayed with him throughout his life."

"Oh," Kennedy replied unhappily. "Does it always mean one of them is about to die?"

"No." He gave a lock of long hair a little tug. "It can mean other things too."

"What if the two people are lovers?" Her father's eyes twinkled at her knowingly, and she looked down, feeling the heat in her face.

"Ah. I see." He'd already guessed where the conversation was headed and he waited for her to look up. "In that case, it most likely means the two lovers are bound so closely together that they share the same spirit. The spiritual guardian sees them as one, and protects and guides them both."

"Sort of a soul mates thing?" Kennedy whispered.

"Yes. The two spirits do not merely exist side by side, but are entwined." His voice grew very serious. "It's a bond that cannot easily be broken, Shea. It goes beyond the grave."

Misty blue eyes looked up at him. "I don't want it to ever be broken, Pa. I just have to figure out some things, and so does she."

"I know." He leaned over and kissed her on the head. "Don't fret, love. You already walk the same path. In good time the pieces will fall in place, exactly when they are supposed to."

"What if my spiritual guardian appeared to her while I was asleep?" she pressed forward.

"Really?" he answered in shock. "I heard something once." He stopped and pinched his chin between a thumb and forefinger, deep in thought. "I may have to contact one of the elders on the reservation and ask about this. But I can safely say it seems to back up what I already said that the two of you share the same spirit, the same breath of life, if you will. I think, when your spiritual guardian sees you together, or separately, he sees essentially the same soul. Like it or not, Shea, I think forces have come together to bind the two of you very closely."

"That's exactly what she said, that a force greater than us must be working. Thank you." She got her right arm around him, hugging him close. "I have the best example I could ever want, Pa, of what love is. All I ever had to do was look to you and Mama. I need to go find Carson."

"I should say you do." He watched her leave, his eyes troubled. The last time Joseph had heard of a spiritual guardian appearing independently to two lovers had been many years before when he was a boy growing up on the reservation. The couple lived a long life together, and long after he'd left, he heard they also shared their last breath, dying together peacefully within minutes of one another.

CARSON SAT ON the back porch, surrounded by the dogs. Talia's littermate lay close to her side, guarding her in Kennedy's absence, and keeping the other dogs from crowding her too much. The rest of the pack waited eagerly in a polite semi-circle as she one by one fed them rounds of doggie biscuits. The dachshund crept closer than the others, his nose resting on the toe of her hiking boot, as he took proprietary claim on her as one of his new favorite humans.

"Think they've had enough time yet?" She looked back over her shoulder at the closed screen door and sighed, her shoulders slumped over slightly. After Kennedy talked with her father, Parker was going to drive Carson to the sheriff's office to get the fingerprinting over with, but she'd insisted on waiting until the big talk was over, in the event Kennedy needed moral support afterward. Aileen had informed her that room cleaning and meal preparation were under control and had shooed her outside for some fresh air.

"I have been inside all day," she muttered. She looked across the yard toward the corral, where most of the horses were out, taking advantage of the bright sunny day. Carson finished distributing the biscuits and got up, swiping her hands down the legs of her jeans before she picked her way across the yard to the fence. It was an old-fashioned corral and she climbed up on the top rail, taking a seat facing the horses. The dogs all followed in hope of more biscuits appearing.

One of the mustangs came over and nuzzled her shoulder,

nibbling at her soft cotton flannel shirt. "Hey, there." She gave it a friendly scratch beneath the ears and received more nuzzling and a contented whicker for her efforts. "I could tell she needed some time alone with her dad." She shifted a little bit, rubbing the horse's neck. "This has to be really different for her, bringing me home and all. And after all she's been though. Lord."

She shuddered, flashbacks running through her head of Kennedy falling after she was shot. She closed her eyes, feeling her insides tense with turmoil. A tear escaped and she swiped it away. "I love her so much," she confessed to her four-legged audience. "I almost lost her twice this weekend." She sniffled, wiping her hand across her eyes. The mustang nudged her stomach, making a low, rumbling noise. "I was so scared. S...so scared. I can't lose anyone else. I just can't. But I can't keep her locked up in a padded room, now can I?"

"I certainly wished I could a few times when she was growing up." Aileen saw her jump at the sound of her voice and placed a hand on her back. "I'm sorry, Carson. I didn't mean to surprise you." She climbed up on the fence next to her, and another horse came over for some attention. "You looked a little lost out here and I thought you might need some company."

"It's okay." Carson drew in a breath to still the tears. "Thank you. It's been a rough few days, huh?"

"Oh, let's see. My daughter gets drugged, I learn my son is doing drugs, my daughter and her partner go missing..." She glanced at Carson. "My daughter gets shot, and my son might have something to do with it. I think I can safely say I've had better holidays." She rubbed Carson's arm. "I've shed more than a few tears myself over all this. Joseph has too, but he doesn't know I know."

"Really?" Carson turned toward her, dropping one leg and swinging it as she talked.

"Caught him in his studio. He's really a very gentle man, but even the softest male souls have their limits. I backed on out before he saw me and let him work it out. If he needs my shoulder to cry on, he'll let me know." She smiled sadly. "I don't think he's cried since he brought Shea home from Houston, after Angela..."

"She's a lot like him, isn't she?" Carson smiled. "After I was kidnapped, she'd never come right out and say she needed comforting."

"But in subtle ways, she let you know, didn't she?" Aileen shook her head in mild amusement. "Yes, she's always been like that. So independent, with personal space a mile wide. Getting her to open up was often like cracking open a coconut. Stubborn, that one is. When she was little, if she was hurt, or something bad happened, she usually ended up out in the barn in the loft, or up in that round window in her room. The only way I ever knew she needed any mothering was when she'd come find me, maybe sitting on the couch, or standing at the counter in the kitchen, and she'd snuggle up under my arm. Now mind you, I almost never just sit or stand, so whatever I was doing—cooking, or mending, or folding laundry—she'd pretend she was there to help, but I knew better."

Carson laughed lightly. "She's gotten a little better than that. Now she'll snuggle up without needing any busy work, and if I ask the right questions, I can usually get her to talk to me."

"Well, that's good to hear. I supposed it's easier to snuggle up to your girlfriend with no pretense than to your mother." She watched Carson redden and look down. "Does that make you uncomfortable, Carson?"

"I...um..." Carson's tongue felt too big for her mouth and she suddenly found it hard to breath. "I think it's way cool how accepting you are. It's real different from how I grew up, is all."

"I don't mean to embarrass you." She patted Carson's arm again. "I can't tell you how thrilled I was when Parker told us about you, and the first time I talked to Shea about you...her voice...it did my heart good to hear that lighthearted, playful tone in her voice. It had been years since...Carson?"

The blush turned deep red as Carson scrubbed at her own neck, looking everywhere but at Aileen. "I'm okay.   I...I remember that call..."

"Oh." Aileen chuckled. "I forgot about that." She touched Carson's shoulder, giving her a friendly little shake. "Listen to me. I'm an old married woman. I have three children, and I can assure you they were all conceived in the conventional way. I am well aware that none of my children have ever had any Puritan tendencies. You've seen our family interact, and that includes my oldest and his wife. I'm happy he found her, and I'm happy my daughter found you. I want her to have love in her life."

Carson continued to feel the heat in her face, but forced herself to look up. "You don't know how glad I am to hear that. Give me some time. All this might take some getting used to. My family was pretty reserved about stuff like this. I...I like it though, that your family is so open with each other. I hope, with all that's happened..."

"I've gone back and forth, trying to decide which is worse, helping Shea through Angela's death, or this." Aileen pushed an errant lock of red hair behind her ear. "Because I fully believe my daughter was close to suicidal during that time. She got so thin and she wasn't taking care of herself. She caught a cold while she was with us then that I thought she'd never shake. But this..." Her lower lip trembled and she blinked hard. "I think this is even harder, knowing my son may have knowingly had a part in doing harm to my daughter that could have gotten her killed.

"We tried to raise our children to understand that they could talk to us about anything. Now I find myself wondering where it all went wrong, all over again. How did things get this bad without me knowing about it?" She laughed bitterly. "This too, shall pass, or at least I hope it will. But it may take a very long time, and Pete's place in this family is on very shaky ground right now. Usually, in the big things, we always eventually sat down and talked about it. Even my hardheaded daughter and her even more reclusive younger brother. Pete's been a puzzle to me most of his life. I'm left wondering what all I missed after he left home. He always did keep to himself a lot. Made Shea look downright outgoing."

"Wow," Carson commented. "That's tough to imagine."

"Hey." A slightly hoarse voice called across the yard.

"Speaking of stubborn," Carson mumbled to Aileen, then turned, straddling the fence post. "You done talking?"

"Yeah." Kennedy grimaced as she walked down the steps, her left leg stiff with pain. "Ugh." She hobbled across the yard and tucked up under Carson's arm, resting her cheek against her side. Aileen and Carson observed the snuggle and exchanged glances, then simultaneously laughed. "What?" Kennedy pouted. "Did I say something funny?"

"No, honey." Carson ruffled her head. "Your mother and I were just talking, is all."

"Oh." Their laughter was still confusing, but she smiled a little and shrugged it off. Digging in her pocket, she produced the keys to the 4Runner. "You ready?"

"Kennedy! This morning you were knocked out on half a bottle of ibuprofen and barely coherent. I don't think you should be driving just yet. Besides, your leg and arm..." Carson tried to take the keys, and surprisingly, Kennedy let her. "I thought Parker was going to drive me down there."

"Nah, I told him I wanted to go with you instead. Besides, I'm not driving." She flashed a charming smile. "I was hoping you might do the driving. Please? I just need to get out for a little while."

Aileen watched the exchange and chuckled. "Did I mention she got a lot of mileage out of those baby blues and pearly whites as a child?"

"Hey!" Kennedy's tone was comically indignant and the

pout returned.

"She still does," Carson replied, her voice resigned. "All right, but we come directly back here afterward. You need to rest, get your strength back up."

"Fine." She agreed much too quickly. "Works for me." She glanced at her watch, which she'd switched to her right arm. "Let's get going."

Carson hopped off the fence and stopped as Aileen tugged at the back of her shirt. "Hmm?" She leaned in, listening.

"She's got something up her sleeve," Aileen commented.

"Oh, don't you know it." Carson shook her head and shuffled to keep up. "Slow down. You're injured, remember?"

"Long legs, remember?" Kennedy mimicked her tone, watching Carson's face, knowing by her embarrassed smile she was recalling their conversation on the hiking trail. "Hah. Made you look at 'em!"

"You are such a brat!" Carson caught up and stopped just short of swatting her on the behind.

"Girls, be careful," Aileen called after them.

"Yes, ma'am," they answered in unison, then looked at each other and laughed.

Aileen watched them climb in the truck and drive away. Yes, her daughter was going to be just fine. She glanced up at the third floor window of Pete's empty bedroom. Her son on the other hand... *One down, one to go.* She sighed and went back inside the house.

THEY DROVE INTO town and through it, stopping once at the coffee shop. Carson glanced over at Kennedy, who, despite their earlier playful mood, was now in full-brooding mode, a storm gathering in her eyes as she looked out the window. Careful to avoid the gunshot wound, Carson reached across and hesitantly touched her on the leg, leaving her hand there when she received a silent sad smile.

"You wanna tell me what's going on?" Carson cleared her throat, deciding to ask about her talk with her father when she was in a better mood.

Kennedy nodded toward a low brick building a few blocks down. "While you're getting fingerprinted, I need to have a little chat with someone, if you don't mind."

"Pete?" Carson continued to face the road ahead. "You want me to go in with you?"

"No. Rick. I'm not ready to see Pete just yet. Wanna get Rick's story first if I can." Kennedy shook her head. "And I'd like

for you to join me when the fingerprinting is done. Actually, I'll
just wait until it's done. If the setup is the same as last time I was
here, they'll just let us all chat in a room with a couple of tables.
It's not like the movies, with the little room with glass and a tiny
slot to talk through. We don't exactly get a lot of hardened
criminals in Brewster County."

"How many times were you...um...taken there when you
were growing up?" Carson swallowed, still looking toward the
road and the parking lot, as she turned in and found a spot
under a tree.

"Gosh, I'd have to count it up, but I'd guess at least a dozen
times," Kennedy answered casually as she opened the truck door
and gingerly slid to the ground. "Ouch. Dammit!" She hopped
on her right leg a little, holding her left one with her right arm,
making the hop precarious at best. "Aughhh! Landed wrong on
my left leg."

Carson bit off a 'told you not to go out,' and hurried around,
shoving aside her questions about the dozen visits for another
time. "Honey, careful, before you hurt your arm as well." She
got an arm around Kennedy's waist and guided her up a
handicapped ramp and into the building.

"Shea Nocona!" A large Hispanic man in uniform put down
a newspaper and stood up behind a desk. "As I live and breathe.
Heard you were home for the holiday. Should I prepare your
usual room, or are you only here for a few hours this time
around?"

"Hardee-har-har." Kennedy groaned. "Howdy, Miguel.
Carson's here for the fingerprinting, and then we'd like to pay a
little visit to Rick Wolden."

"Oh, I was supposed to call you, but I forgot. Sheriff called a
half hour ago and said they don't need Carson's prints after all.
Said they'd ID'd all the other prints on that brick. They found
them all in the database. Seems everyone else has a record. I
assume you're relieved?" He eyed Carson expectantly, clasping
his hands behind his back and grinning.

"Miguel, this is my partner, Carson. Carson, meet Miguel,
who must be older than dirt by now, considering he was working
here when I was just a babe in the cradle." She smirked.

"Was not!" He kept smiling and held out a hand. "Pleased to
meet you, Carson."

"Pleased to meet you." She returned the handshake, his
large hand swallowing hers for an instant.

"Don't go believing her now." He gestured at Kennedy. "I'm
only about five years older than Shea here. Been working here
since I was right out of high school."

"Yeah, yeah." Kennedy was genuinely smiling herself this time, enjoying the banter. "Can Carson go back to the visiting room with me?"

"Sure enough." He led them back down a hallway and into a fairly small room with four wooden tables and high, mesh-covered windows across one wall. A Coke machine hummed in one corner, and the smell of old burned coffee permeated the air from a coffeemaker. "You ladies pick a table and I'll bring Wolden back. No purses?"

"Purses?" Kennedy laughed. "Have I ever carried a purse, Miguel?"

"No, but if either of you did, I'd have to confiscate them. Rules and all." He jangled a set of keys at his belt. "Be back in a minute."

The heavy door whooshed closed behind him, and Carson wandered over to a table and took a seat, sipping at her coffee shop brew with new appreciation as she glanced over at the mostly-empty pot on the nearby counter. Kennedy walked around the room once as if she were searching for something, stopping at each table and studying the surface. "Place hasn't changed any," she commented. "Even have the same drinks in the Coke machine." She took a seat next to Carson and a smile lit up her face as she traced something on the tabletop with her fingertip. "Ah. There it is."

Carson leaned over and saw the letters 'KSN' carved neatly into the scarred wooden top. "Yours?"

"Yeah." Kennedy sat back and carefully lifted her left leg, propping it up on the table. "Man, that feels better up than down." She was wearing loose sweats in deference to her injury, and she smoothed the soft fleece over the spot that covered her bandage. "Yeah, carved my initials there one time with a pocket knife they failed to confiscate from me. I was bored and waiting for Mama and Pa to come get me. Not like they ever kept any reading material in here or anything."

"What had you done?" Carson asked quietly.

"Don't remember off the top of my head. Probably caught me out drag racing, or drinking behind the school, or lord only knows what. Might have skipped school or something." She looked down, shifting her sling-supported arm until her hands were clasped over her stomach. "Guess you never went to jail, huh?"

"No, can't say as I have." Carson dug in her pocket and found some quarters. "You want a Coke?"

"Yeah, root beer would be good, thanks." She continued to look down, listening as the money clinked into the machine and

the cold can slid into the catching receptacle with a loud thud.
Another click indicated Carson was opening it before she set it
on the table in front of Kennedy and knelt down next to her,
making eye contact.

"I'm not judging you, honey. Just trying to understand who
you were back then is all." She felt a warm hand against her face
and closed her eyes, leaning into it. Kennedy stroked her cheek
with her thumb. "Do my questions make you uncomfortable?"

"A little, yeah." Kennedy hesitated. "Being back here, that
kid inside of me comes drifting up to the surface, and at the
same time, I think about what a hell-raiser I was, and I get a little
embarrassed, knowing you weren't anything like that. I'm not
real proud of who I was back then, Carson. It's just that I did
have some proud moments, if that makes any sense."

"Perfect sense." The door behind her opened, and Carson
turned as Miguel led Rick into the room. His skin was sunburned
and his hair was sorely in need of washing. He wore jeans and a
sweatshirt that appeared to be his own, although the handcuffs
at his wrists branded him as the prisoner he was.

"Shea," he drawled, his eyes going a little wide in surprise,
before a carefully guarded hood slipped into place. Miguel all
but shoved him into a chair.

"I'll be right outside the door, so don't get any funny ideas,
Wolden." He glared at Rick severely, and nodded at Kennedy
and Carson before he left them to talk.

Rick waited until the door was closed completely before he
leaned forward on his arms on the tabletop. "I didn't shoot you,
Shea, I swear it. Didn't shoot Tom either, but they don't believe
me." He swallowed as her eyes went cold.

"They said your prints were the only ones on the gun."
Kennedy watched him carefully, but saw no surprise register.
None was expected, as she assumed he already knew that. "What
were you and Pete doing down in the park near my campsite?"

"I said I didn't shoot you," he muttered sullenly. "Neither
did Pete."

It was gratifying to hear what she hoped was truth. "Didn't
ask if you or Pete shot me. I asked..." She slowly swung her leg
down and leaned forward herself. "What were you doing down
there? I find it hard to believe it was a coincidence."

"Shea, two guys killed Tom. I heard them, but I didn't see
them. I was in the woods hiding." He looked down at his fingers,
flexing them before he folded them together again.

"You ran like a coward?" She snorted. "Figures."

"No, I went to get us some filtered water and they came into
our camp while I was gone. I heard gunshots, Shea. Heard them

talking, but they didn't see me. Sounded like they tracked us down. They were planning to wait for me. So I turned and started walking. They had already killed Tom. What I figure is they got in my truck and took my gun and used it. Maybe they wore gloves or something, but it wasn't me. I didn't shoot Tom, and I didn't shoot you." He held his hands out in a pleading gesture. "You have to believe me."

"Why should I?" she spat. "You and Tom drugged my drink at Armadillo Flats and let me get on a motorcycle. I could've been killed on the road, you moron, and Carson, too!"

"Tom drugged your drink?" He answered so stupidly, it was obvious it was the first he knew of it. "Geez, Shea. I knew he wanted to scare you, but I had no idea They "

Kennedy's eyes bore into him. "What do you mean he wanted to scare me?"

Too late Rick realized his mistake and he sighed. "Look, Shea, here's the whole deal, least what I know of it." He glanced around and lowered his voice. "We were just messing with you at Armadillo Flats, leastwise that's what I thought. Was a time you would've been interested in our goods, am I right?"

"Yeah," she reluctantly agreed. "Go on."

"I honestly didn't know he drugged your drink. What I do know is, next day your little brother came around and warned Tom he thought you were going to the sheriff. Tom only told me it was over us selling to Pete, but I gather you were going to tell them about Tom drugging you as well?"

"Never mind what I was going to do." Kennedy swallowed a rising lump in her throat. Pete had gone behind her back to someone who had tried to hurt her. It was like a punch in the gut and she felt a little ill. "Keep talking."

"So Tom, he threatened Pete. Said if we went down, he'd make sure Pete went down with us. He pretty much intimidated Pete into helping us track you down in the park. Tom decided to go give you a scare. But Pete wouldn't go with us after we found your truck. He stayed behind while Tom and I hiked out to find you." He looked around again. "Tom was mad as a hornet at you, and I think he was spooked. He wanted to scare you enough to get you to back off."

"And you went along with him, why, exactly?" she snarled.

"Come on, Shea. Like I had a choice." Her eyes snapped and he cringed, halfway expecting her to hit him.

"There's always a choice!" she bellowed. "God, Rick, grow up and be a man. Tom was trash. Always was. Now he's drug you and my brother in, too." She drew a breath, her insides shaking furiously.

"Listen, Rick," she talked slowly, trying to resist the urge to choke him. "Since I came home, I've learned my brother is doing drugs. My root beer was drugged and I almost took a tumble on my bike with Carson as a result. I was shot twice, and now I learn my little brother cares more about a couple of bottom-dwelling drug dealers than he does about me. It's been a fucking stellar Thanksgiving, let me tell you." She shoved the table hard with her right hand, pushing it against his chest until he coughed.

"Back off, Shea." He edged his chair back some more.

"Oh, no." She got up and paced as best she could, her leg notwithstanding. "I'm just getting started. Right now, you're the main suspect in Tom's murder. You know that. You have some half-baked story about two guys shooting him. Carson here saw two guys after I was shot, but they were too far away for us to see any detail, so for all I know, it was you and Tom."

"No." Rick's voice trembled. "There were two guys, Shea. I've been trying to convince the sheriff of that, because whoever they are, they're still out there."

Kennedy stopped and turned, his words chasing a chill down her spine. "You really didn't shoot me, did you?"

"No!" he cried out miserably. "How many times do I have to tell you? Shea, I'm scared. You know I sell a bag of pot here and there, but I've never done anything worse than that. Never killed anyone. Hell, I can count on one hand the number of fist fights I've been in."

"Wuss," Kennedy mumbled.

"Huh?" Carson frowned.

"Nothing." Kennedy hobbled back to her chair and sat down again. "I believe you about not shooting me."

"Shea, you don't know how much that means to—"

"Hold it." She held up a finger. "Jury's still out on Tom. All I really have to say to you right now is, if I ever hear you come anywhere near me, my girlfriend, or my brother again, I will personally hunt you down and make sure you live to regret it."

She stood, nervously smoothing her hair back. "Come on, Carson, let's get out of here." She ushered Carson back into the lobby. "I'd like to talk to Pete."

"Can't." Miguel peered up at her from over a newspaper. "They just took him in for his first shower since they brought him in. After that, he has a meeting with a lawyer your brother found for him."

"Oh." Kennedy nibbled her lower lip. "Guess it'll have to wait 'til tomorrow."

"I'll ask him if he's up to a visit after his lawyer leaves."

Miguel laid the paper aside and stood.

"Thanks. I appreciate it." Kennedy nodded at him, and they stepped outside and got into the truck. Kennedy sat back in the seat, her head spinning from pain and anger, and something else she couldn't quite identify. "Carson?" .

"You need any Advil or anything?" Carson started the truck.

"I need to go home to Austin, that's what I need." Kennedy released a long breath. "But I can't just yet." She rolled her head to the side, her face grim. "I do believe him, and if he's telling the truth, there are still two guys out there who shot me, and who may have already killed Tom."

"Do you really think someone is after you? Any idea who?" She put the truck in gear and steered it back to the road, wondering if her jittery nerves were from caffeine or from fear.

"Don't know now. If Rick is telling the truth, I can't figure out who would be after me. Tom is dead and the guys who kidnapped you are in prison. Besides, it's a little farfetched they would go to the trouble to hunt me down in the middle of a national park and shoot my ass. Seems like it would be a lot easier to just run me off the road in Austin, or something. And then there's Pete..." she trailed off, her face more forlorn than Carson had ever seen it.

"What are you going to do?" She reached across, her hand finding Kennedy's leg for the return trip.

"After I talk to him?" Kennedy growled. "Kick his ass into next week."

"Get in line," Carson growled back.

A BRIGHT ORANGE fire crackled in the fireplace of the third floor family room, and Kennedy leaned a bit closer from her seat on the wide stone hearth, absorbing the warmth. Carson sat on the couch next to her, one hand resting on Kennedy's knee. Aileen, Joseph, and Parker entered the room and took seats in overstuffed chairs across from them. Aileen carried a tray with a carafe of coffee, along with four empty mugs, and a fifth mug full of decaf for Kennedy. She quickly poured cups for herself, Joseph, Parker, and Carson, and sat back, her face a study in worry.

"I talked to Rick this afternoon," Kennedy prefaced her story. "He says he and Pete didn't shoot Tom or me."

"Go on," Joseph replied stoically. "He's at the sheriff's office with his new attorney even as we speak. I hope he has the good sense to tell the truth."

"Hope his lawyer has the good sense to get him a decent

plea if he's involved in any way at all," Kennedy added. Aileen looked down and sighed, swiping at her face before she looked back up, her eyes brimming with tears. "Sorry, Mama. I don't ever want to hurt you, but you need to know what all has been happening down in the park, or at least what I think is happening."

"He's my baby," Aileen answered softly. "The thought he might have done something to hurt you or us is bad enough. The thought he is involved in something that could land him in prison..." she trailed off sadly. "Go on," she continued quietly, echoing Joseph's words. He reached over and took her hand, squeezing it in comfort.

"I'm trying to put together the pieces." Kennedy stirred some honey and soy milk into her coffee.

"Maybe if you put all the pieces out on the table, something else will fall into place," Parker offered. "That has to be what Smothers and the sheriff are doing. I figure that's why they called off getting Carson's prints. They must've found prints of someone who's a sure suspect."

"Yeah, that's what I figure." Kennedy shifted, easing more of her weight onto her right side.

"The first odd thing we saw was that raft of illegals," Carson interjected.

"Does Ranger Smothers know about that?" Parker asked.

"Yeah. I told her about it, and of course there's the empty raft that had the brick of heroin or whatever, in it," Kennedy continued.

"Not too long after that raft of illegals went by, Kennedy was shot," Carson jumped in. "And then I saw two guys standing on the bank after we got away, but they were too far away for me to see any details. Could've been the shooters, or it could've been Tom and Rick. Assuming they aren't one and the same, if Rick's telling the truth."

"Supposedly Pete was back at my truck, waiting for them," Kennedy added grimly.

"Jesus, Mary, and Joseph," Aileen muttered softly, reverting back to a Catholic upbringing she had long since left behind.

"Then they found those two dead women with the ruptured condoms inside." Parker scrubbed his hair back with a swipe of his hand, glad for the caffeine hitting his tired brain. "Seems like there might be a connection there somewhere."

"Do you think Pete might be involved with that?" Joseph asked painfully.

"Dunno." Kennedy stood and joined him. "I plan to talk to Pete and his attorney tomorrow. Hopefully he'll have his plea all worked out by then and he can speak freely with me. I want to look him in the eye and ask him if he knew someone was planning to hurt me."

"I won't believe it!" Aileen rose abruptly. "I can believe he was using drugs. It's not like my other children haven't gone down that path, but I can't believe any of my offspring would knowingly be involved in something so heinous. I didn't raise my children to be criminals. I can't believe my baby helped murder anyone." She burst into tears and swiftly left the room.

"I have to go after her." Joseph clapped Kennedy on her right shoulder. "I'd like to go with you tomorrow when you talk to Pete, if you don't mind."

"Sure." Kennedy nodded grimly. "Go on, Pa. She's seen enough upset from us, that's for sure." Joseph visibly started at her words, remembering other times he'd had to comfort his wife over things their children had done. "Shea..."

"Go on." She turned away, moving to the window and looking out at the bleak cloud-covered sky. She heard the soft padding of his feet against the hardwood floor and looked down sadly, leaning in until one cheek rested against a cold windowpane. She closed her eyes and drew in a long, shaky breath. She knew her mother had suffered because of her, had seen the same scenario at least a dozen times when she was in high school, but somehow her mother's pain had never hit home until that moment.

"You know what I think?" Parker stood, ready to give his brooding sister some space. "I'm beginning to think you two were just in the wrong place at the wrong time. That whoever shot you was after something else, and you got in the way."

"That's crossed my mind as well," Kennedy answered quietly. "At any rate, I have to talk to Pete. I need to hear his side of the story. You gonna go with us?"

"Maybe." Parker moved to her side, clapping her on her good shoulder. "I may stay here if Mama isn't up to being alone. All of this has been extra hard on her."

"I know." She felt off-balance, shades of her teenaged self surfacing from inside. "It always was." Brother and sister simply gazed at each other for a long moment, memories of other bad afternoons and evenings crashing over them with vivid clarity. "Who would've ever figured Pete would outdo you and me in that department?"

"I sure never saw this coming." Parker squeezed her shoulder.

"Me, neither." She looked up at him and impulsively drew him into a side hug. "Thanks again for being here. It means a lot."

"It's my job." He shrugged. "Always was. You're my little sister." He left the room, touching Carson's arm as he passed her.

"Hey." Carson moved into the empty space he left behind, lightly brushing her fingertips against Kennedy's forearm. "I know there's not much I can say, but I'm sorry."

"So am I." Kennedy looked over at her sadly. "So am I," she repeated, so low that Carson barely heard her. Comforting fingers curled around her wrist, and she allowed herself to be led back to the hearth, where Carson urged her to sit back down.

"Com'ere." Carson took her into her arms, rocking her gently. Sometimes, Carson reflected, when you don't know what to say, a hug could speak volumes. Even she couldn't believe Pete was involved in the shootings, but if he was, she vowed to see Kennedy through, just as Kennedy had helped her through her own crisis not so long before.

FIVE FIGURES SAT around the county jail break room table. Pete and Kennedy merely glared at each other. Carson looked down at her hands folded in her lap, and Joseph sat quietly, feeling twice his age. Only Pete's attorney scribbled furiously away on a yellow legal pad, the scratching noise sounding unusually loud in the otherwise quiet room.

The hum of the Coke machine interjected itself over everything until Kennedy finally got up and stalked glumly over to it, inserting a few coins and punching one of the buttons. Nothing happened and she pushed it a bit more forcefully. When nothing happened, she backed up, swung her right leg back and gave the machine a savage kick, causing not one, but two Dr Peppers to come rolling out. She grabbed them up and sat back down, slamming the drinks down on the table before she quietly slid one toward Carson.

"Thanks." Carson eyed her warily.

"Welcome." Kennedy fixed her gaze back on her brother, who shot daggers back at her with his eyes. She picked up the drink and began pulling at the tab.

"Kennedy. Maybe you should..." Carson trailed off, too late, as Dr Pepper spewed out of the can, spraying both Kennedy and her brother liberally.

"Dammit!" Kennedy shot out of the chair and knocked her left elbow against the table in the process, hitting her funny bone and sending jolts of pain up into her still very tender shoulder. "God-dammit!"

"Serves you right!" Pete shouted, rising along with her and

grabbing at a handkerchief in his pocket. He wiped the sticky cold beverage from his face and neck and sat back down.

"I didn't do anything!" Kennedy shouted back at him. "Just wanted to come home and have a nice holiday with my family and my girlfriend. You had to go and ruin all of that, now didn't you?"

"Shea..." Joseph briefly touched her arm, pulling back when she swung around instinctively, almost slugging at him before she realized it was her father and not Pete.

"Sorry, Pa." She raked her fingers back through her hair, inadvertently knocking her sunglasses off her head. "Son of a..." She knelt down and retrieved them, placing them in her shirt pocket.

"I understand your anger at your brother." Joseph studied her intently, his tanned face lined with worry and frustration. "You have plenty to be angry about, just with what happened out at Armadillo Flats with your drink. But you shouldn't assume the worst without having all the facts."

"Shea," Pete addressed her, his voice filled with angry frustration. "I had nothing to do with those dead people in the park. I had nothing to do with them drugging your drink, and I sure as hell didn't have anything to do with you getting shot. I know you don't believe me." He looked down, pounding the tabletop with his fist a few times.

"No. I don't," she answered matter-of-factly. "You've got complete immunity, right?"

"Yes," his attorney answered for him. "In exchange for your brother's complete cooperation, the district attorney is dropping all charges."

"Then you'd better start talking, son." Both children jumped at the force in their mild-mannered father's voice. "You're very close to losing your family. I hope you understand that. Your mother's so upset she couldn't even bring herself to come down here and hear you out. She's taken to her bed with a migraine."

Pete looked down, tracing the scars in the old wooden tabletop. "It's like this." He finally looked up, sighing in resignation. He'd already shared his story twice, once for his attorney and again for the DA. "I've been buying drugs from Rick and Tom since I was in ninth grade."

Kennedy swallowed and reddened in shame. She'd found her own sources at his age, and wondered, briefly, how she'd escaped sitting where he was at the moment. "I wish I'd known that," she answered softly.

"Anyway, after I left for Austin and joined the fraternity, I started supplying the house with weed, coke, and Ex. It was easy money. I was able to keep up with the guys that way, to buy the clothes and the cool toys that I needed to have to fit in."

"You could've come to me." Kennedy sighed. "I might not have bought you all the toys, but I would've heard you out."

"You would've just told me to get longer hours at work!" Pete snapped back at her. "You and I both know that. I know you, Shea. You had to scrape through college, so you'd expect me to do the same. Austin isn't fucking Santa Fe. Hell, you know how it is there with the sorority girls. If your purse and shoes don't match, you're out. Well, the guys are almost as bad."

"That's true," Carson mumbled softly. "But there's other places to find fun. Greek isn't everything."

"It is for the guys," Pete responded mournfully. "Your frat brothers are a network you can call on for the rest of your life. It's a foot into a better life. I don't have my sister's brains. Grades always came so easy for her. Me, I've always struggled, just to keep a C-average. I probably won't be winning any big jackpot lawsuits."

"Doesn't justify dealing," Kennedy answered evenly. "And it sure as hell doesn't explain what you were doing down in that park. Keep talking."

"This past summer, when I came home for a month, I spent a lot of time with Rick and Tom. At first we just went to Armadillo Flats, got high and cruised chicks. I didn't do any dealing while I was here, and I never have. I won't sell to junior high and high school kids, but I found out Tom had Rick going by the schools almost every day. He's dangerous, Shea, or he was. The one time I tried to talk to Tom about dealing to kids, he just laughed at me. Said selling to school kids was nothing compared to his mother lode business over the border."

"What? He was into smuggling?" She knew it happened all the time on the border, but knowing her brother might have been involved was unthinkable.

"Yeah." Pete wouldn't meet her gaze. "He had connections in Mexico and was helping bring coke, weed, and heroin over the border."

"And you just sat back and did nothing?" Joseph asked sadly. "It was one thing to learn you were taking drugs. But selling them and being involved with smugglers."

"There was no talking to Tom about it," Pete pressed on. "A million times I wanted to go to the sheriff, but I was already in too deep due to dealing in Austin." He looked down. "And I warned them about you, Shea, mostly because I was afraid if they got arrested, they'd drag me in." He looked up, his eyes full of fear. "I never met the guys Tom was working for, and I wanted nothing to do with them. But Tom, he used to say..." He looked down at the table, trailing off.

"He used to say what?" Kennedy slapped her good hand on the table, right under his nose, making him jump.

"Dammit, Shea!" He ran a shaky hand through his hair. "Tom used to tell me I was a dead ringer for one of them. He said one of them was a Spaniard with dark skin, black hair, and blue eyes. He used to joke if they ever pulled in a lineup involving the guy, they'd probably round me up, too. Thing is, I don't think he was joking. I got the feeling it was a threat of some kind. I..."

"You thought they might sacrifice you for the other guy if anything ever went down?" Kennedy finished for him.

"Yeah." He looked at her sadly. "I was scared when I went to them, and then he reminded me of that resemblance again right before he asked me where they could find you."

"You led them to us? Did they have guns when they went after us, Pete?" Carson resisted the urge to lunge across the table and choke him. "Are you sure Tom and Rick didn't shoot her?"

"Not if Rick was telling the truth." Her face was red with rage, and Pete edged back out of her reach. "He was terrified when he found me after Tom was killed. I think Tom was his shield from the others. Rick had come to despise Tom, but I don't think he would've killed him. He's too afraid of the guys over Tom's head. To hear him tell it, he and Tom were running from the same shooters that were after you two."

"And he told you this when, exactly?" Carson felt a strong hand at the small of her back, holding firmly to her belt loop. He didn't answer, and she took her own turn, slapping both hands on the table. "When?"

"Did you leave town knowing your sister needed help?" Joseph stood over his son. "Answer me now, boy." He stepped back. He'd never struck any of his children, but was afraid of what he'd do after the answer he knew was coming.

"Rick didn't tell me Shea had been shot. He just told me they'd seen you two escaping down the river holding onto a tree branch, and figured maybe those guys with the guns had scared y'all, too. After that I panicked. I knew the park rangers had our names, that Tom was dead out there. All I could think of is how guilty we both looked leaving the park like that." He swallowed. "I ran away. I was afraid. I didn't know you'd been shot until Parker found me in Austin. Honest."

"I've heard enough." Kennedy stood. "Every time I turn around, you're connected to people who tried to hurt us...kill us. You gonna be out of the garage apartment by the time I get home?"

"Yeah," he muttered sullenly.

"Good." She looked over at Carson. "Let's go."

Carson stood quietly, casting a final sympathetic glance at Joseph. She looked Pete directly in the eyes and shook her head sadly. "I spent several days wanting to just beat the stuffing out of you."

"I—"

"Hush!" She crossed her arms over her chest and rocked back on her heels. Pete's jaw clamped shut. "Twice this week I've almost lost the most important person in the world to me." She looked over at Kennedy. "One of those times we know you were partly responsible. The other..." She looked down, studying her hiking boot laces. Looking back up, she allowed the full force of her anger to surface. "And then you just left us out there, knowing we were in trouble. Didn't bother to call anyone. Didn't tell anyone. You do anything else to hurt her and you will answer to me for it!"

She turned and left the room, brushing past even Kennedy, who watched her in stunned silence before her feet caught up with her brain, and she took off after her. She stepped outside and saw only her 4Runner and her father's truck parked side by side in the parking lot. They'd taken the two vehicles so Kennedy and Carson could stop off for coffee afterward. "Carson?" she called out softly.

"Over here," Carson called back, not moving from her spot next to the truck.

Kennedy made her way down the steps to join her. Carson was leaning against the cab, arms crossed, looking up at the sky. "Looks so big," she remarked as Kennedy closed the distance. "Blue sky. Fluffy clouds. Looks so peaceful. Like no one should have a care in the world."

"Carson..."

"You know what?" Carson turned to face her.

"What?" Kennedy reached across, brushing Carson's bangs off her forehead.

"I'm glad I'm an only child." She made a fist, pressing it against the sun-warmed metal door, still feeling waves of anger coursing through her body. "I wouldn't have done well with sibling relations, I don't think."

"Sweetheart, no one would do well in these circumstances." Kennedy's own anger began to dissipate. "I want so badly to believe him. Bad enough he was dealing in Austin, and that he warned Tom about us going to the sheriff, and worse that he led them to us. But leaving us out there, not calling anyone to go look for us. Maybe I don't know him at all."

"You think he was in a lot deeper, don't you?" Carson

leaned back again and Kennedy joined her.

"I don't know what to believe." Kennedy shifted, moving so the sun wasn't in her face, then pushed her sunglasses down into place. "He never was a very good liar. None of us were. His eyes shift downward just a bit when he answers some of my questions. And he does this thing with his face...it gets too wide open, as if he's straining every facial muscle to keep from giving himself away. He was doing that a lot in there."

Carson dug the truck keys out of her pocket. "You want to head on back home?"

"No, I think I'd like to go talk to Ranger Smothers down in Rio Grande Village if you don't mind." She glanced at the sun over the mountains. "I'd like to get her impression of Pete's behavior that night."

"You want to go down there now?" Carson also studied the sun. "It's a two-hour round-trip, isn't it? Your leg up for that long a ride in the truck?"

"Yeah, let's go and get it over with before it starts getting dark. I'd like to have one evening of peace tonight if that's possible." She moved around to the passenger side and climbed in.

Carson started the engine and steered the truck out onto the highway, driving in silence toward the road leading down to the park.

Kennedy reached over, dropping her hand down on Carson's thigh as she drove. "Sorry. This is just something I need to do."

"No problem." Carson flexed her leg muscle slightly, enjoying the sensation of Kennedy's fingertips as they absently trailed up and down against the soft denim.

Kennedy leaned over and turned on the radio, cuing up the country music station before she sat back, humming along with the music. It felt good to just sit back for a moment and block out everything save the music, the motion of the truck, and Carson's steady presence next to her. She smiled as she heard Carson join in, harmonizing with her to a timeless love song. It was a sweet moment and she allowed it to soak in, overriding everything that had happened in the past week.

They were going to be all right. She glanced over at Carson's utterly serene face as she quit humming and began to sing out loud, a declaration of love that was a soothing balm to Kennedy's soul. Carson looked over at her for a split second before turning her eyes back toward the road again.

Yeah. Despite everything, they were going to be just fine. Neither woman noticed the two cars that had pulled out across the road from the sheriff's office and fallen in well behind them.

Chapter
Eleven

THE PARK ROAD was rough, more rutted and bumpy than usual after the recent rains. Maintenance on the back roads was negligible at best, and anyone driving less than an SUV was usually in for a teeth-jarring experience. Luckily, the four-wheel drive vehicle took the ruts easily, although jostling of its occupants was unavoidable.

"Urgh." Kennedy tried not to complain as a particularly deep crater sent jolts through her still-injured leg. She looked over at Carson, who was doing her best to avoid the pitted parts of the mostly vacant back road. They'd stopped in Panther Junction for coffee and hot chocolate and talked and sung most of the way up to Dugout Wells, but driving and the monotony of the autumn-brown landscape had driven them both to silence mostly, save the occasional comment if there truly was anything noteworthy to see outside.

"Sorry," Carson slowed down. "Didn't see that one until we ran through it."

"No worries." Kennedy idly caressed her leg, feeling the slight tension as Carson kept proper pressure against the gas pedal. "Don't mean to be such a big baby."

"Honey." Carson laughed lightly. "If I'd been shot twice, drugged, and had to hike several miles with a migraine, while trying not to bleed to death, I'd probably still be lying somewhere out in the middle of the desert."

"No. I would've carried you." Kennedy smiled, patting her leg.

"Or killed me." Carson turned the steering wheel abruptly, dodging another deep pothole. "'Cause I would have been a pain in the behind if I'd gone through all of that."

"Was I?" Kennedy frowned. She couldn't recall much of the time after she was shot, up until she was in the helicopter on the way to the hospital. Most of it was starting to fade into the recesses of her memory, she suspected as a defense mechanism.

"Oh, gosh no," Carson practically chirped. "You kept trying to be so heroic. You were so heroic, come to think of it." She smiled a little bit, shaking her head. "Good to know that you're an easy patient. You must've been a dream for your mother to take care of when you were sick."

"Didn't get sick much." She sat back in the seat, propping her good leg up on the dashboard. The seat was pushed back as far as it would go, in deference to her long legs. "I don't remember missing much school due to illness. Due to fun is another thing, though. If there was even a remote prospect of something more interesting going on outside of school, I always found a way to sneak out."

"And still graduated top of your class. Amazing." Carson tried hard to picture the hellion her lover had been growing up. Even hearing some of the stories Aileen and Joseph had helpfully shared she still couldn't reconcile the relative juvenile delinquent of Kennedy's youth with the model citizen she'd shaped into as an adult. The woman had so few vices she was hard-pressed to even think of one, other than cursing, perhaps. Sweets on occasion, and more recently, Kennedy sometimes consumed caffeine, mostly in the form of a Coke, or the hot chocolate she was currently nursing. She frowned, trying to think of anything else.

"What's wrong?" She traced a line up Carson's leg. "You look like you have a bad taste in your mouth. Is my derelict childhood bothering you that much?"

"No." Carson's features relaxed. "Actually, I was trying to think of your vices and can't come up with much other than a bit of salty language and that there hot chocolate. I swear, you have it so under control in every area, it puts most of the rest of us to shame."

"I can think of a few things I have a voracious appetite for." Kennedy grinned frankly as her hand meandered higher, her fingertips just brushing against the side of Carson's breast. She laughed as the expected blush appeared on Carson's cheeks.

"You saying I'm a vice?" Carson collected herself, capturing the hand and kissing the knuckles before she released it.

"Yep." Kennedy nodded gravely. "One there is no twelve-step program for. Not that I'd follow it if there were. Some vices make life worth living."

Carson smiled a little, keeping her eyes on the road. It still surprised her, this turn of events in her life. She couldn't recall anyone before in her life making her feel as special as Kennedy could with just a few words, or a look, or a touch. A part of her greedily soaked them up, these little endearments and turns of phrase, tucking them into a place that she knew had needed love for a very long time. Now she had it in spades, and the warmth and surge of energy it brought to her was almost overwhelming at times. Like right now, she had the sudden desire to just pull over and park the truck and jump Kennedy's bones, quite honestly.

It was mortifying on a level, yet it made her feel wondrously alive and primal, all at the same time.

"You know what I'd like to do?" She glanced over at Kennedy, who was watching her with keen interest, her eyes shining with something akin to adoration.

"Uh-huh." She trailed her finger across a still-flushed cheek. "Me too. Hold that thought for a few more hours, and I promise I'll make it up to you."

"All this open space, and no one around for miles to see us if we were to pull over for a while." Carson peered at her hopefully.

"No one except those guys up there." They'd just come around a bend, and Kennedy gestured toward a car that was pulled over to the side of the road. "Probably blew a tire on this miserable excuse for a highway."

"Man, that would suck." Carson forgot her lust for a moment, squinting to make out the car and the figures next to it, one of them kneeling behind it with what appeared to be a spare tire propped up next to him. "Glad I know how to change tires."

As they drew nearer, one of the men stepped into the road and flagged them down. Carson sighed and slowed, pulling up next to the car and putting the truck in park, as Kennedy lowered the electric window on her side.

"Need some help?" She draped her arm over the open window edge, studying the vehicle and the two able-bodied men. "Our cells won't pick up out here, but we're headed to the ranger station down at Rio Grande Village. We can make a call for you when we get there. Got a jack in the back here if you need it."

One of the men approached, the sun reflecting off dark skin and black hair. He drew closer and Kennedy frowned as he looked up, his eyes as blue as her own. In a flash, she remembered her brother's description of the Spaniard. "Carson, go!"

Too late, he drew an automatic pistol from his jacket and pointed it directly at her head. "Stupid girl. We've been following you for miles. You made it even easier when you stopped. Two of us passed you while two of our buddies followed you into the shop at Panther Junction. You won't be going to Rio Grande Village today."

"What the — ?"

"Shut up!" The man's face contorted in anger and Kennedy felt the pistol pressed firmly against her temple. He looked past her at Carson, and Kennedy realized she could hear Carson breathing. "Blondie, if you don't want to see her pretty head splattered all over the inside of the truck, you'd better get out of it now. And no lip, you hear me?"

"Carson, don't." Kennedy didn't dare turn to face her, and she felt a rush of adrenaline as she heard the inevitable click of the automatic locks, the creak of the door opening, and the brush of Carson's jeans as she slid out of the seat. She winced, identifying the crunch of hiking boots against the road's surface, and squeezed the armrest in a death grip as the second man grabbed Carson and pointed a gun at her head.

"Now." The man next to her pulled the truck's passenger door open. "You too. No talking. You both just do as I say and no one will get hurt."

Kennedy licked her lips, her throat as dry as the desert dust. Her eyes met Carson's, which were wide with fear. There was no trace of the former blush, her features drained almost entirely of color, and Kennedy recognized a gray tinge to Carson's face. "She's gonna pass out," Kennedy croaked.

"Catch her, Roberto!" The blue-eyed man commanded, and the man holding Carson just managed to do so, as her legs buckled and her eyes rolled back in her head. "That'll make things easier."

Roberto dragged Carson's limp body toward the car and popped open the trunk. It was an old Chevy Impala with ample space, and suddenly Kennedy realized what they intended to do. Her mind raced, thinking of every safety rule she'd ever known. She mentally cursed herself for breaking the first one: don't ever stop for a stranger. It was a rule that had never applied in the small town of Alpine before. Now it was too late for the first rule, and the second was no good either because there would be no running, not with Carson passed out. Besides, the running rule was only a good idea if there wasn't a gun pointed at your head at point-blank range. Not good odds the shooter would miss.

She steeled herself as Carson was lifted into the trunk with a thud, and commanded herself not to fight as she was shoved toward the car. "I can get in," she muttered, grimacing as rough hands grabbed her wrists and pulled them behind her back. She felt something wrapped around them, though what was binding her, she couldn't tell. Her shoulder screamed in agony at the angle of her left arm, and she bit down on her lip until she tasted blood. She was part lifted and part pushed over the trunk's edge as they shoved her next to Carson, and then darkness closed over her with a loud thunk as the trunk was closed.

It was pitch black inside, and her senses careened off track as claustrophobia threatened to choke her. Her breathing went irregular, and she could feel sweat against her skin, beneath her long-sleeved shirt and jeans. With both of them in the trunk, the space was tight. Her knees were shoved up almost beneath her chin, and she had unfortunately landed on her left side with a great deal of her weight pressing against her injured shoulder.

She could feel Carson behind her and gritted her teeth, reaching backward with her fingertips, straining her arms until she felt what she identified as Carson's leather belt, along with one denim belt loop. They were back-to-back. She heard the door to the Impala open and close, and mentally reviewed their situation, waiting for the inevitable rumble as the engine started up. Her nose wrinkled at the stink of exhaust fumes, and she braced herself as the car was set in motion, its poor shocks making her feel every bump in the road as if she were being pounded against them.

She thought about what to do. Carson would eventually come around and would surely be terrified, so she had to be prepared to deal with that. The bumping and rattling of the car was making her shoulder ache and her hands were tied. She tested the bonds, feeling around a bit until her fingertips closed around the dangling end of a piece of rawhide twine. She pulled at it and succeeded in tightening it more around her wrists. "Great," she muttered.

Her eyes strained in the darkness but found nothing. Not a single pinpoint of light. Maybe if she could turn over she could see light from inside the car. She attempted to flip over, but couldn't quite get her knees up and in the right direction, and every time she lifted her body too much, the car hit a bump and pounded her back down again, making her teeth rattle. Releasing a frustrated breath, she reached behind her again, looping one finger through Carson's belt loop and giving it a tug.

One of the safety rules stated that if you ever did find yourself in a stranger's car, to not let them get too far away if you could possibly help it. She tried her best to poke around with her feet, searching for perhaps a trunk release from inside the car, while she continued to give gentle tugs to Carson's jeans. "Carson," she spoke as loudly as she dared. "Come on, sweetheart, wake up."

Kennedy tugged a bit harder and felt a bit of stirring, then heard a gasp followed by a confused whimper. Then another gasp and she felt a tremble in the body pressed up against her. "Baby, I'm here."

"K-Kennedy." She peered into the darkness in confusion. "I can't see. Where are we?" The smell of exhaust reached her nostrils, and they hit a bump that pushed them even closer together, and she quickly remembered everything. "Oh, god, those men. Kennedy!"

Carson's voice rose in panic and Kennedy feared she'd pass out again. "Listen to me." Kennedy pitched her voice to a soothing but commanding level. "We're in their car trunk."

"Oh, god." Kennedy could hear Carson's breathing quicken. "Where?"

"Not sure, but we haven't gone too far, yet, I don't think. You weren't out that long." Another lurch of the car caused her to bite the inside of her cheek. "Ouch! Dammit!" She took a deep breath, realizing she was scaring Carson worse. "Sorry. I'm okay. Sweetheart, I need you to try to do something." She inched her fingers up until she found the small of Carson's back.

"O-okay." Her voice trembled, and Kennedy knew Carson was near tears. "What can I do?"

"Your hands aren't tied. I need you to try to roll over toward me, so your stomach is against me. My back is to you. Can you try to do that?" It was tough not to succumb to her own rising sense of hopelessness. People shoved in car trunks didn't usually live to tell about it. She banished the thoughts as she felt Carson stir and then groan.

"Tight squeeze," Carson muttered. A particularly violent jerk of the car made her hit her head against the trunk. "Ouch!" She saw stars and turned, only to feel something digging into her arm. "Dang! Ouch!"

"You okay?" Kennedy tried to make herself smaller, pressing herself as tightly against the backside of the trunk as she could and bracing herself with her good leg, trying to avoid rolling around as the car continued to rumble over the bumpy back road.

"Yeah. Screw or something scraped my arm, but I...ugh..." Carson pushed against the trunk lid, forcing her body into a strange twisting motion, and suddenly she was curled against Kennedy's back. "Okay, I turned, now what?"

"Try to untie my hands." She felt Carson's breath, warm against the back of her neck, and close as they were, swore she felt the pounding of her heart against her shoulder blade, despite their jackets. Carson's hands pressed against Kennedy's back and moved down until they found her hands.

Carson felt gingerly around, identifying the thin strip of leather. "Hold on." She reached down, digging into her jacket pocket and shoving her hand against Kennedy's backside in the process.

"Hey, save the groping for later." Kennedy managed a small chuckle.

"Not groping, sorry." Carson's hand disappeared, and Kennedy heard the blessed click of a pocket knife. "Hope I don't slice any fingers off," Carson halfway joked. "Hold still, honey, and I'll do my best here. Hopefully we won't get tossed in the wrong direction at the wrong time."

"Baby, I trust you, just do it." Kennedy felt a light brush of lips against her neck and then the cold smooth side of the metal blade against her palm. A tug or two, and then here wrists were free. "Thank god I fell in love with a Girl Scout."

"Honey, you fell in love with a lesbian. Knives come with the territory." She got the knife closed and slipped it back into her jacket pocket as the fear slammed her in the guts all over again. "Kennedy?" she asked softly. "Now what are we going to do?"

Kennedy felt Carson curl against her, her body shivering in the darkness, her teeth chattering from fear as much as the rattling of the car. Carson's arm slid around her waist, just as she lifted herself enough to get her hands in front of her again. Her fingertips had started to grow numb from the tight binding bite of the twine, and she wiggled them until she felt the tingle of blood rushing back into her hands. "Let me feel around here and see if there is some kind of trunk release. You do the same back there, okay?"

"Okay." Anything to stay busy and take her mind off the fact that she was in the trunk of a car in the middle of no where, headed for god only knew where. Carson reached up and carefully ran her hands all along the metal surface that was really much too close overhead. She could feel Kennedy doing the same in front of her, and their breathing became labored as they both strained to reach as much of the trunk lid's surface as they could. The combination of fumes, darkness, and rattling was making her stomach queasy, and she pressed her tongue against the roof of her mouth, determined not to throw up.

"Nothing." Kennedy finally gave up. "It must be somehow between this back part here and the outer part where the lid closes over it. I did find a tire iron, but it's not much good with nothing to pry open."

"You could maybe bust out a tail light?" Carson asked hopefully.

"Those don't go all the way through either. How flat can you make yourself back there? Can you get to where you're on your back?" She grimaced as Carson inadvertently pressed against her left shoulder blade while trying to move.

"Okay." Carson touched her neck with her fingertips, the only skin she could easily get to. "I'm kind of on my back, but it's an awful tight squeeze."

"All right. I'm coming over you, so get as skinny as you can. We need to try to switch places." Kennedy began to roll as Carson made a slight noise that sounded like protest. Whatever she was going to say died on her lips.

"Doing my best." Carson pushed herself all the way against what she assumed was the back seat of the car and braced herself as Kennedy began to climb across her, inch by inch. "Honey, you're taking my breath away in a very bad way." Kennedy was pressing against her, pushing her tightly against the bottom of the trunk, squeezing against her stomach and chest in the process. With each bump of the car, the air was forced from her lungs in a most unpleasant way.

"Sorry." Kennedy shuffled over as fast as she could, ignoring the scraping sensation as her shoulder dragged against the underside of the trunk lid. "Glad we aren't both claustrophobic," she mumbled.

"Oh." Carson reached up, finding her face and touching it. "I forgot about that. You must be miserable."

"I'd say we probably both are right about now." Kennedy groaned, getting half her body over to Carson's other side.

"Well..." Carson shifted in the opposite direction, freeing a leg from beneath Kennedy. "I can honestly say I can think of better reasons to have you lying on top of me, breathing hard."

Kennedy laughed lightly, gasping as her lungs really had no place to expand with the movement. "Oh, god, that hurts." She found Carson's lips, brushing her own against them for the briefest second. "Thank you."

"For what?" Carson gave Kennedy's behind a gentle shove, helping her roll over a little bit more. "You must be hurting. I am, and I'm not injured."

"Thank you for keeping me sane." Kennedy reached her goal, rolling over so she was facing the back of the back seat. "I think I would've gone nuts by now if you weren't in here talking to me."

"Oh." Carson rolled over herself, once more curled against Kennedy's back. It gave them more space that way, spooning on their sides. She felt Kennedy moving around, busy at something. "What are you doing?"

"Trying to see if this seat folds forward." She shoved her fingers into every crevice, stretching and wiggling them, feeling around for any kind of latch. "Ah!" She found one and gave it a test push, and the seat gave way just a little. "Shhh." She felt Carson go completely still behind her. She carefully pulled the seat back until it was latched in place again.

"Carson, I'm going to push the seat open a crack and get my bearings." She shifted, finding Carson's hand against her hip. She curled her own around it.

"What are you planning on doing after that?" Carson kissed her neck again. There wasn't much else she could do.

"I'm going to force them to crash the car. I wish..." her voice trailed off in regret.

"Where's your Glock?" Carson suddenly remembered the gun had been with them nearly constantly since Kennedy had gotten out of the hospital.

"In the truck, unfortunately." Her fingers curled around the cool metal tire iron. "Gonna use this iron if I have to."

"You be careful. They have guns." Carson felt the car jerk sharply and felt her already upset stomach twist into a knot. She tasted coffee mixed with bile at the back of her throat, and a cold, fearful sweat broke out along her forehead and upper lip. *No*, she mentally chastised herself. *You will not throw up back here.*

"Carson, listen, I might have to—"

"You do whatever you have to," Carson cut her off.

"But..."

Carson wrapped her arm around Kennedy's waist, conveying as much comfort as she could. "I don't want you to kill anyone."

"I—"

"Hold on. Let me finish." She nuzzled Kennedy's hair. "I don't want you to kill anyone because of what it will do to you inside. But if you have to, just know that it isn't going to change how I feel about you." She felt a tremor run through Kennedy's tense body, and she squeezed her for a moment. "I got you, honey. And nothing in the world can make me let go."

Kennedy nodded, Carson feeling the motion. "All right." Her voice shook and she took a breath. "Once I get this seat down, you have to be absolutely quiet. And brace yourself. My goal at best is to get them to stop the car. At worst, to crash it. We have to get them to stop before they get to wherever they're taking us. Our chances are better now. They get us somewhere even more remote, or they get to a place where they have reinforcements, they might..." She stopped, realizing what she was going to say.

"Kennedy." Carson found her ear and got one hand up, stroking the thick hair in the darkness. "I don't want to die. I promised you I'd grow old with you, so just do it. I'll be right here if you need me."

"Okay." Kennedy almost lost it as Carson pecked the back of her neck one more time. "Hang on, and be quiet."

"I love you," Carson whispered, fervently hoping she'd get to say it again real soon.

"Love you too." Kennedy patted her leg, then inched forward, once again jamming her fingers into the space where the seat latch was located. She worked it up and carefully pushed the seat forward, grateful to discover only half the seat moved, rather than all of it. She peered past the slight crack she made, squinting as bright sunlight nearly blinded her.

Sure enough, both men were in the front seat. The driver had one hand on the wheel, the other on a cigarette that hung out the partially open window. The man on the passenger side was fiddling with the radio, making a racket of static as he hunted for a station in the empty vastness of the West Texas airwaves.

Okay, she made mental dialogue, *now or never*. She edged the back of the seat down, inch by careful inch, until it was lying as flat as she could make it, holding her breath lest she make the slightest noise that might cause one of them turn around. She slowly began to ease her way through the small opening and felt a squeeze to her calf. It almost undid her for a moment, realizing just how much hung in the balance. Her chest felt tight with anguish at the mere thought of failure.

Well then I just won't fail, she resolved, and continued to crawl forward, amazed they didn't hear her. She realized she needed a plan, and decided quick and decisive was her best option. Once her hips were past the opening, she pushed up with her knees and grabbed the driver around the neck, jerking his head back against the headrest as she shoved the tire iron against his throat.

"Stop the car!" She watched the man in the passenger seat as he jumped up just as the driver gurgled in surprise and tried to struggle.

"Dammit! Jose! Guns are both in the back window." He started for it, only to get a sideways head-butt from Kennedy that slammed him back against the passenger door.

"Don't even," Kennedy snarled. "One move in this direction, and I'll crush his windpipe and then slam this baby into your face." She hoped the threat was good enough. There was no way she could turn around to look for the guns herself and she drew in a long breath, only releasing it after the passenger meekly sat back, facing the road.

"What the fuck!" Jose almost lost control of the car, and it slowed just a little. "Get off me, bitch! Roberto, you get your gun. She can't fend off both of us."

The truth of his words hit home, and Kennedy fought back a wave of panic. "I'll kill you, I swear I will!" She pushed the metal tighter against his neck.

"I can speed up, bitch!" He pressed the accelerator into the floor, and Kennedy watched the speedometer edge up until they were doing ninety on the bumpy road. She fought to keep her hold on him, cursing as Roberto reached for her right arm. Her left arm ached at the effort of keeping Jose's throat pinned, but she dug in with her feet, pressing them against the seat and bracing herself.

Roberto grabbed hold, and she felt her grip on the iron slacking. "Dammit! Don't make me kill him." She tried to elbow Roberto, as Jose renewed his own efforts to free himself of her. Roberto's hand slid up her arm, coming perilously close to the iron, and she smelled liquor on his breath as he drew nearer.

"Let go of her."

Kennedy and Roberto both jumped as Carson moved in next to Kennedy, her own hand wrapped firmly around the handle of a gun. She pressed it against Roberto's neck until he gave in and sat back in the passenger seat in defeat.

"I can still go faster, chica." Jose increased their speed, and the entire front end of the car visibly vibrated in protest. "You ain't about to shoot me while I'm driving."

"Don't be so sure," Carson hissed.

A wave of pain shot through his left hand as Kennedy slammed it with the tire iron, and Jose screamed, jerking it from the steering wheel as bright red blood streamed off it.

"Next time, I'll just shoot you, you bastard." Kennedy ignored his continued screams of pain. The car was weaving dangerously back and forth and she assessed the terrain, realizing that there were trees and boulders around, but thankfully no canyons or other drop offs. "Stop the damned car. Game's over, asshole."

Jose looked up in the mirror and glared at her. "No." He slapped at her with his injured hand.

"Jose!" Roberto's eyes widened, realizing the real peril that they might crash. "Jose, stop!"

"No!" Jose pressed down on the accelerator.

Kennedy looked over at Roberto. "You wanna die?"

He shook his head vigorously. "Dios mio, no!"

"You better be prepared to grab the wheel, then. Carson, drop the gun and get down in the seat." Her eyes met Carson's and the blonde woman complied. Kennedy's nostrils flared and she quickly clobbered Jose's other hand. He screamed in pain, but let go of the wheel, and she managed to keep him from falling forward, as Roberto stared dumbly for a split second. "The wheel, idiot!"

Roberto sprang into action, taking the wheel most ineffectively, as the car skidded off the road and headed for a small strand of trees. Memories of a two-lane highway and another crash filled Kennedy's head as she saw the trees coming up toward them way too fast. "Carson!" She let go of Jose and dove to the side, shoving Carson down into the floorboard and covering her, just as the car impacted the trees with a sickening crush of twisting metal and breaking glass. The front seat pushed back against them, pinning them against the back one, and Kennedy felt a shower of glass fly back, landing on her back.

Just as quickly, everything grew still, and she heard a moan coming from the front seat. "Carson?" She pushed up, squeezing past the two very close seats, until she was sprawled on top of the back one, looking down. "Carson?" The fear rose up, closing her throat, as she noted a pool of blood on the floorboard next to Carson's face. "No!" She got a hand on Carson's shoulder just as she felt her move.

"I'm okay." Carson coughed and began to roll over.

"Careful." Kennedy brushed aside some glass. "You..." she reached down as Carson flipped onto her back. Blood was smeared across the side of Carson's face. "Sweetheart, be still. I think you're hurt."

"Don't feel hurt." Carson reached up, finding the warm, sticky substance on her face, and suddenly the smell of it hit her. "Kennedy?" A hundred thoughts ran through her mind, remembering tales of people who were severely injured and didn't even feel it.

"Hold on." Kennedy's lips were grim, and she carefully checked very inch of Carson's face, head, and neck, a puzzled expression growing ever larger as she thankfully found nothing. "Hmm." She studied the blood and realized it was pooling from a trickle that ran under the seat from the front. "Don't think it's yours. We need to get out of the car, baby. I can smell a gas leak."

"Okay." Carson gingerly sat up, feeling battered, but otherwise unharmed. "You all right?"

"Fine," Kennedy grunted, as she tugged Carson up and they

managed to shove a badly-bent back door open. They crawled out and away from the car, huddling together in the dirt, and just holding each other for a minute. Kennedy could feel bruises on her bruises, and she was certain the stitches in her shoulder had split yet again, but none of it mattered.

"You sure you're all right?" Kennedy's hands wandered gingerly all over Carson, feeling for any bumps or broken bones.

"I'm fine," Carson answered shakily. "Just catching my breath." She snuggled up against Kennedy and closed her eyes, too weary and shocked to do anything but sit there until Kennedy was satisfied she was okay.

Finally her hands stilled, and Kennedy simply hugged her close. Carson was okay, and solid, and warm in her arms, and her own personal nightmare subsided, trickling back into her mind and away to a dark place that she hoped never to revisit. She took the edge of her own shirt and cleaned the blood off Carson's face, then tucked Carson's head under her chin and kissed it, feeling tears streaming down her own face. She sniffled and swiped at them quickly before wrapping her arm back around again, holding Carson tightly against her.

"Think we should check on them?" Carson finally looked up, eyeing the car and the open gas tank. She studied the gas that had splattered down the side of the car, but it otherwise did not appear to be leaking. "I think it's safe, unless the radiator explodes or something."

"I think it would have by now if it was going to." Kennedy reluctantly got up, remembering that there were still two guns in the car, and one, if not two, injured bad guys. "They can go to hell for all I care."

"Kennedy." Carson touched her face and then ran her hands lightly over Kennedy's arms and body, mimicking her earlier motions, checking her for any injuries. The thick leather jacket made much of an inspection difficult and she carefully pushed it down, stopping when Kennedy released a gasp of pain. "You're hurt."

"Just busted stitches, I'm pretty sure." Kennedy got up. "I'll go check on them."

"I'm going with you." Carson slowly stood, feeling wobbly for a moment after the confinement in the car and the rush of blood back to her limbs.

"Might not be a good idea." Kennedy was already headed toward the car and she sighed, realizing Carson wasn't going to back off. She gave the driver's door a tug and then a kick, and it popped open and fell to the side, hanging by only the top set of hinges. She peered inside and made a face. "Ugh. I think

Roberto's dead."

Carson looked in over her shoulder and was sorry she had. Roberto's neck was snapped back at a very odd angle, shoved into Jose's stomach by the steering wheel, which was lodged against Roberto's head. She doubled her courage and looked up again, feeling Kennedy pulling at bits of the inside of the car. Jose was passed out, but she could see his chest rising and falling. The entire front of his shirt was soaked in blood, both from his own wounds and Roberto's injuries.

"He's wedged in." Kennedy withdrew from the car. "They'll need the Jaws of Life to get him out, I think." She eyed Jose's hands and wrinkled her nose. She'd smashed his right pinky flat, and the left was covered in so much blood, she couldn't tell what she'd done to it. "Guess I should wrap up his hands."

Carson went around and popped the trunk, and found some rags in the back. She'd thought she felt them earlier and now she pulled them out and handed them off to Kennedy. They made quick work of the bandages and retrieved both guns, then backed away from the car. Both of them drew in deep lungfuls of clean air, purging the stench of blood, gasoline, and sweat. Kennedy looked down the long road and groaned. "Guess we should start walking. I think we're closer to the ranger station than we are to the truck. Plus, I'm not sure where the keys are, and I don't want to move Jose to see if they took' em."

"Let's stay close to the side of the road, honey, in case the other two they mentioned are out here and we need to take cover." She looked behind them in reflex, but the road was empty of anything other than dirt.

"Good idea." Kennedy wrapped a hand around Carson's waist and they set out. She looked around, trying to gain her bearings, and smiled. "Well, how about that?"

"What?" Carson did her best to support her, mindful of her healing left leg.

"Son of a bitch went so fast, I think it's only another mile or two to the ranger station." She looked over, swiping a remaining bit of blood from Carson's face. "There. Better."

Carson looked up at her and pushed some hair out of her eyes. "Lead on, then. I feel a hot bath and a warm bed in our near future."

"Oh, yeah."

"YOU READY FOR this?" Ranger Smothers ushered Kennedy and Carson into an observation room, a relatively new feature of the Brewster County Jail, one taxpayers had grumbled about, but that the sheriff took great pride in. One wall was floor-to-ceiling glass, overlooking not one, but two interrogation rooms. Both rooms were equipped with communication equipment that connected back to the observation room. On a side wall was yet another one-way sheet of mirrored glass, which looked into a currently dark lineup room.

"Ready as I'll ever be." Kennedy automatically placed one hand at the small of Carson's back, guiding her to a comfy padded couch where they could see the goings on in both rooms. In one room, Rick Wolden sat at a table, nervously twiddling his thumbs and staring pointedly away from them. In the other was a still-bandaged Jose, who glanced suspiciously at the mirrored window from time to time, in between taking large gulps from a can of Coke.

"How're his injuries?" Carson winced slightly, remembering the smashed pinky finger.

"He's had a few days to recover enough. Other than some broken bones in his hands and fingers, he got lucky, just like you two." Smothers took a seat next to them. "How're you doing, by the way?"

"A lot better." Kennedy rolled her shoulder, mindful not to do anything to loosen her stitches. "Leg's just about good as new. Doc said as soon as I get back to Austin to start hitting light weights at the gym again. The shoulder...he said he'd like me to do a little PT, just to make sure I get the muscles working back the way they should."

"Great." Smothers shuffled through a folder. "Let's get up to speed here. At present, we have federal agents closing in on a house a little east of the park. Your buddy Jose there started singing like a canary once he realized his choices were limited. We haven't even really finished cutting any deal with him just yet, but when his lawyer explained deportation and the intricacies of our lovely prison system, he became real co-operative."

"What house?" Kennedy shifted in her seat, draping an arm across Carson's shoulders.

Carson glanced toward Jose, who for a moment appeared to look directly at her. She shivered, remembering the cramped confines of the trunk. "He can't see us, right?"

"Right." Smothers reviewed her notes. "Seems Roberto and Jose were working for a couple of bigger guys up the chain. We found some guns in an old shack he directed us to. Ballistics on one matches the slug they took from your shoulder. Roberto's prints were all over it, so there's a good chance your shooter is dead."

"Really?" Kennedy appeared somewhat relieved. "Where does Rick fit in?"

"He's just become a lot more willing to talk to us." Smothers set her folder aside. "He saw us bring Jose in and immediately called his lawyer. All of this, you getting shot, the rafts of illegals, and the dead girls in the park, it's all connected."

"Wow." Carson sat back and drew a long breath, the information a bit overwhelming. "How did we end up in the trunk of that car? And why were they shooting at us in the park?"

"Near as we can tell, you two were just in the wrong place at the wrong time." Smothers turned as Sheriff Waters entered Rick's room, along with his attorney, and sat down across the table from them. "Here, let's see what he has to say." She fumbled with a switch, which piped sound from the interrogation room into the observation room.

"Richard Wolden." Waters read briefly from a piece of paper before he set it aside and looked up. "Your attorney here has cut a pretty sweet deal for you. In exchange for you telling us everything, and I do mean everything, you know about your buddy Jose over in the next room, and why you were in the park the night Thomas Mackey was killed, you will get five years' probation, which will include weekly community service for the duration. You will also enter a drug treatment facility for the first part of your probation period. Do you agree to these terms?"

"Yeah." Rick turned to his attorney, who whispered something too low to be heard. After a bit of discussion, Rick signed some papers and looked up. "Here's the deal." He sat back, pushing hair out of his eyes. "Tom hired me to deal locally, that's all. Most of my clients were at Armadillo Flats. A couple of kids at the high school. That's it. I still had my job at the gas station. Just did the dealing on the side for extra cash. Never meant to get mixed up in no murders or running illegals or nothing."

"I see." Sheriff Waters studied his notes. "So you, Thomas, and Peta went to the park to scare Miss Nocona and Miss Garret?"

"Yeah. Just wanted her to get her nose out of our business was all. I wasn't going to hurt no one, honest. Just give them a scare and tell them to butt out." Rick studied the glass for a moment and Kennedy detected a hint of a sneer, her own lip curling up in response.

"Bastard." She clenched her left fist, the knuckles turning white, until Carson gently took her hand and tucked it against her.

"What do you know about the shooters in the park?" Sheriff Waters glanced toward the window himself, well aware of who was on the other side.

"There's some other guys involved, but I only met them a few times, hanging out at Armadillo Flats." Rick's words came slowly at first, and he stopped, taking a sip of coffee. "Tom knew them. I think that's how he ended up dead. I think those guys killed him. He was getting sloppy, and I think he got to where he knew too much."

"Too much about what?" The sheriff checked a tape recorder, which was running next to him on the table.

"Them guys, they was using the illegals to smuggle drugs into the country. Tom was helping them get the illegals past the park and through it sometimes. They used the river to run them. But Tom, he was a cocky son of a bitch. Got to where he told me he was making demands of these guys for extra money and stuff. Damned fool. Those guys are dangerous. They got connections all the way to New York, from what Tom said. I think they might be mafia or something. Anyway, I met Jose and his buddy Roberto through Tom. Roberto, he's a sharpshooter, or he was. I think he might be the one who shot Shea."

"And why do you think that?" Waters continued to scratch on a pad of paper.

"Tom said they had a deal going down in the park that day. Those guys were into some ugly stuff." He hesitated, hoping immunity meant what he thought it did. "They weren't just running drugs, they were selling those people. They were into human trafficking. They'd fool a bunch of Mexicans into thinking they had jobs for them, then when they got them here, he sold them. Women and children sold into prostitution all over the country."

Kennedy's mind reeled, going back to the raft of terrified people they'd seen on the river. A touch to her arm made her turn. "That raft," Carson gasped. "I remember now. There were no men on board. Only women and children. Dear God." She buried her face in her hands. "Those people."

Rick stood for a moment and walked toward the mirrored window. He glanced at it uncertainly then sat back down. "Who's in there?" He gestured toward the glass.

"Never you mind about that." The sheriff made a few notes. "Just keep telling the truth."

"You got anything else, Rick?" his attorney interjected. "You have complete immunity at this point. It'd be in your best interests to make sure these fellows have all the information you can give them."

"I didn't shoot Shea or Tom. And I never got involved with selling people. Hey." He paused. "How come you were willing to let me off a possible murder charge?"

"Two can play the holding back game, Wolden." The sheriff closed his notepad. "Your prints were the only ones on the gun that killed Tom, but we took plaster casts of footprints around your truck. Once we hauled Jose in, and Roberto's body, turns out those casts match up with their boots. More importantly, we found shell casings from your rifle in the glove compartment of the car that crashed. Seems Roberto gathered souvenirs. We even matched one case up to the bullet we took out of Tom. His prints were all over it. But the clincher was, we found some of Roberto's prints on Mackey's belt buckle."

"I'll be damned." Rick turned, staring at the sheriff. "So I was never a suspect?"

"Didn't say that," Waters drawled. "But the full scope of our investigation seems to back up your story. For that, count yourself lucky."

"Damn." He sat down again and finished his coffee. "Bet Shea will kill her little brother for talking to us, huh? Damned fool kid caused all this trouble, all over a measly few bags of pot laced with coke."

Kennedy stiffened in her seat, her mouth going dry. She held her breath for a moment, unsure if she wanted the questioning to go any further. She sighed as it did just that. "Guess I might as well know everything now," she muttered.

Carson took her hand and squeezed it. There was little she could say to make it better. If Kennedy had any remaining threads of trust in her younger brother, Carson knew after this they were severed.

"Ah, Peta Nocona." Sheriff Waters made an effort not to look toward the glass. "What was his involvement in all of this?"

"Other than being a damned fool user and dealing to them sissy boys over in Austin?" Rick grinned for a moment. "Not much. He warned Tom his sister was going to call you, and Tom scared him into leading us to Shea's truck down in the park. So we followed her and her little lesbo girlfriend on their hike. I was floored when I heard those guns going off and saw her fall. Ol' Shea just walked into the wrong place at the wrong time."

"So to your knowledge, Peta Nocona wasn't involved in any of the drug or human trafficking in the park?" The sheriff appeared relieved, wiping a hand across his brow.

"Hell, no." Rick shifted in his chair. "That boy doesn't have enough sense for Tom or no one else to have hired him to do anything. Tom was afraid he'd mess up and get caught as it was.

Even if he wanted to be involved, Tom would never have hired him for any of the really big deals."

"I'll kill him when I get home," Kennedy replied evenly. "I can't believe Pa let him move back in. If he knew about the human trafficking, I swear I will kick his bony behind all the way back to Austin."

"Honey, it's only for a few days until his apartment in Austin is ready. He had nowhere else to go." Carson reached over, smoothing back a lock of hair. There was little else she could say. After yet another trip to the emergency room, they'd spent two days recovering from the car crash, holed up in the family room with Aileen waiting on them hand and foot, both of them avoiding Pete at every possible turn.

"I know." Kennedy released an agitated breath and sat back in her seat. "But it's a few days too many." She turned toward Smothers, as the activities in the interrogation room came to an end. "So who are the feds closing in on?"

"A couple of guys that Jose told us about... We think they're the ones who've been running the illegals through the park and using them to transport the cocaine and heroin. Then they were handing them off to the pimps. He says they're the ones who had them follow you around that day. Apparently they sat outside your folks' house all day, a ways down the road, waiting and hoping you'd come out. Then followed you to the jail and waited, then followed you when you headed down into the park. They had two cars, so when you stopped, one car stopped with you, and the other went on by. That's how they ended up waiting for you where they were. If you hadn't continued toward them, the other car was going to keep following you and run you off the road. Seems those guys wanted to talk to you, find out who all you had talked to about all of this. That's why they didn't just kill you on the spot." She fished a tape out of her pocket and popped it into a recorder on a table. "His lawyer had us interrogate him privately yesterday. Said he wouldn't work with us if there was anyone in here at the time. We'll finish up this afternoon, but here's what we got. You want to listen? Most of it's in Spanish."

"Sure." Kennedy's interest was piqued. After so much confusion, it seemed surreal that the answers to all her questions might be on a tiny little micro cassette.

"Will you interpret for me?" Carson frowned, wondering if she wanted to hear what all might be on the tape.

"You betcha." They sat back, and Kennedy tilted her head to one side, listening carefully as she sorted out four voices, the sheriff, his interpreter, Jose, and Jose's lawyer. The tape went on for several minutes before it trailed off into static, and Smothers popped it from the recorder, putting it back in its case.

"So, what did he say?" Carson curled her fingers around Kennedy's hand.

"Damn," Kennedy spoke softly. "Just like they've been saying, we were basically in the wrong place at the wrong time. Seems Jose and Roberto were our shooters in the park, if what he's saying is true. They were there trying to round up a group of illegals who had escaped. That explains that runaway raft we used to get to Rio Grande Village. We got in their way, and because we saw the rafts, that's why they tried to kill us. They were afraid we'd go back and report the raft to the authorities. And with those dead girls out there, they didn't want any murder charges being pinned on them. Their bosses sent them after us again after we escaped. They were afraid we were going to eventually get someone to talk who would implicate them. They're still trying to track down all their escaped illegals and the drugs they had ingested for them."

"Yeah." Smothers jotted down a few more notes. "He said they had plans to take out Rick, too. Meanwhile, we're afraid we may be finding some more dead bodies before this is all over. He said he isn't sure all the illegals even knew what they were swallowing."

"What about my brother? Were they gonna come after him as well?" Kennedy immediately forgot her own threats to kill him.

"Don't know." Smothers studied her in sympathy. "We'll keep an eye on your folks' house for a while, until we're certain we have everyone in custody that we need to. We've been watching the house at night, as it is."

"Thanks." Kennedy's heart skipped a beat, wondering where her folks were at that minute. She knew it was grocery shopping day, and so they had both gone into town to buy all the food needed to run the bed and breakfast. "Wonder if I should get them to come stay with us in Austin for a while?"

"You know they won't," Carson interjected. "Your mom said they're full up with guests for a while. And what with the horses and dogs and all."

"I know." Kennedy sighed. "I still won't rest easy until those guys are caught."

Smothers glanced at her watch. "Should have them in custody by now. The agents headed out before dawn this morning. Wanted to surprise them while it was still dark. Jose assured us they weren't planning to move on until they had exhausted their search for their illegals and their drugs. But with him in custody, we needed to start moving as soon as we had our information. Didn't want them to have time to get spooked and run."

"When will you be finished with him?" Kennedy nodded toward Jose, who still sat quietly in the other room.

"Another hour or so. Tuesday is hell day at the county courthouse. You got all the guys who were hauled in on Saturday night, got a chance to talk to lawyers yesterday, and are now busy pleading out before the judge. Jose's lawyer got caught up down there, and he'll be in as soon as he finishes up with another couple of clients. You plan to stick around and listen in?" She looked from Carson to Kennedy and back.

Kennedy studied Carson, who had been relatively quiet for most of the morning. It was the anniversary of Carson's mother's death, but they'd been so busy, they'd had little time to talk about how Carson was doing. Now she looked up as Kennedy's hand ran gently against the back of her head. "You wanna stay here or go find a milkshake somewhere?"

Carson found a small smile. "I've heard enough. Let's go one better. Let's go back to the house and make milkshakes, okay?"

"You got it." Kennedy stood, taking Carson's hand and hauling her to her feet with her. "You need us to stick around for anything else?"

"No, although we might have some follow up questions in a few days. I just figured you'd want to be up to speed for now." Smothers also stood, shaking their hands. "I have a mile of paperwork to fill out back at the office. I do wish these guys could have stayed out of my park to do their dirty work. It's hell on my supply of computerized forms."

"I can imagine." Kennedy pulled Carson to her side, giving her a little squeeze. "Let us know when you get those guys and what you find out." She handed over a business card. "We'll be here a few more days, and even after we go home, I won't be back in my office until Monday, but my partners will forward you to me, or you've got my cell number on the card as well. It actually works in Austin." She smiled.

"Will do. I imagine your folks will be glad to maybe have a few quiet evenings with you before you take off." Smothers pocketed the card.

"We'll see you in court, most likely." Kennedy glanced at Carson. They already had court dates in their future related to Carson's kidnapping in Dallas. Enough was enough, she thought wearily. "They'll probably have us in to testify if they end up trying anyone, huh?"

"Yeah, you can count on that." Smothers escorted them back outside, watching thoughtfully as Kennedy helped Carson into the truck. She smiled as Carson immediately slid over next to Kennedy once they were both inside. "I do hope she doesn't kill her brother," Smothers fretted. "That's just way more paperwork than I care to deal with on top of everything else."

NIGHT SOUNDS DRIFTED up through the window, which was open a crack to let in fresh air. Even in winter certain night birds and bugs still clung to life, chirping and shuffling about in the bits of brush that surrounded the house. Milkshakes had long since been consumed, and they'd gone on a horseback ride and spent some time with some baby chicks in the barn, after which they'd shared an uneventful dinner with Parker, Aileen, and Joseph. Pete had chosen to eat his dinner in his room.

During all the afternoon and evening activities, Carson had remained somewhat detached, though guardedly interested in what was going on. Parker, Aileen, and Joseph had ensured no lull in conversation, incredulous as Kennedy shared with them what they had learned at the jailhouse. If any of them noticed Carson's relative silence, they didn't comment on it.

Now they were in Kennedy's room, straightening up a few things. Kennedy folded up a couple of T-shirts, laying them on top of the other clothing in her suitcase, and then shut it, zipping the flap closed before she set it down at the foot of the bed. She looked over where Carson was idly staring out the window. Carson's face was impassive, her thoughts obviously a million miles from Alpine, Texas. "You've been awfully quiet today," Kennedy commented.

Carson turned and attempted to smile, but it didn't reach her eyes. "Have I? Sorry. Didn't mean to be."

"It's all right." Kennedy moved to join her, and hesitantly wrapped an arm around her waist. She looked out the window, trying to figure out what Carson had been studying so intently and decided it had probably been nothing at all. "Just figured, what with today being...what it is...maybe you needed to talk or something."

"No. Not really." Carson made an effort to brighten her mood, but it fell short. She just felt numb more than anything else. Truth be told, so much had happened she'd had little time to think about her mother and that was starting to weigh on her. She wasn't sure exactly why, it just seemed all wrong to not spare some time to just remember. She sighed and laid her head on Kennedy's shoulder. "Guess I'm just tired. You ready to go to sleep? I know it's early and all, but I don't have much energy left."

"Sure. We can go ahead and sleep." Kennedy glanced at the clock, which showed it to be all of 9:45 p.m. "Kinda early, but it's been a long day." She moved apart long enough to shuck her clothes, and started to climb in bed, when she noted Carson removing her own clothing before she shrugged into an oversized T-shirt. Kennedy frowned, as they'd been sleeping in the nude for quite some time. Still, she could go with the flow. She quickly located a T-shirt of her own and donned it before she slipped under the covers, lying back against the pillow with her arms crossed under her head.

She watched as Carson took her time, puttering about the room before she finally turned and made her way to the bed. Her eyes were so sad it broke Kennedy's heart, yet she was loath to say anything. Carson had made it pretty clear she didn't want to talk about it, and Kennedy thought that perhaps talking about it would make her feel worse, and she'd be damned if after everything they'd been through, she was going to add to it by forcing Carson to talk if she didn't want to.

Carson sat on the edge of the bed and tugged her socks off, then leaned over and clicked the lamp off, leaving them in what was always the shocking darkness of a West Texas night. Kennedy felt Carson move, and the brush of air as she lifted the covers and settled under them, mimicking Kennedy's pose, lying apart with her head on her own pillow. Slowly, objects in the room began to take shape, and faint starlight twinkled in through the open curtains. Kennedy had always liked it that way, being able to see the stars outside from her bed.

"Can't believe everything that's happened," Carson broke the silence. "I wish we could just go home."

"Yeah, me too. Just a few more days, sweetheart." Kennedy started to reach out and stopped herself. For whatever reason, Carson was putting up barriers. Wearing the T-shirt, keeping the foot or so of space between them, sent clear signals that for some reason, she needed some space. Kennedy was unsure of what to do or say. She was fairly certain she hadn't done anything. Still..."You sure you're okay?"

"Yeah," Carson answered, her voice not certain at all. She thought about the night in Austin, when she'd had the nightmares while sleeping in Kennedy's guest room and Kennedy had come to her and she'd bared her soul, sharing about the night her mother died. She hadn't shared so much with anyone, and she remembered how raw and exposed she'd felt the next morning, unsure if she'd dumped too much on her new friend.

But Kennedy had been a rock for her and had accepted everything she'd had to say without judgment, and with just the right amount of comfort and support. She felt badly now, knowing Kennedy was lying so close, wanting to be there for her again. Her emotions were so mixed up and so close to the surface, and with everything they'd been through, she was afraid if she started thinking too hard all of that might spill out. She sighed heavily. It was hard, trying to hold it all together when she wanted so badly to...just...there, Kennedy's hand was on her head, gently brushing her bangs back off her face.

Carson closed her eyes, soaking up the touch greedily. She let the feelings come then, thinking about her mother, and about the night she died, and even allowing the guilt feelings that she'd spared so very little thought for her on this, the anniversary of her death. It had been three years, and maybe she wasn't supposed to feel it so strongly, but it was there, and she released another trembling sigh, followed by an unexpected sniffle, as the first tear squeezed out of her eye and tracked down her cheek.

"Come here, baby." Kennedy's voice was soft and non-threatening, not demanding, just an invitation to go to the one place she wanted to go more than any other. She rolled over, crawling into long, open arms, burying her face against a strong shoulder as those arms wrapped around her, holding her close while soft lips brushed against her cheek.

She wasn't sure how long she cried. It wasn't the hard, wracking sobs she'd cried when her mother died, but more a steady, sad stream of memories that bubbled up one by one, swirling around as others pushed them aside. "I miss her so much sometimes," she finally whispered.

"I know." Kennedy kissed her forehead. "I know, sweetheart. I wish I could have known her. She must have been a very special person to have raised a daughter like you."

"She was the kindest, gentlest soul I've ever known," Carson replied softly. "You would have loved her. Everyone did."

"I know I would have." Kennedy rubbed her back, feeling the tears slow and subside. "Carson, I'm sorry we didn't take some time today to just honor her memory. I promise you next year I'll make sure we do."

"It's all right." Carson sniffled. "We're doing that right now, aren't we?" She slipped a hand inside Kennedy's T-shirt, rubbing circles against her belly with the flat of her hand. "I think maybe one of my biggest regrets is that I'll never get to introduce you to her. It's sad the two most important women in my life will never meet."

"I think I meet her every day." Kennedy reached up, stroking Carson's head. "I've seen her pictures, Carson, and I see her in your eyes, and in your smile. I bet you move and talk like her too, don't you?"

"Yeah." Carson smiled against the darkness. "Yeah, I've been told I do."

"She was a very beautiful woman," Kennedy continued. "And the apple didn't fall far from the tree, far as I'm concerned. I think she'd be very proud of how you've handled things these past few years."

"You think so?" Carson asked timidly. Sometimes it was easy to feel like she hadn't coped well at all.

"I know so." Kennedy pulled her closer, finding her lips, engaging in a series of soft kisses that were meant to comfort and reassure more than anything else. She pulled away and hugged Carson close again, smiling sadly as she felt the tension slowly drain from her body. "I hate that you hurt so much. I wish I could make it all better."

"Just hold me," Carson answered, snuggling up and kissing a bit of bare skin at Kennedy's neckline. "There's something else you can do." She suddenly rolled almost on top of Kennedy, nose to nose, peering earnestly into surprised wide eyes that were mostly colorless in the darkness.

"Anything." Kennedy's eyes felt like crossing as she tried to focus on Carson's face at such close range.

"I almost lost you a few times this past week." Carson touched her nose with her fingertip, smiling as a set of white teeth playfully snapped at her finger. "Stop it, I'm being serious here."

"Sorry." Kennedy smiled anyway. "Go on."

"I almost lost you," Carson repeated herself. "So you promise me not to be putting me through that again any time soon, okay? I don't think I could stand it."

"I'll do my best." Kennedy grew sober. "I don't ever want to cause you any pain, Carson."

"And I don't want to cause you any either, so we need to just make up our minds to live a good long time." She smiled, ducking her head and quickly pecking Kennedy's lips before she settled back down, curled up against her side. She snuggled closer as one long arm wrapped around her and resumed rubbing her back. "That feels nice," Carson mumbled sleepily, her eyes growing heavier and heavier by the minute.

"Good." Kennedy nuzzled her hair. "Wanna make you feel nice all the time." She shoved down an overwhelming wave of tenderness, knowing Carson was just about to fade out on her. Morning would bring a whole new day, and a whole new outlook, she was certain of it.

KENNEDY HOBBLED INTO the bedroom after breakfast, and lay cross-wise on the comforter, her right arm drawn across her face. She shifted and groaned as sharp pain shot through her left shoulder, but otherwise she remained quiet.

Carson stepped quietly into the room behind her and closed the door, leaning back against it as she studied the silent figure on the bed. She sighed and moved over to the bay window and pulled back the curtains, staring out at the sun chasing cloud shadows across the ground below. "Nice day out there."

"Mmm." Kennedy removed her arm from her face long enough to glance over at Carson's back. "It was until I passed my sorry excuse for a brother in the hallway out there."

"Maybe you should talk to him. Clear the air, one way or the other." She turned and sat down on the cushioned platform under the window, crossing her legs.

"Can't face him right now," Kennedy mumbled.

"Then why don't you stay here and rest while I go talk to him?" Carson leaned forward a bit, resting her arms loosely on her crossed legs.

"I don't think I can live under the same roof with him at present." One sad blue eye appeared momentarily, before the long arm covered it again. "These last few days have been hell on strained relations around here."

Carson puzzled over that, watching Kennedy's chest rise and fall with her breathing. Despite her reclined position, she could tell Kennedy's body was tense, whether from pain or stress or both, was a toss-up. She knew they had to stay a while longer, only a few more days, while Smothers and Waters wrapped up the case. Besides that, she knew Valerie and Serena had promised to hold down the fort at the law office for the rest of the week, and the one after that if necessary. The horses would be fine at the boarding stables, and the place they had boarded the dogs and cats was the equivalent of canine and feline Club Med, complete with video of birds and fish for the cats to watch to their feline hearts' content, and large, open running space for the dogs.

Damn it, she silently punched the thick cushion she sat on. They needed a break. The trip to Alpine was supposed to be fun and relaxing, but for the most part, it had been anything but. *Well, maybe except for our time in the waterfall cave, and the day before that*, she admitted to herself with a tiny smile. They'd even missed Kennedy's birthday, and that...she huffed out a frustrated breath...that was simply unacceptable. It was time to remedy the situation.

She shoved decisively off the cushion and slipped over to

the bed, sitting down on the edge. "I need to go make a couple phone calls downstairs, honey. You want me to bring you anything when I come back?" A guardedly interested blue eye reappeared, and Kennedy scooted over, until her head was in Carson's lap.

A mildly contented noise escaped Kennedy's lips, and she felt a gentle stroking touch to her hair, as Carson carefully ran her fingers through it. "Just bring back yourself." She closed her eyes again. "Maybe some cookies."

"I can do that," Carson soothed softly. "Are you going to be okay?"

"No," a grumpy voice answered. "Maybe later, after all this is over." She released a long trembling breath. "Why does it hurt so much?"

"Because you don't expect family to betray you," Carson answered quietly. "Because he's your baby brother, and you love him."

"Don't know why I expected more." Kennedy looked up at her. "Not like I set him a real good example."

"Don't start down that path again, please." Carson rubbed her head. "You've set him a plenty good example the past five years or so. Pete made his own poor choices, and you know it."

"I don't know much of anything right now." She snuggled into the thick down comforter and allowed the soothing touch to seep in and begin to heal the pain, just a little bit. "Except that I don't think I can stand to look at my own brother."

"Tell you what, let me go make those calls, and maybe when I get back, I'll bring you cookies and an even better surprise." She slid toward the edge of the bed. "Deal?"

"You gonna come back naked?" Kennedy looked up hopefully.

Carson simply burst out laughing, glad for the unexpected humor. She leaned over and kissed Kennedy's head, and received a gentle nuzzle to her belly. "You are something else, Kennedy Shea." She kissed her again, this time brushing her lips. "I think loving you is going to be one heck of an adventure."

"Like it hasn't been already, eh?" White teeth flashed in a genuine smile.

"That it has." Carson carefully slipped out from under her, sliding a pillow under Kennedy's head. "You want me naked, do you now?"

"Naked is always good." Kennedy batted her eyelashes playfully.

"Can't promise that just yet, but maybe I can work some nakedness into the rest of the surprise." She couldn't resist kissing Kennedy's head one more time and leaned over, gasping a little when Kennedy tickled her ribs, before she cupped Carson's face, stroking it with her thumb.

"Do I get to get naked with you?" A little color was returning to Kennedy's cheeks, along with a familiar sparkle in her eyes.

"Oh, I think that can be arranged." Carson reluctantly pulled away. "I'll be back in a bit."

Kennedy frowned. "I think I'll just take a catnap while you're gone."

"Okay." Carson stopped in the now open doorway. "Sweet dreams."

Kennedy blew her a kiss. "They will be."

Carson shook her head as she padded down the hall and traipsed down the two flights of stairs that led to the first floor. After making a few calls her plans were set in motion, and she collected a platter of cookies, one glass of regular milk, and one glass of soy milk, and carefully carried her tray back upstairs. As she passed Pete's room, she noticed the door was cracked open. She was certain it had been closed on her way downstairs and she stopped, wondering if it was an invitation. "I'll probably live to regret this," she murmured as she set the tray down on a hall table and knocked softly at the door. "Pete?"

"Come on in," a contrite voice answered.

She stepped inside and waited, leaning against the wall. Pete sat in a window similar to the one in Kennedy's room, both knees drawn up with his arms wrapped around them. "Can I sit down?" She indicated the empty space next to him, and he nodded slightly, not looking up. She settled down and swiped slightly sweaty palms against her jeans-clad legs. "I've been debating ever since Parker brought you back from Austin. And I don't know whether to talk to you or beat the living daylights out of you." Her shoulders slumped in defeat, and she fought her own tears. "I hate feeling this way. You're her brother. How could you betray her like that? How could you?"

At the sound of her shaking voice, he looked back up and swallowed. "Didn't mean for things to turn out the way they did. I didn't think—"

"No. You didn't, did you?" She stood and began pacing the room. "Let me tell you something, Pete. I'm an only child and both my parents are dead. My family, the family I knew growing up, is gone. You have the most amazing family. Do you have any idea how lucky you are?" She moved closer, doing her best to keep a lid on her rage. "Do you?" Her voice rose and she fought the urge to slap him senseless.

"I..." He looked back down. "I just didn't want to go to jail is all."

"Do you understand what you've done, Pete? What you almost did?" Carson picked up a decorative pillow and hurled it across the room. It hit the far wall and bounced to the floor. "Your friend, if you called him that, Tom...he's dead now. And your sister." She clenched and unclenched her fists. "Your sister, the love of my life, very nearly died because you had to open your big mouth. You knew we were in trouble and you just left us! You almost killed her. Just turned her over to a couple of guys who would kill for a bag of cocaine." She found another pillow and it followed the first one. "Or maybe you just don't care. I swear, the way you've been acting, maybe you wanted her dead."

"I—"

"Shut up!" She whirled around and faced him. "Despite everything, I think she still loves your sorry ass. God knows why, but she does. Now, if you'll excuse me, I'm going to take her out for a nice birthday celebration. We'll be gone a few days, so you can shove your attitude. Won't be anyone around to use it on."

"I never meant for her to get hurt. You have to believe me," Pete pleaded. Large eyes brimmed with tears, and he swiped his hand across his face.

It took the wind out of her sails and Carson slumped back against the wall, shoving her hands into her pockets. "I do." She looked up. "But that doesn't undo what you did. She's pretty bruised right now. You cut her pretty deep, and it's going to be a while before she'll get past this. Broken trust is a tough thing to mend."

"Should I go talk to her?" He started to stand, but Carson held up a hand and he sat back down.

"I wouldn't just yet. Give her some time." She pushed the door open and stepped partway out. "Hopefully she'll come back in a few days in a much better mood. Meanwhile, you have some pretty big problems of your own to deal with."

Shades of a twelve-year-old boy surfaced in his tanned features and Pete fought the urge to cry. "Carson," he answered softly. "I was so scared. More scared than I've ever been in my life. I don't know how things went so wrong."

"Sounds like you have a lot to think about." She gazed at him intently and he shrank back in reflex. "She's been in this place before, you know, at least as far as being hooked on drugs goes. Give her some time, and she just might have some words of wisdom for you. We have to stay here for a few more days, but I think it will be best for all of us if you and she aren't under the same roof. We'll be leaving in a little while and be back in a few days." She opened the door wider. "I have to go."

"Can you tell her I'm sorry?" He looked up hopefully.

"Sure, I can do that." She slipped out the door and retrieved the tray, making her way back into Kennedy's room.

"Hey." Kennedy studied the tray and perked up noticeably. "What you got?"

"Cookies and soy milk." Carson set the tray down. "Eat up, 'cause you and I have some reservations this evening to go celebrate your birthday."

"Aw, Carson." Kennedy managed to sit up. "That's sweet, but I'm not sure I'm up for an evening out, just yet."

"How about an evening in?" Carson tugged her suitcase out from beside the wall. "How does you, me, a really nice room, and some excellent room service sound? You won't have to do anything more strenuous than maybe take a nice long bath."

"That sounds perfect." She edged closer, snagging Carson's belt loop with her right hand, and pulling her around to face her. Carson ended up standing between her legs, one hand resting on her right shoulder, while the other tilted her chin up. Kennedy looked up at her earnestly, her thoughts a jumble. "You really do take good care of me."

"That's my job now, isn't it?" Carson's insides fluttered, remembering things they talked about before Kennedy was shot and the direction their conversation was leading. She swallowed and shoved down the attack of nerves, covering it up with a little wink.

Kennedy felt the tremor in her hand and captured it, kissing her knuckles. "Can't think of anyone better for the job."

"Come on then." Carson forced herself to step back. "Let's pack up a few things and go celebrate, birthday girl."

THE STRONG SCENT of oil paint and turpentine assaulted Carson's nose as she poked her head inside the studio. It was a bright, sunny room, considering it was in the basement, with a row of windows circling the room just below the ceiling, letting in the outside sunshine. Various sets of lights also hung from the ceiling, and she noticed an impressive row of dimmer switches next to the door. Stacks of canvases, some finished, some in progress, and some untouched, leaned against two walls, while others adorned half a dozen easels scattered about the room.

A sink and long counter graced half of one wall, while a

large cabinet and a set of shelves covered the other half. A table in one corner bore several instruments, some she recognized and some she didn't, although one appeared to be a machine for stretching canvas. The room had a warm, busy, yet cozy feel to it, and soft, new age music flowed from a boom box on the table.

"Hi." Carson stepped all the way into the room. "Am I interrupting you?"

"Ah. Come on in." Joseph's back had been to her, but now he turned to face her, setting aside a tin of paints and a brush, and wiping his hands on a rag that hung from his belt. His shirt was clean and free of paint, as were his shoes and the floor around him. Carson recalled experiments in painting and was impressed with his ability to confine the paint to the canvas.

"What are you working on?" She moved closer, studying a wide painting on an easel next to him that had the beginnings of the mountains and trees of Big Bend colored in along one side.

"Something my daughter mentioned." Joseph gestured toward the un-painted side of the canvas, where he had sketched in bits of scenery to be painted. "It struck an inspirational chord and wouldn't leave me alone, so I came down here to capture it."

"Oh." Carson spotted something that was surely a buck, and she stepped closer to study it. Unpainted, it was anyone's guess as to what color it would be. She noted some faint symbols, possibly Native American, that were sketched in along the bottom of the painting, and again along the top, framing the scene. "What you've done so far is gorgeous." She looked around the room. "All of it. Kennedy has some nice ones on the walls at home, too."

"Home?" Joseph smiled, his tone slightly teasing.

Carson blushed and looked down. "At her house, I mean..."

"I'm sorry, Carson." Joseph chuckled, feeling badly he had teased her. "I didn't mean to make you ill at ease."

She looked up uncertainly. "Does that bother you? Me calling her house 'home'?"

"No." He gazed steadily into her eyes. "So, Aileen tells me you have a birthday surprise for Shea?" he changed the subject.

"Um. Yeah, I do, actually. I thought it might be a good idea to get away for a few days." She looked at the painting he was working on again. "What color do you plan to paint that deer?"

"White." His eyes conveyed amusement, and Carson realized he was reading her thoughts.

"I see." She swallowed, wiping her suddenly sweaty palms on her jeans legs. "I saw him, you know."

"Yes. Shea told me." He raised one knee, resting his foot on the top crosspiece of his stool, wrapping his hands around his leg. "That sort of thing doesn't happen very often, but I'll let my daughter share my theories with you. I had assumed she would have by now."

"Oh, yeah. Just...we got a little distracted with everything going on and..."

"I'm sure she'll share with you when she's ready." He smiled. "Shea has always been one who had to ponder things a bit and let them sink in. Deep thinker, that one is."

"You can say that again." Carson smiled back. "I just thought maybe if we got away for a day or so, it would give her a chance to relax and maybe emotionally recover some from everything that's happened. Process things. You know."

"Good idea." His gaze became pointed. "What about you, Carson? Do you need a little time away to sort things out?"

Ah. An opening. Thank you. She felt the need to pace and moved over under the windows, her hands clasped behind her back as she sought her words. "I...um...you see, I already did some of that...sorting things out, I mean. I had a lot of time to think while we were in that cave after she was shot. And before that, even." She turned back to face him. "What I figure is, Kennedy, she waited five years to get into a relationship after Angela died. That tells me she doesn't take them lightly."

"That would be true." Joseph nodded in agreement.

"But at the same time, she isn't one to push people into something they aren't ready for." Carson moved closer and leaned back against the counter top across from him. "All along she's told me to take my time, figuring out if I wanted to move to Austin, figuring out if I wanted to look for my own place."

"No matter what she really wishes for, I'd wager," Joseph encouraged her.

"Yes!" Carson smiled. "That's exactly it. She's never pushed me, sir."

"Carson, please." He smiled warmly. "Joseph will be fine."

"Oh. Right. Joseph." The infuriating blush returned, warming her cheeks. "Your daughter...Kennedy...I think she wants all the things you have with your wife, you know? A home. Security. A family."

"Love?" Joseph added helpfully, watching the blush turn crimson.

"Yes," she whispered. "That most of all. I do love her, sir...Joseph...sorry." She paused in frustration. "I do. She means more to me than anything, and I'd do just about anything for her. I just want her to be happy."

"Do you think you make her happy?" The question was harsh, but his tone was kind.

"I...I try to. I hope so. I..."

"Carson," his voice was very gentle. "I know you do. I see it in her eyes every time she looks at you. Nay, every time she mentions your name. My daughter glows with her love for you. You didn't know her before, so you can't see the difference you've made in her, but I surely can."

"Is it a good difference?" Carson crossed her fingers behind her back.

"Good in every sense of the word," he assured her. "Shea has been alone for much too long and I could feel the emptiness she felt. I couldn't be happier you've come into her life."

Carson felt almost faint with relief. "Well, good, you see, because Kennedy, I don't think love alone is good enough for her. She deserves that security and all that other stuff I mentioned. She deserves to know that if she gives her love to someone, that she won't wake up one morning and find that person has left her and thrown that love away. She deserves to know that whoever holds her heart will cherish it, and honor it, and take care of it." She paused, taking a deep breath. "Am I making sense?"

"Absolutely." Joseph nodded gravely, only his lips twitching in amusement. "Go on."

"Mr. Nocona...sir...oh, drat!" Carson sputtered. "Joseph." She released a long breath. "My intentions toward your daughter are honorable. I love her, and what I figured out in the past few days is, I want to be with her always. I...I know we can't get married. Not legally. Maybe someday we will, but...but I want to ask you, sir..." Her eyes flashed with a bit of pride, daring him to correct her on her choice of words at such an important moment. "...that if I ask your daughter to spend the rest of her life with me, that you will give us your blessing."

There. She'd said it. Now she only hoped it had made sense.

"Carson, come here." Joseph beckoned her with a crooked finger, his face expressionless. She walked slowly toward him, hoping he wasn't planning to smack her into next week when she got within reach. Instead, he opened up his arms and welcomed her into a most unexpected hug, along with a kiss to her cheek. "I'd be proud to welcome you into my family." He released her. "And for the record, my daughter would be foolish to reject such an offer."

"You don't think she'd...?"

"Not in a million years," he answered. "And yes, you have my blessing. You didn't need to ask, but I'm honored you did."

Carson flung her arms around his neck again. "Thank you. You won't live to regret it."

"Of that I have no doubt." He smiled as she stepped back. "Go and take her to her surprise."

"I will." She turned toward the door. "I'm sorry for everything that's happened here. I know it can't be easy for you and your wife."

"Yes, and all the more difficult because I've had to make some choices. I have to do my best to hold my family together, if that's possible." He sighed. "What my son did is almost unforgivable. But he is my son, and I will always love him. Just as I will always love my daughter. My son made some bad choices, and those bad choices led to more bad choices. I believe him when he says he felt trapped and afraid. My daughter also made bad choices in her past, and she will never know for sure if one of those choices led to the death of someone she loved. You know about all that." Carson nodded. "As a father, if I step back, both my children did things that hurt other people. It's just that in Pete's case, it hurt another member of the family. My daughter is not in a place to see things in that same light."

"I hadn't thought of it like that," Carson murmured. "I don't think I can think of it like that. I love her and he almost got her killed. I understand they're both your children and you love them, but in this, I have to take her side."

"And I would expect no less from someone who wants to spend the rest of their life with her." He smiled sadly. "It seems I am about to pass the job of taking care of her on to you. I think she's in more than capable hands." He swiped a tear from Carson's cheek. "And, Carson, make sure she tells you about the white buck. You have a much higher blessing than mine."

She opened her mouth to ask another question and then closed it, thinking better of it. "All right." She sniffled and gazed at him in puzzlement. "Thank you. I will."

She mounted the stairs and stopped in the guest powder room long enough to remove traces of tears from her face, then slipped through the first floor of the house, and out the back door where Kennedy sat on the porch swing, gazing out at the horses in the padlock. "You done with your super-secret meeting?" Her tone and her face were more than a little grumpy.

"Yeah." Carson held out a hand and waited, while Kennedy slowly reached out and accepted it, allowing herself to be pulled up. "You ready to go?"

"Been ready," she grumbled. "Still don't see what you had to talk to Pa about that is so all-fired private. He probably gave you all kinds of advice on how to deal with me when I'm hurt, didn't he?"

"Nope." Carson patted her cheek and she scowled. "All in

good time, honey."

"I coulda told you about the buck," Kennedy ventured.

"Didn't ask him about the buck," Carson shot back. "But he did tell me to ask you about it, so I told him I would."

"He...he did?" Her eyebrows disappeared under her bangs. "How on earth did that come up?"

Carson simply smiled and helped her into the truck.

Chapter
Twelve

KENNEDY LAY STRETCHED out on a doublewide leather chaise lounge, staring out the window in contentment at the view from their cabana window. Before her were miles and miles of Lajitas Resort, a plush little hideaway tucked against the southwest side of the park, just on the edge of the Mexico border. The resort had the best Big Bend had to offer: green golf courses, man-made ponds, natural mountainscapes, horseback riding, wildlife, spa facilities, fine dining, shopping, and best of all, the peaceful, pricey accommodations Carson had rented for them for three days.

They were in one of the Cavalry Post Cottages, a stand-alone facility with a private patio, kitchenette, and a tub she was certain Carson must be lost in at the moment. Carson had insisted on a combination of both the romance package and the pampering package. Next to the lounge on a sturdy antique oak table was a stoneware vase, painted with Native American designs and filled with a bouquet of fresh flowers, some local and some imported from elsewhere. Next to the vase was a container of chocolate-dipped strawberries.

Kennedy plucked up one of the juicy red pieces of fruit and bit into it, closing her eyes in bliss as the combination of tart strawberry and sweet chocolate washed over her tongue. She lazily opened one eye and noted she'd only eaten three of the dozen strawberries. *Heh.* She smiled. That meant three more were hers for the taking.

She heard singing coming from the bathroom along with a splash of water, indicating that hopefully Carson was emerging from her bubble bath and would join her soon. They'd tried to bathe together, but because of the need to keep her shoulder and left leg dry, she couldn't fill the tub very full. It had become too complicated trying to keep her injuries above the water line and actually try to bathe.

They'd finally given up, admitting that sitting in four inches of water with her shoulder covered in Saran Wrap and her leg propped up along the rim of the tub wasn't the most romantic or comfortable way to get clean together. Carson had gotten out and helped her bathe, washing her hair and treating her to a scalp massage. After getting Kennedy situated on the chaise, wrapped up in a thick terry robe the resort provided, Carson had refilled the tub and added some agave bubble bath. She'd been in there for twenty minutes, which seemed much too long to her waiting companion.

It was surreal after all they'd been through over the past few days, to find herself suddenly sitting in the lap of luxury with a virtual plethora of culinary and carnal pleasure to look forward to. A massage therapist was scheduled to visit them for two hours each day, and more fresh flowers and strawberries would arrive each morning, and a bottle of champagne each evening. Carson had even convinced her to go for a manicure and pedicure treatment, while Carson had signed on for something called an "Egyptian mud wrap." Kennedy chuckled at that. She wasn't sure about the wrap part, but she was looking forward to seeing Carson covered in the mud. It was oddly appealing, and she tried to remember if she'd ever actually watched any female mud wrestling. Maybe.

It was easy for the moment to forget about shootings, dead men, and drug dealers. A little less easy to forget about Pete, but Carson had told her he said he was sorry. It was precious little consolation after what he'd done, and she still hadn't forgiven him, but...she sighed. She knew that eventually, she would. He was her brother after all, and she did feel responsible for him on a certain level. Still, she decided it wouldn't hurt to let him stew for a few days, wondering, before she bothered to talk it out with him.

It hurt. More than she really wanted to admit to herself, much less to Carson. Little brothers were supposed to look up to their big sisters. It was all so wrong. The hatred in his eyes. She'd seen that look many times as a trial lawyer and as a prominent openly gay figure within Austin's increasingly conservative legal community. She'd just never expected to see that expression on the face of a family member.

She plucked up another strawberry. Somehow, warm and clean and wrapped up in that robe, consuming the tasty treat and looking out on the mountains, it was hard to think about Pete too much at the moment, and so her thoughts drifted elsewhere. Friends had taken her out to lunch and dinner on almost all her birthdays. A few times Heidi had even traveled down from Dallas to take her out on the town. But this was the first time a lover had ever swept her away for a weekend of decadent pampering.

It was a dual celebration, really. Carson's birthday was now less than a week away. They'd both done a little shopping when they first arrived at the resort, just to unwind and wait while their room was being prepared, since Carson had called them only a little while before they drove down. She'd secreted away a few items for Carson's birthday, assuming she could hold out that long before giving them to her. In one soft, suede leather bag, lined in satin, was a simple pair of diamond stud earrings, a half carat each, and set in platinum. In another similar bag was a matching diamond tennis bracelet, also set in platinum.

Carson still had not asked about the buck. It was a relief to have a little more time to think about how to explain that they shared the same spirit. It made sense, given some of the intense emotions that ran between them. She remembered how it felt, sitting on the rock outside the cave, watching the buck together. Her body still tingled, remembering how close she had felt to Carson, as if they were one and the same. If she closed her eyes she could still feel Carson, as if she were breathing from Kennedy's lungs.

Her eyes popped open as she felt warm breath against the top of her head, followed by a brush of Carson's lips. "Caught you daydreaming, didn't I?" Carson's lips moved lower, capturing Kennedy's own willing ones and engaging her in a lengthy exchange. Carson was leaning over her, one hand braced on the arm of the chaise lounge, and the angle offered Kennedy just the slightest peek at a couple of her favorite assets.

A bubbling, throaty laugh escaped, and she reached across, giving Carson's robe ties a gentle tug, causing the front of the robe to spill open. Carson also laughed as Kennedy's hand slipped inside the robe, wrapping around her waist and pulling her forward until she was reclining against Kennedy on the lounger.

"Careful." Carson gently touched Kennedy's left arm. With a promise to be good and keep still, they'd left the sling off, with the robe only draped over her left shoulder, her arm inside it, but not in the sleeve.

"Don't wanna be careful." Kennedy nipped at an earlobe, then moved lower, nibbling Carson's neck. She slipped her hand inside the robe again, sliding up and finding sensitive spots that made Carson practically purr against her lips as they met in another dizzying kiss.

"Honey." Carson came up for air. "Are you sure this is a good idea? Your shoulder and leg. I don't want to..."

"My arm and leg may be out of commission," Kennedy interrupted. "But I can assure you all the body parts necessary for this are fully functional and standing at attention at present." She took Carson's hand, pulling it inside her own robe. Carson's fingers brushed over a hardened nipple and Kennedy's eyes closed as she groaned in appreciation.

"I see." Carson continued to touch her, her hand sliding gradually lower and nudging Kennedy's legs apart. "Yep." She kissed Kennedy, her lips trailing across the upper swells of her breasts as her hand continued to explore. "I do believe you were telling the truth about them there body parts, Miz Nocona." She withdrew her hand and Kennedy made a disappointed mewling noise.

"Please, baby." She took Carson's hand, intent on dragging it back where it had been, only to have Carson pull away.

"Hold on." Carson hovered over her, pushing back the robe from Kennedy's left shoulder. She grinned wickedly and pulled the tie from her own robe, and quickly secured Kennedy's left arm to the wrought-iron arm that decorated the chaise on one side. "Wanna make sure that arm stays still if we plan to take this any further."

"Why, Carson Garret, you little dominatrix." Kennedy peered over at her lover's handy-work. "How did you know I was fantasizing about you tying me up and taking advantage of me?"

"I just had a feeling you were that kind of girl," Carson teased back. "Next thing, you'll be asking me to flail you or something."

"Ooo." Kennedy's eyes glinted, testing her lover's reaction

Carson's skin prickled in mild alarm. "You weren't really fantasizing about me tying you up, were you?" She felt Kennedy's right hand trail up her thigh, pushing her robe up in the process.

"No, sweetheart." The hand found her behind, giving her a sensual squeeze. "At least not the tying up part, but I did have a nice daydream or two about you while I was waiting for you to get out of that tub in there."

"Did you now?" Carson's smile returned and her hands began to wander again, pushing Kennedy's robe the rest of the way open. She slid up the long body, finding Kennedy's earlobe and suckling it thoroughly, as her hand nudged the impossibly sexy legs apart again. "What kind of daydreams, exactly?" she whispered before blowing over a spot she'd just tasted, watching chills raise up on Kennedy's skin.

"Oh, god." Kennedy's eyes slammed shut as Carson began

stroking her, teasing her lightly with her fingertips, while her lips performed a simultaneous assault on her neck and throat. "Reality beats the daydream every time, darlin'."

"Shhh." Carson found her lips. "Too much talking." She kissed her lightly, pulling back and gazing into sultry eyes that burned right through her. "So damned beautiful," Carson whispered, not breaking their connection, her own eyes conveying the same passion. "I love you," she whispered again, closing the distance and ratcheting up the heat, both with fingers and lips.

Kennedy closed her eyes again, getting lost in the sensation until her body rose up, arching against her lover before she crashed over the edge, her climax washing over her in waves that left her gasping for air, her heart pounding in her chest.

Carson kissed her again, light nibbles all over her face and lips, her own body just beginning to heat up. Kennedy's hand was still splayed across an ass cheek, urging her closer, as Kennedy slid down from her partially-sitting up position, to a fully-reclining one. They kissed again, Carson almost, but not quite, lying on top of her, as Kennedy's hand edged inward.

Full lips moved to Carson's neck, and then to her ear before Kennedy released a sigh of frustration. "I don't have enough hands." She nipped Carson's nose. "Can't hold you and touch you at the same time, and I sure as heck can't trade places with you, because I'd need the one good arm to brace myself."

"It's all right. We'll just do what we can. This is really nice." Carson soothed, kissing her soundly. They got lost in the exchange again, Carson's own passion rising to a maddening level that demanded relief. She felt Kennedy's hand slide up and over her hip and warm breath against her ear.

"Flip around and over me, baby." Kennedy bit down, taking a tiny fold of skin between her teeth, leaving a mark almost irrelevant at that point. "Please," she whispered.

Carson kissed her again before she complied, nibbling her way down Kennedy's body in the process. It was a new position for them and a strange sensation at first, being unable to see Kennedy's face. Carson felt the loss of their intimate connection for only a second until the first warm breath brushed against her inner thigh. She gurgled something unintelligible and simply dropped down, her cheek resting against Kennedy's belly.

She could smell Kennedy's warm musky scent, and feel her skin all up and down her body, not to mention what her mouth was doing. It was hot and easily one of the most erotic sensations she'd ever felt. She moaned softly, wishing she were just a little taller and could reciprocate.   A soft, insistent tongue eased inside her and all thought vanished, save the physical sensations. She cried out softly, burying her face into Kennedy's stomach, as wave after pleasurable wave washed over her.

Somehow she ended up turned around, cradled against Kennedy's side, while Kennedy kissed the top of her head and made little nonsense noises, talking her back down to earth. "Better than any chocolate covered strawberries." A husky voice burred into her ear, vibrating almost inside of her. "Remind me to become incapacitated more often."

Carson slowly opened her eyes partway, peering up at Kennedy. "No need for incapacity." She smiled. "I can just tie you up."

Their eyes locked before they both burst out laughing.

"Oh, god, I love you so much." Kennedy pulled her to her as tightly as she could with one arm. "I never knew making love could be as hot and as fun as it has been with you." Her arm slid up and she pushed the hair back from Caron's face. "I could stay right here like this forever."

"Mmm." Carson rubbed her belly in circles with the flat of her hand. "Forever sounds good." She nuzzled Kennedy's chest as they settled into a blissful semi-conscious state.

Forever. Yeah. Kennedy looked down at the blonde head, kissing it tenderly one more time before she closed her eyes again.

CARSON STRETCHED, HER body gradually coming back to life. She slowly opened her eyes to find Kennedy missing, though the leather surface next to her was still warm, so she couldn't have been gone long. The room was quite a bit darker than it had been when they'd fallen asleep, and a fire was now burning in the gas fireplace. She looked around for a clock.

Instead, she saw an orange-red sky outside the window and noticed the door to their private porch was open a few inches. *Ah. Bet that's where she went.* She sat up, twisting her body from side to side before she stood, her feet hitting the cabana's cool hardwood floor. Socks were in order, and she padded into the bedroom and spotted Kennedy's robe hanging from one of the tall bedposts.

Carson shucked her own robe in favor of a pair of thick navy blue sweats and warm socks. Over the socks she slipped on a pair of well-worn moccasins, and then made her way into the kitchen, where their bottle of champagne sat in a bucket of ice. She grabbed it up, along with two tall crystal flutes, and moved to the patio door. She pushed it open and stopped, smiling at the sight before her.

Kennedy had donned a pair of white sweats, and sat at the very edge of the patio on a wide padded high-backed bench. She'd pulled it around facing the sunset and long golden rays of rich warm sunlight spilled over her, setting her hair afire with burnished mahogany highlights. Her face was a study in utter serenity, her eyes closed, and her dark brown skin taking on a golden-red sheen. Carson shook her head, wondering if a time would come when Kennedy wouldn't take her breath away.

She sure hoped not. But if it ever did...she shook her head again, for a different reason. As she continued to observe Kennedy, there was no longer denying that what had started out as a tiny spark of lust in a seminar conference room, had grown into a huge warm ball inside. It was something she could barely describe, which filled her up and threatened to bubble up and spill out onto the flagstone patio before her.

Would it last? This feeling that made her want to dance and sing and shout out to the mountains beyond the patio? Was it realistic to expect to always feel the way she did at that very moment? Looking inside herself, she knew the truth. And the truth was that she was in love. Not just lust anymore, and not infatuation, but a bone-deep love that had soaked into every fiber of her being. Even if the overwhelming feelings of euphoria passed, it had knitted itself much too deep inside of her to ever go away.

She stepped the rest of the way out the door and as she closed it, Kennedy opened her eyes, raking them up and down her in frank appreciation. "Hey, sleeping beauty. You gonna join me for the rest of this gorgeous sunset?" She eyed the champagne bottle. "We celebrating something?"

"Maybe, birthday girl." Carson set the flutes down and neatly popped the cork on the bottle before pouring up two healthy measures of the sparkling, bubbly liquid. She took a sip and sat down next to Kennedy. "Mmm. Nice and dry and not too sweet. Just like I like it."

"It is good stuff." Kennedy took a long sip and swirled the champagne around her mouth, smiling at the tickly sensation of bubbles bursting against her tongue. She felt Carson's fingers gently playing with her hair, and closed her eyes, deciding it just didn't get much better than that very moment. "Feels nice," she murmured.

"It's all red and silvery-looking in the sunlight." Carson continued to arrange Kennedy's hair, running her fingers through it in idle pleasure. "But no real silver ones just yet."

Kennedy opened her eyes and studied her carefully. "That'll

take a long time," she repeated her words from their
conversation in the cave, her gaze locked with Carson's.

"You'll be beautiful with gray hair," Carson repeated her
own words from the cave, her eyes soft and shining, offering up
her heart as a silent gift. "Tell me about the white buck," she
whispered.

"All right." Kennedy shifted, placing both feet on the stone
and leaning forward slightly, her forearms draped loosely over
her thighs, her right arm favoring her weight. She looked away
from Carson, out toward the lengthening shadows beyond the
patio and the warm red and pink sky over the mountaintops.
"You know the buck is my spiritual guardian."

Carson nodded, remaining silent, as she continued to play
with Kennedy's hair.

"He protects me and gives me guidance on the important
things in life." She swallowed and took a deep breath. "It's
supposed to be a very personal and private thing."

"Does it bother you that I saw him too?" Carson's eyes stung
with irrational tears. She didn't feel sad or anxious, and she
wasn't sure where the emotion was coming from.

"No." A tiny smile tugged at Kennedy's lips and she glanced
over at Carson before returning her gaze toward the mountains.
"It just surprised me. That's why I had to ask Pa about it. He
said..." She paused, closing her eyes as Carson moved closer and
placed a single kiss against her neck, her fingers still combing
through her hair. "He said it's a very rare thing for two people to
see a single spiritual guardian at the same time, much less for
you to have seen him while I was asleep. It can mean a few
things, but in the case of two lovers..." She paused again to
regard Carson, who blushed very nicely.

"He called us lovers?" she squeaked.

"God, you're adorable." Kennedy kissed the top of her head,
her eyes sparkling in the fading sunlight. "Not us, specifically.
He was speaking in general terms about the buck. But..." She
smiled. "Pa's not stupid, Carson. I think he knows we're doing
more than just sleeping in that bed we've been sharing."

Carson covered her eyes for a moment and sighed, slowly
regaining her composure. "I know. I just don't like to think about
him thinking about us...like that."

"It's what we are, isn't it?" Kennedy took Carson's hand,
brushing her thumb across her knuckles. "Lovers?"

"Lovers. Best friends." Carson agreed. "Soul mates," she
added softly, watching Kennedy's eyes sparkle in surprised
wonder.

"Funny, you should say that." Kennedy looked down at

their joined hands. "Pa said when two lovers see a spiritual guardian together it most likely means they are bound so closely together that they share the same spirit. The spiritual guardian sees them as a single being and protects and guides them both."

"Wow." Carson sat back a bit, allowing the words to sink in. "And I'm not even Comanche." Kennedy peered up, her face as wide open and vulnerable as a child's.

Was it too much? Carson appeared to be stunned and Kennedy sighed unhappily. *Time to do the right thing.* "Carson, listen. I had a pretty good fever going back in that cave after I was shot. I know we said a lot of things. And Pa...he's full of the old ways. I...I don't hold you to anything. It was cold and dark, and we were both pretty miserable at the time. I..." A soft kiss to Kennedy's lips silenced her.

"Do you believe your father?" Carson peered anxiously into her eyes, reading the truth.

Kennedy broke her gaze, looking down, her eyes brimming with tears. "I do." A thick lump in her throat hurt so badly she could barely speak. "But I don't want you to feel like you have to..." Two fingers against her lips hushed her again.

"No one ever made me do much of anything I didn't want to." Carson twined their fingers. "I remember reading somewhere that it takes a second to notice someone, an hour to like them, a day to fall in love, and a lifetime to forget them." She inched closer. "And I know if I walked away right now, I would never ever forget you."

"Is that what you're doing?" a pained voice asked. "Walking away?"

"No. Oh no, honey. Not at all." She tilted Kennedy's chin up. "Oh, sweetheart." Tears flowed down the tanned cheeks and Carson quickly brushed them away. "I'm not doing a real good job of this, but please hear me out, will you?"

Kennedy nodded uncertainly. "Sorry."

"Don't be sorry." Carson kissed first one cheek and then the other and then briefly brushed Kennedy's lips, smiling against them. "Better?"

"Some." A charmingly shy, uncertain smile appeared.

"I may not follow much of my Southern Baptist upbringing anymore." Carson continued to hold Kennedy's hand, giving it a little squeeze. "But there's one thing that stuck solidly with me, something one of the youth pastors said one time. He said love is not a bunch of warm, fuzzy feelings. Love is a decision and a commitment. He said that when you fall in love, if you want it to last, you'd best just decide it will. Because there will be days when you don't always feel those warm fuzzies, and those are the days you commit to loving someone anyway. Those are the days you just decide you will love them, no matter what."

Slowly, Carson slid off the bench and dropped to her knees, taking Kennedy's hand between her own. "I think I fell in love with you the first time we danced." She looked up hesitantly.

"Me too," Kennedy responded softly, her eyes shining warmly over Carson.

"Things happened so fast between us, it sometimes makes my head spin," Carson continued. "And maybe it's too soon to be saying all of this, but I keep going back to that decision and commitment thing."

Kennedy reached up, stroking her cheek. "Not too soon," she whispered. "You've had my heart from the moment I first held you in my arms."

"I know." Carson smiled sadly. "And you've been so patient with me."

"How could I not be?" Kennedy blinked, sending another scattering of tears down her cheeks. "My heart gave me no choice."

"I knew I loved you," Carson continued, gently swiping at Kennedy's tears. "I knew I felt all those wonderful feelings. But during this trip out here, I decided to love you. Do you understand what I'm saying?"

"Yeah." A slight nod of her head as Kennedy eased off the bench, joining Carson on her knees. "Maybe we should do this together."

A happy little yelp escaped and Carson found herself crying. She carefully gathered Kennedy to her, mindful of her shoulder as she held her close. "I made you a promise back in that cave, that I would hang around and grow old with you. Remember?"

"I remember," a rich voice burred in her ear.

"Will you let me make good on that promise?" Her lungs felt so tight she could barely draw a breath.

"Yes." With a single word, Kennedy felt all the tension drain from Carson's body, and felt warm tears against her neck. "You want to hear the rest of the story of the buck?" Carson nodded against her, and Kennedy carefully guided them both back onto the bench, where they curled up together in a ball of pure happiness.

"Pa said when two people share the same spirit, it means they do not merely exist side by side, but are entwined." She kissed Carson's head and pulled it down to her shoulder. "He said it's a bond that cannot easily be broken, that it goes beyond the grave."

"I felt that when I saw him, when we were sitting on that

rock." Carson closed her eyes, remembering feeling Kennedy as if she were inside her. "I felt like we were one and the same. Your father said we had a higher blessing than his. Now I understand what he meant."

"Is that what you were talking to him about?" Kennedy's whispered in utter surprise.

"Yeah," Carson answered sheepishly. "I...um...kind of went to him to let him know my intentions toward you are honorable and to get his blessing on our relationship."

"Carson." Kennedy sat back, just enough to look into her eyes. "That means more to me than I can adequately express. And I know it meant a great deal to Pa."

"You're his only daughter and he loves you very much." Carson shrugged, and snuggled back down against her shoulder. "It was the right thing to do, to put his mind at ease. At least I hope that's what I did."

"I know you did." Kennedy ducked her head, finding her lips for a long while, feeling the same merging of spirits they had felt on that boulder in the park. She deepened the contact, pulling Carson close against her and getting lost in a warm, euphoric wave.

When they finally broke apart the sun had long since set and a blanket of stars covered the dark blue sky overhead. As they watched in companionable silence, a star shot across the sky, burning out somewhere beyond the mountaintops. Two pairs of eyes closed for a moment before they turned and looked at each other.

"Did you make a wish?" they asked in unison, then both smiled.

"Wow." Carson rested her head on a sturdy shoulder. "Wonder what your father would say about beginning your life together by wishing on a star?"

"Don't know." Kennedy pressed her cheek against her lover's soft hair. "Maybe it depends on what we wished for."

"Maybe." Carson looked up at her again, and Kennedy found herself lost in a pair of shining gray eyes.

She kissed Carson again and found her ear. "Know what I wish right now?" She nipped at her earlobe. Carson smiled, and without a word, took her hand and led her inside to the warmth of the fire, glad that some wishes were easily fulfilled.

THE FIRE CRACKLED low in the stone fireplace, two figures stretched out lazily before it in a nest of blankets and comforter that had been dragged off the bed and into the sitting room. Carson was fast asleep, curled into a ball under the down coverlet, her arm tucked under her head. Her face was serene, her lips hinting at a smile. Kennedy reached over, barely touching the top of her head, smoothing her hair back.

Next to the hearth were two mostly-cleared plates and a completely empty bottle of champagne. Warm lassitude seeped into her every pore, and it was difficult to muster up the energy to do anything other than observe Carson while she slept. They'd made love and ordered room service, then shared their meal and made love again. She couldn't recall spending that kind of intensive time together since they'd gone to Fredericksburg.

It was deliciously decadent, and she stretched, curling herself around Carson, inhaling and drawing in her scent. It sent chills tingling pleasantly across her skin, or maybe it was her full stomach, or way too much champagne, or maybe...

She shook her head and smiled, wiggling her toes and looking up at the ceiling for a long moment. Maybe it was this amazing head over heels sensation of being completely in love for the first time in her life. Maybe it was the wonder of that love reciprocated. Maybe it was something too magical to explain.

Carson had proposed to her. She knew they were getting very close to that line, knew there was that tension, the good kind of tension, when you are about to take something to a higher level. They had been so close in the past few weeks and during their time in the Big Bend area and with her family, despite everything that had happened, she had never felt more in tune with Carson.

Her heart was so full, she thought it might burst. She'd been hoping for what seemed forever that Carson was ready to be in a fully committed relationship. True, it had really only been a few months, but Kennedy had known, almost from the start, that this was it for her...the love of her life.

Love had crept up and bitten hard and without mercy. When she said she had no choice, she meant it. It had become a bittersweet pain, loving someone as much as she loved Carson, waiting and hoping that Carson would find her way to that same place.

And now she had.

Kennedy's vision grew blurry and she reached up, swiping her hand across her eyes. "Damn," she murmured softly. She sniffled, and nestled back down beneath the covers. It was full dark outside and probably close to midnight. They really should drag the bedding back into the bedroom and take advantage of having a nice king-sized mattress to sleep on.

"Hey." Carson gazed across at her solemnly. "You crying? I hope those are happy tears." Kennedy nodded and Carson reached over and touched her cheek. "Who knew you were such a romantic softy?" She brushed her thumb against the soft skin. "Guess I should have been clued in when I started receiving a dozen roses every Monday morning after we met, huh?"

"I was so afraid it was going to be too much, that first time I sent them." Kennedy smiled, the firelight painting her face in interesting shadows.

"No, it was wonderful. No one ever did anything like that for me before." Carson continued to trace the high cheekbones and leaned closer, finding Kennedy's lips and sampling them for a long moment before she pulled back and stretched and yawned. "Ooo. Sorry, honey. I'd like to move this into the bedroom, but unfortunately, it's so we can get some sleep. The fire is nice and all, but this floor is a bit hard and I'm starting to feel it, even through all these blankets."

"Read my mind." Kennedy carefully rolled up. Her shoulder was feeling pretty good, but she didn't want to take any chances.

They re-made the bed after a fashion and tumbled into it, landing in the middle curled up in a happy warm tangle of arms and legs. Kennedy sighed in utter contentment as Carson extinguished the bedside lamp, leaving only the faint glow in the doorway of the remaining fire from the living room. She had banked it and it would be cool ashes by morning. She felt a series of tiny kisses to her jaw line before Carson settled down, curled tightly against her right side.

"Love you," Carson crooned softly.

"Love you too." She reached out in the darkness, twining their fingers.

"Shoulda had a ring for you," Carson muttered. "But I didn't exactly plan on doing this when we came out here."

"Ring? Oh." Kennedy laughed lightly and lifted Carson's hand, kissing it in the darkness. "Kinda glad you didn't actually. Not that I wouldn't love whatever you pick out."

"Why glad?" Carson felt another kiss to her knuckles before Kennedy tucked their joined hands just under her own breast.

"I had this kind of silly notion that if we ever did take this step, we might pick out matching ones together." She chuckled a little bit nervously, wondering what Carson thought of the idea.

"I like your silly notion very much. I...um...think it would be awesome to look down at my ring finger every day, and know that wherever you are, you are wearing a ring that matches mine." She squeezed Kennedy's hand. "I like the idea of belonging to you."

"Likewise." Kennedy kissed the top of her head. Thoughts of rings led to thoughts of all that went with a ring and she hesitated, but only for a moment. "Did you want to have some kind of commitment ceremony? I know we can't legally marry, but..."

"Can I just say how unfair that is?" Carson pouted. "I'd marry you in a New York minute. I'd take your name, you know. Maybe I'll change my name. Carson Nocona sounds nice, don't you think? I'd really like to be married to you." She suddenly felt like crying, wishing more than anything in the world that their relationship could be the same as any other couple that falls in love and decides to spend their life together.

Kennedy felt the slight tremor in Carson's body and she shifted, rolling to her right side and carefully reaching out with her left, stroking Carson's head once, and letting her hand come to rest on her shoulder. "Listen to me. I will protect you with everything I have. Everything I am. We can draw up papers, Carson. Wills...medical powers of attorney...joint bank accounts. We'll do everything we can, sweetheart, and if the day comes when we can marry, you bet we will."

"I...just..." Carson rolled to her left side, peering into the darkness. "If we have kids, will they let us adopt them together? And what about the kids' last name?"

"I'll check it out when we get home and find out how the adoption laws are set up. But we can draw up papers for that, too. And how about we both change our last name to 'Nocona-Garret'?" Kennedy felt Carson grow still for a moment.

"You'd do that?" Her voice was full of wonder.

"Carson." Kennedy laughed lightly. "Don't you realize there's almost nothing I wouldn't do for you? If you asked me to go get a Mohawk and dye it purple, I would."

"I appreciate the sentiment." Carson giggled. "But I love your hair just like it is." It felt good to lighten the mood and she relaxed back against the pillows. "Sorry to get all serious on you. You asked me a question, and the answer is yes, I'd like very much to have a commitment ceremony. Maybe somewhere in Austin, huh? Invite our closest friends and your family?"

"I'd like that very much." Kennedy leaned over and kissed her thoroughly. "We could do it just like a wedding, you know. Have the flowers and cake and all."

"Mmm. Nice idea." Carson trailed one fingertip down Kennedy's cleavage. "Which one of us is going to wear the white dress? You, maybe?"

"Um...how about a white tux?" Kennedy captured the wandering finger and nipped it.

"Ooo. Bet you'd look nice in that, too. How about we both pick out something we want to wear and surprise each other at the ceremony?" She traced a pair of full lips.

"Now that idea, I like." Kennedy smiled then, an all-out flash of white teeth that Carson could clearly see, even in the darkness. "You're amazing, you know that?" Carson ducked her head, burrowing into Kennedy's chest and just listened. "No, really. I know we have a lot of stuff to deal with after this little interlude is over, but this is just what I needed, and somehow you knew that."

"Just wanted to get you into a happier place," Carson murmured. "Proposals are extra."

Kennedy laughed for a long moment, ducking her own head until their foreheads were touching. "If that was extra, then I look forward to a lifetime of extras."

"You got it." Carson looked up, cupping her face and gazing into her eyes. "Always."

KENNEDY STARED INTO the darkness, trying to determine what had woken her up. The night creatures had all gone silent, and a glance at the digital clock showed it was 2:00 a.m. Carson was pressed tightly against her, a little too tightly as a matter of fact, and she smiled, realizing one of Carson's hands had a firm grasp on her breast. "Mmph." She hissed as Carson gave her a bit of a squeeze. "Gotta remove that."

"Mmm." Carson mumbled in her sleep, and Kennedy's attention was redirected to her hip, which Carson was grinding against. She had one leg draped across Kennedy's legs, doing a pretty good job of holding her in place. "Mmm, feels so good," Carson continued to carry on in her sleep and Kennedy chuckled, enjoying the impromptu entertainment.

"Hope I'm part of this one, whatever it is," she whispered. "Sounds like a good one." Carson shifted a bit, continuing her assault on her hipbone. "Feels like it's a pretty good one for you, too."

"Mmm, Kennedy." Carson's hand wandered to her other breast and Kennedy stifled a yelp as she gave her nipple a pinch.

"Well, at least it is me you're dreaming about." She managed to get hold of Carson's hand, which immediately settled down.

"So full. Feels so good." Carson's voice grew low and breathy, something that Kennedy always enjoyed during their lovemaking, and she found her own body starting to respond.

"Okay," she reasoned with the ceiling above her. "Your girlfriend is obviously making love with you in her dreams." She looked down again. "Do I wake her up and help her out?" She felt a distinct wetness against her skin and smiled. "Not that she seems to need my help at this point. Or do I just let her keep dreaming?" She let go of Carson's hand, deciding to see what would happen next. Then she groaned as it wandered lower, gliding between her legs.

"Vroom vroom," Carson mumbled.

"Vroom vroom? Okay, now I've got to wake her up." She trailed a hand up Carson's thigh, finding her backside and giving it a squeeze. "Hey there, hot stuff, wake up." She ducked her head, locating Carson's lips and kissing her soundly, her own heartbeat picking up as Carson readily returned the kiss, deepening it and moaning as she slowly came awake.

"What the?" Carson pulled back, looking around in confusion as she assessed her situation, then released a long frustrated sigh, flopping back on her pillow with one arm over her face. "God almighty, I'm turned on right now. Was I doing what I think I was?"

"That would make two of us, and yes, you were." Kennedy laughed and rolled to her side, prying Carson's arm away from her face and finding her lips again. "You were dreaming, sweetheart. Pretty damned good one, judging from this nice big wet spot on my hipbone here.

"Oh, god," Carson groaned and tossed her arm back over her face. "I'm sorry."

"Don't be sorry." Kennedy began tracing circles against Carson's stomach. "It was incredibly sexy. Can you tell me about it? I'm especially curious as to why you were making engine noises."

"Oh, sweet Jesus." She felt Kennedy's hand continue to wander upward, brushing across her breasts. She gave her a playful slap. "Please, can you let me maintain what's left of my dignity?"

Kennedy laughed outright, but stopped. "Sweetheart, there's no need to be embarrassed. I really am curious as to what you were dreaming about. It was incredibly cute."

"Cute?" One distrustful eye appeared. "Me humping your leg was cute?"

"You humping my leg was getting me hot and bothered. The things you were saying and the noises you were making were cute. Come on, share." She kissed Carson again, grinning as the felt her relax a little bit.

"What was I saying?" Carson finally broke off.

"Well, you said you felt good, you said you were full, and you said 'vroom vroom' right before I woke you up. I'm particularly intrigued as to where that came from." Kennedy's hand began to wander again and this time there was no resistance. "You wanna pick up wherever you left off?" She managed her most charming smile and was rewarded with one in kind.

"Be kind of hard to do in here," Carson's voice was sheepish, and she could feel the blush across her cheeks, glad of the darkness to hide it. "Okay." She gathered her courage. "I just don't want you to be appalled or anything."

"Carson." Kennedy's fingertips circled an enticing breast, pleased when she felt Carson's ribs expand sharply at her touch. "First of all, you were dreaming, and you can't help what you dream. But let me assure you, there is very little you could dream or fantasize about that would shock me or make me think any less of you. I was getting turned on just listening to you a minute ago. I can't wait to hear what was going on in that lovely head of yours."

"Well..." Carson grabbed her hand. "You're distracting me." She smiled. "In a good way, but I can't talk when you touch me like that."

"Okay, I'll try to be good." Kennedy kissed her way along a collarbone for a moment. "But it might be real difficult. Go on." She propped her head up on an upraised hand.

"We went for a ride on your motorcycle, and while we were riding I kind of unbuttoned your shirt and was playing with your breasts." Carson reached over, touching one of the body parts in question while she spoke. "I think in the dream, I made you come while we were riding."

"Ah, a woman of many talents." Kennedy smiled, rolling even closer and pressing her knee between Carson's legs. "Then what?"

"We got back to the barn and I guess you were packing," Carson mumbled the last part so low, Kennedy barely heard her.

"Come again?" Kennedy leaned closer, listening.

"Haven't come the first time yet, thank you very much," Carson replied, giving a nipple a pinch.

"Hey!" Kennedy grabbed her hand. "I could swear you said I was packing in your dream."

"You were." Carson blushed furiously and covered her eyes with one hand for a moment before Kennedy removed it.

"Why does that embarrass you?" Kennedy smiled, and tilted her head curiously.

"I'm not sure. Maybe it's the rest of the dream. You basically got off the motorcycle, pulled my jeans down, bent me over the seat, and um..." she trailed off, hiding her eyes again.

"Went to town?" Kennedy supplied helpfully. "That's one very hot dream. I like it." She pulled Carson closer and kissed her soundly. "I've actually had a fantasy or two that involved you and a dildo. Is that something you'd like to try sometime?"

"Maybe. Especially if we both get to use it," she finished quietly. "You still not appalled at me?"

"God, no." Kennedy rolled on top of her, insinuating her own leg more firmly between Carson's. She rocked against her a little bit, smiling as a low groaning noise rumbled up from Carson's throat. "I think we're going to have a fun and hot time together, for a very long time, that's what I think." She ducked her head, closing her mouth around one of Carson's nipples, feeling her own body on fire once more as Carson clutched at her shoulders.

"Oh god, don't stop." Carson buried her face into the crook of Kennedy's neck, holding her close. She nipped at warm skin and moaned softly as Kennedy's hand trailed down her stomach and nudged her legs further apart.

"Don't have any toys with me right now." Kennedy found her ear, flicking an earlobe with her tongue. "But I can improvise if you want me to."

"Mmm." Carson's hands trailed down her back, landing on her ass and pulling her closer.

"Guess that means you want, huh?" Kennedy chuckled and began playing Carson in earnest. She smiled as little noises of pleasure continually bubbled up from Carson's lips. As she continued to stroke her lover, her lips wandered leisurely from Carson's neck, down her body, stopping at all kinds of interesting places in the process.

"Grrrrr." She hummed against warm salty skin. "Vroom vroom."

THE SUN WAS just coming up over the mountains as Carson stepped outside on the patio with a steaming cup of coffee in her hands. Kennedy was already out there, her own hands curled around a cup of hot herbal tea, its faint mint scent wafting up and mingling with the pine and sandy scent on the wind. It was chilly, and Carson was grateful for the heavy sweats they both wore.

"Hey." She sat down on the padded bench and smiled, nudging Kennedy to the side a little bit. "You look awfully serious for this early in the morning."

"Mmm." It was their last morning at Lajitas. Kennedy sipped from her mug, inhaling the fragrant tea as she swallowed.

"Just thinking about everything we face when we get back to the house. And trying not to think about them."

"Mostly we're just going back long enough to pack up, say goodbye, and leave, aren't we?" Carson sat back, taking a giant gulp of her coffee.

"Yeah. I guess we need to get moving, huh?" Kennedy sidled up to her. "Let's go order up breakfast." They wandered inside, and Kennedy picked up the room service menu and leaned against the counter. "You want the egg, bacon, and hash browns?"

"I'll have whatever you have," Carson answered absently. She drizzled honey into her second cup of coffee, followed by a generous helping of real cream.

"Sweetheart, you don't have to become a vegetarian just because I'm one." She moved to the snack bar that separated the living area from the tiny kitchen and straddled one of the leather-covered bar stools.

"Not becoming one, but can I make a confession?" Carson stood across from her on the other side of the bar. "I've discovered I feel a lot better when I follow your eating routine. I just have more energy and I've lost some fat, but my muscle tone has improved with all the running around we do taking care of the horses and the boats and stuff."

"Funny." Kennedy smiled lazily in her direction. "I feel a lot better too, and my diet hasn't changed. I figured it was all those love-induced endorphins dancing around in my bloodstream."

"Ooo." Carson leaned over until they were almost nose-to-nose. "Then I must be feeling extra good, 'cause I've got those *and* this new healthy lifestyle."

Kennedy closed the distance and pecked her on the lips several times in succession before tilting her head for a more lasting contact. They separated and she smiled, smacking her lips together as she identified the taste of Carson's lips. "Coffee." She shook her finger at Carson in a mock gesture. "That is not part of a healthy lifestyle."

"It's for darned sure part of your healthy lifestyle." Carson grabbed the finger and squeezed it. "Because living with me would be hell without it."

"Good point, shorty. Hey!" She shook her finger as Carson released it after another strong squeeze. "Fine. One order of warm mixed grain cereal, fresh fruit, and organic yogurt for you."

"Sounds great," Carson answered demurely. "You ordering breakfast? I'll hit the shower first if you do."

"Or I could order it and then join you." Kennedy's eyes

sparkled mischievously.

"I'll get the saran wrap for your shoulder." She finished off the coffee, set the mug in the sink, and sashayed toward the bathroom, swaying her hips suggestively. She looked back over her shoulder and grinned, her eyes roaming all over her partner. "Don't be long with that breakfast order, and tell them to take their time."

A sexy low growl was her response.

KENNEDY STOOD NEXT to the Harley as she looked idly around the barn, taking in the warm mixed scents of hay, horseflesh, oats, and leather. She wrinkled her nose, detecting a hint of the chicken coop at the far end of the building. Looking down at the Harley, she smiled, remembering Carson's dream and their resulting lovemaking. She leaned over a little, bracing her hands against the bike's saddle, testing to see if the height would work for Carson's fantasy.

"You ready to go?" Joseph entered the room, raising his eyebrows slightly as he spotted her. "Surely you two aren't thinking of riding that back to Austin, are you?"

"Um. No." Kennedy stood up abruptly, blushing at her own thoughts. She cleared her throat and suppressed a smile. "Our bags wouldn't fit. Someday, though, I might have to take the bike to Austin."

"I thought you believed it wasn't safe to be riding it in the city." Joseph frowned.

"Mmm." She smiled mysteriously. "True, but it might be just fine riding it around out by the lake. Listen, Pa, I wish we could stay longer, until things are more settled around here."

"Despite everything, the two of you did good for those people," Joseph commented quietly.

"I still can't believe when the federal agents went to raid that house, they got there right when they were loading all those illegals into a truck." Kennedy turned, leaning against a support post. "Ranger Smothers said if the timing had been just a little off, they would've been headed for the streets of New York. And I'll rest a lot easier knowing they've broken up the ring in this part of the state, at least for now. But yeah, if there's a silver lining in all this, it's rescuing those people from sexual slavery. I just wish our family didn't have to pay such a heavy price for it."

"It's been a hard time for all of us, but your mother and I, we'll be fine. Parker has gone home to be with his family, and you need to do the same. You need to take your partner home and start living your lives together." Joseph placed an arm across her shoulders, hugging her close to his side.

"My life partner." Kennedy laid her head against his shoulder. She looked up, meeting his gaze. "Pa, I can't thank you enough for the way you've accepted Carson as one of us."

"She's a beautiful woman, both inside and out. I couldn't wish for someone better for my cha-nawoonit ecka-peta to spend her life with." He looked down, kissing her head. She closed her eyes and sniffled, feeling him tilt her chin up. "You are happy, aren't you?"

"Oh. Oh, yeah." She opened her eyes. So much had happened, it was difficult to process. "Pa, I just want you to know you and Mama didn't do anything wrong. You did just fine with me and Pete. And Parker. I know I was so angry at you growing up, but, Pa, I shouldn't have taken things out on you. You tried to teach me to be proud of who I am. I...I just wanted you to know that now I am very proud to be your daughter, proud to be Comanche and all that means."

"And Irish," Joseph supplied. His eyes swam with unshed tears, and his heart threatened to burst with emotion he couldn't express with words. He sighed heavily and hugged his daughter. It was worth it. All the heartache and the worry, the late nights, the phone calls from the sheriff's office. It was all worth it, for this one moment when he could hold a daughter who made him so proud.

"And Irish," Kennedy parroted back at him. She hugged him in return, smelling the warm cotton of his flannel shirt and the lingering scent of tobacco from the pipe he still occasionally smoked. "I won't forget, Pa. You and Mama, you done good."

Joseph held her in silence for a moment more as sunshine spilled over them from a high window, dust particles dancing around them as if they were live flying creatures. Finally, he pulled back, clasping her shoulders at arms' length. "Shea, I know you had to do what you had to do, with regard to Pete."

"Pa, I can't have him in my house with drugs. I just can't. It would—"

"Shhh." He smiled at her, a gentle expression indicating he wasn't angry. "I know. Let me finish, please."

"Sorry." Kennedy looked down, her hair covering her face as she tilted her head to one side, listening.

"Before he left yesterday we had a long talk. He's deeply afraid, Shea. And genuinely sorry for everything that happened. He said he wants to talk to you when you get back to Austin. He knows he's not welcome to live with you, but I think he's afraid he's no longer welcome in your life." He pushed back her hair, searching her face, and finding a swirling brew of emotion there.

"Your brother needs you. I think he's reaching out for help."

"Pa, it's not that easy. What he did...I just found Carson and we plan to make a life together. What he did almost killed both of us. I'm finally happy, Pa, truly happy, for the first time in my life. I feel complete with her and he could have snatched that away." She shook her head angrily and crossed her arms over her middle. "I'll talk to him if that's what he wants, but that's all I can promise."

"And that's all I can ask of you." Joseph brushed his hand against the back of her hair once and let her go. "We probably need to get going."

"Yeah." She looked around one more time and chuckled softly, patting the Harley's handlebars on the way out the door.

"Something amusing about your bike?" Joseph ushered her toward the house.

"Oh, maybe." She glanced at him, her eyes twinkling mischievously. "But nothing I can share."

"Ah." He smiled. "I see."

They reached the back porch just as Carson and Aileen came out the back door and set their bags down next to the swing. "Hey. We were wondering where you wandered off to." Carson approached Kennedy, holding out her hands and taking Kennedy's, pulling her toward her and giving her a quick peck on the lips. She laughed as Kennedy unexpectedly engulfed her, holding her close and kissing her cheek right next to her ear.

"Guess you've lost some of that shyness around my folks, huh?" Kennedy whispered.

"Been having a nice chat with your mother," Carson whispered back. "Been hearing some cute and interesting stories about you."

"Oh?" Kennedy straightened and peered at her mother. "Mama, please tell me you didn't pull out the photo albums."

"I most assuredly did." Aileen gave her a swat on the behind. "Figured Carson should know what she's getting herself into."

"Mama, not the naked baby ones!" Kennedy wailed piteously.

"Especially those." Carson giggled. "I must say, it was creative of you to take off your Tigger outfit in the middle of the Halloween party. Bet you won best costume after that."

"Mama!" Kennedy glared at Aileen. "I was two, Carson. Two! It was hot at that damned party."

"Uh-huh. Still using that excuse out on the boat too, even in the dead of mmpphh." She glared in outrage as Kennedy clamped a hand over her mouth.

Aileen and Joseph both burst out laughing, giving their daughter knowing glances. Kennedy could feel the heat flushing her cheeks, and blew out a frustrated breath, ruffling her bangs. "I think it's time to head for Austin." Kennedy pulled together her shredded dignity. She carefully uncovered Carson's mouth and received an innocently charming smile for her effort. "And you..." She tweaked Carson's nose. "You are in so much trouble."

"Promises, promises." Carson grinned as she bent over and hefted her bag into the back of the 4Runner.

Kennedy followed suit, and then they shared hugs all around. "Safe travels." Aileen pressed a wrapped bundle into Kennedy's hands. "Cookies for the road."

"Thanks, Mama." She leaned over and kissed her mother's cheek. "Everything's gonna be fine," she whispered.

"In time, yes." Aileen blinked back tears.

Joseph released Carson from a bear hug. "Welcome to the family, such as it is at present." He gazed at her, his eyes full of sorrow, and for a moment Carson felt all the pain he was feeling over his fractured family.

"I've never been more honored..." She kissed his cheek. "...than to be included in this family."

Kennedy moved in behind her, touching her on the arm. "You ready?" Carson nodded and followed, climbing up into the truck and settling into the passenger seat. The door thunked closed, and Kennedy walked around, joining her. They both turned around and waved one last time, then turned to face each other.

"Kennedy." Carson reached across, resting her hand on a firm thigh. "Let's go home."

"For good?" Kennedy leaned across, kissing her lightly on the lips.

"For better or for worse." Carson rubbed noses, then kissed her one more time before settling back, facing the driveway that led to the long road home.

FORTHCOMING TITLES
published by
Yellow Rose Books

And, Playing the Role of Herself

by K. E. Lane

Actress Caidance Harris is living her dreams after landing a leading role among the star-studded, veteran cast of 9th Precinct, a hot new police drama shot on location in glitzy LA. Her sometimes-costar Robyn Ward is magnetic, glamorous, and devastatingly beautiful, the quintessential A-List celebrity on the fast-track to super-stardom. When the two meet on the set of 9th Precinct, Caid is instantly infatuated but settles for friendship, positive that Robyn is both unavailable and uninterested. Soon Caid sees that all is not as it appears, but can she take a chance and risk her heart when the outcome is so uncertain?

The leading ladies and supporting cast of this debut novel by newcomer K. E. Lane will charm you, entertain you, and leave you with a smile on your face, eager for Ms. Lane's next offering.

Coming February 2007

Butch Girls Can Fix Anything

by Paula Offutt

Kelly Walker can fix anything—except herself. Grace Owens seeks a stable community of friends for herself and her daughter. Lucy Owens wants help with her fourth-grade math. As their stories unfold in the fictional town of High Pond, N.C., each must deal with her own version of trust, risks, and what makes someone strong.

Coming February 2007

OTHER LINDA CRIST TITLES

The Bluest Eyes in Texas

Kennedy Nocona is an out, liberal, driven attorney, living in Austin. Once a player in the legal community, a personal tragedy for which she blames herself causes her to re-evaluate her life. Seeking redemption, she loses herself in her work, strict discipline of mind and body, and the teachings of Native American roots she once shunned.

Dallasite Carson Garrett is a young paralegal overcoming the loss of her parents, and coming to terms with her own sexual orientation. After settling her parents' estate and examining her failed past relationships, she is desperately ready to move forward. Bored with her state of affairs, she longs for excitement and romance to make her feel alive again.

A chance encounter finds them inexplicably drawn to one another and after a weekend together, they quickly find themselves in a long distance romance that leaves them both wanting more. Circumstances at Carson's job escalate into a series of mysteries and blackmail that leaves her with more excitement than she ever bargained for. Confused, afraid, and alone, she turns to Kennedy, the one person she knows can help her. As they work together to solve a puzzle, they confront growing feelings that neither woman can deny, complicated by outside forces that threaten to crush them both.

ISBN 978-1-932300-48-2

Galveston 1900: Swept Away

Forced to flee from her family at a young age, Rachel Travis finds a home and livelihood on the island of Galveston. Independent, friendly, and yet often lonely, only one other person knows the dark secret that haunts her. That is until she meets Madeline "Mattie" Crockett, a woman trapped in a loveless marriage convinced that her fate is sealed. She never dares to dream of true happiness, until Rachel Travis comes walking into her life. As emotions come to light, the storm of Mattie's marriage converges with the very real hurricane of September 7-8, 1900, the storm that destroyed Galveston. Can they survive, and build the life they both dream of?

ISBN 1-932300-44-9
(978-1-932300-44-4)

OTHER YELLOW ROSE TITLES

You may also enjoy:

Learning to Trust

by J. Y. Morgan

Jace, the director of a college Achievement Center, has a new graduate assistant, Taryn Murphy. Both women cannot avoid spending time with each other, as they are part of an extended family. Both have their secrets and reasons not to trust, but when they find themselves opening up to each other, they realize their problems are very similar. Can a friendship develop between them or will their pasts haunt them forever?

ISBN 978-1-932300-59-8

Tropical Storm

by Melissa Good

From best-selling author Melissa Good comes a tale of heartache, longing, family strife, lust for love, and redemption. *Tropical Storm* took the lesbian reading world by storm when it was first written...now read this exciting revised "author's cut" edition.

Dar Roberts, corporate raider for a multi-national tech company, is cold, practical, and merciless. She does her job with razor-sharp accuracy. Friends are a luxury she cannot allow herself, and love is something she knows she'll never attain.

Kerry Stuart left Michigan for Florida in an attempt to get away from her domineering politician father and the constraints of the overly conservative life her family forced upon her. After college she worked her way into supervision at a small tech company, only to have it taken over by Dar Roberts' organization. Her association with Dar begins in disbelief, hatred and disappointment, but when Dar unexpectedly hires Kerry as her work assistant, the dynamics of their relationship change. Over time, a bond begins to form.

But can Dar overcome years of habit and conditioning to open herself up to the uncertainty of love? And, will Kerry escape from the clutches of her powerful father in order to live a better life?

ISBN 978-1-932300-60-4

OTHER YELLOW ROSE PUBLICATIONS

Georgia Beers	Thy Neighbor's Wife	1-932300-15-5
Carrie Brennan	Curve	1-932300-41-4
Carrie Carr	Destiny's Bridge	1-932300-11-2
Carrie Carr	Faith's Crossing	1-932300-12-0
Carrie Carr	Hope's Path	1-932300-40-6
Carrie Carr	Love's Journey	1-930928-67-X
Carrie Carr	Strength of the Heart	1-930928-75-0
Carrie Carr	Something to Be Thankful For	1-932300-04-X
Carrie Carr	Diving Into the Turn	978-1-932300-54-3
Linda Crist	Galveston 1900: Swept Away	1-932300-44-9
Linda Crist	The Bluest Eyes in Texas	978-1-932300-48-2
Jennifer Fulton	Passion Bay	1-932300-25-2
Jennifer Fulton	Saving Grace	1-932300-26-0
Jennifer Fulton	The Sacred Shore	1-932300-35-X
Jennifer Fulton	A Guarded Heart	1-932300-37-6
Jennifer Fulton	Dark Dreamer	1-932300-46-5
Anna Furtado	The Heart's Desire	1-932300-32-5
Gabrielle Goldsby	The Caretaker's Daughter	1-932300-18-X
Melissa Good	Eye of the Storm	1-932300-13-9
Melissa Good	Thicker Than Water	1-932300-24-4
Melissa Good	Terrors of the High Seas	1-932300-45-7
Melissa Good	Tropical Storm	978-1-932300-60-4
Maya Indigal	Until Soon	1-932300-31-7
Lori L. Lake	Different Dress	1-932300-08-2
Lori L. Lake	Ricochet In Time	1-932300-17-1
J. Y Morgan	Learning To Trust	978-1-932300-59-8
A. K. Naten	Turning Tides	978-1-932300-47-5
Meghan O'Brien	Infinite Loop	1-932300-42-2
Sharon Smith	Into The Dark	1-932300-38-4
Surtees and Dunne	True Colours	978-1-932300-52-9
Surtees and Dunne	Many Roads to Travel	978-1-932300-55-0
Cate Swannell	Heart's Passage	1-932300-09-0
Cate Swannell	No Ocean Deep	1-932300-36-8
L. A. Tucker	The Light Fantastic	1-932300-14-7

About the Author:

Linda Crist was born and raised in Dallas, Texas, has also lived in Nacogdoches, Port Aransas, and Austin, and is back in Dallas, where she lives with two spoiled rotten cats. When she's not working her real job or writing, she enjoys scuba diving, hiking, camping, golf, sailing, snow skiing, biking, traveling, reading, sketching, photography, making music videos, listening to music, and chilling with her friends.

She is currently the evening shift supervisor in the Legal Response Department at the U.S. Small Business Administration, and is a former section editor at the *Dallas Times Herald*. She has a Journalism degree from The University of Texas at Austin, where she was awarded a scholarship position with the Lady Longhorns sports information office. She began writing while in preschool, drawing picture stories on the bulletin during church. Her foray into lesbian romance writing began with several volumes of alternative *Xena* fan fiction, for which she has won numerous online writing awards. She was on the Orlando BardCon staff during its four-year run and wrote two episodes for the *Xena Subtext Virtual Season*.

Her first novel, *The Bluest Eyes in Texas*, made the Open Book's top ten best-selling list for 2002 and spent several months on the top twenty list at Libertas in the U.K. After *Bluest Eyes*, Linda went on to publish her second novel, *Galveston 1900: Swept Away*, which was named one of the top ten lesbian novels of 2005 in San Francisco's East Bay Voice, was a finalist for a 2006 Goldie Award, and was the July 2006 selection for the Dallas Border's Lesbian Book Club. She has contributed short stories to two charity anthologies, *At First Blush*, and *Telltale Kisses*. This novel, *Borderline*, the sequel to *Bluest Eyes*, makes her third novel. She is currently working on her fourth, a sci-fi romance set 200 years in the future.

Her e-mail address is texbard@earthlink.net and her website is http://home.earthlink.net/~texbard.

VISIT US ONLINE AT

www.regalcrest.biz

At the Regal Crest Website You'll Find

- The latest news about forthcoming titles and new releases

- Our complete backlist of romance, mystery, thriller and adventure titles

- Information about your favorite authors

- Current bestsellers

Regal Crest titles are available from all progressive booksellers and online at StarCrossed Productions, (www.scp-inc.biz), or at www.amazon.com, www.bamm.com, www.barnesandnoble.com, and many others.

Printed in the United States
67269LVS00005B/1-15

9 781932 300628